SPITTING GOLD

www.penguin.co.uk

SPITTING GOLD

Carmella Lowkis

doubleday

TRANSWORLD PUBLISHERS
Penguin Random House, One Embassy Gardens, 8
Viaduct Gardens, London SW11 7BW
www.penguin.co.uk

Transworld is part of the Penguin Random House group of companies
whose addresses can be found at global.penguinrandomhouse.com

First published in Great Britain in 2024 by Doubleday
an imprint of Transworld Publishers

A CIP catalogue record for this book
is available from the British Library.

ISBNs
9780857529466

Typeset in 11.5/15.75pt Adobe Garamond by Falcon Oast Graphic Art Ltd.
Printed and bound in Great Britain by Clays Ltd, Elcograf S.p.A.

The authorized representative in the EEA is Penguin Random House Ireland,
Morrison Chambers, 32 Nassau Street, Dublin D02 YH68.

Penguin Random House is committed to a sustainable
future for our business, our readers and our planet. This book is
made from Forest Stewardship Council® certified paper.

dedication

PROLOGUE

15 JULY 1866

I AM WORKING on a pair of gloves. They are for a man. I wonder who he will be, if he will know where his gloves began their life.

Really, I do not need to do this: we mere accused are not obliged to do any work. Most of us choose to, even so. The sewing is something familiar to cling to in this place. From aristocrats to slum-dwellers, we women are all united by our ability to wield a needle and thread. There are no distinctions in Saint-Lazare: all the accused are housed together in the common dormitory. Regardless of crime or class, we all rise together at five a.m., we pray together, we eat the same broth – which includes meat only on a Sunday – and we exercise in the same yard. There are prostitutes, drunks, thieves, vandals, swindlers – some of them children no more than twelve – and murderesses, like me. Word gets around quickly about us, and we are left to ourselves, so I am not bothered by any of the petty in-fighting I sometimes see among the others awaiting sentence.

This is a kind of purgatory, for none stays here long. We all wait to hear where we will be sent next. If we are lucky, it may be hard labour in the provinces; if we are unlucky, the Grande Roquette, and the guillotine that resides there. But I do not need to rely on luck.

I am going to walk free.

PART ONE

'Look what comes out of your sister's mouth whenever she speaks! Wouldn't you like to be able to do the same thing?'
— 'The Fairies', Charles Perrault, tr. A. E. Johnson

CHAPTER ONE

3 April 1866

THE FIGURE HAD been standing across the street for an hour now. When I first noticed it through the window, I had passed it off as simply another pedestrian, perhaps someone waiting for a friend. I was sure that the rain, just starting, would keep it from loitering about: Paris in the rain was a miserable place. The streets would be transformed from pleasant thoroughfares into swamps, churned to mud beneath shoes, hooves and carriage wheels. Grime seeped into the seams of dresses and clung to the legs of urchin children. Watching this from my room, separated from the squalor by only a thin pane of glass, I was thankful for the protection of my warm apartment.

The figure proved hardier than I had imagined. When next I glanced outside, it was still there. Standing in the same spot. The cloak gave it an uncertain shape which seemed to waver at the edges where raindrops blurred the scene. Tall. Reasonably broad. The silhouette of a woman. No clues further than that; nothing to suggest that she was anybody of my acquaintance, but as time wore on I became increasingly convinced that whoever it was, she was waiting for me.

I would get like this sometimes, even as a child: sure that the world was conspiring against me. Papa had called it paranoia; Mama, intuition. I supposed that which parent was correct depended upon the outcome. Which of them would prevail this time?

I leaned in to look closer, but my breath soon turned the pane as misty as a storm glass. All that I spotted before my exhalations obscured the view was a glint of pale skin beneath the shadow of the hood: her face appeared to be turned towards my building. The sight made me jump, and I stepped quickly back out of sight.

My boudoir was suddenly cold. The fire had burned low, and a creeping sensation was starting across my forehead where it had been pressed to the window. Silly nonsense. Letting my imagination run away with me. A fine habit for a child, but not one suited to a fully formed woman. I would not look again. The figure was surely awaiting an appointment, or perhaps was one of those women of a *certain trade* – although, granted, the shapeless cloak did not seem to match this latter theory. But what other explanation?

Whether by the grace of this line of thought, or by the gloomy atmosphere of the day, memories of fairy tales and ghost stories began to stir. I could almost hear the whisper of Mama's voice in my ear as she told the midnight secrets of the graveyard. But this morbidity would not do. I rang for the housemaid, Augustine, and directed her to build up the blaze. A good heat would soon evaporate these phantoms.

The girl set about stoking and piling and conducting the little manoeuvres that one employs to coax a fire. It was an alchemy I knew well – better than Augustine, judging by the trouble she was having with stacking the kindling. The fires back at home had normally been built by Papa; though, when we were older, my sister and I had taken our turn as well. But now I had servants, and it would have been improper to correct them on their technique. A lady should not know how to perform such menial tasks; to demonstrate my knowledge could have raised doubt about my position. Eventually, Augustine managed to get the fire alive.

Besides her difficulty with this, she was an otherwise competent girl of sixteen, who had been in my service for about six months now; a hard worker, if a little timid, and with a troublesome habit of neglecting to dust in the corners. Sensible, though. Yes, this would be easy to settle, I thought as I watched her work. Once the fire was satisfactory, I beckoned her over to the window.

'Do you see that person standing across the road, Augustine?' I attempted nonchalance in the tone of the question, but the accompanying gesture of my palm rubbing across my forehead likely betrayed my unease – something that I realized only once it was too late. Augustine peered out in the direction I indicated and, when I saw that she had noticed the figure, I said, 'Yes, that one. Please send Virginie to enquire of the porter who it is.'

That done, I hid myself a little behind the curtain, and watched to see what would happen. Presently, the porter hove into view. He was a stout man with large red whiskers: unmistakable even through the rain. As I had requested, he crossed the road and shared some words with the woman. After a moment, she raised one arm and pointed directly at my window.

My heart gave a savage leap against my ribs; I was forced to hurry out of view. Who could this stranger be? And what could she want? My husband always warned me to be cautious: a man of his position was sure to make enemies, sure to merit blackmail. Every secret that I had ever held churned within my brain, as I tried to find one that would explain this strange apparition.

That this person wished me harm, I was certain, as if gripped by premonition. Erring on the side of Mama.

When a knock came at my door, I almost cried out in fright. Then I realized that it was Virginie, my lady's maid. I smoothed my hair and called for her to enter.

'What word from the porter?' My voice managed somehow to remain steady despite the gasping of my pulse.

'Monsieur Coulomb sends his apologies, Madame,' Virginie replied, 'but the lady outside would give neither her name nor purpose. She did, however, request that I bring you this visiting card. Only, she directed that neither I nor the porter was to look at it.'

Virginie held the card face-down so that the lettering could not be seen. I took it from her and turned away. It was a simple design, with none of the fashionable miniatures or messages that many of the upper class preferred. All that it bore was a name and address: *Mlle C. Mothe, 34 rue de Constantine, Belleville*.

At the familiar words, the thrumming of my heart gave way to a strange tranquillity. I lowered the card. There was a mahogany writing desk against one wall of the boudoir, with a drawer that could be unlocked only by the key that I wore about my neck. I crossed to this now, opened it, and placed the visiting card inside. Then I fetched a coin purse and took out a couple of francs.

'Please show the lady into my rooms,' I said, moving back over to Virginie. 'Make sure that my husband does not see – perhaps the servants' stair would be best.'

Virginie bobbed her head. 'Of course, Madame.'

'And Virginie . . .'

'Yes, Madame?'

I reached for her hand, pressing the money into it. 'You will not tell anybody of this?'

'Of course not, Madame,' Virginie replied. Her expression was unreadable, just as any good servant's should be. Frustrating when one wished to gauge a reaction, however. I would have to trust that the money would out-value the social capital one might gain from such gossip. And Virginie was not known to be a gossip.

While I awaited Mademoiselle Mothe, I relocked my desk, and then examined myself in the looking glass. It had been over two years – oh, how I had changed in that time! A smattering of grey had already begun to appear in my hair, and my waist was threatening a decline beneath my stays. This was the price of having a paid cook to hand! But my wardrobe was considerably better, my posture more refined: I looked a respectable, well-bred woman.

Taking a seat on the Turkish divan, I tried to arrange myself as impressively as I could, and awaited Virginie's rap at the door.

When it came, I called out, 'Enter!'

Virginie led the cloaked figure into the room. This latter was dripping with water from where she had stood so long in the rain, but, appearing now in the warm boudoir, she looked far less ominous.

I directed Virginie to take the cloak and hang it before the fire – which seemed to take an age – then finally dismissed her.

At last, I was alone with the woman who had waited hours to catch my attention. 'So you found me, Charlotte,' I said.

Charlotte only smiled in response. Her smile hadn't been at all altered by the years. My resolve softened at the familiar features: her square jaw in contrast to my rounded one; her blonde hair honeyed where mine was ashen; her thick, clumsy wrists the disappointing twins of my own. Yet she was in some ways entirely different, more haggard. There was a recent wound upon her brow, about the length of a little finger and not quite healed. Her under-eyes were dark, her face sallow.

My pose on the divan felt suddenly absurd. I rose hurriedly, leaning to kiss Charlotte's cheeks in order to disguise the awkwardness.

'I am truly pleased to see you,' I told her. 'Certainly, I should have preferred . . . Well, you are here now; I see no use in quarrelling over it.'

'I weren't sure if I should come,' said Charlotte, all in a rush. 'I kept turning back, then changing my mind and whirling round again – I must've looked like a spinning top! Then I couldn't get up the nerve to approach that porter of yours. I kept thinking, what if he sends me right away without even listening to what I've got to say? Truth told, I thought that's what he was coming to do just now.' She finally paused long enough to take a breath. 'But here we are.'

'Here,' I said, 'come closer to the fire. It will be no wonder if you have caught your death. You never were one to behave sensibly, were you?'

Charlotte allowed me to guide her to the hearth. Her skirts immediately began to steam. 'I s'pose not,' she said, but she sounded distracted. 'You don't need to talk to me like that, you know.'

I smiled thinly, refusing to be goaded. 'I have no idea what you mean.'

'La-di-da,' she replied. Her eyes were roving around the room, taking everything in. 'You've got a beautiful house. Almost like the ones that we used to play-act. You remember those?' She adopted a silly, girlish voice for a moment. '"When I am grown up, I shall have a carriage with horses, and twenty servants, and a hundred dresses, and I shall eat Turkish delight every day."'

She paused, peeling off her gloves to warm her hands before the flames. 'Do you? Eat Turkish delight every day?'

'Charlotte . . . Why are you here?'

She hesitated, and then said, 'Papa's ill.'

'Not dying?' I asked, then winced at my own bluntness. It was not as if my sister would have come for anything less, not after how we had last parted. My nerves were beginning to buzz again. I could feel them like gnats in my skull.

'I . . . I don't think so, no, for the time being. But if the doctor stops treating him . . .' Charlotte was looking very carefully at her hands. 'I've burned right through my savings; the man's good, but very expensive with it. I've done everything else I can think of, Sylvie, but I can't pay the bills any more.'

I shifted uncomfortably. 'If you have come to ask for money—'

'That's not why I'm here, I swear,' Charlotte said, holding up a finger to urge silence. 'I know you can't withdraw all that without the Baron asking why. But I'm desperate. The kind of piecework I've been sewing just ain't enough. Do you know what it pays? And to think that you and I used to make as much in a day as I now make in—'

Having already realized Charlotte's meaning, I jumped in to interrupt. 'That is entirely out of the question.'

'It'd only be one more time,' said Charlotte. 'I've already found a client.'

'I want no more to do with all of that.'

'I don't remember you being so particular about "all of that" when it was paying your dowry.'

I avoided her eyes. That had been a different time, of course. A time when consequences were something that happened to other people, never to us.

13

Charlotte reached a hand towards my shoulder, but changed her mind halfway through and let it fall limp between us. 'Please, Sylvie, you know I wouldn't ask if I'd got another way out of this. Believe me, it weren't easy to find you again.'

With good reason. It had been no accident that Charlotte had never received the change-of-address card.

We were silent for a moment as Charlotte repositioned herself to dry her back. 'Do you never miss it?' she asked. 'The thrill, the excitement.'

'The danger of being found out.'

Charlotte gave a devilish smile. 'But weren't that part of the fun? And now here you are: *you*, Sylvie Mothe—'

'Baroness Devereux.'

'A society lady. A pretty wife. Tell me, how is it that you've spent your day? Embroidery?'

'I happen to find embroidery quite stimulating,' I told her sharply. But Charlotte's words had stirred up the memories that I had carefully hidden away, like the visiting card I had just locked in the drawer of my desk. I put a hand to the key about my neck.

'We were the best in the game,' said Charlotte.

'Yes, we *were*,' I said.

I had meant this to highlight the past tense of the statement, but Charlotte seemed to interpret my words as agreement. She said, '*You* were. Sylvie, I understand your worry. I do. Your husband—'

My husband. That was a thought that instantly dispelled any nostalgic reminiscences. 'Alexandre is a wonderful man,' I said, a little sharply. 'An important man. You cannot possibly realize just how influential one's reputation comes to be in our circles. Even the smallest whiff of scandal . . . It does not bear

thinking about. I have to consider his career. And our future.'
I absently placed a hand across my midriff as I thought of all
that the word entailed.

Charlotte gave me a funny look. 'You ain't—?'

'No,' I said quickly, heat rising in my cheeks at the misunderstanding. 'Not yet, but I mean that one day I hope to be.
This is what I want, Charlotte. I know that you never wanted
a life so . . . so ordinary. With your grand dreams of fame and
adventure—'

'*Our* dreams,' Charlotte corrected me. 'You played those
make-believe games as much as I did.'

'But they were of your invention,' I insisted. 'And my point
is that those games of yours no longer fit into my life. So you
understand that I am no longer at liberty to take the kinds of
risks that you propose.'

Charlotte had wandered nearer to the mantelpiece now, and
was fiddling with the ornaments kept there. I watched to make
sure none went into her pockets. 'Course I can see why you
don't want to put all this at risk,' Charlotte said. Her face had
the appearance of composure, but there was a slight twitch at
the very corner of her mouth. It was the same twitch that always
appeared when she was mocking someone.

Surely our first meeting in over two years need not end in
a quarrel? With some effort, I ignored the jab at my pride. 'I
wish that I could be of more help,' I said firmly, 'but there is
nothing that I can do.'

Charlotte did not seem to mirror my qualms about falling
into an argument, as she curled a lip and said, with a curdling
tone, 'I knew family meant nothing to you, but I never imagined
even you would turn your back on a dying man.'

There was a moment of silence, as if we both were too struck by the audacity of the accusation to continue our conversation. Rain pattered like fingers at the windowpane.

'You will leave my house now,' I said at last.

'I—'

'You will leave, and you will not return.' Saying this, I crossed to the bell and rang. 'Virginie will show you out. If you do not go quietly, then I will be forced to call for the constabulary and tell them about the statuette in your pocket.'

Charlotte sneered and thrust a hand into her skirts, pulled out the statuette and then threw it to the ground. A porcelain Eros with bow and arrow. Luckily, it did not break – it was a favourite of mine, a gift from Alexandre in the early days of our marriage. It was spared from any further acts of destruction by the arrival of Virginie.

'Please escort this woman back outside,' I said, raising my eyebrows to indicate that it might prove a difficult task.

'Cast me from your house, then!' Charlotte exclaimed. 'But I hope you enjoy hellfire, Sylvie *Devereux*, because the Lord'll surely cast you from his.' As damnations go, it was an impressive one, but Charlotte only believed in the Lord when it suited her purposes. She shouldered her way past Virginie, who was forced to hurry after her.

Then I was left alone with my anger. And oh, was I angry! It was a swelling, sickly wave in my chest. How dare she come crashing back into my life with *this*? To talk of family and dreams and God! Charlotte was a hypocrite through to the bone. To suggest that I should feel any hint of filial duty to our father, after all the ill treatment I had endured, years and years of it, before I had managed to escape . . . And now it transpired that my sanctuary was not safe from it all; my old life could come striding in at any time, dripping on my carpets and pocketing my ornaments. I looked down at the statuette and felt a sudden wave of disdain, as if Charlotte's touch had somehow sullied it. Before I was quite sensible of what I was doing, I had plucked it up and cast it against the wall. There was a satisfying peal as it splintered into pieces.

And as for Charlotte's visiting card, that could go too. I fumbled to unlock the desk drawer, hands shaking with barely contained emotion, and yanked it open, setting the contents rolling out of order. Where had the damned thing got to? I rummaged among my knick-knacks, intending to chuck the card into the fire. I could not find it. It must have skittered under something. I lifted items out, hoping to uncover it: a pair of scissors, a notebook, a little velvet pouch. This last gave me pause. I considered it, and then tipped it up so that the contents fell into my palm with a *chink-chink*. A locket on a chain. It was a pretty thing, although the silver was tarnished and the hinge was stiff when I eased it open. Inside was a miniature – our mother. A high-browed and pale-skinned face with beautiful dark eyes. Not that the image could capture even a fraction of what her eyes had been in life: those deep, inky irises that seemed to contain other worlds, like windows on to the night sky. Neither I nor Charlotte had inherited these; we had our father's river-water grey. No, our mother had been an exceptional beauty; a beauty that could occur only once, that could not be passed on.

Gazing into this paltry representation now, I knew what she would say. *Be kind to your sister, and forgiving to your father. They need your care more than ever now I am gone.*

I thought of all the trouble that Charlotte could get herself into: with her clients, with Papa, with the law. There was good reason that we had always worked as a pair in the past. And as the elder by six years, it had been my duty to watch out for her for as long as I could remember. But even if I *wanted* to help, how could I? There was my husband's position as a deputy prosecutor to think of. Alexandre must be my first loyalty now: he was my new family.

But the locket felt warm, skin-like, under my thumb. Mama's head was tilted at a slight angle, as if patiently awaiting the answer to some question.

It was probably too late to catch Charlotte. Even if she had put up a fuss, she would have been chased off by now. Would she not?

Shoving the locket into my skirts, I hurried out of the apartment and downstairs.

On the street, there was no sign of my sister. Luckily, Coulomb was there, leaning against the porter's lodge. A pipe curved out of his lips.

'The woman who was here,' I said, dispensing with the usual pleasantries, 'which way did she go?'

Following Coulomb's smoke-choked response, I hurried down the street. I hadn't run like this since I was a child. What on earth would Coulomb be thinking? And I had not even stopped to put on outside clothes. I was still in my house slippers! Never mind; with luck, I would catch Charlotte before I caught cold. Was that her there? The hem of a cloak turning a corner – yes! I called her name desperately, voice hoarse.

Charlotte turned, a look of surprise painting itself across her face as she recognized me. This was immediately replaced with one of chagrin. 'Oh, for fuck's sake, if it means that much to you, you can have it back,' she snapped, pulling a paper fan from her pocket with a flourish.

I stared at it blankly for several moments, before I realized that I had last seen it decorating a nook in the entrance hall. Christ, when had Charlotte even had the chance to take it? 'Never mind that,' I said, then had to stop when a sharp pain hit my chest; knives of cold exploding within me. I held up a hand: a signal to give me a moment. Once my lungs had stopped screaming, I tried again. 'I wanted to ask— Not that I definitely will— I still have to— But if I *did*— What is the job?'

'You've changed your mind?'

'Yes. No.' I drew in another breath, concentrating on the feeling of my lungs expanding like a pair of bellows. Expand, contract. 'I need to know more,' I said. 'But not now; we cannot talk here. And it will be dinner soon. Can you meet me tomorrow?'

'Even better,' said Charlotte, 'I've got an appointment to meet the clients. Come with me. If it's too much, you can pack the whole thing in then and there. And if not . . .'

We both let the silence trail on.

'Very well,' I agreed at last.

Once we had negotiated a time and place to meet, we said our goodbyes, and Charlotte departed once more. She melted so effortlessly into the bustle of the streets, it would have been easy to imagine her insubstantial. But I knew well enough that even the insubstantial could wield a great deal of power.

Returning to my rooms – giving Coulomb a civil nod when I passed, as if nothing untoward had taken place – I tried not to dwell on the way my afternoon had unfolded. Best to put it out of mind until tomorrow. Seeing the state I was in, Virginie hurried to assist me in changing for the evening meal. Glad as I normally was of her company, that day I sent her away as soon as we were done, preferring to brood alone. I took up a pattern that I had been embroidering, but, before even a minute had passed, I had thrown it down again in disgust. All that I could hear was Charlotte's teasing voice. *And now here you are: you, Sylvie Mothe.* The people who had known me by that name would hardly have believed where I was today. And the people who knew me as the Baroness Devereux, well . . . They never needed to know the details of the rock out from under which I had crawled.

I ought to have been frightened. After everything I had done to reinvent myself, here was the threat of exposure if I committed even the tiniest blunder. Yet that was the thing – underneath the anxiety and irritation, there was a tremor of excitement, just as Charlotte had said. I could feel it fluttering in my midriff like a caged songbird. It had been locked away for over two years, but now it was ready to sing.

CHAPTER TWO

4 April 1866

I MET WITH Charlotte the following day in the Jardin du Luxembourg. From there, we took a hansom cab to the clients' apartments on the place des Chevaux.

'You are a real Cendrillon. I am quite unaccustomed to such luxury,' Charlotte joked, using the affected voice she normally adopted for clients. The one into which I had now trained myself on a permanent basis. 'You had better be careful lest I get used to it.' She had walked all the way from Belleville.

'You really ought not to travel without a chaperone,' I told her.

Charlotte cast me a look, as if to say, *And just who d'you propose for that job?* Whom indeed? Mama was dead; Papa ill; myself gone. But surely Charlotte had friends? As a girl, she had always had some female intimate or another, always some whirlwind friendship with an inseparable companion, until the turbulent attachment would be broken by a 'lovers' quarrel'. And then how she would wail and mope! Like a young Romeo thwarted in pursuit of his paramour. She always did get too invested in these entanglements. I was a solitary child by contrast. Secretly, I had preferred it when Charlotte suffered such break-ups; at last I would have my sister to myself again, and would no longer have to feel jealous or excluded. At least until the next charming young thing came along.

But what if there were no more charming young things? Had they been replaced with nothing but loneliness? I had never paused to wonder to what manner of existence I had left my little sister – or, more accurately, when I *had* wondered, I had put a stop to it when I did not like the conclusions to which it led.

'Even so,' I said, 'you would not want . . .'

'People to get the wrong idea?' Charlotte quipped. And the unspoken: *Or the right one?* 'Anyway, you don't need to worry – I've always got my knife on me.'

The implication of this sentence settled over me as slowly as a morning frost. 'You carry a *knife*?'

'Don't you? Really, Sylvie, you've got to have the tools to protect yourself.'

I could think of no suitable response to this.

Not yet fully rid of my anxiety that I might be observed, I insisted that the hansom stop some streets away so that we could walk the final stretch. This was the Marais district: the roads here were a far cry from those around my house, all haphazard corners and irregular cobblestones; we might have stepped back into medieval times. Charlotte remained silent as we walked. I wondered if I had said something to upset her.

Underfoot, there was a squelch from yesterday's rain. The air was heavy with rich decay and the sharper, slicing whiff of sewage. Despite this, the streets were busy, and I found myself checking my pockets every few steps for fear of thieves, hugging my reticule tightly to my side.

It was a relief to reach the place des Chevaux, a square of buildings surrounding a compact park. One half of the square was medieval, the wattle-and-daub now fronted with limestone, giving its structures a sombre look. The other half was of a later era: four stories of red brick with blue slate roofs in the Louis XIII style, reminiscent of the place des Vosges, if one were to remove the arcades and allowed for dilapidation. It had clearly once been beautiful, pre-Revolution, but had now gone the same way as the ancien régime nobility who had previously inhabited it. There was rubbish strewn across the cobbles, suspect-looking shopfronts, and the park was unkempt. I spotted an inebriate tottering into one of the alleyway offshoots.

'What a place,' I murmured.

It did not seem to bother Charlotte. She led me to one of the buildings on the red-brick side and rang at the door. There was a wait – long enough for me to examine the paint peeling off the doorframe – and then a porter or some other domestic answered.

'Charlotte Mothe,' Charlotte informed him, using her high-society voice and presenting one of the now-familiar visiting cards. 'I am here to see the Dowager Marquise. She ought to be expecting me.'

My first impressions of the de Jacquinot family were not entirely favourable. They received us in a dark little parlour, and perhaps some of the room's shabbiness discoloured my view of them. It was furnished sparsely, with certain marks upon the floor that made me suspect there had once been more pieces, since removed. Pale outlines on the wallpaper suggested paintings that had similarly disappeared.

'The Mothe sisters.'

It was our hostess, Madame de Jacquinot, who announced us to the room. Between the silver cap of hair on her head, her grey dress and her squat figure, she reminded me distinctly of a pepper pot. Although I understood her to be the Dowager

Marquise, her clothing was modest and had a low-pointed waistline not popular since my mother's days. This was evidently an aristocratic family fallen upon hard times.

'Mesdemoiselles, please, do come and sit with us,' she went on, beckoning to the settee. This was a funny way to phrase it, as the other members of the family were seated as far apart from one another as was possible. It was as if each had chosen a point on the compass and stuck to it. 'How was your journey today?'

As we traded niceties, I eyed each of them. The north was occupied by the Dowager Marquise's son – the current Marquis de Jacquinot. He was maybe twenty or twenty-one; he looked about the same age as Charlotte. Fairly attractive: tall but not particularly broad, with auburn hair and a neat little moustache on his upper lip. Instead of joining the conversation, he was reading a book. Or, rather, he was pretending to read a book, as I caught him sneaking glances at me over the pages.

To the east was a bloodless girl, a little younger than the Marquis, who reminded me for all the world of a wilting flower. This was Madame de Jacquinot's daughter, Florence. Her features were pretty, but pretty in the way that one had seen hundreds of times before.

Finally, the south was home to an old man, so tucked away in a shadowy armchair that I barely noticed him until he was pointed out as 'Comte Ardoir, my father'. He might have been a skeleton already, for all the flesh he had upon him.

This left the western portion of the room to Charlotte, myself and Madame de Jacquinot. The three of us were obliged to share an undersized settee, making it rather hard for Charlotte and me to drink the coffee that had been offered to us without elbowing one another.

'Now, then,' said Charlotte, once a polite amount of time

had elapsed. 'I think it will be best if we approach this directly. Madame de Jacquinot: I believe you are being haunted?'

'In fact, we all are,' said Ardoir, in the churlish tone of someone who resented being overlooked.

Charlotte adopted a saccharine smile. 'Yes, of course, Monsieur.'

Madame de Jacquinot, with a glance at her father, said, 'Well, I do feel a little silly when you say it out loud . . .'

'Please put aside all notions of "silly",' said Charlotte. 'My sister and I are here to listen to whatever you have to say. You have . . . sighted a presence in this building?'

'Oh, not sighted, no,' said Madame de Jacquinot. 'I would not say sighted. But I have *sensed* her, here in the apartments, you understand? She wakes me often at night with all manner of noises: knocking, banging. In the morning, we rise to find things out of their rightful place. And . . . oftentimes, I will feel a chill, as if somebody is breathing upon my shoulder.'

'Naturally, I would have thought it a case of female over-imagination,' said Ardoir, 'but I have felt it too, in fact.'

'Naturally,' Charlotte agreed, managing to sound mostly sincere. 'You know, temperature fluctuations are frequently an indication of spiritual activity, Monsieur.'

The young de Jacquinot coughed behind his book; it was well hidden, but I thought he might have been suppressing a laugh. Apparently Ardoir held the same suspicion, as his fingers tightened, claw-like, upon his armrest at the noise.

There was a stirring from the daughter, Florence. 'I have seen her,' she whispered. 'She comes into my room at night.'

I shared a quick look with Charlotte at this. To have a manifestation before we had even set to work . . . Well, it was no wonder that Charlotte had been so confident about this endeavour! It seemed almost that there was no convincing to be done on our part at all.

'What is it that she does, when she is in your room?' I asked.

Florence kept her face turned down towards the floor, but she did for a moment lift her gaze up to meet mine. Her eyes were pale, with barely a glimmer of spirit in them. 'She cries,' she replied.

'Cries? You mean to say that she wails?'

'Not at all: she is perfectly quiet. She stands at the foot of my bed and weeps in silence.'

Unusual – in all the stories, weeping spirits were more likely to be heard than seen. I nodded thoughtfully, and waited for Charlotte to take note of this. 'Have you attempted to touch her?' I then asked. Lord knows why anyone would want to, but there were always the oddballs who did. And more besides: I was struck with the unwelcome memory of a woman who, having been visited by a handsome young male spirit, claimed to have . . . Well, it did not bear repeating.

'She runs away.' The daughter rubbed at her elbow with one hand, as if thinking. 'Or disappears; it is hard to tell. Grandfather has seen her too.'

'I have also seen her,' Ardoir agreed, magnanimously providing his male credibility.

The son gave a proper laugh this time, setting his book closed in his lap – I saw that it was a volume of Darwin's work, telling me all I needed to know. 'Well, there is your evidence: an old man and an unwell girl—'

'Maximilien!' cried Madame de Jacquinot.

'I am sorry, Mother,' he said, 'but you know my feelings on the matter. What Florence needs is a doctor, not some *spiritist*—'

'This "old man" is running out of patience with you, boy,' snapped Ardoir. 'You will not take such a tone with your elders.'

De Jacquinot opened his mouth as if to protest, but then thought better of it. 'Of course,' he said. 'I am sorry, Mother. I did not mean to speak so rudely. But my point is that Flo—'

Ardoir cut him off again. 'You would do well to remember under whose roof you are living.'

'But it is nothing more than superstition!'

I thought it best to forestall any further bickering and confront de Jacquinot on his 'point' directly. 'So you do not believe in spirits at all, Monsieur?' I asked. A cynic in one's midst is no trouble, so long as one can identify him as such and discredit his protests from the outset.

He looked me candidly in the eye. 'I am afraid that I find the entire concept to be drivel. Science, now *that* – he tapped the book with one finger – 'is what I believe in. The observable phenomena of the real world.' He gave a sly smile. 'If you will excuse me.'

Charlotte cleared her throat. 'If I may, Monsieur de Jacquinot,' she said, 'as a matter of honour—'

'Please, I do not believe in titles. Call me Maximilien.'

Not only a cynic and a man of science, then, but also a Republican. Lord have mercy upon us.

Charlotte gave a thin smile. 'Very well, Monsieur *Maximilien*: as a matter of honour, I feel I must defend my profession.

'I assure you that there is no "drivel" about our work. Certainly, there are charlatans out there who will take your money in exchange for their fakeries, but all professions have their crooks, and one does not dismiss the entire field of – for example – medical science as drivel, simply because one has had the misfortune to be tricked by a spurious sawbones. No, one overlooks such anomalies and believes in the abundance of evidence in favour of the field. It is the same with we spiritists.

For every crook, one hears countless stories of successful contact with the souls of the departed. Why, though only through recent advances have we been able to perfect the art, it is hardly a modern science. Since time immemorial, there have been reports of the existence of spirits, of visitations and possessions. Now, I have no way to prevent you from dismissing every single account as drivel – as people lying or being tricked – but, I put it to you, Monsieur, that it is far more likely, given the overwhelming number of cases, that these accounts are authentic. As the law of parsimony states, the most likely explanation is the simplest. And is it not simpler to believe in the existence of spirits than to dismiss an entire profession as "drivel"?'

Maximilien did not look convinced, but he was also unable to find a response. Charlotte's arguments often had this effect on people – particularly on men, who were not used to hearing a woman defy them so confidently and with such strong rhetoric. Papa used to say that she could have talked Louis Philippe off the throne, if only the Republicans had not got to him first.

Ardoir harrumphed in approval. 'There, boy,' he said, 'may we now return to the reason that we have, in fact, invited these two' – he paused to find the rest of his sentence, beady eyes appraising us for an unpleasant amount of time – 'charming young ladies into our home?'

Keen to move along, Charlotte turned brightly to Florence. 'So, Mademoiselle, are you able to tell me when it was that you first became aware of the spirit in the apartments?'

'It was just after . . .' said Florence, but then trailed off. I noticed her eyes kept returning to the cut on Charlotte's forehead, as if the sight of it disturbed her. She was either squeamish or highly empathetic. Either way, it did not speak for a strong stomach; we would have to be careful with her.

Madame de Jacquinot sniffed loudly. 'Florence has not been quite well this past year,' she said. 'She is only now recovering from a period of ill health – she spent many months in bed. It was shortly after the end of her indisposition that the spirit first appeared to her.'

'You see why I consider this a medical matter,' said Maximilien.

Ignoring his input, I asked Madame de Jacquinot, 'And did you also notice the spirit at this time?'

'No.'

'In fact, I did,' said Ardoir.

'It is good to get the *facts* down,' said Charlotte. I caught a definite glimmer of mischief in her words – a mockery of Ardoir's repetition, which I hoped the others would not notice. I had been right to join her on this visit.

Madame de Jacquinot nodded in agreement. 'At first, it was only my father and Florence. I thought that . . . Well, naturally I assumed it to be a . . . sort of shared hallucinatory state brought on by . . . certain stresses. But then I myself experienced it.'

'Leaving me the only sane person in the house,' muttered Maximilien.

Charlotte smiled again. 'Some people are simply not as finely attuned to the spiritual world as others,' she informed him. 'It is often the sign of an inferior psyche, I am afraid.'

'Perhaps a tour?' I suggested, standing up so quickly that I knew my knees would regret it for days.

Before the mansion had been converted into apartments – around the time of Madame de Jacquinot's adolescence, she informed us – it had originally had a squared-off horseshoe as a footprint. When the building had been segmented into parts, not only had it been separated vertically, with different floors under different ownership, but it had also been bifurcated horizontally, so that all that was left to the family was a half-horseshoe on the first floor.

This remaining L-shape comprised seven main rooms, or eight if one counted the hall, which was certainly large enough to be a room of its own. Two further doors led out of the parlour, and it was through one of these that Madame de Jacquinot now guided us.

This far room was a dining room, furnished with tasteful varnished pieces, although like the parlour it seemed despondently sparse. Madame de Jacquinot drew our particular attention to the table – an Italian import – and to the pianoforte, both of which had been in the family for over a century.

From the dining room, we entered the library. Books lined three of the walls, dusty and fat with unappreciated knowledge. The third wall was home to a trio of windows that looked out on to the main square. The spaces between them were overrun with ancestral portraits: the same high, supercilious brows recurring over and over, the same wide shoulders and elegant necks. I spotted one that was clearly the old man – Comte Ardoir – some decades ago, his flesh fuller but his look as mean and shrunken as it was now. However, my eye was soon caught away by the centremost portrait. This was an aristocratic woman, finely dressed in a peacock-blue gown with pink trim. Her hair was piled atop her head in the fashion of the last century, most likely augmented by a hairpiece. The pouf had been powdered a lavender grey; however, it was clear from her eyebrows that she naturally shared Florence's bright coppery tresses. Woven throughout this arrangement, and spilling about the woman's neck, across her hands, up her arms, from her earlobes, were countless precious gems, filling the portrait with light like the reflection of the sun upon open sea. But what struck me most was the woman's expression – a knowing, enigmatic smile, with just a touch of cruelty to it. Almost as if she were mocking the viewer.

'That is the Comtesse Sabine de Lisle,' said Madame de Jacquinot, noticing where my attention had fallen. 'Was she not a beauty?'

Charlotte came to look as well. 'She resembles your daughter somewhat,' she said. The same hair and shape of face, maybe, but it was hard to descry the meek Florence in this passionate countenance.

'My father believes the spirit to be hers. It is something of a family legend, you see, about lost treasure. The Comtesse was executed during the Terror, and her brother – which is to say, my grandfather – and his family only escaped by fleeing Paris in disguise. Father was just a boy at the time. When they returned later to reclaim the building, they found it entirely untouched and with no signs of entry. All the silver was still in place, the art, the books, everything of value. However, the Comtesse's vast collection of jewellery was nowhere to be found. Father has always believed that she managed to hide it just before she was taken.'

'And now she has returned to show him where to find it?' suggested Charlotte.

'One can only hope so,' said Madame de Jacquinot.

On the ceiling was a fresco of turquoise sky against which a flock of snarling, winged women thronged. The Furies, perhaps? They were too faded to tell. A table and several reading chairs were clustered in the centre of the room, overlooked by a mounted stone bust.

Charlotte stopped to note something down in her pocket-book – I was close enough to read *library: marble bust – valuable?* When Madame de Jacquinot inclined her head inquisitively, Charlotte said blithely, 'I am just noting that I feel the presence particularly in this room, Madame. I expect we will experience some interesting phenomena in here.'

Out through the other door in the library, and we were back in the parlour. As Madame de Jacquinot led us through into the hall, I avoided Maximilien's gaze. I did not trust young men – they had not had the time to mature into worthwhile individuals. Give me an older man like my dear Alexandre any day of the week. I had always put stock in experience over vigour. Indeed, my husband's years of wisdom were a daily blessing in my life.

The adjacent wall of the hall opened into a gallery, spanned on one side with windows and on the other side with bedroom doors. At its far end was a servant's stair, the entrance disguised to blend into the wallpaper. I made a show of retrieving my thermometer and taking the temperatures outside each room. There were no major fluctuations, although the end with the servants' stair was a little cooler than the rest. However, this did not prove anything in particular, as the servants' stair was very likely draughty.

'Whose room is this?' I asked, indicating the door nearest to the stair's entrance.

'That is Florence's.'

'I am not surprised your daughter has experienced such penumbral disturbances,' Charlotte remarked. 'The servants' stair is an unbalanced space. One should never overlook the power of architecture to affect the spiritual activity of a house. Private space repels spirits, whereas thresholds are more threatening to the natural order of the world. These stairs afford movement not only between floors, but also between social spheres.' It was a pleasure to see Charlotte in her element once more; it had been so long that I had almost forgotten how good she was. I felt a glow of pride as she went on, 'It is through architectural features such as these that rooms and their inhabitants communicate with one another. Inhabitants both living . . . and dead.'

Madame de Jacquinot gave a sharp intake of breath, one hand coming up to hover at her breast. Such willingness to believe.

The inside of Florence's room was a sad space – not for lack of adornment, but there seemed a melancholy in the air, as if it still carried the memory of her former sickbed. Had she really been confined to such a cheerless room for months on end? It was no wonder she looked such a pale sap of a thing. There was a faint floral smell that reminded me of – what was it? Orange blossom, I thought.

The room next door belonged to Maximilien. It was a typical bachelor's space, lacking the feminine touches that make a chamber homely. It had taken such a battle to convert my husband's room into something attractive when we had first married – and still he enjoyed a good-natured grumble if I added too many dried flowers or had the maid tidy his shaving tools.

There was a portrait on the wall, an oval in watercolours of two children sitting side by side in the suggestion of a summer garden. They were a boy and a girl, both with reddish hair and plump cheeks. The boy was holding a sailing boat in one hand; he had about him the stiffness of a child made to pose for a long period of time, despite the artist's best efforts (I am sure) to conceal it. The girl in her turn held a posy of flowers. It was not a particularly good piece: too crowded in the oval – it was a scene better suited to a rectangular canvas – and the limbs gave the impression that the painter was more used to depicting adults than children. As Maximilien could therefore not be keeping it for its artistic merit, I surmised that it must be of sentimental value.

'Are these your children, Madame?' I asked.

Madame de Jacquinot stepped over to look alongside me. 'My, it seems like it was so recent. They were such sweet little things, and so close to one another. I remember when we first sent Maximilien off to school – there he was, all dressed in his smart new uniform and ready to leave, but we couldn't find Florence anywhere to wish him goodbye. We feared she had run away in protest! But then we thought to check inside Max's trunk, and of course that's where she was, playing stowaway. It took three of us to drag her out. Indeed, I seem to remember she bit the governess.' She paused to chuckle. 'Oh, she was inconsolable for weeks after he left without her.'

How curious – if I had been asked to guess at Florence's childhood character, I would never have pictured such a spirited little girl.

Madame de Jacquinot smiled at us both. 'Well, I am sure that you understand that sort of devotion, as sisters.'

I glanced at Charlotte. 'Oh yes,' she said. 'We can hardly bear to be parted, even today.'

In Ardoir's chamber – the master bedroom – we found no fewer than ten crucifixes affixed to the wall, directly above his headboard.

'Your father is very religious?' asked Charlotte.

'I suppose,' said Madame de Jacquinot, as if she had never put much thought into the matter. 'He has become more so in his old age.'

Ardoir had not struck me as a particularly religious fanatic thus far, and the positioning above his bed was intriguing. It was almost as if they had been placed there as a protective ward. Against what? The ghost? But then why would a man so certain that he was being visited by a beloved aunt take such extreme measures to prevent her from approaching him?

There was a Bible at his bedside also, which had scraps of paper tucked in to mark certain pages, so that it had swollen to what must have been twice its original size. I smoothed a hand over it, feeling the bumps of old leather through my glove. Glancing up to check that Madame de Jacquinot was not watching, and finding her well occupied in sharing reflections upon ageing with Charlotte, I chose one of the marked pages at random. A passage from Deuteronomy. Select words had been picked out by an ink pen:

> There shall not be found among you any one that maketh his son or his daughter to pass through the fire, or that useth divination, or an observer of times, or an enchanter, or a witch, Or a charmer, or a consulter with familiar spirits, or a wizard, or a necromancer. For all that do these things are an abomination unto the Lord: and because of these abominations the Lord thy God doth drive them out from before thee.

It appeared Ardoir had been researching our profession. I wondered what it meant that the old man had read we were abominations in the name of the Lord, yet still allowed us to conduct our work in his house. There was clearly something at stake that he valued – or feared – more than the word of God.

Finally, there was Madame de Jacquinot's chamber. This was

more to my taste: soft furnishings, pleasing tints of colour, elegant hints of lace and silk. The chest of drawers was an obvious antique, and a few glittering ornaments were arranged upon it. Whatever sacrifices had been made in the rest of the house, Madame de Jacquinot had managed to hold on to some of her fripperies. When she was not looking, I surreptitiously stroked a weighty, silver-backed hairbrush.

'Madame,' I said, withdrawing my hand, 'may I ask: what made you first suspect that the spirit was specifically that of the Comtesse?'

Madame de Jacquinot did not need to think long on her answer. 'Well, it was because my father said as much. As the only one of us to have met the Comtesse – in her living form, that is – I trust that he is the most capable of identifying her.'

'I see,' I said. 'So am I correct in saying that, besides Comte Ardoir's word, you have not – shall we say – *personally* observed any evidence as to her identity?'

This caused a small frown to appear. 'But who else would have business with us?'

'Spirits can be tricky,' I replied. 'One should never take anything for granted. Which is why Charlotte and I will make it our first priority to discover the identity of your unseen guest – whether the Comtesse or otherwise. Would you please remind me which of you was the first to see her? And can you remember precisely when it happened?'

Madame de Jacquinot gave a polite sort of cough. 'Forgive me, Mademoiselle Mothe, but have we not just been over all of this?'

Indeed we had, but – as Charlotte now explained to her – we wanted to be sure that we had all the information properly recorded. And – although we kept this part to ourselves – we wanted to look for any discrepancies in accounts.

'Well,' said Madame de Jacquinot, accepting this logic, 'the first of us to mention her presence was Florence. She asked one morning, had we had a guest in the house? And when we said that no, of course we had not, she appeared confused and said, in that case, who had been the woman in her room when she awoke? Of course, I assumed this was simply an after-effect of her illness – there was some mental incapacitation, you see. You could not know the half of it, but she had all kinds of fancies in those days. Such inventions! The paranoia also; she accused us – her own family – of such dreadful things.'

Charlotte made a sympathetic noise, although I noted a slight squint to her eyes, as one might adopt in response to a chill breeze. 'And when did you say that this was, Madame?' she asked.

Madame de Jacquinot's nose scrunched up as she tried to recall. 'Let me see . . . I suppose it would have been mid-February. No more recently than the start of March, that is certain, because I remember clearly that it was only just over a year since the . . . the episode which really triggered this bad phase of Florence's illness. She had seemed to be recovering for a few months, but then the anniversary came, and I thought that must have been what was causing her to see . . . such things. However, my father then revealed that he had also been visited by this presence, on more than one occasion.'

The reference to some past 'episode' pricked my interest, but when I enquired further, Madame de Jacquinot bristled and became reticent. 'Oh, it was simply one of these things,' she said.

The whole line of questioning seemed to turn her against us in some way, and we got little more out of her before we reached the parlour once more.

'Thank you again for your hospitality, Madame,' said

Charlotte as we entered. 'We have some compelling information to be getting along with.'

Maximilien had sloped off somewhere in our absence, leaving Ardoir and Florence to one another's company. The latter was now standing near the mantelpiece. I noticed she had Maximilien's book in hand, which she was turning over with mild curiosity, but she looked up from it at our entrance. 'I told you they would help, Mama.'

Madame de Jacquinot nodded in acquiescence. 'Your involvement was Florence's idea,' she explained to me.

'Well, they would hardly have supposed it to be Maximilien's,' said Florence, offering a glint of humour.

I caught Charlotte hiding a smile.

'If it is agreeable to you, Madame,' I said, 'my sister and I shall go now and discuss our first impressions of your case. Then, if convenient, may we return next week – say, Monday at eight o'clock – to hold a night's vigil?'

'Perhaps Maximilien would prefer not to attend,' added Charlotte.

Once we were clear of the building, I warned Charlotte against angering the young Marquis.

'Oh, but Sylvie, he was a right arse, wasn't he?'

This was but one of the labels I would have applied to Maximilien. There was also arrogant, self-aggrandizing, rude, oily, and a damned great thorn in one's side. But beyond stubbornness, it appeared that at least some of his opposition came from genuine concern for his sister. I could feel a kinship in that – it was, after all, the same reason that I had accompanied Charlotte there.

'He does pose a problem,' I said, 'and one which will need to be handled with delicacy.' In cases such as this, one had either to convince the disbelieving party, or to ensure their exclusion. Our profession was fragile enough as it stood – to have someone constantly alert for any hint of a trick, for the tiniest sleight of hand, could prove disastrous.

Charlotte shrugged. 'I s'pose you're right.'

'As do the jewels.'

'Oh?'

I raised my eyebrows at her. 'When Madame de Jacquinot asks our spirit for their location, and we've to come up with an answer, what are we supposed to say?'

'Maybe Comtesse Sabine de Lisle will tell us.'

'Please be serious.'

We were separated for a moment as we dodged a knot of street urchins.

When I caught up to Charlotte again, she was rolling her eyes. 'We'll just have to say the revolutionaries *did* take them. And the Comtesse would like the family to know that true wealth is not located in some hidden treasure, but in the love they have for one another.'

I thought of Comte Ardoir's hissed insults. 'I doubt them to be the type to settle for that.'

'We'll think of something,' said Charlotte. 'Besides, there's a more pressing problem to discuss.'

'And what should that be?'

Charlotte looked at me pointedly.

'Me? What am I supposed to have done?'

'Absolutely nothing!' said Charlotte. 'That wasn't the Sylvie Mothe I knew in there.'

'No, it was the Baroness Devereux.'

'Well, it ain't the Baroness I need,' said Charlotte. 'If we're going to convince Maximilien – and the others – then I need *you* back. If we're going to exorcize their grief, to heal them of their spiritual woes, I need your otherworldliness, your mysticism; you know you're the better medium by far!'

I had not been up to my usual form, Charlotte was right, but I had been years without practice! It was hardly reasonable to expect me to remember it all overnight. Still, I would have to try, seeing as in the heat of the moment I had somehow agreed to returning. And I had to acknowledge the truth: I was enjoying myself. So long as I was careful, and discreet, and up to my old standard, then there would be no harm in this one last case. We would string the family along on the story they had already so generously concocted for us, hold some dark circles and maybe stage a possession or two, and then be on our way once they were safe in the assurance that their restive relative had been brought to peace. And then Charlotte would get her fee, and in turn pay the physician, and we would part once more, back to our separate lives. I quashed the tingle of sadness that accompanied that thought. It was how things had to be.

Charlotte and I said our goodbyes at the place du Château d'Eau, where I was finally able to hail a hansom. Feeling a kick of sisterly affection, I did offer to have the cab drive Charlotte home first, but Charlotte insisted that she had business nearby. A jangling in her pockets suggested that she meant a trip to the pawnbroker's to divest herself of whatever she had picked up in the de Jacquinot apartments. With luck, the family would attribute the loss to ghostly activity, I thought as I watched Charlotte scamper away.

CHAPTER THREE

5 April 1866

MY POSITION IN society gave me a wide social circle of recurring faces who could be considered friends. I had only one, however, who was close enough to serve also as a confidante – and even she did not know the full truth of my family history.

To the Vicomtesse Sarah Coupart, my past life was unremarkable, impoverished and unworthy of discussion. In short, I had been a nobody, and as such had entered society as an outsider. This, she could understand. Her father had been a commandant in the Algerian conquest, from which he had returned with a four-year-old daughter. The story he put about was of a Christian wedding ceremony to a French general's daughter, who had subsequently died of the cholera. The darkness of Sarah's skin suggested an alternative narrative. Still, she had been raised as a legitimate child, with all the privileges concurrent with her rank; and while there were those who thought the circumstances of her birth worthy of derision, there were a similar number who found the subject fascinating. She had once confided in me that she thought both groups equally tiresome.

When Sarah had married Guillaume Coupart – over ten years ago now – tongues had started wagging more than ever. Many would have despaired, retired from society, gone abroad.

Not Sarah. She had a shrewd mind and had quickly realized that the best way to prevent people from gossiping about her past was to create far more spectacular opportunities for gossip in the present. She had grown calculatedly extravagant: hosting wild parties, wearing eccentric outfits, voicing unlikely opinions. And, as she had undoubtedly intended, these extravagances had made her popular. These days, she knew everyone who was anyone – and, more importantly, they knew her. She had taken public scrutiny and fashioned it into celebrity; but such a position was a precarious one, always at risk of toppling a person back down to the place where they had started.

Whether Sarah had looked upon me with sympathy as another outsider, or marked me out as a curious accessory, she had immediately approached me with welcome at a time when others disapproved of my match with Alexandre. Some vile things had been said about me: that I was nothing but a social climber, that the only motivation I could have for marrying an older man was his money. It had broken my heart that anyone could question just how much I loved him. But Sarah's influence had secured my acceptance within the upper echelons. As such, she was the friend I valued most, and the only person I felt able to turn to for advice on my current situation. Albeit a situation that I could reveal to her only in part.

When I called upon her to do so, I found her in a highly animated mood, worked up by some grievance or other.

'This business with the estate in Lozère. Such a bore! I am sick and tired of Guillaume harping on about it. It's all down to this blasted cousin of his who claims some kind of ambiguity in the inheritance.' She was reclining on a blue velvet chaise longue, nibbling at a biscuit between exclamations. 'By the way, I have read the legal papers myself, and the man is full of . . .

42

well, better not say; but certainly there is no ambiguity as far as I can see.'

'What a cheek!' I sympathized. I was seated across from her on a canapé that was purple and clashed horribly with the blue. This was the general decorative tenet of Sarah's parlour. It was much like herself: friendly, vibrant and self-knowingly exhibitionist.

Sarah swept her hand in an arc. 'Well, that's the whole point of the matter, darling. Honestly, I do not give a flying toss. As I said to Guillaume: if the miscreant wants the estate, give him the damned thing. What do I care about some wretched estate in *Lozère*? I mean, do *you* know anyone who lives in Lozère?'

I had to confess that I did not.

'Precisely! But Guillaume keeps going on about principles and rights, and anyway my opinion is not to be counted at the moment as I am somewhat out of favour.'

'Oh dear. What have you done?'

'Not a damned thing!' declared Sarah. 'Only had the gall to suggest that every so often he could spend an evening at home with his wife, rather than whichever tart it is at the moment. But apparently that is none of my business; though, of course, if the situations were reversed . . .'

'Sarah! You have *not*!' I cried, half scandalized, half thrilled.

'What? At my age? Goodness, I hardly think so!'

I raised an eyebrow at this; Sarah had only just turned thirty.

'Yes, well, you wait until you get to thirty and see how you feel, darling. But do hold that thought – I think we had better get some fresh coffee.'

In with the coffee came a neat little spaniel, much to Sarah's delight. 'Oh, come here Gévaudan! Good boy!'

Gévaudan loped over, tongue lolling in joy, and allowed

himself to be scooped into Sarah's lap. 'Isn't he looking pretty today?' asked Sarah, smoothing back his ears.

I found Gévaudan no more remarkable than any other dog – although perhaps he was slightly smellier. But one did not say such things to a dog's mistress. Not if one wished to remain her friend.

'Are you my favourite boy?' Sarah was saying. 'Yes! Yes, you are!'

What her two sons would think of this assertion, I did not know.

Gévaudan comfortably seated, Sarah settled herself back into position on the chaise longue and resumed. 'Now, where were we? Ah, yes: infidelity!'

It felt odd to discuss such things in front of a dog. I had to remind myself that he could not understand a word we said, despite what his bright, watchful eyes might have suggested. 'Does Guillaume really . . .' I began. 'I mean, are you certain that . . .?'

'Oh, entirely. The man cannot spell "discretion", let alone exercise it.'

How Sarah could make such a statement without so much as a ruffled feather was beyond my powers of imagination. If Alexandre ever . . . But I could barely envision such a thing; it was my good fortune to have a husband who was enduringly loyal. When we had first begun courting, I had speculated – only naturally – about the women he might have known before me. I did not expect a handsome bachelor of his age never to have taken a lover. So picture my surprise on our wedding night when I saw that he was even less experienced than I! I do not believe he had ever so much as glanced at another person, before or since.

'How dreadful for you,' I said now. 'Not just for it to happen, but for you to have to know about it, about all those other women.'

Sarah gave me a long look, as if considering something. 'To tell you the truth of it,' she said, but then stopped and shook her head. 'Never mind. I had better not say.'

'I had better not say' could mean anything from 'I want very much to say, but I want us to pretend that you have to convince me first', to 'I don't actually know anything on the subject but don't want to admit to it'. I did not feel in the mood for playing along with the game this time. If Sarah wanted to tell me something, she would have to choose to do so of her own volition.

'Affairs of the heart aside,' I said, leaning forwards a little, 'tell me, do you ever . . . well, keep things from Guillaume?'

'Ha! All the time. Whoever heard of telling one's husband the truth?'

'Hmm.'

'Indeed, I am quite convinced that secrets are the key to a happy marriage.'

With Sarah it was often hard to discern whether she truly believed her declarations, or if she merely said them for shock value.

'But suppose—'

Sarah raised a finger. 'I see what this is about, you naughty little thing! What have you done, then?'

It would have been impossible to tell the whole of it. As far as Sarah was concerned, I had no sister. Alexandre had put about that I was an orphan of good lineage, raised as the ward of his extended family in Dijon – never mind that my 'r's were distinctly Parisian. However, it did occur to me that the more information I had on the de Jacquinots, the better equipped I would be. And if anyone were going to have information on the family, it would be Sarah.

I began to spin a story about a debt at the clothier's and not wanting to admit it to Alexandre. This was familiar ground to Sarah, who suggested several ways to raise funds and recommended a discreet pawnbroker I could use in the meantime. Should I like her to accompany me?

'Oh, it is not all that much, really,' I averred. 'The clothier's were very accommodating. Now, that reminds me, I did make a curious new acquaintance while I was there. A gentlewoman, though I had never heard of her before – the Dowager Marquise de Jacquinot. Do you know of her?'

Clearly this was worthy of remark, as Sarah's face lit up and she straightened a little, unsettling Gévaudan's perch. 'Goodness! But she is never seen in society of late. And at the clothier's! Why, I wonder? Do you think this means she is about to resurface from wherever she has been hiding? My, what news!'

'Is it that compelling?' I asked.

Sarah helped herself to another biscuit, as if she needed fortification for the coming reply. 'Well,' she said, 'there has been some talk about the family. You know how people *will* say things . . .'

'And what do they say about the de Jacquinots?'

'Where does one start? The Dowager Marquise is a self-important termagant; the Comte Ardoir is a fanatic who lives in the past; and the daughter is a lunatic. They keep her locked up, you know?'

'And the Marquis, the son?'

'Pleasant enough in small doses, but prone to pig-headedness.'

I had to stifle a laugh at this. 'I see.'

'Yes, the son is the only one I have seen about, although he is never very conversational. One would think, with a daughter of that age, the family would be more invested in finding her a husband. How they expect ever to succeed in marrying her off is a mystery, if they keep her sequestered so. Although I suppose the chances of finding a match for a madwoman are not particularly high.'

'Why do people think her mad?' I asked. Certainly, Florence had seemed wilted and wan, but this was in her favour: such a feeble body seemed unlikely to contain the power required for a display of lunacy. But then, Madame de Jacquinot *had* mentioned a certain mental incapacitation surrounding her illness . . .

'Well, that *is* a story! She came out at fifteen and was a perfectly jolly and pretty thing. And with that striking hair and those elegant limbs, of course she attracted suitors, some of them quite spectacular matches. Do you know the Duc de Polane? No? Well, never mind, but suffice it to say that he is set to inherit quite the sum. But despite her beauty, there was something repulsive about her – chilly, even. No matter who courted her, eventually he would lose interest – and the girl never seemed particularly moved by it, either! But then there was the most recent, a young lawyer, a friend of the brother's. Vasseur was the name, I believe. I forget if he was a vicomte or a baron. Again, he pursued, she rebuffed, but then when he dropped her and left for the country, a terrible change came about her. One could easily not have recognized her! She took no care in her appearance, she was sullen and withdrawn, and on two occasions I have heard it on good authority that she was observed weeping in public.'

This was more like the Florence whom I had encountered.

'Goodness,' I said. 'Do you think the girl was in love with him after all, then?'

'She must have been,' said Sarah, with a shrug. She offered Gévaudan a portion of biscuit, which he snapped up directly from her palm. 'Heartbroken. Well, then suddenly the family locked her away, and she has not been seen since. I have never been able to get anything out of the brother – the story he has been putting about is that the girl suffers a wasting sickness, but I am sure it is in truth a mental affliction.'

'I couldn't possibly say,' I said, apologetically.

'Well, of course not,' said Sarah. 'I hardly expect Madame de Jacquinot would have told you all about it! But listen: if you have made her acquaintance, then that is something quite remarkable. Oh, Sylvie, you must try to get an invitation into her house! I would give a fortune to have the chance! You shall have to be my agent on the inside.'

'It really was the briefest of encounters . . .' I objected.

'But you must! Please, I implore you – for me, your dearest and truest friend. Oh, and I shall invite the son to my party – next week, you haven't forgotten it? – and then you can force him to have a real conversation with me for once!'

I could not help but smile in fondness. 'But Alexandre would hardly approve of my becoming an intimate of such a scandalous family,' I said.

'You could always tell him that you have been with me,' said Sarah. 'You know I would speak in your favour. In any case, it would almost be true, as you would be doing it out of friendship for me.'

If I was honest with myself, this offer was what I had come to Sarah to secure – indeed, I had already told Alexandre that I had spent the day with her earlier in the week, to account for my visit to the de Jacquinot residence. Although I did not enjoy deceiving my husband, I had no other option, and an adequate account for my time was therefore a necessity.

'You would do that for me?' I asked.

'If you can find out the whole story, I will do anything you please!'

'I am making no promises that I can.'

'Oh please, please, please!' She hoisted the dog up as if he were the one speaking. 'How can you say no to this little face?' Gévaudan's eyes bulged vacantly back at me.

'It's impossible,' I agreed.

49

CHAPTER FOUR

9 April 1866

I THOUGHT OF the rumours Sarah had shared with me, as I readied myself to return to the de Jacquinots' house. Florence's alleged madness and the strain it must have put on the family did go some way to explaining the tension I'd observed upon our first meeting. It was commonly held among spiritists that hidden resentments could give rise to poltergeist activity; this seemed the best avenue for Charlotte and me to explore. How had we approached similar cases in the past? It was amazing how quickly such things could slip one's mind, replaced by fashion plates and dance steps. I had a quick rummage through my old papers – kept locked in the desk where Alexandre and the servants could not accidentally discover them – to refresh my memory. Among them, I once more came across the locket containing Mama's miniature. Thinking that perhaps her memory would do something to inspire me, I slipped it around my neck.

It was through Mama's line that Charlotte and I had inherited what she called the 'family gift'. Whenever we had questioned her about its nature, she would tell us that, while the principal role of a medium seemed to be the ability to commune with the dead, our true purpose was to help the living. We had the power to comfort, to chase away grief, to heal those pains that were beyond the reach of medical science – and if we were obliged to use some level of trickery, surely this was excusable in light of its positive effects? The trickery was the part that we had inherited from Papa – a petty criminal in his youth. Papa held no sincere belief, but Mama had never minded this: his contributions elevated her craft beyond what she had ever achieved alone. They had been the perfect match, and the combined talents had always treated Charlotte and myself well.

But these clients, the Dowager Marquise and family, wanted to gain more than comfort and healing; they wanted to gain something tangible. If it had not been for Papa's plight – well, for the idea of Mama's celestial disapproval in the face of Papa's plight – I would already have insisted we could be of no help.

A knock came at the door. I was so absorbed in my thoughts that I nearly jumped from my skin, before hurrying to lock everything away.

'Come in,' I called, hanging the desk key back around my neck to rest beside the locket.

It was Alexandre, damp-haired and smelling of the office when he stooped to kiss me – other men's cigar smoke and cologne. His gaze fell on the key and locket. I hurriedly tucked them into my bodice, out of sight.

'Just got in?' I asked.

'Yes, and out again shortly, I am afraid.' The wince that accompanied this was genuine – beneath his baronic mask, Alexandre was a shy man. Indeed, it had been his social discomfort that first brought us together. I had been at a ball hosted by one of our clients, and, as I slipped out to the gardens to set up a trick involving a magic lantern, a tree and a good length of rope, I had collided with a figure in the dark. After reassuring me that he was not a murderer, Alexandre had introduced himself and explained that, having misplaced the friend with whom he had arrived, and knowing nobody else, he had decided to hide outside to avoid further embarrassment. He had been out there for almost an hour. Feeling sorry for him, I had felt obliged to abandon my equipment and accompany him back inside, where I had found him to be rather handsome. His refined physiognomy, the mature greying hair and spectacles – even the awkward demeanour – were strangely endearing.

'Are you expected at the club?' I asked, tilting my head back as he smoothed my hair.

'Yes, I promised Pinard. But look . . .' There was a paper package tucked under one arm, which he now brought out to show me.

'Oh! Not for me?'

'I saw it in a shop window and thought you would like it.'

I took the present from him, running my fingers over the brown paper to hear the crinkle. It was a rectangular shape and fairly heavy – a book, I thought.

'Go on, do open it.' He was grinning, looking almost boyish in his excitement. He had confided in the past that he felt at times self-conscious about the gap in our ages – he was closer in years to Papa than to me – but he had such a youthful spirit that I often forgot the difference entirely.

Thanking him for the gift, I tore back the paper to find a book bound in red leather. The gold lettering on the cover revealed it to be a volume of Perrault's fairy tales; a new illustrated edition. With a queasy sort of guilt, I remembered Charlotte's reference to Cendrillon the other day.

'Do you like it? I remember you once told me it was a child-hood favourite. I thought . . . for the nursery? I can just imagine you reading it to our children one day.'

I leaned up to peck him on the cheek, doing my best to show delight. 'Yes, of course, darling. How thoughtful of you.'

'You deserve no less! Anyway, I must go and change. You will not be too bored this evening?'

'Ah, I am paying a call myself – Sarah has invited me, as it happens. I may stay the night, if we end up talking until anywhere near as late as we normally do.'

He raised his brow at this. 'Sarah? Have you not visited her twice in the past week already? I wonder that you have anything new to say to one another!'

I flapped my hand vaguely. 'Oh, you know how we are.' Another guilt-pang, but I swallowed it down, telling myself that the falsehood was a lesser betrayal than the truth. On the subject of my family, Alexandre had always made himself explicitly clear.

For a moment, I thought I saw an expression of doubt cross his face, but this must have been my own self-projection, as he quickly smiled again and said, 'Very well. If you see Guillaume, do *not* mention Lozère; he has been hounding me to look at his papers for days, and I can only avoid him for so long.' Alexandre and I both found Sarah's husband a terrible bore. 'Do enjoy yourself, and take the cab if you like.'

As I waited for him to depart, I flicked through the plates of my new book, not really seeing them as I did so. Yes, I could picture myself reading to a child – should one ever come. We had been married two years with no luck. This fact may in part have contributed to Alexandre's anxiety about the gap in our ages, but I knew of many men who had become fathers later in life.

My gaze came to rest on an illustration from 'The Fairies'. A docile girl drawing water from a pump. I supposed this was the good sister. It had been a while since I had read the tale in full but, as I remembered it, it was about two sisters: one good, one bad. Despite being the kinder, prettier and milder-mannered of the two, the good girl was treated poorly by their guardian, whereas the bad one was the favourite. Because of this, it was always the good sister who was sent to the well to collect water. One day, as she was fulfilling this task, she was approached by an old woman who asked her for a drink. Being of a charitable disposition, the girl poured out a draught for her. Once the woman had drunk her fill, she revealed that she was in fact a fairy, and she would repay the good sister for her kindness by casting a spell that made gold fall from her mouth every time she spoke. When the bad sister learned of this new gift, she too went to the well to seek an old crone. However, this time the fairy had disguised herself as a wealthy young noblewoman, so that when she asked for water, the bad sister did not recognize her and replied rudely that she had not come there just to fetch some aristocrat a drink. On hearing this discourteous outburst, the fairy cursed the girl so that every time she spoke, a toad fell out of her mouth. Eventually, the good sister met a prince who fell in love with her charms and her ability to spit gold, whereas the bad sister was spurned by all, and ended up dying alone in the woods.

I had always been certain, as a child, which one I was. Now, I was not so sure that it was not both Charlotte *and* myself who were full of toads.

The de Jacquinot apartments were somehow more pleasant by night – the shabbiness disappeared under the gentle light of candles, and heavy shadows furnished the empty spaces. Sitting at the table in their dining room while Charlotte unpacked our equipment, I fancied I could see how the room had been before times grew hard – shining bright and filled with beautiful, lively people. Dressed in the latest fashions, ladies bubbled with laughter over the scandals of their peers. Men in immaculate dinner suits debated politics and arts. How many romances had begun within these four walls? How many had ended? The dramas of the aristocracy, shimmering and golden, had played out night after night. And at the helm of it all, there was Sabine in her full glory, glittering with the otherworldly light of a fortune of gemstones. Leaning forwards to drop an intimate secret into an open ear. Tinkling with champagne laughter in response to a joke. Pointing out this dish, that portrait, these new earrings from Milan. Sitting at the piano and playing a sonata as smooth as honey. Standing at the window to admire the sunset. Rising from her chair, glass in hand, preparing to make a speech, preparing to be given a voice.

'What is all this?' Madame de Jacquinot asked. Her words extinguished the mirage soirée, returning the room to its threadbare reality. She was watching carefully as Charlotte removed items from the old leather bag that I had once been so used to seeing at Papa's side.

Trying to regain my old confidence, I began to explain the different items to our audience: Madame de Jacquinot, Florence and the Comte. Maximilien had evidently taken Charlotte's advice.

There was the divining rod – a Y-shaped piece of wood, about as long as my forearm. It could be used to detect all manner of things, I told them, such as hidden water, buried treasure, unmarked graves, and the invisible lines of spiritual force that encircled the entire globe. I picked it up to demonstrate its use, holding the two forked ends loosely in my hands, palms facing upwards. This one had been in the family for generations; our great-grandfather had once used it to hunt witches.

Then I showed them the storm glass. Ardoir recognized it as such immediately, and asked why on earth it would be in a spiritist's bag. 'It is most unusual to see a woman handling scientific equipment; I wonder that you know how to use it at all.'

'As is often the case with our tools,' I told him, forcing a polite smile, 'a storm glass has more than one use. Of course, as a well-read gentleman, you will be aware that ordinarily such items are used to detect the change in atmospheric pressure that augurs a storm. Well, when the veil between worlds is stretched thin enough for a soul to pass between them, do you really think that the atmosphere is *not* affected?'

He narrowed his eyes at this. 'In fact, I had not given it much thought.'

'You would be amazed to know how many pieces of scientific apparatus and even everyday objects have a spiritual application,' I told him. There was the thermometer, which could detect the fluctuations in temperature caused by a spiritual presence; the compass, to measure how the field of magnetism became warped by passage from one world to the next; the set of bells for summoning and banishing; a candle, whose flame could be discoloured by spiritual activity; and, of course, a bowl of sea salt.

'Sea salt?' asked Madame de Jacquinot.

'There are times,' I told her, 'when spirit visitors can be difficult to regulate. Although Charlotte and I do our best – with the help of our spirit control – to prevent the passage of undesirable spirits into our realm, sometimes one may still break through.'

There was a gasp from Florence here.

'Do not be so melodramatic, girl!' snapped Ardoir. But there was a shake to his voice, and I recalled the wall of crucifixes in his bedroom. He was just as scared as she was.

'There is no need to be alarmed,' I told them. 'We have every defence at the ready should such an unlikely incursion occur: sea salt and iron' – here, I gestured to a metal rod that Charlotte was unwrapping – 'are fatal to the substance of a visiting spirit.'

'And I believe you mentioned a spirit control?' asked Madame de Jacquinot.

'A spirit medium cannot call directly upon the world of the spirits – to communicate with them, she must have a spiritual accomplice, with whom her soul is linked by the threads of Fate.' Here I paused, touching my locket – which I had untucked from my dress so that others could see it. 'For Charlotte and myself,' I went on, 'our spirit control is the soul of our mother.'

This always had an effect upon older women, and Madame de Jacquinot was no exception. She touched a trembling hand to her bosom and, with a waver to her voice, asked when Mother had passed.

'A short time after I was born,' said Charlotte, who had now finished assembling our paraphernalia. A short time of ten years.

'You poor thing,' said Madame de Jacquinot.

'But you see,' said Charlotte, 'I count myself very lucky. Unlike so many others, I was still allowed to know my mother.' She dropped her voice to a whisper. 'Indeed, she visits me every day.'

These objects, of course, were no more than scene dressing. For this was the true skill of a spirit medium: to create a credible show. It did not matter whether or not one could summon a spirit; it did not even matter whether one believed in the existence of spirits – what one's success truly came down to was one's ability to convince the clients, *in that moment*, that a spirit was present. Without that ability, one might summon every soul in the catacombs and still be denied a fee.

Once Madame de Jacquinot had been comforted, our party spread itself about the dining table, with Charlotte and I sitting opposite one another.

'In a moment,' said Charlotte, 'I shall put out all of the candles, bar one. When I am seated again, I ask that everybody join hands, and then you all must remain entirely still and silent so that Sylvie and I can establish a connection with our spirit control.'

There were noises of agreement, and so Charlotte set about extinguishing the candles. As she blew out the last one – save for the candle remaining at the centre of the table – the door opened, and Maximilien slipped into the room.

'I apologize for my late arrival,' he said. 'I was dining with Clement and we quite lost track of the hour.'

I tried to keep the dismay from my face that, whoever this Clement was, he had not been able to distract Maximilien longer. 'Not at all, Monsieur,' I told him. 'If you would be so kind, please take a seat and remain silent while my sister and I call upon the spirit world.'

He seemed in a more amenable mood this time, refraining from making any snide remarks as he groped his way to the chair next to mine. His expression, however, was hard to read in the low light.

A hush set about the room, and I held out my hands, one to Maximilien on the left, and the other to Madame de Jacquinot on the right. We remained in silence for several minutes, with only the sound of the dining-room clock ticking to mark the passage of time. One had to judge this just right: summon a spirit too soon, and people would think it too easy to be worth the fee; leave it too long, and they would simply get bored.

Just as Maximilien was beginning to shuffle, a knock reverberated throughout the room.

'Mother!' I cried. 'Is that you?'

There was another knock. Madame de Jacquinot's hand tightened around mine.

'One knock indicates a reply of "yes",' Charlotte whispered to the de Jacquinots. 'Two means "no".'

'Mother,' I went on, 'please tell me: is there another presence in this house?'

Knock.

'Is this presence the soul of the Comtesse Sabine de Lisle?'

Knock.

'Anybody could be making that noise,' muttered Maximilien.

'Quiet, boy!' returned Ardoir.

I pressed on. 'Is the presence in this room with us now?'

Two knocks.

'Are you able to help us to bring her into the room?'

There was a pause. Then one knock.

A gasp came from somewhere – I assumed from Florence again, although I could barely see her – drawing everyone's attention to the candle. Where it had previously been burning a jolly, yellow flame, it had now turned icy blue.

This was an ingenious discovery of Charlotte's: if one mixes a little calcium chloride into melted wax, the resulting candle will have a blue flame. It takes only some careful designing to make a candle that changes between colours as it melts.

A moment later, the table began to rattle. Florence shrieked, and there was the scrape of her chair as she tried to move away.

A hidden hook up my sleeve, slotted under the tabletop. In a pinch, one could also catch one's toe around the table leg – I had even known mediums who simply kicked the underside of the table, but I found this inelegant.

'Do *not* break the circle, Mademoiselle!' cried Charlotte.

I felt Madame de Jacquinot jerk Florence – who was at her other side – back into place.

Then an unmistakable scent unfurled itself into the room: orange blossom. A smell taken straight from an ancien régime perfume recipe. I thought this a very clever touch from Charlotte, whom I presumed to have a scent bottle secreted somewhere about her person.

'Is the Comtesse Sabine de Lisle here among us now?' I called.

Knock.

'Auntie!' called Ardoir, the tremor still present in his words. 'Auntie, is it really you?'

Knock.

'Rot,' muttered Maximilien, but I could feel the pulse racing in his thumb where our hands were joined. A mouse's heartbeat.

'Does the Comtesse have a message for the living in this room?' I asked.

Knock.

'For whom, Auntie?' asked Ardoir. The outline of his head was just visible, turning back and forth across the table as he searched the shadows for her form. 'Is it for me?'

A scream rent the air, and Florence shot from her seat, her face pale as a corpse in the blue half-light. 'A hand!' she cried, her voice cracking. 'There was a hand, a cold hand at the back of my neck!'

'You have broken the circle!' shouted Ardoir, and I caught the movement of his own hand being wrenched from Charlotte's as he lunged towards Florence. 'You stupid girl!'

I was not sure if he intended to strike her, or merely to shout in her face; before I could find out, the movement overbalanced him and he toppled forwards against the table, knocking over the candle. Its light went out.

Florence screamed again. Madame de Jacquinot's hand left mine; in contrast, Maximilien's gripped tighter, so tight that I felt the bones of my fingers might crack.

'Keep calm!' Charlotte commanded. 'Please, everybody remain calm! The circle is broken; Mother has departed.'

'But Auntie?' asked Ardoir's voice.

'She has also departed,' I said. 'We are alone once more. Can you not feel the calm in the air?'

Whatever was in the air, it was not calm: there were Florence's sobs; a series of fumblings as somebody tried to strike a match; and the final, lingering traces of perfume.

At last, there was a flare of brightness. Charlotte had lit a taper. She went around touching it to the candles in the room. As the shadows were pushed back into the corners, everyone seemed to relax. Maximilien, realizing he was still clasping my hand, muttered an embarrassed apology and let go. For an odd half-second I could still feel the drumming of his pulse, as one sees the outline of an image at which one has been staring, even after looking away.

'Goodness,' said Madame de Jacquinot, giving a shaky laugh.

Ardoir's cheeks were mottled – red flush against a stricken white. 'You have ruined it, girl. I will make you regret—'

'Not at all,' Charlotte hurried to say. 'This was extremely successful for a first attempt at contact, Monsieur. Why, I imagine that with a few more evenings like this, we may progress to a genuine manifestation.'

Florence shuddered. 'I see her frequently enough as it stands,' she said. Her face was puffy, glistening either from perspiration or from tears. I could not help but recall Sarah's assessment of her – but she looked more spectre than madwoman at that moment.

'There,' said Maximilien, 'she does not even want to continue. Come on, Flo, let's put an end to this nonsense and—'

'Will you please stop being so contrary?' said Madame de Jacquinot, finally pushed into losing her patience. 'And Florence, for heaven's sake, go and wash your face.'

Florence did not move.

'Florence . . .' said Madame de Jacquinot.

'Am I to go on my own?'

'Really, you are a grown woman!'

Charlotte cleared her throat delicately. 'Shall I accompany you, Mademoiselle?' she asked. 'I will bring the salt, look. And we can ask your housekeeper for a nice glass of wine before we return.'

I tried to catch her eye, wary of her motives; either she did not see, or – more likely – was avoiding my gaze.

A little calmer now that Florence was out of his sight, Ardoir watched as I packed the equipment back into the bag. 'Fascinating,' he said, staring at the now-foggy storm glass. Silver nitrate and acid, shaken together. 'Truly fascinating.'

I took the opportunity to ask a little more about his contradictory attitude towards the Comtesse. 'If it is not too upsetting a subject, Monsieur,' I began, 'may I ask what you know of the circumstances of your aunt's death?'

There was a quiet moment as Ardoir collected himself, sucking in his lips as if to seal them permanently. How old was he, I wondered? If he had been a child at the time of the Revolution – even a very young one – he must have been at least seventy now, perhaps older still. All the years he had seen, all accumulated in that shrunken head of his. If only one could have cracked it open – what hidden secrets of the past would have come flowing out?

At last, beckoning me to sit back down across from him, he said, 'What do you want to know of it?'

'Well . . . Why do you not start with something simple? For example – where is the Comtesse buried?'

Something in the Comte's face ticked: a suppressed flinch.

Suddenly aware of a hush in the room, I glanced up to find both Madame de Jacquinot and Maximilien averting their gazes. 'Forgive me, have I caused some kind of offence?' I asked.

Ardoir's hands were fidgeting like a pair of pale spiders. 'It is just that I do not know the answer,' he said at last. 'I was only a boy. In fact, my parents and I had already left Paris by the time . . .' It was easy to forget that the Comtesse had been a real person whom Ardoir had known and loved. The old man sitting before me with his papery skin and liver spots had once been a frightened child, fleeing for his life without understanding why there were people who wanted it over in the first place.

Of course, I was proud of my country for overthrowing those who had kept us in shackles, for winning our freedom and asserting our inalienable rights, but when I thought of the blood that had brought these victories to pass, I could not help but shudder.

'When was this?' I asked, trying to sound gentle. 'By "the Revolution", do you mean 1789 itself, or are you referring to the Terror?'

'Let me see . . . We left in the summer of 1792. Auntie and Uncle had intended to join us some time later. We received word from Auntie in 1793 or '94 – it was certainly winter – that she and my cousins would come without the Comte. Now I think of it, it must have been '93, as I remember being excited that they might be with us in time for Christmas. But they were not; we heard in the summer of 1794 from a family friend that Auntie and Uncle had been executed as enemies of the people. 'It may not have been in summer that it happened, but that was when we heard.' The Comte gave a series of rapid blinks. There was moisture in his eyes. 'I never learned where they were buried, nor the fate of my cousins.'

I made a sympathetic noise in my throat. 'Ah, I am sorry for your loss. Have you ever checked for the family's names at Picpus?' Once, many years ago now, Mama had taken Charlotte and I to dowse atop the pit at Picpus Cemetery. Over a thousand headless bodies had been tossed there between June and July in 1794 – our client at the time had been sure that at least one belonged to a lost relative. Mama's results had not contradicted the theory, even though the list of names on the church walls had.

'We could never find them,' said Madame de Jacquinot, coming over to hand a handkerchief to her father.

'Thrown into a hole with the common muck,' Ardoir shuddered. 'It does not bear imagining.'

Madame de Jacquinot turned back to me. 'Could this be connected to why the Comtesse has returned?'

'It is possible,' I said. 'An improper burial can make for an unquiet spirit. Ghosts will sometimes make contact so they can be laid finally to rest.'

'So that is why she visits me,' said Ardoir. Something about his words made my skin crawl.

We regrouped in the parlour, where Florence and Charlotte had set up with glasses and a jug of wine. Despite my misgivings, Florence appeared tranquil now; Charlotte had evidently managed to reassure her. Well, Charlotte or the alcohol.

I took my seat beside Charlotte, who poured a glass and passed it to me with a smirk. She knew I could not abide the smell, and now I would have to drink at least some so as not to appear rude to my hosts. This was her idea of a great joke, I was sure.

Settling into his armchair, Ardoir nodded at Florence. 'They look alike, in fact. That is how I recognized Auntie so quickly, even after all these years. I would know those eyes anywhere. And the hair, like copper. No, Florence' – he held up his hand to reject the glass she offered – 'I will pour for myself, thank you.'

Madame de Jacquinot looked as if she were going to say something in response to this strange preference, but held her tongue as the old man got back up to pour his own drink.

Hoping to steer him back to our former subject, I asked, 'You learned of the Comtesse's death from a family friend, you said. Did you learn anything of its nature?'

There was a bob of movement in Ardoir's throat: the Adam's apple shifting as he swallowed. 'It is not a pleasant story for the delicate ears of young ladies,' he said.

Charlotte's mouth pressed into a tight line. 'But it may be a necessary one, Monsieur.'

Ardoir seemed to look into the distance, his eyes like two bright crystal balls. 'I was not meant to hear it, in fact; I had been sent from the room, but I crept back to the door and listened in. The man – the friend, although I did not think of him as such at the time – told my parents all. He had arranged for the Comte de Lisle and his family to be smuggled from the country, disguised as wine merchants. My cousins were to hide in the barrels. Imagine that – children squeezed into barrels so they would not be murdered. But such was the heartlessness of the Republicans.

'Then something went wrong – the Comte must have been betrayed. I hope the thirty pieces of silver were worth it to whichever Judas took them! As the family tried to escape through the garden – our garden – there was a great ruckus from the other side of the wall. Shouts and men's voices, the sound of danger approaching. The gate was thrown open, and in spilled an angry mass armed with pistols, carbines, work tools and a makeshift red flag mounted on a pike. The children began to cry in terror and Auntie pulled them back to stand behind her. She asked the mob to grant her passage. They demanded to see her papers. When she offered none, they accused the family of attempting to flee the country illegally, of being traitors to the cause.'

He stopped to take a gulp of wine, as though steeling himself for what came next. 'Three or four of their number surged forwards and grabbed Auntie, pulling her away from the children and throwing her to the floor. The friend tried to intervene but was knocked aside and pinned down by some brute. One man leaped upon Auntie and snatched at her skirt, claiming to be in search of papers, until the fabric ripped open, revealing (if you will excuse my recounting such foul treatment of a lady) her petticoats. She cried out and tried to twist away, but the movement dislodged a clatter of gold coins from her skirt lining – it had been the Comte's idea to conceal them so. The man who had torn it cried out that she was escaping with the property of the people. Although the Comte tried to catch hold of the children, fierce hands tugged them from him. He was struck with the barrel of a pistol and fell unconscious to the floor. My cousins – Hélène and Luce were their names – were dragged away from their mother, screaming all the while. Our friend did not see what happened to them beyond that: they were simply gone.

'Auntie began to wail, but a woman told her she must remain silent, or they would silence her – and so Auntie (such a poised and respectful woman at all times, but now forced to resort to the only language these brutes could understand) spat in her tormentor's face. "It seems Madame is full of nastiness," said the woman. "Why don't we help her to change that?" At this signal, Auntie was hauled on to her knees and her jaw pulled open. The woman scooped up a fistful of coins and dirt from the ground and shoved it all into Auntie's mouth, then her accomplices forced Auntie's lips together again, even though she could barely close them around their contents. She began choking, but her mouth was held firmly shut. Our friend tried to scream for help but was throttled before he could do any good. One of the men stepped forwards, a dagger in his hand, and held it to Auntie's throat. Whether he acted out of mercy or out of impatience, I will never know. He drew the blade across, and only as the blood flowed out of her did her captors loosen their grip on her jaw. The last thing our friend saw before the horror of it all caused him to lose consciousness was Auntie's mouth, spitting out a tumble of gold.'

I looked away politely for the duration of the time it took Ardoir to dab at his face with his handkerchief. What did one say to such a story? Commiserations did not seem adequate.

But still . . . that left one thing unexplained. 'If I may, Monsieur . . . How is it possible that the Comtesse left behind concealed treasure, if the insurgents caught her in the act of smuggling away her gold?'

Ardoir looked at me as if I had asked the most foolish of questions. 'Well,' he said, 'naturally, she had more gold than one could fit in a single dress.'

'Oh,' I said. 'I see.' I ran a quick mental calculation: even if I put together all the gold finery owned by both myself and Alexandre, *and* the jewels I was set to inherit from his parents . . . even then, it was probably not quite so heavy that I could not have sewn it all into one dress. It would certainly have been uncomfortable – but by no means impossible. In that case . . . just how rich *had* the Comtesse been?

'That went well,' Charlotte observed. She was in the process of unbuckling the straps that had kept two wooden discs fastened to the inside of her knees all evening. It was by knocking these together that she had produced our spirit raps. They were impossible to detect beneath a set of voluminous skirts, although one did have to walk carefully when wearing them.

'I think so too,' I said, as I climbed into Florence's bed. Florence had surrendered her room to us – so we could be on the watch for any paranormal occurrences – and would be sharing with her mother that night. 'Shall I put the light out?'

Charlotte knocked the discs together once for 'yes', then stowed them away before she joined me in bed. 'God, what a story from the old man.'

I leaned over to extinguish the candle. 'It does almost make one feel sorry for him.'

'What? No, I don't believe that rot for a second. And even if the insurgents *were* that brutal – which sounds exaggerated – don't forget what they'd suffered for generations thanks to people like the Comtesse. Anyway, I don't believe they'd have murdered children like that. It's just anti-Republican fearmongering, if you ask me.'

I was not so sure: just because a story is not politically convenient does not make it fiction. I wondered briefly what Alexandre would make of it – he always had an intelligent stance on such questions – but then remembered with disappointment, and a small pang of guilt, that I could not ask him.

'But overall, it went well,' Charlotte said again.

'Yes. Although, the spectral hand . . . I felt that was a sight premature.'

I could just about make out a movement on the other pillow, which may have been a nod. 'Yes, at least on Mademoiselle Florence. Next time, maybe try someone more robust.'

'Why on earth did you pick her?'

Charlotte was silent for a moment. 'I didn't pick her, Sylvie,' she said at last.

'Pardon?'

'Pardon yourself!'

I shifted to face her, not that there was enough light to make out her expression. 'I dare say that you must have picked her,' I said, 'seeing as you put out your hand and touched her, rather than anyone else.'

The simplest method of manifesting a spirit limb depended on very low lighting and dexterity of movement; a medium could slip her bare hand out of a pre-cut slot in her clothing, while her glove, stitched to the end of her sleeve, remained atop the table for all to see. For further effect, she may have previously tied a tourniquet about her arm, or dipped her hand into water to give it a ghostly chill when touched. But, now that I thought on it, Charlotte could not have performed this trick tonight – we had all held hands for the duration of the circle.

'Me?' asked Charlotte. 'Sylvie, it was *you* that touched her, wasn't it?'

I realized what was happening, and let out a groan. 'Do not start on that silly business, trying to scare me,' I said. 'It was not funny back then, and it is not funny now.'

'I'm not!'

'You know that I was not at all near enough to Mademoiselle Florence to touch her.'

'Well, I didn't either!'

I had always found it best to ignore Charlotte when she teased like this, so turned to face the other way. The bed smelled musty and of something that I supposed must have been Florence. No, it was the orange blossom again. The residue from Charlotte's perfume trick. 'The scent was clever,' I said.

'But Sylvie, that wasn't—'

'Oh, stop it.'

Charlotte laughed softly. 'Whatever you want to believe.'

Then we were both silent, nothing but our slowing breaths and my own heartbeat in my ears. *Tap-tap*, *tap-tap*, like the knocking of a ghost at a table. But, of course, there were no ghosts; it had always just been us.

CHAPTER FIVE

10 April 1866

THE GOUGES WERE inches in diameter – some up to three feet long – crossing back and forth as if forming strange hieroglyphs. There was no arrangement to them, no logic. No meditated act: this was pure, unbridled rage; concentrated loathing unleashed upon architecture. Great swathes of the library's wallpaper had been torn down, rags of it peeling away from the wall like skin from burst blisters. The most violent marks had gone deeper, ripping out chunks of plaster, even exposing the dark, intestinal cavity of the wall in places. Plaster dust lay white over the furnishings. Every one of the de Jacquinots' ancestral portraits had been cast upon the floor. Many of the canvases were torn to ribbons – particularly the faces.

No, not *every* one. A single portrait had been spared. Keeping her place in the centre of the wall, Sabine de Lisle overlooked the carnage with a secretive smile.

The weight of this violence crawled up my throat. My stomach felt full of pebbles, cool and heavy. The Furies above scowled down at the scene, as if such destruction was an affront even to their natures.

Maximilien cleared his throat, making me jump. I had forgotten that he was there behind us. 'I do not know what is going on here,' he said, voice oddly tight, 'but I think you ladies had better come up with a good excuse if you do not wish the blame to fall upon you.' Without waiting for our response, he withdrew, as if to let us stew alone in the echo of his words.

'"Mene, mene, tekel, upharsin,"' said Charlotte, laughter underneath her voice. The biblical writing on the wall, warning Belshazzar that his kingdom was soon to fall.

'Is that appropriate?' I hissed.

Charlotte looked at me with glittering eyes, which were lost beneath a frown when she understood that I was serious. 'Well, forgive me for trying to lift the mood,' she said.

'Is that really your first thought?' I asked. 'You see this' – I cast about for a word strong enough to describe the butchery that stood before us – '*this*, and your immediate response is to try to "lift the mood"?'

An eye roll. 'I don't see why you're so cross. It's not like *I* did it.'

The pebbles in my stomach began to wriggle; not pebbles at all, but toads. Fat and viscous. They were croaking words, and what they said was this: Charlotte had slipped from the room the previous night and come into the library and— But how could she have? I was a habitual light sleeper and would surely have heard her rise. As it stood, I had slept soundly all night – better even than normal, after such an evening of excitement. And even if I had slept through this, someone would surely have heard the commotion in the library; it would have been impossible to complete such a project in silence. Madame de Jacquinot and Florence had slept only two rooms away, and claimed to have heard nothing. Instead, we had all learned of the scene only a quarter-hour before, when the day girl had come into the library to light the fire and woken us with her screams.

So why did I feel certain that Charlotte was somehow at fault?

'Charlotte,' I said, the words rasping forth from a suddenly dry throat. 'Please tell me that you had nothing to do with this.'

The look she gave me was righteous with outrage – I would almost have been convinced that it was genuine, if I had not known Charlotte to be such a good actor.

'All I am asking is that you look me in the eye and tell me that you did not come in here last night.'

'I'm sorry?' asked Charlotte. 'You mean, you think I somehow snuck away from you, made it down the corridor without anyone hearing, came in here and used – what? My sewing scissors? – to savage this wall?'

'Well, did you?'

Charlotte's eyes looked ready to pop out of her head. 'What in God's name is wrong with you, Sylvie? Are you completely incapable of trusting another human being? Or is this all specially for me? You've known me twenty-one damned years, and *this* is all we've got to show for it?' She gestured to the space between us, as if she could see there some physical manifestation of our sibling bond. Fraying and decayed.

I knew that I should give up, but I could not shake that sick feeling. 'All I am asking—' I began.

'No!' said Charlotte. 'There: are you happy? No, I didn't! And I don't s'pose it's crossed your mind that I could well ask the same question of you. But I won't, because the accusation's completely mad.'

I may have been the one to insist Charlotte make eye contact, but by the end of this outburst it was I who was unable to meet my sister's gaze. 'I . . . I am sorry, Charlotte,' I said softly. 'I was not thinking rationally.'

'Sylvie, if we're going to work together on this, then you need to trust me. I know we've had our differences over the years, but we're sisters. If we can't trust each other, then who can we?'

To believe in Charlotte as I had as a child, despite what had happened two and a half years ago . . .? But then, Charlotte was willing to put that behind us.

'So if you had no hand in this,' I said, 'I mean, *as* you had no hand in this, then who did? And *how*?' Perhaps we should have been treating this as a crime scene. But Charlotte and I were no detectives. We had no idea where to start.

'Not Madame de Jacquinot, surely?' said Charlotte.

'No, that seems unlikely. And the grandfather is far too frail.'

'So's Florence,' said Charlotte.

'That could be an act.'

'You think she enjoys being locked away as an invalid?' Charlotte asked incredulously. I had filled her in on Sarah's gossip beforehand.

'I suppose not,' I said. 'So Maximilien? He was late to arrive to the circle. What if he and his friend were plotting this very trick as they dined together? If he was even telling the truth about that.'

Charlotte grimaced. 'But why would he do it?'

For that matter, why would anyone? 'Perhaps someone else, someone who holds a grudge against the family? One of the servants, or a neighbour. I am sure they must have earned themselves some enemies over the years. One hardly imagines that Ardoir has lived so many decades without upsetting anyone with those manners.'

'Or . . .' Charlotte stopped herself, biting her lower lip. Her eyes flitted from the wall to me, then back to the wall.

'Or what?'

'Well,' said Charlotte, 'it'd take a great amount of strength to do something like this, wouldn't it?'

'Yes, I suppose so.'

'You might even say . . . a supernatural amount of strength.'

I laughed, this time glad to hear a joke. 'Yes, very funny.'

'I ain't joking,' said Charlotte. Her face was solemn; a Sunday-in-church face.

'A spirit?' I asked.

'Well, why not?'

'Why not?' I lowered my voice further. 'Because *we* are the spirits, Charlotte. You and I.'

Charlotte frowned and paced closer to the damaged wall. Slowly, as if it were a wounded animal and she was afraid it might bite, she reached out a single finger and traced along one of the gouges. 'D'you remember how you used to play sick to get out of visiting that old woman up the road?' she asked suddenly. 'You always said she smelled of beef. What was her name again?'

'Madame Rambon,' I said. 'And it was ham.'

'Oh yes, Rambon the jambon!'

'How I hated those house calls.'

Charlotte turned back to me and raised her eyebrows. 'My point is, you always played sick, and then one day you actually *were* sick, and Papa wouldn't believe you and made you go anyway.'

I winced at the memory, one hand reflexively reaching to stroke the underside of my jaw. 'And I fainted and cut my chin on her front step,' I said. I could still feel the bump of a scar, although Alexandre always assured me he could see nothing there, that my beauty was unmarred. Clearly a lie, but one that I never tired of hearing.

'Exactly,' said Charlotte. 'Just because you'd been lying all those other times, that didn't mean you weren't actually ill that day.'

I thought I had managed to catch up with the analogy. 'Charlotte, I hardly think that a head cold and a ghost merit the same level of credulity.'

'I'm just saying we shouldn't rule it out.'

So, this was it: somewhere in the two years of separation, Charlotte had finally succumbed to her imaginative tendencies. I had heard of such spiritists before – those who became so entrenched in the fiction that they managed to convince even themselves that it was fact. It was never a story that ended well.

'I think, perhaps,' I said, newly cautious, 'we should exhaust our earthly options to begin with.'

Before the discussion could progress any further, there came a polite rap at the door, followed by Madame de Jacquinot's head, hairs curling anxiously out from beneath her day cap. 'I am sorry to disturb you, ladies,' she said, peering in at us with undisguised curiosity, but clearly unwilling to extend any other body parts across the threshold unless it was absolutely necessary, 'but I wished to know, have you come to any conclusions so far?'

'Let us step into the parlour with you,' said Charlotte, ushering our client along with her hands.

The whole family was gathered together. I took a quick inspecting look at each of them, searching for any sign of dissimulation. All that I saw was dishevelment.

Madame de Jacquinot was fussing with her cap. 'My, you must think us quite ridiculous to be so worked up. I am sure that to ladies of such experience as you, it will seem quite the trifling matter, but nevertheless . . .'

Charlotte batted a hand soothingly. 'No, Madame, it is quite . . . a mess.'

'A mess!' Maximilien scoffed, but even he looked unnerved. He was at Florence's side, one hand resting lightly on her elbow as if in support. I could almost feel, for a moment, the flutter of his pulse against my hand once more. For all his talk, he was clearly terrified. Perhaps less of the spirits themselves as much as of the potential that spirits might exist after all – a fact that would force him to reassess everything in which he had hitherto believed. Ghosts were not as scary as being proven wrong.

Ardoir also seemed deeply troubled, twitching whenever anyone spoke, as if he expected to hear a spirit voice at any moment.

Charlotte had clearly noted this as well; she turned to Ardoir and said, 'Monsieur, I believe you were of the initial opinion that your aunt had returned to lead you to her missing fortune?'

'Yes.'

'Is that still your belief, even now?'

A moment of hesitation, then, 'Yes.'

Charlotte leaned forwards, gaze fixed upon him. 'If it is not too impertinent a question, Monsieur, may I ask why, then, you have so many crucifixes in your bedchamber? I could not help but notice it when your daughter showed us around.'

Ardoir's lips pursed slowly, like withering fruit. 'I do not see how that is any of your business, young lady.'

'My apologies. I did not mean to sound interrogative. I merely wondered if you had assembled them for . . . spiritual protection.'

It seemed as if some internal debate was playing itself out in Ardoir's brain: his eyes flicked to and fro and his mouth quivered wordlessly. At last, he inclined his head. 'That is true,' he said.

'From the unseen guest?' asked Charlotte.

'Do not be ridiculous,' Ardoir said immediately. 'Auntie is here to help. But . . . I know it cannot be she who plays such wicked tricks as the one in the library. Auntie would never so deface her beloved house.'

'I am sorry,' I said, 'do you mean to say . . . you think there is another spirit here?'

'I do not know what I think,' said Ardoir. 'That is why we are paying you ladies. But I see no reason not to take precautions.'

Charlotte and I glanced at one another again.

'And this . . . other spirit,' said Charlotte. 'Let us just say for the sake of argument that there is another one; if it is not here, like your auntie, to help – then what else?'

'Do you think it could be seeking help for itself?' I suggested.

Ardoir shook his head. 'I think . . . to harm us.'

Florence stifled a squeak.

'Please do not alarm yourselves,' I said quickly, looking between the family members. 'What happened in the library certainly seems easy to explain as an act intended to cause harm, but often when spirits behave in such a manner it is not out of ill will, but to attract attention.' Even as I spoke the words of reassurance, I did not know whether they were true – if some enemy of the family had really come into the house to destroy the portraits, then malice was far more likely a motive. I could not stop thinking of the Comtesse's portrait, left unscathed. Left with that knowing smile.

'Unless,' said Charlotte, interrupting my thoughts, 'you can think of a reason that a spirit would wish to hurt you?' She paused. 'There is not something you know about that may have upset them, is there?'

'I . . . No. There is nothing. I was merely disturbed by the library.' Ardoir smoothed his lapels.

I dropped my voice to a confidential level. 'If there *is* something, Monsieur Ardoir, it is essential that you—'

'Do your ears not work?' he snapped. 'I said there is nothing.'

He was not about to budge. But I could sense something just out of reach, like a figure shrouded in mist. What was it that I was missing? What were the family hiding? And why, for the love of God, would they not just tell us if they wanted our help?

Charlotte, now done with Ardoir, was looking around with a frown. 'Where has the day girl got to?'

Did my sister think the day girl a suspect? But, again, how could one young woman manage to cause such destruction on her own, and without being heard by the slumbering household?

'The poor thing was quite shaken,' said Madame de Jacquinot. 'All pale and trembling, and going on about witchcraft or what-have-you. You know how superstitious her sort can be. I sent her down to the kitchen for a drink and said she might go home.'

Charlotte nodded her understanding. 'How *generous* of you, Madame.'

All was a-bustle as Charlotte and I stepped into the kitchens at the base of the building: whistling kettles, sizzling pans, dense, damp air and the smell of yeast as breakfast was made ready. The day girl was sitting at the vast wooden table – short and slender, probably about twenty but already crooked in her back. Such is the price of a life of domestic labour, of averted eyes and silent curtseying. It didn't escape me that, in another life, this could have been my own fate.

'Willemijn?' asked Charlotte, drawing out a chair across from her and taking a seat.

The girl looked up from an open bottle of beer. 'Good morning, Mademoiselle,' she said. Her accent was Dutch.

I dipped my head in greeting, sitting beside Charlotte. 'I do not believe we have been properly introduced,' I said. 'I am Sylvie Mothe, and this is my sister, Charlotte. We were Madame de Jacquinot's guests last night.'

I could not help but notice how calloused Willemijn's hands were, all cracked and red at the knuckles. Catching me looking, she withdrew them, back into her lap.

'I know,' Willemijn said. 'You're the spiritists, ain't you?'

'Yes, and we'd like to ask you some questions, if you don't mind?' asked Charlotte, setting her notebook out on the table. 'About what you saw in the library, and your work here. It's just to help us understand what's been happening upstairs – we won't tell anyone else a thing you say. You can be honest with us.'

'And please do not omit details even if you think them to be insignificant,' I added. 'What you consider insignificant, we may recognize as something more.' I paused, noting her hesitation. How good was her French? 'Do you understand everything so far?'

Willemijn nodded brusquely, while Charlotte shot me a frown. 'But I can't be long. Madame de Jacquinot said I can take the day off, and I'd like to get back to the children in that case.'

'You have children?' I asked.

Willemijn squinted at me, not answering. Wondering why the likes of me wanted to know, no doubt.

'Sorry,' I said. 'I do not mean to sound like I am prying. I meant only to be friendly. I love children.'

'You have them?'

'Ah . . . Not yet.' Was I blushing? Silly to feel so embarrassed by the subject! There were many wives who did not produce an heir in the first years of a marriage. There were some, at least. I was not ashamed of it – though I did hate to feel judged. Un-womanned in the eyes of some stranger. And I could sense Charlotte eyeing me up.

'Siblings,' Willemijn said. 'The little ones; they ain't my own.' Then, after taking a swig of her beer, she added, 'My man says there's no such thing as spirits. He says Madame and all are a family of idiots to believe in them.'

I shook my head. 'I have made my livelihood off spirits since I was a child, Willemijn. They are as real to me as . . . well, the dust and the fireplaces and such which make up your work.' I regarded her closely, watching for any sign of recognition. Was that a hint of irritation as she shifted her posture? 'Now, I do not believe that you are in agreement with your . . . gentleman friend. You have seen something yourself, have you not?'

'You're talking about this morning in the library?'

'Yes, if you like.'

Willemijn shuddered and gripped her beer bottle, fingers melting circles in the condensation upon it. Noticing my attention, she said defensively, 'I wouldn't normally be drinking this early, just so you know. But I needed it after what I saw. What's happened in there . . . It's evil, that's all I know. The room felt evil. I felt it before I even lit the lamps to see by.'

There was the sound of pencil on paper as Charlotte noted this down.

'Have you ever felt anything like this before in the house?' I asked.

Willemijn shook her head. She wore her hair back under her cap, with two barley-curls framing her face on either side, bobbing like catkins in a breeze as she moved.

'So this is the first time such a thing has happened?'

'Oh, I can't say either way. I've only been in service three months.'

'I see. Well, what about the other staff? Have they said anything on the matter?'

'There's only me and Caroline, the housekeeper,' said Willemijn, 'and she's newer than me.'

I had seen this Caroline about the de Jacquinot apartments a little – a middle-aged woman with a face the texture and colour of a blancmange.

'Do the family have trouble keeping staff?' asked Charlotte.

Willemijn shrugged. 'Don't see why that'd be. Aside from the ghost, they're no better or worse than most others. No, it sounded more like they dismissed their old housekeeper a year or so back. Lily, I think her name was. I don't know why she went, though, or why it took them so long to replace her. Maybe they just didn't have money to keep her no longer.'

'So you do not mind working here?' I asked.

'It's a decent enough job.'

'And you would not remember, then, when the haunting started?'

'Oh, I remember that all right.' She paused to take another sip of beer. She was down to a quarter-bottle now; I surmised that once it was gone, our time would be up. 'I remember because I was setting up for the morning, when I met Mademoiselle Florence coming out her room. She was much earlier rising than normal – she was still weak from that illness she'd had, and tended to sleep in late – and still in her nightdress. So I ask her if she's feeling right, and she says to me, "Did you see her?" So I ask who "her" is, and she says, "The woman that was just in my room. She was just here. She must have come out this way?"

Well, I thought it was very odd, which is why I remember it so well, but I told her I hadn't seen anyone, and after checking down the hall she said it was likely just a dream and went back to bed. I thought that'd be the end of it, but, well . . .'

'Well . . .' I agreed. 'Can you remember *when* this was? I would like to establish a timeline, if possible.'

Willemijn picked thoughtfully at her hand. 'Yes, it was a month or two after I started. The end of February. Maybe even the very start of March, come to that.'

Charlotte tapped her pencil against the table. 'The first months of the year are a powerful time for such things.' There was a glimmer in her eye which I did not much like.

'Is there any other person who often has access to the apartments?' I asked.

Willemijn sniffed thoughtfully. 'The family keep themselves to themselves, mostly. There's Monsieur Maximilien's friend from upstairs, Clement Diagne. He comes by sometimes.'

I wondered whether it would be wise to ask for an audience with this friend, for an outsider's perspective – although, if he was anything like Maximilien, that conversation risked being both unpleasant and useless.

'Next, I would like to ask you a few questions about Mademoiselle Florence's ill health over the past year, and her recent recuperation,' I pressed on. 'Will you have another drink?'

'Thank you, but I'll get back home soon.'

Hopefully not before we had squeezed a little more out of her. 'And we do value your time,' I said, leaning forwards and lowering my voice, 'which is why we will of course pay you for your trouble. Now, do you know anything of the nature of Mademoiselle Florence's illness?'

Willemijn shook her head. Another dead end. But the

mention of money had at least stopped her from shifting so restlessly in her seat.

'Nothing at all?'

'Well . . . I wonder if it was contagious or something.'

Another tap of Charlotte's pencil. 'Why's that?'

'The Comte, for one; he's an odd man . . .' She paused, eyes sliding up to gauge my reaction to this. 'But he won't eat or drink nothing she's touched. It's like he's scared to catch something from her.'

'I see,' I said. Had I not noticed this myself when he rejected a glass of wine Florence had poured?

'And I think it required a lot of bed rest. She was confined to her room for a long time, from what I gather.'

'And how did you "gather" it?'

Another sip of beer gone – too soon, too soon. I needed hours more.

Willemijn squinted. 'Let me see, I s'pose because such a deal was made of it when Mademoiselle Florence started to feel well enough to take walks outside. Really, I think too much of a fuss was made of her. It ain't my place, I know, but I reckon her mother is too protective. She's mentioned to me she finds it a bit . . . suffocating. She spends most of her time out in the garden to get away from it all. Caroline and me feel sorry for her, so we escort her sometimes if she wants to walk out in the streets a bit.'

As she spoke, one of her hands came up to fiddle with a curl. She met my eyes and blinked once, twice, three times in total. I had not spent years of my life as a professional liar for nothing: I knew how to spot when someone else was not telling me the whole truth.

'So, when Mademoiselle Florence makes these outings, she is always in the company of you or Caroline?'

'That's right.' Blink. Blink. Blink.

I leaned across the table again, trying not to flinch when my forearm connected with something sticky. 'We need you to tell us the truth, Willemijn. I promise this will not get back to anyone else.'

Willemijn giggled nervously, but then appeared to accept her defeat. 'All right, I s'pose there's no point keeping it from you. So long as you won't tell . . .'

'On my word.'

A nod. 'Sometimes when I go out with Mademoiselle Florence, she wants to walk alone to have some time to herself. I know I shouldn't really, but how can I deny her when she's been so cooped up? She's a grown woman, after all, and it ain't right to treat her as a child that needs watching at all times.'

'And, of course, you get an hour or so of free time for which you are being paid,' I observed.

At least she had the good grace to flush. 'Yes, I s'pose.'

To mask her embarrassment, Willemijn took up her bottle again and drank the last of it. The conversation was over. 'I'd best be getting on,' she said, already standing and readjusting her shawl. She looked at me expectantly.

'Yes, of course.' I stood as well, beginning to rummage about for my coin purse. 'Before you go, is there anything else you can think to tell us? Anything at all?'

Willemijn shrugged her shoulders. 'I don't know what you're looking to hear,' she said. 'Except that . . .'

'Except?'

'It might not be related . . .'

I gestured for her to continue.

'The other day I went into Comte Ardoir's room to do the bedding, and I didn't knock as I thought he was out. Only he *was* in there' – I had a horrified moment of thinking I was about to hear something lewd – 'and he close to jumped out of his skin. Once he realized it were me, he screamed about knocking and privacy and such, but for a few seconds he looked like he could just die of terror. He must've thought I was the ghost. He's terrified of it, I can tell.'

All of which only went to confirm that Ardoir had been withholding something earlier – he had been afraid of our unseen guest long before this morning.

Nodding, I began shaking out coins, not really paying attention to how much I was handing over. It was clear that Willemijn hadn't caused the damage in the library, but she had given us some things to think about. Yet more mysteries to add to the pile, like bones in a paupers' grave.

CHAPTER SIX

13 April 1866

'SARAH, MY DEAR! What a triumph!'

'Oh, it is nothing,' laughed Sarah, returning my kiss.

It was not nothing: the Coupart house had been transformed into a kaleidoscope of whimsy. Every room was bedecked in dazzling colours and guests – noblemen rubbed shoulders with merchants, actors, writers, politicians, foreign royalty (wherever did Sarah find all these people?) – and conversations trilled like birdsong; the doors between rooms had been thrown open so that their occupants could flow freely from one to another, unhindered by trifles such as wood and hinges, followed by the sweet strains of music coming from a live band, and mingling scents of flowers, pastries, cooked meats and oriental incense. Each area had been set up for ease and pleasure: in the dining room, furniture had been removed to clear space for a dance floor, upon which some couples already twirled; on the other hand, more furniture had been shoehorned into Sarah's parlour so that it was a haven of comfortable seating perfect for intimate conversation. Through all of this weaved a squadron of waiting staff, replenishing beverages and proffering canapés with the sleight of hand usually seen only in street-corner conjurers. It was such a bustle, such an attack upon the senses, that it was a challenge to recognize one's acquaintances, and even more of a challenge to secure them for longer than the time it took to say, 'Oh, it is—! Have you met—?' before one was whisked away to the next attraction.

'And I see you persuaded the Baron to come along,' said Sarah, flashing a charming grin at Alexandre, who was indeed at my side. I had even managed to convince him to wear a rather dashing new cravat for the occasion – Virginie and I had spent an age picking it out in the shop together.

'I would not have missed it for the world, Madame Coupart,' Alexandre declared, kissing the hand she had presented.

'I am delighted. Say, if you see my awful husband, then run the other way, else he will try to talk to you. He is on the warpath!'

When we had caught sight of Guillaume on our way in, however, he had been already deep in conversation with an unfamiliar young man – tall and handsome, with dark skin and elegant cheekbones. He could not have been any more of a contrast to Guillaume, who was stout and pink as a ham.

'But do you know,' Sarah went on, leaning closer to me, 'who else turned up, much to my amazement? Monsieur de Jacquinot!'

My stomach dropped. I had completely forgotten Sarah's threat to invite Maximilien along. Indeed, I had assumed it a joke.

'You must make sure to interrogate him and report back,' she said. 'Now, I had better dash – I need to say hello to—' And then she was gone, sentence unfinished.

Placing a hand on my elbow, Alexandre half turned to face me. 'Whom did she mention?'

'Ah, Monsieur de Jacquinot?'

'Who is that?'

'Oh, nobody, really.' I tried to approximate the dismissive air that Sarah was so good at, praying Alexandre would not see through me. 'I got talking to his mother at the tailor's.'

'You did not mention it.'

'I did not think it important – the name wasn't familiar. The Marquis de Jacquinot?'

'De Jacquinot . . .' Alexandre muttered. 'It rings a bell, but no, I cannot place it.' To my relief, this put an end to the topic.

As I moved through the party, I took the opportunity to fish for gossip around the de Jacquinots whenever Alexandre was distracted. Most of what I heard was old ground – dwindling finances, a broken engagement, a thoroughly unpleasant old man. Plenty of people had their theories about what was wrong with Florence, from simple mania to witchcraft, from arsenic poisoning to heartbreak. One person even told me that Maximilien had almost killed the man who'd upset her, but could provide no further details to substantiate this.

I did not run into Maximilien himself until some time later in the evening. Alexandre having left me for a moment to fetch a drink, I ducked away from the crowds into an alcove formed where the stairs swept round. However, I found that it was already occupied – and almost yelped in surprise when I realized by whom.

'Goodness!' exclaimed Maximilien. 'What on earth are you doing here?'

He was accompanied by one other person – the man whom I had seen speaking with Guillaume earlier.

'Ah, forgive me, I have interrupted something,' I said, immediately trying to reverse my steps.

'No, no,' said Maximilien hurriedly, his neck and ears turning a curious rosy pink. 'Nothing of the sort. Come on in.'

I eyed the space uncomfortably; it would be a snug fit.

Apparently noticing the absurdity of his invitation, Maximilien hurried on, 'Have you met Clement Diagne? This man is my dearest friend. We were students together, and he also happens to live in our building.'

I extended a hand to the man, saying without thinking, 'Sylvie Devereux.' Then, in horror, I caught Maximilien's eye and knew that he had registered the misstep.

'Ah,' said Diagne, flashing a smile, 'I believe I have just met your husband, the Baron – I left him speaking with Coupart.'

'Our sublimely tiresome host?' asked Maximilien. 'Poor fellow. And the wife is so charming. What a waste *that* match is!'

'Entirely. And, you know, he was speaking to me very attentively. One might have thought he was after something.'

'A private stroll in the park?'

'I will say no more,' said Diagne, with a wink.

I cleared my throat.

Maximilien narrowed his eyes in my direction. 'Do tell us, *Baroness*, how you know the Couparts?'

'They are close friends of mine,' I said. 'The Comte works with my husband.'

'Ah,' said Diagne, 'well, I do apologize, Madame Devereux. I was simply making a joke, of course.'

A rather dangerous joke about Coupart's appetites, if indeed I had understood properly. Did he not realize how such rumours stuck? One could ruin a person's life by spreading such malice – I had seen it for myself.

Noting my stony silence, Diagne rubbed his neck sheepishly. 'Max was just telling me how he has been getting along with Darwin's thoughts on the origins of the species – he has my copy on loan.'

I presumed Diagne was referring to the same book I had seen Maximilien reading at our first meeting. I had not picked up a copy myself, but Alexandre had shared the main details of the text with me when it was first translated into French, and that was enough for me to know my opinion on the matter.

'I do not think that Madame Devereux is much interested in the sciences,' said Maximilien, with a smirk.

'Not interested?' asked Diagne, shaking his head as if this was a personal affront.

I gave a cool smile in reply. 'I prefer chemistry to natural history. It has more practical use.'

Diagne would not let this stand. 'But natural history tells us all about the world, about our very existence as humans. Our origins!'

'Clement is a student of human anatomy,' Maximilien informed me.

'It holds all the answers,' said Diagne. 'Have you never wondered how you came to be on this earth, Madame Devereux?'

'I am quite certain that I have two humans to thank for my birth, rather than a pair of monkeys, as you and Monsieur Maximilien would have it.'

For a moment, Diagne looked worried that he had offended me, but then he caught Maximilien's eye and they both burst into laughter. 'I think another drink is in order,' he said, patting Maximilien on the shoulder. 'I will venture forth and find one. Madame Devereux, the pleasure has been mine . . .'

I considered escaping in his wake, but Maximilien's expression made clear that this was not the end of the conversation.

'Monsieur Maximilien,' I said, standing tall and throwing out the words before he could gain the upper hand, 'I have not been entirely honest with you, and for that I apologize. I am, indeed, married to the Baron Devereux. My husband does not know I have been assisting you.' I forced my voice to be stern; I could not appear desperate. 'I would be grateful if you would keep the details of our acquaintance to yourself.'

He was silent for a moment – just long enough for my heartbeat to pick up speed. 'Are you close to your sister, Madame Devereux?'

Caught off guard, I did not manage a particularly convincing, 'Of course.'

'I am close to mine. I would do anything for her; I want you to know that. She is the one soul in this world I cherish above all others. And so I hate to see that soul in pain – I hate to see her wounded, and hate even more to see others use those wounds to their advantage. No – please let me finish, Mademoiselle . . . Madame Devereux. I want to tell you that my sister is more fragile than you may realize. She has been through much this past year or so; her body has endured a lot, physically, and of course such things affect an individual's mental state also.

'I do not blame you for coming to us. You were invited, after all. And even if I find the thought of exploiting the vulnerable so abhorrent, well, I am not free enough of sin to cast the first stone. But take it from me: Florence is not just some easy target. If you continue in this project, then you will break her. Do you understand me? I cannot convince my family to listen, but perhaps I can appeal to your better nature. Think of your own sister – think of what you would wish for her if you saw her being mistreated in such a way.'

This was clearly all spoken from the heart, and perhaps it would have moved me had it not contained so many attacks upon my person.

'May I speak frankly, Monsieur?' I replied, lifting my

chin in a demonstration of how little I had been deterred by Maximilien's words.

'I pray that you do.'

'I promise you that it could not be further from my intentions to see harm done to Mademoiselle Florence. Although I was not honest about my name and rank, I have spoken only the truth on every other matter. It appears that you view me as an unscientific charlatan – and I shall overlook your manifold insults in the assumption that you were so overwhelmed with concern for your sister that you momentarily forgot your manners – but I am a professional. If there is indeed a preternatural explanation for these phenomena, then it is just as much in my interests that we discover it. I would not risk my good reputation by claiming a ghost when there was none.'

Maximilien scoffed, then leaned closer, so that I caught an eddy of his smell – pomade and old tobacco. 'Forgive me if I do not believe you.'

'Believe what you will. Then I may have the pleasure of surprising you. And, I tell you, I intend to exhaust all earthly explanations to be sure that there is no mistake here.' This at least was spoken with all honesty. Because, just like Maximilien, I had witnessed something that I could not believe in the library, and I needed either an explanation . . . or proof.

'I know that it is reassuring to cling to your scepticism,' I said, 'like a child clinging to a blanket because he believes it will protect him from the monsters under his bed. Maybe the monsters are real and maybe they are not, but a blanket has no chance against fangs, Monsieur, and cowering beneath it will not answer the question either way. I am not asking you to believe me in the absence of evidence; I am simply asking you to open your mind enough to *see* the evidence as it is presented to you. What we witnessed in your library cannot be explained away – believe me, I have been trying to rationalize it myself. If you are as concerned for your sister as you say you are, then you will not get in the way of our helping her.'

Almost word for word, it was the twin of a monologue that I had delivered once in a manor near Auteuil that had been victim to a 'poltergeist'. I had spoken it to distract a family from the sound of a pretty young man – the true source of the nightly knocking and moaning noises we had been called to investigate – climbing out of the eldest son's bedchamber. It was funny how what might be a lie one day could be the truth the next.

'What you are asking me to accept . . .' said Maximilien, shaking his head slowly, 'I cannot.'

'You do not have to,' I said. 'You have only not to reject it outright.'

He did not speak for some time.

'Monsieur Maximilien, can I trust in your discretion?'

After a pause, he gave a short, sharp nod. 'In any case, I would rather not have my family name associated with occultism, superstition and hysteria.'

'Then we understand one another entirely.'

Returning to the party, I found Alexandre locked in the inevitable conversation with Guillaume. I approached them gratefully.

'Well, darling, there you are,' I said. 'Monsieur Coupart, would you mind awfully if I stole my husband for a moment?'

Guillaume looked as if he would in fact mind, but he could hardly object. 'By all means,' he said, sweeping his hand towards Alexandre, as if presenting a gift. I could not help but watch him with new eyes – was there something there, a hint of the anti-masculine? No; it was beneath me to listen to such gossip. 'Devereux, I will catch you again later in the evening.'

Alexandre grimaced politely. 'I do hope so,' he said.

'And you must both come to lunch one day – I feel I hardly see your lovely wife any more.'

I only hoped the horror in my heart did not show on my face as I faked a laugh, swiftly pulling Alexandre away. The comment had not passed him by, however. 'Whatever did he mean by that?'

'I think he was being ironic,' I whispered, looping one arm through his and patting his chest with the other hand. 'Well done – you were very brave.'

'My, that was trying.'

I glanced around to check that nobody who might object to an open display of affection was watching, then stood on tiptoes to kiss him on the cheek.

Instead of the intended soothing effect, however, this caused him to frown. 'And who was that earlier?'

'I beg your pardon?'

'That young man with the reddish hair. The pair of you seemed . . . intimate.'

Why, for the love of God! He must have spotted Maximilien and me as we emerged from the alcove. Was this evening to be nothing more than a series of trials? I may as well have stayed home with a pile of thumbtacks and driven these one at a time into my eyeballs – the overall outcome would have been much the same.

'Oh, *that* gentleman,' I said, forcing jollity. 'That was the Marquis de Jacquinot. Yes, it was rather cosy back there; there was a group of us all crammed in. Quite the lark!'

'The one with the mother?'

95

'Oh, yes, I did tell you about that.'

'Hmm . . .' His expression was unfathomable.

'I cannot say I know him well,' I added, casting about for an excuse to change the topic. The last thing I needed was for Alexandre to take an interest in my connection to Maximilien's family – especially not now that Guillaume had unwittingly almost shattered my alibi. 'Shall we dance?' I asked.

'In all honesty, I am feeling a trifle tired.'

'Oh, come along, Alexandre.'

Eventually he relented and we headed to the dance floor. The band had struck up a polka, and pairs of people were spinning here and there in flashes of brightly coloured skirts. I took Alexandre's hand and he put the other about my waist, and, just like that, his dour mood had lifted and he was smiling, the corners of his eyes creasing and his features animating.

Alexandre had always been a good dancer. We had danced that first night we met, after I had rescued him from the garden. It had been two and a half years now – a time both long and short. Some days it felt as if I still barely knew him, other days as if my life prior to this was so far distant that it had faded all to grey. Yes, a wash of grey, greyer still because I had not even known that it was grey, and then there he had been, my man who shone upon the dance floor like burnished gold. He had not known why I was there at the party, had not known me as Mademoiselle Mothe the spiritist. Until then, men had always led with questions about my work. They had wanted to know if I could read their thoughts, know their characters, tell their futures – as if it took a psychic to do that! They had never asked about *me*, the woman behind the medium. I was no more than a thrilling curiosity to them. But Alexandre had not known me as anything else first. He had seen me as a woman and decided that he wanted to know me – not for the novelty, but for the normal reasons that normal people have for falling in love. And that was why he had stood by me through everything that had happened next, why he had still married me despite the risk involved in connecting himself to a family such as mine.

'I love you,' I whispered, lifting my chin to rest it on his shoulder.

He did not need to say the words back for me to hear them.

CHAPTER SEVEN

15 April 1866

THERE WAS NO fire in the library grate on this occasion. When we moved to rearrange the furniture for the sitting, my gloves came away with a thin grey film at the fingers. Dust.

Madame de Jacquinot noticed me looking. 'The servants have been refusing to clean in here since what happened,' she explained. 'They are afraid of seeing the spirit.'

'And yet the person who has seen the spirit the most seems entirely unafraid,' Charlotte said, looking to Florence. 'But then, I suppose, you are composed of hardier stuff than most.' She had always had a knack for gallantry; it was successful with ladies – particularly younger ones – although it tended to alienate men. I had always hoped for Charlotte's sake that she would one day discover a man who proved the exception – though as time went on this became less and less likely.

Florence was clearly quite taken by the whole act; she smiled meekly in reply, two pink circles appearing high on her cheeks. She had one of those unfortunate complexions prone to blushes – so inconvenient to have one's emotions broadcast for the world to see. I only hoped that she would not be *too* taken with my sister, and on Charlotte's part that she would not get carried away with it. One did not need a repeat of past mistakes.

And on the subject of past mistakes, I was still heavily

regretting the comedy of errors that had been Sarah's party. Alexandre had certainly seemed at the limits of his credulity when I had told him that I planned to call upon the Couparts again; I would need to invent a new alibi for the next time. In addition to this, I had noticed Coulomb watching me intently from the porter's lodge as I set out tonight. I wondered for the first time if he had mentioned Charlotte's recent visit to Alexandre. Coulomb had no reason to know who my sister was, but Alexandre was fully capable of putting evidence together – it was, after all, his profession. However, it would do me no good to worry about this at present; I had a job to do.

Once we had formed a circle of chairs around one of the reading tables, Charlotte set about snuffing the candles, so that shadows flickered and died across the ruined walls. I made use of the last of the light to glance about the faces of our sitters. I saw excitement and anticipation, but there was an undercurrent of fear – particularly, as I had expected, from Ardoir. Even Maximilien looked curious this time around, although this was with the hawkish attention of someone watching for the trick behind a magic act. Clearly, I had not fully persuaded him over to my argument at Sarah's party. Unfortunately for his designs, the table prevented him from seeing as I surreptitiously removed the silencer from the bell strapped to my calf.

'Let us join hands,' I said, as Charlotte took her place opposite me. 'And this time, if you please, do try not to disturb the circle.'

'No matter what happens,' added Charlotte.

Ardoir coughed significantly in Florence's direction. She was at my side tonight; I would not let Charlotte spook her prematurely again.

With the circle complete, I sat up straight. Sabine de Lisle smirked at me, dead centre in my sight line – the only portrait left on the wall. I addressed my words to her: 'I call upon the spirits; may they bring illumination to counteract this darkness. I call upon you, Mama, to act as guide. I call upon you, Comtesse de Lisle, to be guided to us.'

Silence. Not one of us seemed even to breathe.

Then came the peal of spirit bells. Only, I had not moved my leg. I looked to Charlotte, but her face gave nothing away.

Just as I was angling my sleeve-hook to shake the table, there was a tug at my hand.

Florence had jolted backwards in her chair. For a moment, I was sure she had fainted in fright, but then I saw her face: pale, eyes fixed upon some spot beyond our circle, lips parted and trembling. The candlelight dancing across her features changed their angles, giving her face a new aspect – many aspects, in fact, like a fresh mask for each shift of the flame. There was something captivating about it. A tension in the air. Her fingers trembled in my grip.

'Florence?' Maximilien's voice climbed up a pitch with worry.

Not looking to him, she opened her mouth as if to speak – but no noise came out, only a soundless gasp. She tried again; another gasp. It was like watching a carp gulping at the surface of a lake. With a shadow of confusion now crossing her face, she tugged her hands free of the circle and raised one – tremulously and so slowly that I found myself watching every inch of its movement – to rest against her throat. Once more, she opened her mouth, and this time there was a noise: not words, but a faint, guttural rattle, which then grew in volume until it became a hacking cough. The force of it wracked her shoulders and sent streams of moisture from her eyes.

'She's choking!' cried Maximilien. He too freed himself from the circle, sending his chair shrieking backwards as he hurried over to his sister. 'Florence!' He gripped her shoulders and gazed wildly around at the rest of us. 'For God's sake, will nobody else help? What should we do? Florence! Can you breathe?'

Instead of responding, she shrugged him off, with more force than I would have expected from her. Was she really choking? Could this be a return of her consumptive illness? But even as my mind raced to find rational explanations, gooseflesh shivered up my arms as my body reacted of its own accord.

'Is it the spirit?' asked Ardoir.

'Florence!' cried Madame de Jacquinot, now standing as well. There was a touch of a wail to her voice.

Charlotte and I would need to resolve this situation quickly if we did not want a panic on our hands. I looked past Florence to meet my sister's eyes – two small beacons reflecting light in the gloom – and widened my own to communicate the need for action.

I was not certain that Charlotte would catch this in the low light, but she must have done, as she abruptly said, 'It is imperative, Madame, that we retain our composure at all times. A visiting spirit will take its cue from the hosts – if we remain calm, it will speak with us cordially; if we show alarm, we risk—' Charlotte broke off mid-sentence, head cocked, and now that she was silent I could hear what had interrupted her: a long, low moan was rumbling from Florence. She was trying to speak. There was a collective sense of electrification as we all leaned in to listen.

'Florence?' Maximilien tried again.

This time it worked. Her head snapped around to face him, as if noticing him now for the first time. A curious wave of chill washed over me. A funeral on a winter morning.

'What is it?' Maximilien asked, but his voice was suddenly hoarse and the question little more than a wheeze of air.

Florence opened her mouth and out of it came a hiss, a snake sound. It was the sound of Lucifer in the Garden; the sound of Evil itself. My insides formed an uneasy knot. And then the hiss rounded off and reconciled itself into syllables, and then words. No: one word, repeated over and over.

'Sabine. Sabine. Sabine.'

Ardoir lurched forwards in his seat and cried, 'Auntie!'

With that, Florence went limp. A true faint this time.

Maximilien was there immediately to stop her falling from the chair. He brought a hand to her forehead, and then paused. Touched a finger to her chin. Slowly drew it away. Alarm came over his face, and I noticed that his hand was suddenly moist, coated in something pale that adhered to it with a sickly glimmer. Pearlescent and thick as porridge. Then I saw that it was about Florence's lips, too, trickling from the corners of her mouth. Vomit, I thought for a moment. But then, no . . . No, I realized that I knew exactly what it was. Accounts of its exact nature varied: some reported it as slimy, as muslin-like, as resembling smoke or dough. I had always used flour mixed with milk. But this was no work of mine.

'Ectoplasm,' breathed Charlotte.

The substance left behind when a medium interacted with a spirit.

'Stay back,' ordered Maximilien. He had taken on a greenish hue, finally presented with evidence enough to spook him. 'Give her some space.'

We all disregarded this, gathering around as he lifted Florence from the chair and laid her down upon the floor. Taking a handkerchief from his pocket, he dabbed at her chin.

The cloth came away with an unhealthy sheen. He looked at it carefully, turning it back and forth in the candlelight, before passing it to me.

'Is it dangerous?' asked Ardoir. He appeared to be quite content with keeping his distance.

'No, not at all,' I reassured him, sniffing the handkerchief as subtly as I could. It didn't smell bilious. I tried to tell myself that maybe this, too, had been Charlotte's doing. I attempted to catch her eye. Had she somehow persuaded Florence to . . . To what? To hold a bag of ectoplasm under her tongue in order to play a trick on her family?

Florence was slowly coming back to herself, head rolling from side to side as if waking from a deep sleep. From under lids that quivered like moths' wings, she looked up at us. 'What happened?' she asked. Her voice was heavy, as if she were recovering from a cold.

Madame de Jacquinot elbowed us all out of the way to lean over her daughter, placing a cautious hand upon her shoulder. 'Oh, my darling, you were possessed by a spirit,' she said, with an eloquent shudder.

'For God's sake!' cried Maximilien. 'Is there no end to this delusion? Can you not see that she is ill? She has merely vomited.' His voice had turned shrill with desperation; I wondered if he believed his own words, or if he was just saying them in the hope they were true. 'You think it does her any good to have you filling her head with these superstitions?'

'But the voice—' began Madame de Jacquinot.

'She is unwell!' snapped Maximilien. 'I can hardly believe I let this farce go on so long. Florence needs a doctor!'

'Never mind about her,' said Ardoir. 'Where is Auntie?'

Madame de Jacquinot ignored both of them completely,

smoothing Florence's hair back from her face. 'Did you feel anything? Are you in any pain? Were you frightened?'

Florence shook her head to all three. 'No, Mama,' she said. 'I just feel . . . a little tired.'

'Will you never listen to me, by Christ?' Maximilien stomped his foot – actually stomped it!

Ardoir sniffed in disgust. 'Will you behave like a man, for once?'

'Oh, for the love of God!'

'And no more of this blaspheming – in the presence of nice young ladies, no less.'

Some of the ladies did not seem to mind – rather, Charlotte appeared to be enjoying the whole exchange. I wished I could say the same for myself.

'Grandfather, please—' Maximilien began to object.

Ardoir cut in over him. 'Not a word more from you, Maximilien, or you shall be made very sorry.' There was a flash of something in his face, a moment of malevolence of which I would not have believed him capable. It put an end to Maximilien's objections, although I could still see that his hands shook with repressed emotion – frustration or fear?

Could Maximilien's suggestion have been right – that this was merely some medical condition? Charlotte and I had been called upon in the past to aid epileptics whose fits had been misidentified as the work of demons or spirits. But if what had happened to Florence was epilepsy, it was a very mild form. And that substance: there was no smell of bile about it, so how could it have come from the stomach cavity?

Ardoir turned to me and cleared his throat. 'So, what is the meaning of all this, then?' he asked. Most polite, as if he had walked in on a minor disagreement at a dinner party, rather than just witnessed his granddaughter in the grips of some other-worldly influence.

'It appears . . .' I began, but then I realized that I had no conclusion to this sentence. I did not know how it appeared at all. Or, rather, I did. Either Florence, a complete novice, had convincingly faked a possession to a professional standard, and for no discernible reason . . . Or . . .

'Your granddaughter was momentarily possessed by a spirit,' Charlotte finished for me.

It was crazy. And crazier still: for a moment, I almost entertained the thought. But no, I could not let Charlotte's silly arguments cloud my senses. Whatever had happened here, there had to be another explanation.

'This is not unprecedented, although certainly it is uncommon for the spirit to bypass the medium and enter directly into another vessel, unless there exists some affinity between them,' Charlotte went on. 'If this spirit is the one who damaged your house, I cannot guarantee that its intentions are as we originally thought.'

'Certainly not!' said Madame de Jacquinot. She looked wounded at the very thought.

I glanced about the room. The Comte was shaking his head with determination. Maximilien and Florence, on the other hand . . . there was something, not quite suspicious, but not altogether *unsuspicious*, in the way they avoided her gaze.

'Do you mean to say,' continued Madame de Jacquinot, 'that my father may be right? That we may be facing a spirit which wishes us harm?'

'Mademoiselle Florence, may we speak to you alone for a moment?' I asked.

*

Florence did not look well. Her complexion was paler than ever – not the fashionable pale of society ladies, but that of an invalid. There were deep shadows beneath her eyes, clear to see once we had her under the brighter lights of the parlour. One might have imagined that the ordeal of being haunted was taking its toll on her – between nightly visitations, possessions and the interrogations of a pair of spiritists, would it really have been any surprise? But I knew better than that.

'How did you do it, then?' I demanded. I could see Charlotte flinching at my tone.

'Do what, Mademoiselle?'

'The ectoplasm. Did you regurgitate it? Conceal a pouch somewhere?'

Confusion and hurt both played across her face. If her innocence was feigned, she was a remarkable actress. 'I do not know. That is to say, it was not my doing. It was as if my body was not my own.' Tears sparkled in her eyes.

Charlotte stepped between us. 'For goodness' sake, Sylvie, just what are you accusing her of?'

I could not answer – especially not with a client listening in. Instead, I held her gaze and said, 'This is not right.'

'No,' Charlotte agreed.

'What is it?' asked Florence. 'Is something wrong?'

Charlotte's expression immediately softened as she turned to Florence, taking one of her hands. 'You are perfectly safe with us, Mademoiselle Florence. How do you feel at the moment?'

'I do not know,' said Florence. 'No different from normal. A little hungry. Tired, perhaps.' I thought I saw a tremor in her fingers where Charlotte pressed them.

'And how was it when the spirit possessed your body?' Charlotte asked. 'Were you still aware of what was happening?'

Florence beetled her brows and thought. 'It is hard to say. It was like dreaming. The images I saw . . .'

'Images? You mean, of what was happening around you?'

'Yes, but also other things. I think . . . that is, I do not know if it is possible, but it seems to me that perhaps they were visions from her. From the Comtesse.'

Charlotte leaned in closer. 'And what did you see?' Her entire body was tensed in excitement. I had thought her talk of real spirits had merely been talk – but could she truly believe all of this?

'I am sorry, Mademoiselle Charlotte,' said Florence. 'They are no more than impressions, really. I thought . . . I saw a face. It looked like the portrait of the Comtesse; the same eyes and cheeks. The same woman I have seen at night. And I saw . . . no, it was more a feeling. I *felt* an anger.'

'You are angry?' I asked, snatching desperately at this possible motivation.

Florence shook her head slowly. '*She* is angry.'

'Perhaps she is merely frustrated that she cannot yet communicate with us clearly,' Charlotte suggested.

'Maybe . . .' said Florence.

'Do you still see the Comtesse de Lisle at night?'

'Most nights.'

'And she is still weeping?'

'Yes, always.' Florence was twiddling one of the buttons on her dress, as if growing bored with our questioning.

'I wonder why she is drawn to you in particular,' Charlotte said. 'Tell me, have you ever had any experiences before this that suggested a certain affinity with the supernatural?'

Florence shook her head.

'No premonitions, visions, unexplained phenomena?' Charlotte prompted.

'I am afraid not. Sorry, Charlotte.' I noted that she was addressing my sister informally – I hoped as a sign that Charlotte had won her confidence, rather than out of disrespect.

'Mademoiselle Florence,' I said, 'forgive me for asking, but I must: your illness. I know that it must be unpleasant to recall, but the spirit first began to appear to you around the time of your recovery. One cannot help but speculate that there may have been a connection. Can you tell us anything about the nature of your ill health?'

'It was consumption,' said Florence immediately.

It was perfectly easy to believe that she was a recovering consumptive. Yet the speed of her reply somehow rang false. I had a certain talent for spotting a liar. Besides, if one had wealth – even the diminished wealth of this family – would one not send a daughter with consumption to the countryside or the coast to recover in the fresh air?

My doubt called to mind Sarah's speculations that Florence's withdrawal from society had in fact been connected to lunacy. Could that not explain things? Just think of all those religious hermits whose pursuit of holiness bore a striking resemblance to madness. Yes, it could all have been delusion, but for the destroyed library, the ectoplasm. Those were real. Those were all too tangible.

'Is it possible,' asked Charlotte, 'that for a time during your illness you were close to death? Such proximity to the other-world could make a person more connected to its inhabitants.'

'I no longer have any idea what is possible,' Florence replied. 'I hope it is your job to tell me?'

Charlotte laughed in response. 'Yes, I suppose.'

But what was possible was quickly slipping from my grasp.

*

Before we took our leave, I stepped out to use the privy. The garden's cool air was welcome against my face, nature tethering me back to the world. *This* was real, this square of space, with its pebble path and pond at the centre. There were flower beds and shrubs shedding their fragrance, and bushes clustering up against the house. Even so, I was on edge, jumpy. I thought for a dreadful moment that I saw a pale face watching me from the garden gate. But it was just moonlight on dead leaves and branches.

When I was done, I lingered a moment longer outside to look up at the building, at the lights glowing from its windows, the reflections of which glittered in the pond. I could see clearly into the dining room: the diminished figures of the de Jacquinots and my sister sitting around, taking one last coffee. They were all in conversation – distracted, I realized. They would not miss me for some time yet.

Hurrying back inside, I muffled my ascent of the staircases and, instead of turning to join the others, I ducked into the long corridor towards the bedrooms. If Florence had engineered ectoplasm, there would surely be some evidence in her room – instructions or ingredients, maybe even some leftover amount. I had to know.

Although it was completely dark by this time, the servants had not yet been through to light the sconces in this part of the building – either that, or they were under instructions not to, so as to save money. The shadowy corridor yawned before me, its far end gnawed by the dark so that it was entirely possible to imagine that what lay just out of my sight was not the entrance to the servants' stair at all, but rather more corridor, stretching forever onwards, and this sense caused a roil of giddiness as if I were facing not in a lateral direction, but downwards as into a great chasm. And just when I thought I couldn't feel any more unsettled – there, right at the furthest brink of my perception before all became obscurity, I swore that I saw something move.

My organs liquefied inside me, yet my exterior had petrified like lightning-struck sand, and I was unable to move – even to breathe.

All was still. I strained my every sense, seeking out any further sign. It had come and gone in an instant, an agitation of the air just a shade paler than it should have been. Roughly the height of a person. The height of a woman. My pulse had juddered to a halt, but now it rallied again into double-time to make up for it. All I could hear was the thrum in my head, like a dismal drumbeat counting down to execution. My eyes smarted from lack of blinking. From underneath the door back into the parlour crept a narrow band of illumination, a tether to the safety and company of others. To turn back or to press on? I took a long, slow breath, filling my lungs: bags of dried lavender at the windows; beeswax on the floor; vinegar and carbolic; and the traces of latent mildew and dust. Scents of the household – distinctive and dependable. Nothing could have been further from the otherworldly. I could not let myself be frightened by the inventions of my own mind, and if I retreated now then I would be forever haunted by what I thought I had seen.

You are no coward, I told myself. There are no spirits. You are no coward. There are no spirits. A mantra, and on the third repetition I moved a foot forwards, slowly, slowly, and advanced one pace down the corridor. No movement – not even a sound. I gained another step. Then another. In such a fashion, I progressed, increasing in confidence and speed as I did so. This continued until what I estimated to be around the halfway point, when my brashness caused me to stumble on some irregularity in the flooring. I let out a sharp gasp that rent the silence and, unwilling to let my momentum overbalance me, allowed it to carry me forwards at a dash, arms outstretched for support where there was none. A moment later, my hands met heavily with wood, damp through my gloves – but, no, that was just the sweat upon my own palms. The door to the servants' stair. I had been much closer to it than I had thought. I turned around and leaned back against it, surveying the corridor. The tether of light from the parlour revealed my starting point.

See? Just a corridor, finite like any other. Empty. All the doors along it shut – and if anything had passed through and closed them, I would certainly have heard. There had been nothing here. Of course not. But I had proved it to myself, and that buoyed me up, the adrenaline of it all going to my head and almost causing me to laugh aloud. First the face in the garden, now a figure in the hall – I was letting silly stories get to me. I inhaled in relief. Lavender, beeswax, carbolic and vinegar, mildew and orange blossom.

I pushed into Florence's room, pawing over the sideboard until I found matches and a candle. The room flared into view.

It looked much the same as it had when Charlotte and I had spent the night in it. Moving quickly, I searched through the usual hiding places. Toiletries, trinkets, embroidery work – nothing that suggested Florence had been brewing ectoplasm. Lack of evidence was not proof of innocence. But I needed proof of guilt.

A creak from behind. I spun around, heart jolting. There was nothing there. But I had tarried too long in any case; I extinguished the candle and hurried from the room, back down the corridor and towards the safe light of the parlour.

*

As soon as I reached home that night, I retired to my parlour to note down all that we had observed. This was my custom after every sitting, and ordinarily the words came easily to my pen, but now I found myself for at least a quarter-hour staring dumbly at the blank page. What was I to write? What had I even experienced? If Florence had faked her own possession, she had done it to a standard of which I would have been proud – I had not spotted a single tell in the whole performance. But how would she have come by the knowledge to achieve this, and for what purpose? When Charlotte and I had spoken to her afterwards, she had truly seemed innocent in the matter. Then again, if she was a good enough performer to stage the possession, this too could have been part of the act. And what was the alternative? That there had been – against all that I had ever known and believed – a spirit walking among us. No. It was a matter for the law of parsimony: which was more likely? The natural explanation.

And yet such bodily terror had come over me in that dark corridor . . .

Surrendering to failure, I returned my notebook to the locked desk drawer. I had taken to keeping all of my case writings here, just to be on the safe side. I doubted that Augustine could read, and neither the butler nor my husband had much reason to be rummaging about in my quarters, but Virginie was another matter – she could be relied upon for discretion, of course, but I preferred to keep what distance from her I could. I had always to be on guard with the servants: if I was too friendly with them, too free, they might see me for what I was. It was a shame, as I rather thought that Virginie and I could have been friends under different circumstances. But then, this was precisely the problem.

Yet I wished I had someone I could talk to about all this. Most of all, I wished that Mama was still here, that I could press my face into the incense-scented folds of her dress and have her stroke my hair. Would she have entertained the idea of a real ghost? I had never been able to put a pin on whether she secretly believed in the spirits we conjured – after all, she had practised the family gift for many years before Papa's tricks had come into it. Yet whenever Charlotte and I had tried to ask her, she had always simply smiled and said that it did not matter. We helped people; that was what was real. That was all I could keep striving to do now.

CHAPTER EIGHT

16 April 1866

'SYLVIE, WAKE UP.' Alexandre's voice drew me from my dreams.

I had returned so late the previous night, then sat up trying to write for so long, that I had opted to sleep in my own bed rather than disturb Alexandre by joining him in his chamber. I had slept long and well – I could tell from the quantity of light that it was now late morning. Alexandre was already dressed in his day clothes, and when I looked at him properly, curious, I saw that he was standing with his hands clasped behind his back, jaw squared. It was his courtroom look: the look he turned upon criminals. Something cold flickered in my stomach.

'I waited up late for you,' he said. Ah, so that was the problem.

Propping myself up on one elbow, I tried to look apologetic. 'I am sorry, darling. Sarah and I got quite carried away with ourselves.'

'Spare me the charade,' he said. 'Please, at least do me that courtesy.'

'Have I . . . Have I done something?' I asked, fighting against panic. Of course he had found out about Charlotte. How had I imagined that he would not? He had found out and now he would forbid me to continue.

'I had Coulomb follow you yesterday.'

Followed? I pushed myself up to a sitting position. That face

I had seen in the de Jacquinots' garden – perhaps not just a trick of the moonlight, after all. A mixture of panic and guilt inched up my gullet, but there was indignation there too. He had had me followed! Did he not trust his own wife? But, God, of course he was right not to have trusted me. What could Coulomb have observed? He would have seen me with Charlotte, and that we had entered the de Jacquinot building, certainly. Could he have caught sight of the dining room from the gate? The scene had certainly been clear enough to me. Christ, could he even have seen into the library windows from the street? No – we had closed the shutters, of course, for the seance. But Alexandre was not stupid; given the facts in hand, he could deduce what was happening. It was such a talent that had made his career, after all. Already, beneath the panic, my reason was weighing its options. I had not been raised to lose my head under pressure. Should I just confess it all now, hope that he would be forgiving if faced with repentance?

'You need say nothing,' said Alexandre, his voice suddenly cracking. 'I can read it all in your face. Did you want to make a fool of me? Or did you really think I would not notice?'

'Alexandre, no! No, this had nothing to do with you.'

Alexandre gave a hollow laugh. 'My wife an adulteress, and it has nothing to do with me!'

The accusation was so unexpected that I almost skipped past it; I had to force my ears back over what they had heard to truly register the words. 'An—? No!' I said. 'Alexandre, you have to believe me; I never—'

'Just stop! I cannot listen to more lies and excuses, Sylvie. I have been telling myself enough of those over the past weeks, but I cannot ignore the truth any longer.' He flexed his fingers, as if casting away the falsehoods. 'This sneaking about, the private notes you keep locked in your desk, those countless evenings spent with Madame Coupart. Is that the arrangement? She lies for you and you for her? Coupart has often told me his suspicions about her, but I never thought . . . Then, when I saw you with that man at the party last week, I just knew . . .'

Dear God, he thought I was running about with *Maximilien*! I scrambled out of bed, feeling intensely the indignity of having this conversation in my nightgown. 'Alexandre, please, you have it all wrong!'

But he was not listening. 'And as for *him* – him, of all people! Sylvie, how could you prefer that blackguard to me?'

'Do not say that!' I was referring to the idea that I would ever choose someone over Alexandre, of course, but he interpreted my words quite differently.

'You defend him! Are you even aware of the truth of his character, of his family's characters? I have remembered now where I had heard the name de Jacquinot – I went back and read the files. A hushed case, kept from the public.'

I should have ignored this tangent, continued to plead my side. But I was not thinking clearly. 'What are you talking about?' I asked instead.

'The shame upon that family, all thanks to Monsieur de Jacquinot and his sister. You know the girl began an indecent affair with the best friend of her brother—'

'Diagne?'

'No, not him. There was a third member to their little fellowship in those days: Vasseur – son to a baron. The two planned to elope, but they were discovered by de Jacquinot. He flew into an animal rage and beat Vasseur to within an inch of his life. Vasseur was ready to press charges, but then the grandfather paid him a fortune to leave town.' Alexandre would not look at me – it was as if he were telling this story to himself. 'Of course, to this point one could place an equal measure of blame upon Vasseur – who might at least have had the good grace to *stay* in the countryside, but he has crept back to Paris again now the drama has been largely forgotten, and even has the nerve to resume his legal practice! But as for the ungrateful girl, when she learned of what her grandfather had done to protect them all, I hear that she tried to poison him. If the maid had not caught her lacing his coffee, the man would be dead.'

Even as I was struggling to find his purpose in recounting this, a disconnected part of my mind had time to reflect that it explained why all the former domestic staff had been dismissed: a silencing tactic.

Finally, Alexandre faced me. His eyes glistened with unshed tears. 'And *these* are the people you choose over me?'

My throat was burning; I could barely even speak up to defend myself. 'I—'

'You know, I cannot even blame you. I refused to listen to those who warned me against marrying someone so young, from such a different social strata. They always said you would get bored of a dull old man like me.'

'That is not—'

'I thought that my love would be enough. Why was it not enough for you, Sylvie?' He seemed to hear the whine in his own voice and, embarrassed, forced himself back to his cold, courtroom guise. 'I thought I was elevating you above the con- ditions of your birth. But instead, you have merely dragged me down into the gutter with you.'

I was struck with greater pain than if his words had been daggers. 'Alexandre, you do not mean that!' Tears pushed them- selves from my eyes like a rash, and I jolted forwards, meaning to cling to him, to make him wake up from this delusion into which he had fallen.

He shook his head slowly and stepped further away from me, as if scared of some contagion. 'I sometimes think I should never have married you, Sylvie.'

It was not true. He had been wounded and was only saying this to wound me in return. But this knowledge did not make it hurt any less.

'You need to leave this house,' he said.

'Leave? For how long?'

Alexandre shook his head. He would not answer – perhaps he did not even know the answer.

'But where will I go?'

'You have an hour.'

I was not guilty – at least not of that of which I stood accused – but I could not convince him of this now, not in the heat of his wounded pride. He needed time to calm down. Then, when he was again able to listen to reason, I would explain myself. I could have Maximilien testify that I had done nothing – but no, why should Alexandre believe that? I would have to involve the other members of his family, reveal the whole story about working with Charlotte once more.

But this was hardly a better prospect. When Alexandre had saved us all from what Charlotte had done, when he had agreed to marry me even so, his one condition in exchange had been that I end all contact with my family. It was for Charlotte's sake that I had accepted it – to keep her from prison – although she had refused to see that at the time. Our estrangement was as much a tenet of my marriage as was fidelity. When considered like that, did it matter which vow Alexandre believed me to have broken? Was I not guilty either way?

I managed to wait until he had left my bedchamber before the tears started in earnest, great grating sobs that jolted my ribs and stung in my throat as I sank to the floor. I did not know how long I wept there, but at some point I heard Virginie's frightened voice asking whatever was the matter.

'Oh, Virginie!' I cried, grabbing at her hand and likely scaring her all the more. 'Oh, I have ruined everything.'

Virginie's body was stiff, but she did move one of her arms to pat me on the back. 'I am sure not, Madame; it cannot be all as bad as that.' She flinched as another sob shook us both.

'Oh, it is that bad. I have been such a fool – how could I think—?'

Making a gentle shushing noise as one might for a baby, Virginie guided me up from the floor and sat me on the end of the bed. 'There, Madame, let it all out, that's it. Shall I fetch you something? A nice cup of milk? Or something stronger – I know you don't normally, but maybe under the circumstances?'

How lovely it would have been to curl up and let someone else take care of me . . . But I shook my head. 'No, there is not the time. We need to pack, and quickly.'

'Pack, Madame?'

I braced my elbows against my knees, forehead against my palms, forming a triangle. I tried to concentrate on breathing. Calm down. Deal with the situation. There would be time for panic and tears later, but for now I needed to focus on what had to be done. First, to pack my things. Then, to find out where I was going to go. One step at a time.

'Please fetch my valise from storage, Virginie, and some crêpe paper for wrapping. Then there will be some dresses to press – we need to be fast, so find Augustine and ask for her help if you need it.'

'But Madame—'

'Now, Virginie, please.'

Virginie bobbed a curtsey and left the room. As soon as she was gone, I crossed back to my desk and unlocked its drawer. All the treasures I would have to leave for now! Countless love notes from Alexandre, from the early days of our courtship. How could I have foreseen then that it would come to this? I took out Mother's locket, the spiritist diaries, the purse of money, and then my hand brushed against something I had forgotten was in there: Charlotte's visiting card. My old address stark like a sign. I had once believed that I would never go back. My departure had been performed in a rush that time, too, flinging possessions into a bag and pushing down my emotions for a later date. I had had fewer possessions then, of course, and no maids to help pack them.

And this was temporary. A week at the most, and then Alexandre would return to his usual disaffected, logical self. It was so unlike him to fly into a fit of passion. At the least, at the very least, this was proof that he loved me. If he had not loved me so much, he would never have been moved to such extremes.

I put aside a pair of walking dresses, one evening dress, and a gown that was a particular favourite of mine, as I had worn it to my first party in society as the Baroness Devereux – though it had been much altered since those tiny-waisted days. Stockings, drawers, chemises, petticoats, camisoles, a pair of kid slippers. I still needed to change out of my nightgown – I could wear my corsetry and crinoline, so there would be no need to find room for them. Then I could even throw on a shawl, cape, gloves and bonnet on the way out – it was too warm for so many layers, but there was only limited space in the case. Some jewellery could be carried in my reticule.

Virginie rematerialized with Augustine in tow, Virginie carrying the valise and Augustine with armfuls of crêpe paper. Once I had indicated what was to be packed, Augustine set about pressing and folding and squeezing it all in as Virginie helped me into my day clothes. We all worked in silence; Virginie had clearly warned Augustine not to ask any questions. Alexandre would be sure to explain it all to them soon enough.

At long last, everything was packed. How much of my time had passed? I realized I had not thought to check the clock before. It was close to midday.

'Augustine, will you fetch Coulomb to help with—' But no, it had been Coulomb whom Alexandre had sent to spy on me. At least let me be spared the insult of having that man's whiskery face with its gap-toothed smile leering at me, imagining that he knew all these lurid secrets. 'On second thoughts,' I said, 'it had better be Thomas. Never mind if he is busy; whatever else he is doing can wait.'

Augustine dutifully pattered away to fetch the manservant.

Virginie, emboldened now that the task was finished, tried once more. 'Madame, please, what's happening?'

I sighed, passed a hand across my forehead. 'You have been a good maid to me, Virginie,' I said. 'I have been eternally grateful for your loyalty and service.'

'Thank you, Madame.' Her face flushed at the unexpected praise, but then the expression cracked and her eyes grew wide. 'Oh, Madame, you are not dismissing me?'

'No! At least, I hope not. I am sorry, Virginie, I cannot be certain of anything at the moment.'

Virginie crossed to my side and took one of my hands. Her fingers were calloused from years of domestic servitude, but warm and comforting. The impertinence could be overlooked, given the sentiment behind it. 'What has happened? Are you . . . unwell?'

I shook my head. 'It is hard to confess,' I said. 'I . . . I have held a secret from my husband, and he has found it out. No, that is inaccurate. He thinks he has found out a different secret – one that is not true – but the act of keeping something from him has been the same, and so I am guilty nevertheless. He has asked me to leave for a time. I do not know how long.'

The fingers squeezed tighter. 'Then I can come with you! You'll still need a lady's maid, wherever you are going.'

I gently slipped my hand from hers. 'I am afraid not,' I said. There was no place for a lady's maid at Papa's.

'But who will dress you? Who will style your hair and mend your clothes?'

A smile of affection snuck its way on to my face, taking me quite by surprise – I had thought it would be a long time before I could smile again. 'You know, Virginie,' I said, 'I lived twenty-five years doing those things for myself. I think I can manage them again for a short while.'

Thomas arrived shortly to take the valise down. No questions from him: Alexandre had clearly already alerted him to the situation.

'Thank you, Thomas. Please will you carry my case to the hansom and I shall be with you in a moment.'

Thomas hesitated, mouth opening as if to speak although no words came forth.

'Well, Thomas, what is the matter? Are you taking that or not?'

'It is just, Madame,' he said, scuffing one toe against the floor and looking steadfastly at this rather than me, 'the master has instructed me to see you down. He said that I was to make sure you went straight to the cab and did not try to find him and harass him further, as he could not abide to hear no more of your lies. Forgive me for putting it so plainly, Madame, but these were his words, not mine.'

So, was I to go to my sentence without the least bit of protest? This was not in my nature. If Alexandre was really to send me from my home, then he could look me in the eye one last time before doing so.

'If they are his words, he can speak them to me with his own mouth,' I said. 'Take my valise and I shall be along shortly.'

Thomas stooped halfway to obey, then paused, straightened, stooped again.

In the end, it was Virginie who lost her patience. 'Just take the blessed case, Thomas,' she snapped. 'Is Madame not going through enough without having to watch you struggle to make a damned decision?'

Thomas turned the colour of a beetroot, but at last took hold of the handle and heaved the offending object from the room.

'I apologize for the language, Madame,' said Virginie, smoothing down her skirts. 'Only, I'm a little upset at present and lost my temper.'

I placed a hand upon her shoulder and looked her in the eye. 'Thank you,' I said. 'Thank you for all you have done.'

Alexandre was still in his study when I found him. The air had a smell of alcoholic fumes – good preparation for what I would shortly find at rue de Constantine. He was sitting at his desk, hunched over with his head resting upon his crossed arms. When he heard me enter, he looked up to reveal red tracks in his face where the skin had been pressed too long against the fabric of his sleeves. His eyes focused on me, but with a bleary quality. I wondered how much he had had to drink.

'I have come to say that I am leaving,' I told him, keeping my head high, back straight. This would be a dignified exit. I was no disgraced adulteress. 'If that is still what you wish.'

'It is.' His voice was a toad-croak.

I nodded. 'Very well. When you are ready to listen to reason, you may contact me at my father's address: thirty-four rue de Constantine, as it was before. Then I will explain everything to you, and you will see that while I have kept secrets from you, I was never unfaithful, and I did only what I thought to be right.'

There was no response.

'Farewell, Alexandre. I love you.'

I turned and left the room. As I was closing the door behind me, faintly, almost obscured by the creak of hinges, I thought I heard him say it back.

CHAPTER NINE

17 April 1866

THE CEILING'S COBWEBBED cracks were as familiar as the whorls on my own fingertips. For a moment, I could have been a child again, waking to the sight that had greeted me every morning of my life. But then it all returned to me: Alexandre, the de Jacquinots, the series of events that had conspired to return me here to my childhood bedroom. I wished I had stayed asleep.

When one looks back upon one's time on Earth – across the span of years and decisions that have carried one from birth to wherever one is now – it is nigh impossible to point out a single particular moment and say, 'Yes, here. This is where it all began to go wrong.' But still one tries. One inspects the tapestry for the pattern, for the loose thread. Had it been when Charlotte had reappeared in my life? Had it been when I had disappeared from Charlotte's? Had it been when Mama had died? Or had it been further still, all the way back to the day on which I was born in this wretched house?

As I thought on it, however, I decided that I might as well say it had all begun that summer of three years ago. 1863: the summer I had been invited by one of our clients to a ball where I had met a baron – an esteemed lawyer who glittered with promise – and glimpsed a world of which I longed to be a part. I had known, then, that I needed to leave behind who I once had been. Spiritism might have been a fashionable profession for the moment, but it was not the profession of a baroness. So I had lied. No, not lied – omitted. I had told Alexandre everything about myself, more than I had told anyone before or since: my dreams, my fears, my interests, my politics, my grief at the loss of Mama; everything but the one thing that seemed at the time to define my life. And it had worked: he had fallen in love with me. Soon he had begun to court me with romantic letters and little gifts. I knew that he would ask for my hand, once he had overcome his shyness – and then he did, came to this tiny house and sat down with Papa to arrange the whole thing. He thought that Papa was a medical consultant.

So it was set. I saw happiness blooming in the future like a fresh rose.

But then, Charlotte.

While Alexandre had been courting me, Charlotte had been doing some courting of her own.

We were working at the time with a charming family, consisting of a recent widow – untitled, but wealthy – and her three unmarried daughters. They had enlisted us to help contact the deceased husband. Back then, Charlotte and I were still the main performers, but it was Papa who ran the business.

It was hard to say whether the idea had been his or Charlotte's; they had hatched it between themselves and only invited me in later: private tutoring sessions with the youngest daughter. 'A natural talent for the supernatural,' Papa had told the widow. For a modest fee, the girl could learn to make contact with the deceased unaided. She was enthusiastic – a pretty, apple-cheeked thing. Charlotte, being of the same age, would be her tutor.

Charlotte and the girl passed a number of sessions together. The progress reports were promising: to the mother, of a quick mind well suited to learning the craft; to Papa and myself, of an unremarkable fool, too flattered by the attention to realize she was being 'had'. We had extra money coming in – enough for a fine dowry.

Then the widow walked in on one of Charlotte's private tutoring sessions.

Charlotte insisted that it was a case of mutual feeling – that the other girl had initiated things, even. And it was not against the laws of the state. Naive as Charlotte was, she thought they were in love, that they were going to run away together one day. She had never been able to accept reality.

The widow's daughter, whether in truth or out of fear, planted the whole thing upon Charlotte – claimed she had become obsessed with her, pursued her without any encouragement. To whom was the widow to listen? Of course, she would choose her own child. There was talk of the police, the court. Charlotte was a corrupting influence who had taken advantage of an innocent girl. And, of course, this led to some conclusions about the credibility of our business practices: if what Charlotte had done had not been necessarily contrary to the law, scamming a bourgeois widow by exploiting her grief certainly was.

Papa was outraged, to say the least. Everything he had worked to build had been ruined in an instant by Charlotte's weakness. How he shouted, called her a whore, a fricatrice, drank himself insensible and beat her and me along with her, because he could not believe there had been no collusion between two sisters.

But I fixed it. I went to Alexandre and confessed all. No, not all: I left myself innocent of the deception, claimed I had truly believed in the spirits but now saw the error in this. Alexandre was so in love that he could not deny me. He stepped in, bribed off the policemen who had been called, paid a hush fee out of his own coffers, stifled all mentions of the case. The only thing he asked in return was that I disassociate myself from the criminals I had called a family; for the sake of his legal career, he could not risk such a connection. This was the only way that he could marry me. And for me, this was a chance to start afresh. A chance to save Charlotte from herself. Who would not have taken it?

Just as I had now done once more, I had packed my bags that day and left my home, ignoring Charlotte's exhortations that I stay.

I could see her still on the kitchen floor, one eye swollen shut and tears coursing down her cheeks. 'Please don't leave me alone here with *him*! Please, Sylvie, he'll kill me!'

As if slipping a pair of trick handcuffs, I had pried my wrist from her grasp. 'I am doing this for you. For both of you.'

'You're doing this for yourself – don't pretend it ain't what you've always wanted!'

'Charlotte, you would have gone to jail.'

'No! She'd never—'

'She already did!' If I had to hear one more word of Charlotte's childish, misplaced belief in the girl who had done this to us, I was going to scream so loud the dead would hear it. 'She does not love you. She does not care about you. She is not going to protect you – that was me! I am the one who saved you. It is time to stop believing in your fairy stories.'

My sister looked like she could kill me; misery turned in a quicksilver flash to rage. 'And you don't? Off to marry your prince. At least my love weren't bought with gold.'

I could not look at her any longer.

As I turned away, I heard her croak, 'If you leave now, I will never, ever forgive you.'

Whatever Charlotte needed to believe of me, I had been given no other option. Leaving her had been the only way to save us all from the law. That did not mean that it had not hurt, that I had never once missed her or worried for her well-being. That it had not felt at times as if a limb had been ripped from my own body. But I had known that she was strong enough to manage without me. I had only done what needed to be done when I picked up my bags and marched away, kept going as her sobs grew fainter and fainter, although they had never quite left my ears. Or my heart.

Now throwing off the sleep haze, I rolled on to my side. There was the wince of ancient springs. Charlotte and I had shared this cast-iron bed for nearly two decades, but when I had turned up the previous afternoon – and after an unpleasant time spent confessing my situation – she had insisted I take the room for myself. Apparently, she now slept in Papa's chamber so she could watch him in the night.

Charlotte had not done much to decorate since becoming sole proprietor of the space: the walls were adorned with the same embroideries that Mama used to make for our birthdays as children. She had been a deft seamstress, whether she had been turning her hand to these decorative patterns or sewing a false lining into an evening gown. Charlotte and I had spent many tranquil afternoons practising our own stitches under her tutelage. I could often hear the memory of her voice even now when I picked up a needle.

My favourite of the embroideries had a pattern of yellow roses surrounding a little cottage. Next to it was a second, almost identical – Charlotte had so coveted mine that she had demanded Mama make another when it came to her birthday. She had always been like that as a child, copying me, jealous and admiring in equal parts. I wondered at what point I had lost her high regard. When had the heroic older sister transformed from an idol into a fallible person?

Presently, I realized that I could hear a low murmur of voices. My room was adjacent to Papa's, and the walls were thin. So, he was awake. He had been passed out when I had arrived the day before – a small mercy.

On tiptoes so as not to make a noise, I got up and pulled a robe over my nightdress. It was Charlotte's robe, but I did not feel too guilty. We had once shared all our clothes.

I crept down the corridor, pausing to listen outside Papa's room. We used to do this as children, whenever our parents shut themselves away to argue. Only, this time, Charlotte was not at my elbow, and it was her voice on the other side of the door.

'. . . am just as angry with her as you are, Papa, but she's still family.'

'She can't pick and choose when to be family.' Papa's voice was hoarser than it had been before, but still recognizable enough to send a chill down my spine. I had genuinely believed that I would never see him again in this life. He was as good as a ghost to me already.

'And neither can you, Papa.'

He made a long, low reply that I did not catch.

'Well, you can say that all to her yourself when she gets up.'

'Is it time for my egg yet?'

Again, I could not hear the reply, but it was swiftly followed by footsteps heading for the door.

I leaped back, trying to hide my eavesdropping, but it was already too late. The door swung inwards to reveal Charlotte.

'Good morning, Sylvie,' Charlotte said after a moment. 'I thought the rich didn't rise before midday.'

'Is he ready to see me?' I asked. Although my chest tightened at the thought, I had to face him eventually; I was staying under his roof, for God's sake! There was a lump of nerves weighing in my stomach like a peach pit, but I reminded myself that things were not the same. I was a fully grown and independent adult, a married woman – and he was sickening in bed. He no longer held any power over me.

So why did I feel a child again, hiding from a scolding that I knew I deserved?

'Go on in,' said Charlotte. 'I'm just getting his breakfast.'

'Is he . . . very much changed?'

It was a feeble ploy to waylay her and she must have seen through it immediately. She shrugged at me. 'He's dying.'

I could do nothing but nod in response.

'You've got nothing to say about that?' Her expression was suddenly, inexplicably aggrieved, with colour high on her cheek-bones and something ticking in her jaw. 'D'you know,' she asked, one finger wagging as if scolding a misbehaving dog, 'that you've not even asked what's wrong with him? You've had weeks, and you never thought to ask. Worse: you don't even ask how he's doing. There's a boy who sells papers at the end of the street – just some boy, I don't even know his name – but whenever I buy one, *he* asks. And you, his daughter . . .' She waved her hand in a flourish of disgust, unable to finish the thought.

The sermonizing rankled with me. As if Charlotte had a leg to stand on when it came to morals! 'If you are trying to make me feel guilty, it will not work,' I said. 'We always knew it would be the drink that did for him, so why should I ask when I know the answer already?'

Charlotte powered past this. 'And did it ever cross your mind to visit? Any ordinary person would've come to see their father on his sickbed.'

'I owe him nothing!' I fought to keep my voice down, aware that it would carry all too easily into the room.

Charlotte's lips had formed a single tight line, like a stitch. 'I don't owe him anything either,' she said, 'and yet here I am nursing him, day after thankless day, completely without help, without money, without anything. I can't leave the house unless Adèle next door will watch him for a while.' Her voice was cold and steady as a blade. 'He's in so much debt that when he dies, I'll lose my home. I won't even be able to pay to bury him. But what choice have I got?' It was not a rhetorical question: she locked eyes with mine and challenged me to respond. How had I not noticed before that the impish face of old had become so tired?

It was I who looked away first.

Charlotte cleared her throat, smoothing a hand over her chest. 'Go and talk to your father.'

It was clear the argument was over – and Charlotte the victor, although I could not have identified the moment when she had begun to gain the upper ground, or even the point at which the quarrel had started in the first place.

As she turned away down the corridor, she threw a half-glance back at me and said, 'It weren't the drink, you know.'

It took me a moment to understand her meaning. 'Oh?'

'A tumour growing in his brain – big enough you can see it up his nose, the doctor says. It'd be the same whether he was sober or not.' With that, she disappeared into the kitchen.

Taking a deep breath, I went into Papa's room.

Papa was tucked up in the bed he had once shared with

Mama. Someone – Charlotte – had propped him upright with a host of pillows, against which he lolled as if he hadn't the strength to hold his back straight. The pigeon-grey which formerly flecked his temples had now spread to colonize his entire head, and his facial hair, which he used to keep neatly trimmed into a moustache and side whiskers, had been allowed to flourish into a full beard. His nose was the colour of port and swollen with papules, made all the more prominent by the pallor of the rest of his skin. His eyelids and cheeks sagged. Two rheumy eyes blinked out at me, their whites yellowish and speckled with veins. Although it was April and barely chilly, the bed was piled with blankets, obscuring Papa's shape from view, but for his face and the two arms peeping out of the covers like chicken legs. He'd lost so much weight.

Unlike the rest of the house, the room was very tidy, with everything organized into neat stacks. Despite this, it had a smell to it – a blend of stale breath, old sweat, alcohol and stasis. A commode had been placed in one corner.

I took a few steps forwards. There was a photographic portrait above Papa's bed that had been taken the year before Mama's death, depicting all four of us. We had worn our smartest clothes and the portraitist had arranged us carefully in front of a backdrop that made it look like we were in the countryside. Really, it had been a painted sheet. Just another illusion in the lives of the Mothe family.

Mama was at the very centre, sitting elegantly upon a stool. Her hair shone and those dark eyes drew the viewer's attention like a dare. She looked very beautiful. One hand was folded over the other in her lap – I remembered that she had had a wax burn on the one that was hidden. She had been terrified that it would ruin the portrait. Indeed, she had fretted over most things, in that last year – it was as if a dark cloud had descended over her spirit without our realizing, preventing any light from shining into her life.

Charlotte and I were kneeling on either side of Mama like mirror reflections, each with a posy in hand. Charlotte looked plump and happy, her fair hair arranged like a halo about her face. The lights had been very bright and I had been trying not to squint, causing my image to have a sly aspect to it. Good sister and bad sister. At the back of the portrait, standing in a dark suit with one hand resting on either side of the chair back, Papa loomed over us.

The man who greeted me now seemed less real than that image. 'Is that you, Sylvie?' he asked.

I moved closer so that he could better see me. There was a sense of apprehension as I approached, as if my body was prepared at any moment for Papa to leap out of the blankets and cry, 'Tricked you!' I reached the side of his bed but did not know what to do next. Should I sit? Take his hand? Kiss him? Instead, I stood awkwardly, shifting my weight from foot to foot. His breathing was raspy. The smell of alcohol was stronger this close.

'Come back with your tail between your legs?' said Papa.

I did not know the correct answer to this. A plea for forgiveness, perhaps? But I had done nothing which required forgiveness, as far as I could see.

Papa groaned and shifted in place. 'My legs are like eels,' he said.

'I'm sorry?'

'Eels! You never did listen to me. From all the lying down. Your sister won't let me walk.'

'*Can* you walk?'

He glowered and smacked his lips.

I looked around for something to say. There was a stack of books at the bedside. 'Would you like me to read?' I asked, nodding in their direction.

Papa turned to glance at them and snorted. 'Where's my egg?'

'Charlotte is fetching it.'

'She always overcooks them.'

'She is trying her best.'

He shook his head, beard rustling against the neck of his nightshirt. 'It's on purpose.'

I was about to ask why on earth Charlotte would deliberately overcook his eggs when the woman herself returned, carrying a tray with a hard-boiled egg in a cup, a spoon, a pear and another of the tin mugs.

'It's to punish me,' said Papa.

Charlotte carried the tray over to his bedside and placed it atop the novels, then she turned to Papa and began rearranging the pillows until he was properly upright, more as if he were a doll than a man. 'You having it in your lap?' she asked.

He grunted in reply.

Charlotte broke open the egg with the spoon, then picked up the tray and balanced it across Papa's knees. She took his right hand and guided it to the spoon, then took his left hand and guided it to the mug handle. She was shaping up to be quite the nurse.

Papa clenched his left hand around the mug in a clumsy grip, ignoring the handle completely, and shakily lifted it to his lips. A little liquid dribbled out of the corner of his mouth and soaked into his beard. It was red in colour.

'Should he really be drinking that?' I hissed.

Charlotte shrugged. 'What? In case it's bad for his health?'

Papa had begun to eat the egg. The yolk was firm and powdery. Overcooked.

'So what's your plan now?' Charlotte asked me. She drew a knife from her pocket to slice the pear, depositing the segments on Papa's tray as she went.

I did not want to have this conversation in front of Papa. I did not want to have it at all. 'I will think about it today,' I said.

Charlotte nodded and began dabbing at Papa's face with a napkin, cleaning up the wine dribbles and egg flecks. He sat peacefully while she did so, eyes drooping, but then suddenly he came alive again and grasped at her wrist with his knobbly fingers.

'Charlotte,' he said urgently, 'I need to—'

'Yes, yes,' said Charlotte. She put down the napkin and moved over to the commode, which she dragged out of its corner. 'Go on, Sylvie, you can leave.'

I knew it was cowardly, but I fled the room.

'Right,' said Charlotte, emerging once the task was complete. 'I've got to go out for a bit now, see someone about a bill. You don't mind, do you?' She was already lacing up her outdoor boots. 'I s'pose we could ask Adèle, if you'd like to come with me, but I'm guessing you want to stay put here in case your husband . . .'

I wanted desperately to cling to Charlotte's skirts, say, *Don't leave me alone here with him!* But this was not the behaviour of an adult woman. I could not admit that I was afraid to be alone in the house with my own father. Especially after Charlotte had been on her own at his side for so long. 'Of course not,' I said, watching as she tied the bows. I'd taught her how to do that. 'Charlotte . . .?'

'Hmm?'

'Has it been hard? Caring for him, I mean.'

She looked up at me, then stood to her full height. 'What d'you think?'

'I think that Mama would be proud of the young woman you have become. No, I mean it! And I am too. I wish that I could have been here to help you more.'

Charlotte snorted. 'We both know that's a damned lie!'

'Very well,' I conceded, 'but I am here now, and I will take my turn. You go out for as long as you need.'

She rolled her eyes as she left. I hoped she appreciated my words deep down.

As it happened, Papa was mercifully in and out of conscious-ness for most of the day, leaving me plenty of solitude to think on what I should do about my situation. First things first, I dashed off a letter to Sarah, telling her I would be out of town for a while and not to believe anything she heard about me in the meantime – not that she was the sort of friend to pass judgement over a scandal. Alongside this, I composed a note to Alexandre, pleading for his ear so that I might explain my innocence.

I remembered all in a rush the other of his allegations: that Maximilien had almost killed a man. I had been so caught up in the charge of infidelity that I'd fully forgotten the rest. But had I not heard a similar piece of gossip at Sarah's party? I had dismissed it then as well; I could barely believe Maximilien was capable of such a thing. He was arrogant, that was certainly true, but I had never imagined him to be violent with it.

I needed to speak privately with Maximilien, I realized. I had to tell him of Alexandre's suspicions – he would not be at all pleased to be thus accused – and persuade him to defend my position. It was his reputation in question, as much as mine, if word got out. His family could hardly afford to be implicated in *another* bout of defamation.

All this correspondence, yet nobody with whom to speak. For the two years I had spent as the Baroness Devereux, I had never lacked for company; at the pull of a bell, I could summon Virginie to my side – even if only to discuss the weather. I thought of her cursing at Thomas, lip pouting in impatience, and suddenly missed her horribly. Still, I told myself, it would not be this way for long. Soon enough, Alexandre would come to his senses and appear at the door to call me home. I knew that he would come.

CHAPTER TEN

19 April 1866

I WAS IN agonies waiting for Alexandre's reply over the follow-ing period, rushing to the window at every small sound from the street, my heart galloping with hope only to dash itself time and again against the disappointments of reality. So when a cab did finally draw up two days later, I experienced a mix-ture of strongly competing emotions upon seeing that it was Maximilien whom it discharged on to our doorstep.

'Who's that?' yawned Charlotte, heading to answer his knock.

She had been equally restless these past days, and I had heard her pacing about at all hours the night before, so that I doubted she had slept a wink. I supposed this was down to my pres-ence, which surely awakened as many old memories in her as it did in me.

I was not fast enough to get to the door before Charlotte. I had not told her of my invitation to Maximilien, thinking it too unlikely that he would accept, so the moment she saw him now, the colour drained from her face in terror.

'Good morning, Mademoiselle Mothe,' said Maximilien, his gaze slipping past her to fix on where I loitered in the corridor. 'Madame Devereux.'

There was a small squeak of surprise from Charlotte, who clearly thought that we had been found out entirely.

'Monsieur Maximilien,' I said quickly, pulling Charlotte aside and squeezing her shoulder surreptitiously to let her know that there was no cause for alarm. 'I appreciate your responding so quickly. Will you come inside?'

Maximilien followed me through the entrance and into the kitchen, glancing curiously at Papa's open door – from which the sound of snoring issued – as he passed.

'Our father,' I explained. 'He is unwell.'

Offering Maximilien a seat at the kitchen table, I set about making a pot of coffee.

Out of the corner of my eye, I could see him looking around the kitchen with undisguised curiosity. There was the table, a sturdy slab of oak that had belonged to Papa's parents, scored with marks where generations of Mothe women had neglected to use a chopping board. One wall was taken up completely by a dresser, the everyday china hidden away and the best on display with its pink blossom pattern. When she was herself, Mama had always kept the space bright and clean; however, Charlotte must not have inherited this skill. The floor was dusty in the corners. The range was grubby. A smattering of mould fuzzed the exterior wall, near the ceiling. The window was streaked with grime.

'I do not mean to be rude,' said Maximilien, 'but I had assumed that I would be visiting you at home, Baroness.'

I had finished with the coffee tin, so I returned it to the cupboard. I took out a trio of matching coffee cups and their saucers. There was a crack in one, so I swapped it for another of the same set. They had an orange pattern and, I seemed to remember, had been a Christmas surprise from Papa one year, when he had still thought of such things.

'This is our father's house,' I said. 'I left it when I married Alexandre – the Baron. But, yes, I am back here for the time being.' I took the cups and saucers and placed them on the table, sitting opposite him.

'Thank you,' said Maximilien.

'That is why I have asked you to come here.'

His face was blank with incomprehension. 'I beg your pardon?'

Charlotte – still standing, and thankfully out of Maximilien's eye line – looked about ready to stab me.

I sighed and twisted my cup around in my hands. 'This is awkward to admit . . . No, it is *very* awkward. I do not know quite how to say it. You recall I told you that my husband was not aware that I had come out of retirement to help your family?'

'Ah,' said Maximilien. 'So he found out?'

I shook my head. I could not look him in the face and say it; it was too embarrassing, too ludicrous. I watched my own hands instead as I spoke. 'Worse. He indeed found out some of the facts, but the conclusion he drew from them . . . He believes me to have been dishonest.'

Maximilien did not catch the meaning; it was clear from his face when I dared to glance up.

'Dishonest with him about *you*.'

'Oh.' I knew from his beetroot flush that now he understood. 'Oh.' He shuffled in his seat.

'He will not listen to reason, and I fear I will only make things worse if I bring spiritism into it. He has never approved of the career.'

Maximilien cleared his throat. 'I should not have come,' he said. 'I thought you had something to discuss about your employment, perhaps.' He glanced over his shoulder at Charlotte, as if to gauge her opinion. 'But this . . . My being here makes it look worse. Surely you see that?' He made as if to rise from his seat.

'Wait! Please. Of course I see that, but you are the only person who can help to clear my name.'

He hesitated, still half-standing. 'I do not wish any harm upon you, Madame Devereux. But I need to stay out of this; I do not want to make myself look guilty. I cannot afford to have charges pressed against me. You are the one who chose to keep secrets from him; it is not my responsibility if you are now facing the consequences.'

'You would lecture me on secrets?' I asked, a laugh almost creeping into my voice. 'As if you and your family have kept no secrets from us. I have asked on multiple occasions if you can think of any negative emotions that may be attracting tumultuous spirits, and yet none of you chose to mention the business with Florence!'

'Sylvie!' Charlotte protested.

'What do you know about that?' The question came like a whip. If he had been a dog, his hackles would have been up and his teeth showing.

'I know that your sister attempted to elope with a friend of yours and fell into hysteria when she was stopped. I know that you nearly killed Vasseur yourself.'

A vein twitched in Maximilien's forehead. 'That man was no friend of mine.'

'But you do not deny the rest of it?' I asked.

'If you are trying to blackmail me into fighting your corner, Madame Devereux, I can assure you that it will not work.' He had lowered his voice to an undertone, enunciating each word with great care. 'Any legal case was dropped a long time ago.'

'Yes, when your grandfather bought everyone off. Look where that got him. Nearly murdered by his own granddaughter.'

This time, Charlotte strode towards me to cut me off.

'Monsieur Maximilien, I am so sorry for my sister. I do not know what can have got into her! Sylvie, will you please—'

'No, no,' said Maximilien, 'I would love to hear what your sister thinks that she knows. Where did you hear all of this, Madame Devereux?'

'My husband. He is in the law, after all.' I was not black-mailing, but I could not keep myself from putting a special emphasis on 'law'. It was not a threat. There was no intentional implication – for example, that if Maximilien did not help me, he might face legal repercussions both over the alleged affair and over things further in his past. But if Maximilien chose to imagine there was an implication, then it would be . . . how had he put it? 'Not my responsibility.'

Maximilien sat back down, running a hand through his hair with the manner of somebody weighing up his options. 'I have no obligation to tell you what I am about to,' he said, 'but I cannot bear to hear these allegations against my sister. I will tell you the truth, but you must swear never to speak it to anyone else. Either of you.'

Intrigued, but not wanting to appear too keen, I leaned for-wards in my chair, propping my elbows on the table. 'If you like,' I said, as nonchalantly as I could.

Maximilien nodded, picked up his coffee and took a draught as if to prepare his vocal cords. 'Florence is no murderess . . . It was not my grandfather whom she was trying to poison – that is a nonsense my mother chose to believe because she preferred it to the truth. I do not know how the rumour spread further.' He paused, throat bobbing as if swallowing back some emotion. 'Florence was trying to poison herself.'

Something flipped in my stomach. Murder was quite one thing, but suicide . . . My impressions of Florence were shifting around in my head to resolve themselves. The motives of a murderess, I could understand – particularly as I had met Ardoir and could see why one might wish him dead. But the motives of a suicide were something that I had spent many years pondering, and I was no closer truly to grasping them now than I had been when the question had first arisen. What drove a woman to take her own life? Was it despair, as people often said, or was it the same wrath as a murderess feels, only with a different direction? Unlike a murderess, one could not ask after the crime had been committed.

'She must have been very much in love with Vasseur,' I said.

Maximilien's expression darkened as if crossed by a storm cloud. 'She was not,' he said.

'Well, she must have—'

'She was a young girl, taken in by his charm,' he said abruptly. 'She soon saw him for what he was when he abducted her and . . . misused her.'

'I assume you mean he forced himself upon her?' said Charlotte, her bluntness making me wince. A slight inclination of Maximilien's head told us she was right.

'And is that what caused her to . . .?' I gestured non-specifically with one hand, unable to say the words.

'Florence was with child,' said Maximilien.

My immediate response was shock, but the shock was more because Maximilien had admitted such a thing, rather than because of the thing itself. After all, hadn't I suspected that consumption was not the true explanation for her period of 'ill health'?

'She could not face the thought of bearing it,' Maximilien went on. 'Not at first, in any case. By the end, she had changed her mind. I think she was looking forward to having something to take care of; she had this vision of a life in the countryside or abroad – somewhere she could live anonymously – with a precious daughter as a constant companion. I only wish . . .' He trailed off with a sigh, pressing his fingertips to his temples.

I fiddled with my coffee cup. 'Then what happened?'

'She lost the child; it was born dead. But Florence could not accept this – she was convinced that my grandfather had taken it away alive, that it was still breathing somewhere. Thankfully, that delusion has now passed, but I fear she is still not back to her old self. If only you could have seen her as she was then. She had this vibrancy, this force of spirit that lit up our home. However, I cannot say I am surprised that it has left her, after all she has suffered.' He was staring at the wall now, but his eyes seemed to look past it, back to Florence as she had been before.

'And what did you do to help her?' asked Charlotte, her tone markedly accusatory.

Maximilien looked up at her in surprise. 'We have tried to start afresh. Removed belongings, dismissed old servants. A new start. But it has been so difficult for us all.'

I tried to imagine how I would feel if the same thing had happened to Charlotte – but I could not imagine it. Charlotte was too hardy for anything of that sort.

'I am telling you this,' said Maximilien, 'and trusting that you will keep it as a secret, only to clear my sister's name. And, of course, to ensure that you are properly equipped to banish the ghoul that is haunting us.' He extended his hand across the table, as if he expected us to shake on it.

'So you have decided to believe now?' asked Charlotte. She was swiping at her eyes as if moved to tears by Florence's suffering.

'It seems I have no choice. We have all seen things we cannot explain in any other way. Even I cannot ignore the evidence of my own senses.'

He had done a fair job of ignoring it so far! '*Have* you seen something, Monsieur Maximilien?' I asked.

'I . . . I feel silly saying, but if I cannot tell a spiritist, then I suppose I can tell nobody.' He still had his hand extended stupidly before him, but he remembered it now and curled it back in to his chest. 'As I was lying awake last night, I was struck with a sense of guilt for having dismissed my sister's claims, and, knowing her also to be often awake in the small hours, I determined to go to her rooms and apologize. However, no sooner had I reached the threshold than I heard voices from the other side of the door – too hushed to make out clearly. Fearing she may have been in danger from a night burglary, I put my eye to the keyhole and saw my sister speaking animatedly, although I could not see her interlocutor. Surprised, I stepped back and my foot caught upon a creaky board. Knowing that Florence must have heard me, I knocked and asked who was there with her. She replied, "Nobody." A chill ran down my spine. I opened the door, but it was just as Florence had said – she was alone. But I heard a second voice; I know I did.' He paused, watching my face with an expectant air. The story had unnerved me – it seemed a reflection of my own fearful encounter in the corridor outside Florence's room – but I did not want him to see it. 'Well?' he said. 'It must have been the spirit, do you not agree?'

'Certainly,' said Charlotte, 'and, Monsieur Maximilien, I swear that we shall get to the bottom of this for you. Let us come to your house for a sitting tomorrow, now that we know the full history. I am sure that these misfortunes are what have drawn the Comtesse back to your family. Was it not Florence who saw her first, after all, and who speaks with her still? If we can only understand the connection between them, and what it is the Comtesse wants from you, we will be able to return her to her peace. And perhaps we can bring Mademoiselle Florence to peace, too.'

'Yes, my heart truly goes out to her,' I agreed, not wanting to sound like I was not equally moved. 'Going through something so dreadful – being attacked by Vasseur and then losing her child – and all the time knowing that the man who caused her this pain is continuing with his life as normal.'

Maximilien dipped his head. 'Your sympathy means a lot,' he said. He ran a hand through his hair again: a nervous tick. 'I feel . . . Well, I owe you both an apology for my behaviour. I have not been . . . the most cooperative. In fact, I fear I have given you rather a lot of trouble.' He paused – if he was waiting for us to contradict him, he would have to wait a long time. 'I may be in accord now, but that does not negate my past behaviour. As you can appreciate, I am sure, it was only ever because I was trying to protect my sister. But I see that you are on her side. On my side. So I am sorry.' He looked up at me, bashful as a child asking forgiveness for his misbehaviour.

One would have had to be heartless to have rejected him. 'And we accept your apology,' I said.

Maximilien gave a half-smile. 'Good. I can get carried away when it comes to Florence. Well, you know what happened . . . before.' He flexed his fingers, as if the knuckles still ached from what he had done to Vasseur. 'It is little consolation, but at least I know he did not go completely unpunished.'

It must have been infuriating for Maximilien to know that Vasseur's paid exile had lasted only a brief while, when Florence's pain still went on. 'It does seem without any justice,' I said, 'that he has been able to return so soon to his life without

147

any repercussions. To think that any one of us could bump into him!'

A crease appeared in Maximilien's brow, slowly, like fragmenting ice. 'What do you mean by that?'

'I was just thinking, it must be frustrating to know that he is back now in Paris – practically on your doorstep – and happily pursuing his career as if nothing had happened.'

Maximilien had been looking at me blankly, but now, as I watched, a dawning comprehension filled his features. His eyes widened; his nostrils flared. His knuckles drained of colour where he clenched his hands.

'But . . .' I said, now uncertain. 'But you already knew that?'

'Tell me this is a joke.' His voice was surprisingly steady. 'Tell me that . . . that *bastard* has not dared return to Paris.'

'Oh, Maximilien, I am sorry.'

He did not say anything for several moments, although his throat was working as if there were words trapped inside it that wanted to jump free. Then he stood quickly. 'Thank you for the coffee,' he said. 'I must go now.'

I followed him out of the kitchen, into the corridor. 'Are you sure that you are quite all right?' I asked.

He opened the front door himself, ignoring the question. 'Good day, Madame Devereux, Mademoiselle Mothe.'

Watching helplessly as he marched away, I realized that we had not managed to arrange how he would deal with Alexandre – all I had gained was a non-specific promise, and the feeling that I had only waded in further out of my depth.

'Now,' said Charlotte, closing the door firmly behind him. 'D'you want to tell me what the fuck you were thinking?'

CHAPTER ELEVEN

20 April 1866

FOR THIS SITTING, Charlotte and I were taking certain pre-cautionary measures: reciting prayers, keeping several Bibles to hand, pouring a salt ring upon the floor. All the things one should do when summoning a volatile spirit. My mind kept turning to the figure I had glimpsed in the long corri-dor the other night, to Maximilien's claim that he had heard a ghostly voice, to that hateful destruction of the library. And didn't all these precautions look so flimsy? How could salt and a stack of books really hold back a will so unstoppable that even death had not put a halt to it? I tried to push these thoughts away. There was no spirit. It was impossible that there was a spirit.

What put me more on edge: Maximilien was absent.

'Should we proceed without him?' I wondered.

Ardoir scoffed. 'Of course. You must have realized his char-acter by now.'

Strange, he had seemed so sincere the previous day when he had spoken of the spirit. So destabilized by the news of Vasseur. I found myself hoping that he was not in any sort of trouble.

Florence was given a cup of wine to loosen her senses, and then we were ready. We were in the dining room tonight, the table pushed to one side and the chairs moved into a ring – save for one, which stood at the centre. An island. A target. This was Florence's, of course. She was the vessel.

It was already dark outside, so there was no need to draw the curtains. The reflections of candles and our own faces in the glass gave the room an eerie aspect – but then, the room would have had an eerie aspect either way. It looked as if the flames and our heads and hands – well, the hands of those of us who wore pale gloves – were floating in a black pool. I was reminded of the Russian tradition in which young girls would sit before an arrangement of mirrors on Christmas Eve, holding a candle so that it was reflected over and over in an impossible tunnel – and at the end of it, one was supposed to see the spectral figure of the man one would marry. With a pang, I thought of Alexandre. What was he doing this evening? Was he thinking of me in return?

While the others took their seats, I circled the room, extinguishing flames until only one lit candle remained in a chamberstick. This was placed on the floor before Florence.

Madame de Jacquinot went to her daughter and smoothed her cheek with one hand. 'Are you frightened, darling?' she asked.

Florence glanced at me, as if embarrassed to admit as much in the presence of an almost stranger, and then gave a slight nod.

Charlotte stepped in – both figuratively and physically, crossing the floor and causing Madame de Jacquinot to shift aside so that she could look Florence in the eye herself. She enacted a stern expression. 'Mademoiselle Florence,' she said, 'I have every faith in you. You must take heart, and – I know that we are asking a lot of you – but you must try to control the phantom when it comes. If you believe that you can, you will make it so.'

Florence's eyes grew wide. 'I cannot,' she said. Her voice was high but quiet. 'I am not able.'

One of Charlotte's hands fluttered dove-like to rest on Florence's forearm. 'Yes, you can. Do not forget that I am a professional in matters of the spirit. I can see yours, Mademoiselle Florence; I can see how strong it is. A spirit like that can stand up to far more than one would expect – I can see that it has withstood so much already. You would not be here today if you did not have a spark of fight deep within you.'

Looking at her pallor and her waif-like proportions, this was hard to believe.

'What you must do now,' Charlotte was saying, 'is fight to bring her to obedience. She must not be allowed to overwhelm you again; we need her to remain long enough to answer our questions.'

'Can you do it, Florence?' asked Madame de Jacquinot. 'Darling, will you try?'

Florence looked around at her assembled family members, then at Charlotte and me. I hoped she could not see the anxiety on my face. At last, she bit her lip, and then nodded, once, quickly.

'Good girl,' said Ardoir.

We took our places in the ring, linking hands: myself, Charlotte, the Comte, then Madame de Jacquinot. The absence of Maximilien felt strange – and I wondered if the change in our arrangement would change the nature of the circle. There was a different energy in the room. Perhaps this was just because we were now closer to Florence, practically embracing her, due to the loss of one link in our chain.

'Are you ready, Mademoiselle Florence?' I asked. My voice felt dry in my throat. I was glad to have my sister's solid presence at my side tonight.

Florence's lower lip was quivering but she raised her chin in a show of bravery. 'I am.'

This time I took the summons, the words rattling up from old memories within me. They were words that I had heard Mama speak many times – so many that I could almost hear the echo of her voice beneath my own. 'Our Virgin Mary, we call upon you to allow the spirits of your celestial escort to descend for a moment among us, so that we may question them – not to subject them to impious tests, but in order to come to the discovery of truth.' I kept my eyes on the candle as I spoke, willing the smoke that braided above it to carry the message beyond. The brightness of the flame left a hazy shape in negative across my vision. Yet another ghost.

As the silence deepened, I realized that I, too, had been waiting for the spirit to knock. Something small and cool flipped over in my stomach.

Madame de Jacquinot, positioned to my left, was breathing loudly through her mouth. There were the noises of an old building, rattlings and rustlings and far-off creakings as the other inhabitants went about their evenings. But no knocking. Had Charlotte forgotten that it was her turn? The atmosphere was straining. Sweat budded at my hairline.

I looked to Florence and felt my heart stop, my lungs refusing to draw air. I was certain that it was not Florence who looked back at me. For the first time in my life, I truly believed. Her appraisal raked over me like a chill wind – who was I, to call her to me? And – yes – we had not introduced ourselves on the previous occasions, never given our own names or intentions. Was it not one of the cardinal rules that one should treat a spirit with respect?

'Good evening,' I said, but my voice caught on the words.

I cleared my throat and tried again. 'My name is . . . Sylvie Mothe. This is my sister, Charlotte Mothe. We are spiritists. We have been contracted to speak with you on behalf of this family, whom I believe may be your family too.'

There was no response. I could see Ardoir twitching and shook my head to indicate that he must try to hold his silence for the moment. Please, please would he hold his silence.

'Am I speaking to the Comtesse de Lisle?' I asked. 'To Sabine?'

At this, a keening noise started up in Florence's throat. She bulged her eyes at me, as if she were trying to move forwards while remaining fixed in place.

'Sabine?' I asked again, fighting not to flinch away. Her mouth opened now to reply, and again there was the hissing.

'Please,' cried Charlotte, 'we need to *speak* with you. Please, Sabine, Florence, try to work together.'

Florence shook all the more, and then, with one violent heave, the hissing cut off. Her throat was working furiously, as if in silent conversation. At long last, the mouth opened again. I prepared for a second onslaught, or for ectoplasm. Neither came. Instead, all that Sabine said was, 'Yes.'

I exchanged a horrified look with Charlotte.

'Auntie?' said Ardoir.

'Your kin,' Sabine agreed. Her voice – or perhaps just the way she used Florence's vocal cords – was deep and guttural, with an odd lilt to the accent that was clearly not modern.

'Then your family wishes to help you,' said Charlotte, 'but we do not know why you have come here, or what it is that you want from us. Please, will you help us to understand?'

There came no reply. Perhaps the question was too complex to answer.

'Allow me to ask a different question, then,' I said, though I wanted nothing less than to have her attention turned back to me. 'Have you come here because you need our help, or have you come to offer yours?'

'Yes.'

Madame de Jacquinot had a tight grip on my hand.

'"Yes"?' I repeated. 'To both?'

No response.

'Have you come to us regarding the family inheritance – the gold?' I asked.

'I would see my relations receive that which is due to them.'

I caught the Comte's expression: it was a look of pure avarice. Between his leathery skin and the sharp, gap-filled teeth of his smile glistening in the candlelight, he resembled above all else a lizard. A flash of dark tongue darted from between his lips to wet them. His head twitched. His nostrils flared. A dragon sick with gold-lust.

'Will you show us where to find it?' I asked.

'In time.' Sabine paused to give a sly smile.

'When?' asked Ardoir.

'Patience,' said Sabine. 'Be assured that there is much in store for you.' I did not like the way she pronounced this – there was a tilting humour to it, as if she had told a joke that none of us had yet comprehended.

Before Ardoir had the opportunity to speak again, I hurried to ask, 'Why now have you chosen to reach out to us?'

'Because I was called.'

'By whom?'

'By one who needed me. By one who was in pain.'

When Charlotte and I had played the role of spirits, we had dealt in such vague messages, believing them more intriguing as well as harder to debunk. But now that my own questions were being met with these answers, I would have found it vexing had I not been so terrified.

Sabine had not finished. 'I saw this family in its ruins, fallen low beneath where it ought to be. Enacting violences against itself. Enacting violences against me.'

My eyes fell to where Florence's bare hands rested upon the chair arms: her fingers had crooked like claws and the nails dug into the wood, leaving tiny sickle scars. She was losing control.

'Injustices!' said Sabine. 'Injustices! Injustices!'

'You mean in the Revolution?' asked Madame de Jacquinot.

'Where is the gold?' demanded Ardoir.

Florence's head snapped backwards to face the ceiling, the marble column of her throat stretched taut and eyes rolling up to show the whites. Her hands gripped so tight that I heard something pop within her.

Charlotte cursed under her breath.

A moment later, Florence's face tilted back towards us. She opened her mouth to speak, but instead of words, something was bubbling out. Ectoplasm once more. It was impossible to look away as the fluid slithered like worms from the corners of her lips, dripping down her chin and neck. Her pupils were still invisible beneath quivering, half-shut eyelids. Then the keening recommenced.

'Florence, you must try!' cried Charlotte.

'She is doing it on purpose,' Ardoir declared. 'She wants to keep Auntie from speaking with us!'

'Father, that is ridiculous,' said Madame de Jacquinot. She was trying to keep her tone reasonable, but the noise coming from Florence clearly disturbed her. Her hand trembled in mine – or perhaps it was my own that shook. 'Why would Florence do such a thing?'

'Because she is ungrateful!' snapped Ardoir. 'She wants nothing but to destroy this family! She has always blamed her own failings on the rest of us.'

Florence's keening had grown louder, higher, and she was jerking about in the chair. The candle at her feet guttered, almost went out.

'Stop it!' said Ardoir. 'Stop it, girl!' Ripping himself free of the circle, he lurched a step forwards and raised an open hand, ready to slap.

'Don't you dare touch her!'

To my horror, this came from Charlotte. She had leaped from her own seat and was now facing Ardoir with a look of complete, unbridled hatred – an emotion so intense that she had lost sight of all else.

Before any one of us could recover enough from the shock to react, there was an intake of breath from Florence, sharp like a kettle's whistle. The circle had been broken. The summons was ended.

Relief flooding through me, I stood to place myself between Ardoir and my sister. 'Please, this is not necessary! Look: she has stopped. Charlotte, you will––'

And then Sabine continued to speak.

'You think you can threaten me, you foul old man? Why – are you scared of what I will say? What I may know? Because I have been here all along; I have seen many things. I saw you when you thought that no one was watching. I know what you did.'

'Silence!' cried Ardoir. His voice was a bird screech – but, yes, beneath his anger I could now make out fear. 'Make her stop!'

What did Sabine know? What was Ardoir so scared of hearing?

I did not know what to do. Salt? Iron? Would they work on a spirit that was protected by human flesh? 'Mademoiselle Florence,' I called, 'if you are still able to hear us, please, please, you must try to fight her.' The way the candlelight shone up from the floor created a demonic mask of shadow over her features; it was almost impossible to recognize Florence in the woman before me. 'We were wrong: she does not come in the name of friendship; I fear she is not who she claims to be at all. This is an imposter – a wicked spirit here to torment us.'

'Torment!' said Sabine, followed by a chilling discordant-violin laugh that cut through the darkness. 'You know nothing of torment, *Baroness*. Torment is a child ripped from its mother's hands, torment is betrayal by one's own blood!'

Ardoir reached out as if to grab her.

'Stop!' I cried, before Charlotte could get herself into more trouble. 'It is not safe.' Possessed as she was, this was still Florence's body; I could not stand by and watch a man harm his own kin, and it was clear that Charlotte would not either.

'Then do something, you useless shrew,' he snapped. 'Make her stop.'

'We are trying!' I replied.

But this was not true: Charlotte was still fixated on Ardoir. 'Do you not want to hear what she has to say, Monsieur?' she asked, lip curling.

I would deal with this later – for now, how had Mama used to combat possessions when we had staged them? But Charlotte and I had always been the ones possessed, not the ones banishing the damned spirit! There would be holy water in our equipment bag, but was it genuine holy water, or just a draught taken from the pump? Well, it had to be better than nothing . . . I made for the bag, where it had been left on the dining-room table. Groped around for it in the dark. The holy water was kept in a small silver flask, similar to the one Papa used for his gin. God, I hoped it was not gin in this one too.

'The insurgents murdered my children before my very eyes,' Sabine was saying. 'Savages! Barbarians! What mother should have to suffer such a thing? And now, again—'

I had managed to get the top off the flask. I raised it aloft, ready to fling its contents upon Florence.

Just before I could act, there was a torrent of knocking. Rapid-fire and jarringly loud, coming not from within the room but without. Was it the Comtesse? Some new spiritual intruder?

The door from the parlour burst open. Clement Diagne pushed in, an indignant Caroline following close behind.

At the same moment, Florence collapsed limp in the chair, her body sagging. Sabine had fled. Whatever she had to say, it was for our ears only.

Ardoir's eyes popped like eggs. 'Diagne!' he cried, leaping away from his wilted granddaughter. 'What the devil are you about?'

Clement had clearly been running; his forehead glistened with sweat and he was panting for breath. Clutching his side, he tried to form an answer. 'Maximilien' – gasp – 'been shot' – gasp – 'tried to stop him—'

'Christ!' cried Ardoir as, at the same moment, Madame de Jacquinot exclaimed, 'Shot?'

Florence stirred.

Ignoring the fresh commotion, Charlotte hurried over to her, removing a glove to lay a hand on the girl's forehead, feeling for her temperature.

Clement was nodding rapidly to indicate that he would explain all, just as soon as he was able. 'He' – gasp – 'a duel.'

My stomach dropped like a stone through water. I knew the

name Clement would speak next before he had even reopened his mouth.

'Baptiste Vasseur,' he said.

The effect was instantaneous, like a ripple travelling through the room.

'Florence, I am so sorry, but he is back,' said Clement. Seeming only now to notice her state, he added, 'Are you quite well?' Then, noticing Charlotte and myself too, 'What is happening here?'

Madame de Jacquinot looked as if she might begin to puff smoke. I had never seen her this angry, never would have believed she even had the capacity for such emotion. 'Do not mind that! What do you mean, he is back?'

'He would not dare,' said Ardoir.

'He did,' said Clement. 'He is.' He had caught most of his breath now and was, at least, able to stand upright. 'Maximilien found it out – he heard it from—' Clement stopped midsentence, his eyes falling back to me. I wondered how much Maximilien had told him. 'I do not know, from some acquaintance or another – and tracked him down. Challenged him to a duel. I agreed to be his second . . . Heaven forgive me, I did not even know it was with Vasseur until it was too late. I tried to talk Maximilien out of it but I could not stop him.'

'But what has happened to Maximilien?' asked Madame de Jacquinot, clutching at her cheeks like a comical illustration.

'Vasseur got him in the ribs. He is at the hospital.'

'Then we must go immediately,' said Ardoir.

Madame de Jacquinot began to whimper, the noise grating like chalk on a board.

'For God's sake, pull yourself together, woman. You, Caroline, go and fetch our cab.'

'I had mine held,' said Clement. 'Are you sure Florence is—'

'Then we shall go at once,' interrupted Ardoir. 'I will need a stick. Fetch a stick, Caroline. Oh no, I do not think so . . .' This last was aimed at Florence, who had begun to rise shakily from her chair. 'You will stay here, girl. I hardly think you need any more excitement.'

'But Grandfather!'

Ardoir threw her a broiling look that left no room for argument.

'Am I to stay here alone?' asked Florence. She was already crying, tears leaking from eyes and nose alike. 'With the ghosts?'

'Stop being so hysterical,' said Ardoir, clasping the stick that Caroline had just procured for him. 'Can you not see we have more pressing worries at the moment?' He was brandishing it more as a weapon than a walking aid. 'Diagne, lead the way.' In a dark undertone directed towards Charlotte and I, he added, 'You will sort this out, or I will know the reason why. And do not think your behaviour tonight will stand.'

A moment later, the bustle had left the room. All that remained to us was an uncomfortable silence, punctuated by Florence's sniffling.

Not knowing what else to do, I relit a number of the candles. I was brim-full with all that had happened during the circle, as if I would burst from the internal pressure. What had we just witnessed? And what had Charlotte been thinking? But the news of Maximilien had superseded such concerns. Pushing aside my first impulse to rail at Charlotte, then, I attempted to find some words of comfort for poor Florence. Thinking she worried for what might become of Maximilien in her absence, I said, 'You could do nothing to help your brother even if you went along.'

I had thought these words a kindness, but they prompted a fresh bout of sobbing from Florence.

Charlotte glared at me and snapped, 'For God's sake, Sylvie!'

I returned the glare and mouthed, 'I was trying to help.'

'If you want to help, why don't you go and fetch her a glass of water?'

As I left the room in search of a servant, I just caught behind me the sound of Florence repeating, 'This is all my fault, this is all my fault,' and Charlotte making soft shushing noises as if putting a child to bed.

Caroline had somehow disappeared in the few minutes that had passed – she was not about the apartments and did not respond to my pull of the bell either. I wondered if she had gone with the family and Clement for some reason. Despite myself, I could feel a mounting dread setting in. I had taken a candle with me, but the dance of shadows at its periphery was more disconcerting than total darkness would have been. What we had experienced . . . It could not have been real, and yet I felt it, deep within me, to have been real. And had it truly been Sabine? I had read of evil spirits and demons that took on the guise of a loved one in order to gain a medium's trust, all the better to wreak harm on their victims. We should have demanded some kind of proof, asked a question to which only Sabine would have known the answer. I wandered from room to room seeking a pitcher of water, feeling the entire time that I was being observed. Who could say whether the spirit was lurking here still – following me, even? Her words . . . What did they signify? And she had called me by my title. Baroness. How could she have known such a thing?

There was no water here for Florence; I would have to go

down to the kitchens and ask Caroline for a jug. I was at the far end of the building, by Florence's chamber and the door to the servants' stair. I remembered the previous occasion when I had seen – or thought I had seen – a figure standing in this very spot.

I opened the little door. The stairwell was like a throat: walls painted a deep pink, slightly damp with condensation from the kitchens below. I took the steps down into the belly of the house.

At the bottom I was faced not with one single door as I had expected, but two: one into the kitchens, and one into the garden. A servants' exit, separate from the grand doors intended for use by the family of the house. I hesitated. The door was most likely locked. No – there were scuffs around the keyhole, and there, on the floor, a hairpin bent out of shape. Someone had been sneaking out.

When I tried the handle, it turned. The door opened silently and with so little resistance that it seemed almost to move of its own accord. As if it *wanted* to be used.

The evening air entered like a gasp. Not too chill, but crisp and refreshing. It carried with it the garden smells of earth and pollen, grass and manure.

Now that I was outside, the house at my back felt even more menacing, like a cat unleashing the mouse she'd been playing with only so that she could have the pleasure of capturing it again. Shuddering, I walked over to the pond. A flat black disc, it was like a dead eye staring back at me. Unblinking. How deep was it – deep enough to drown?

I had often wondered how it had been for Mama in those last moments. Had she been afraid as the water filled her lungs? Had she thought at all of me and Charlotte, of the daughters she was leaving behind?

As my brain pursued this thought, my eyes lifted of their own accord up the face of the building. Most of the windows in the de Jacquinot apartments were dark, except for the glow of candlelight in the dining room. As before, I could clearly see inside, see the furniture and Charlotte and Florence. They were as poppets in a dollhouse. Florence was leaning partly against the dining table as if she had lost the energy to hold herself upright; however, there was an uncharacteristic animation to her gestures as she spoke to Charlotte, one hand waving about as if casting a spell. It was more alive than I had ever seen her looking before. For her part, Charlotte was standing close by, head nodding as she listened to whatever it was that had so invigorated Florence.

Then, as I watched, Charlotte took hold of the gesturing hand and gently held it to the side. She leaned even closer to Florence – I thought for a comforting embrace – but then Florence lifted her chin, face tilting into Charlotte's path. Their lips met in a kiss. Not a kiss between friends or sisters: this was hard, passionate. This was the past repeating itself. This was everything all over again.

I flew back to the house, my hands fumbling against the now-resistant door. For a moment I thought I had managed to lock myself out, but then realized that I was trying to push a door that opened outwards. I grasped the handle and yanked it open, throwing myself up the stairs almost in the same action, not caring if the door shut properly behind me. Up the stairs, along the corridor, into the entrance hall, the parlour, and then the dining room.

Charlotte and Florence looked up as I came in. They were still close, but no longer touching. Charlotte took an almost imperceptible step backwards. A guilty movement.

'Ah, did you find it?' she asked. Her chest and neck were flushed.

'You . . .!' I cried. I did not know what to say. I could feel moisture on my cheeks, hot and heavy. Words kept getting tangled on my tongue. 'You!'

A frown beginning, Charlotte took another step back. 'Is something the matter?'

'After everything that happened the last time!'

'Sylvie, I—'

'I saw you.' My voice was shrill even in my own ears. I jabbed a finger towards Charlotte, then at Florence. 'What you did to her.'

Charlotte's face turned pale, but to her credit she did not twitch a muscle. 'You need to calm down. Just let me explain—'

I had expected Florence to begin crying once more, but her face remained dry. She was perhaps in shock.

'After everything this girl has been through, you want to add *this* to her list of worries? My God, what is wrong with you?' I was overcome with the urge to grab Charlotte by her jacket and shake her until that look of defiance was wiped from her face. 'To endanger yourself like this – again! Are you deranged?'

'Oh, shut up, Sylvie.'

It took me long seconds of stunned incomprehension before I realized the words had come from Florence. She moved to stand between us. Her mouth was a stern line and her hair framed her face with a profane light – she was a Fury sprung straight from the library fresco. My mind scrambled to make sense of this sudden metamorphosis; it could not.

'Good,' said Florence. 'Now, listen very carefully. You will not ruin this for me. Do you understand? If you breathe a word, then I will go directly to your husband, the Baron Alexandre

Devereux, and I will tell him all about your plan to defraud my family . . . and give evidence of your affair with my brother.'

'How dare—'

'This is no empty threat, Baroness.'

The sluggish pieces were still crawling into place, but slowly something was taking shape: an understanding, a figure in the mist.

'Sylvie, I swear I never wanted to hurt you with this,' said Charlotte.

And so there was no spirit. It had been Florence all along.

PART TWO

'Toads, what you do that for, I'm not toads inside, it's you that's toads.'

— *The Skriker*, Caryl Churchill

CHAPTER TWELVE

27 February 1866

IT WAS HAMMERING down something awful. I could scarce hear my own thoughts over the percussion of rain against rooftop, the moaning wind, the deep, cymbal-like rumble of thunder at a distance. It could've been the growl of a massive beast, and the restless sky its heaving hide. I thought it must be minded to tear up the city and – what's more – make sure we all knew about it in the process.

So when the knocking started, at first I took it for just another effect of the weather. But then it went on longer and I realized it was somebody at the door. Somebody outside in the deluge.

I rushed to answer before Papa woke up – though if he could sleep through all this racket, a bit of extra knocking wouldn't exactly make a difference. Steeling myself, I opened the door just a tad, jamming a foot behind so it couldn't be suddenly forced in. I'd learned this lesson the hard way.

A young woman was on the front step. She had a heavy cloak clutched round her, the blue velvet material soaked through and plastered with mud at the hem. Just the sight of her was enough to make you shiver to your bones.

'Are you Mademoiselle Mothe?' she asked. Though her voice shook, the shape of the vowels was cultured and smooth as honey. I couldn't see a great deal of her, what with the cloak and the overcast sky: just her pale face, its expression drawn and anxious. Eyes round as coins.

'And who're you?' I asked. Then the unspoken question: *What's a fine lady like you doing here, and in this weather?*

She glanced about, wary. As if anyone else were fool enough to be out on the street to overhear. 'May I come inside?' she asked.

I squinted at her. She didn't look like a debt collector or someone Papa would've cheated at cards. It was possible she had men with her, hiding just out of sight. They did that, sometimes: came to your house pretending to be pedlars or beggars, or even sending a child to say it was lost, then, as soon as you opened the door, they'd leap on you, quick as hounds. You could be robbed blind, if you weren't careful. Not that there was much in here to rob – but you didn't know what else they might try with you besides.

Still, she looked too pathetic to be threatening, and I couldn't stand to close the door on her. What if she died of exposure? It was anyone's guess if she was pale with cold or just had a naturally wan complexion, but her skin was the shade of goose fat – a little blue at the corners, too. It made her copper hair stand out like a brand. She had pretty lips, though, with good colour in them.

'Who are you?' I asked again.

'Forgive me for intruding,' she replied, 'and I will give my name in due course, but first I need your word that it will go no further. Nobody must learn that I am here.'

A large ask from a stranger on your doorstep. 'I'm not about to promise you anything,' I said.

She lifted her chin, refusing to be put off by my abrupt tone.

'That is understandable,' she said. I got the sense she was taking me all in, noting – no doubt – my chapped hands, my much-repaired apron. 'Which one are you?' she asked at last.

'How d'you mean?'

'There were two Mothe sisters. Which are you?'

Something stuck in my throat, right at the divot where my collarbones met. 'Charlotte,' I said. 'My name's Charlotte.' Then, because she continued to look pitiful, I said, 'All right, you can come inside just for a minute, but you've got to be quiet in the hallway.'

She followed me in, mirroring my tiptoeing past Papa's door. His snuffling snores crept through the wood.

Better not wake him. He wouldn't take kindly to my inviting some unknown woman inside – though I clearly weren't unknown to her. I was still puzzling on how that came to be as I led her into the kitchen, where I closed the door and lit a candle. The range glowed from the morning's fire, but for her benefit I added a new chunk of wood, sending up a hiss of sparks. Didn't want her turning to a block of ice. 'You might as well sit down,' I said as I worked. 'Take that cloak off; you'll be at death's door.'

The woman did as told, hanging her cloak across the back of another chair. Nice and polite.

'Are you going to tell me who you are? It's only fair, since you've got my name in your possession.'

She spun her fingers together as if making a knot, then separated them back out and placed them flat on the table. 'I am Florence de Jacquinot, sister of the Marquis de Jacquinot and granddaughter of Comte Ardoir.'

The names didn't mean anything to me. Still, nice to be on a more equal footing.

I went to stand at the chair opposite her, leaning with my hands on the top rail. 'Well, Mademoiselle Florence,' I said, 'I'm sorry to be a source of disappointment, but I am afraid I cannot help you.' I could feel my voice slipping automatically into the higher register I always used with clients, even as I turned her down.

Florence looked up at me through golden lashes. 'I have not yet said why I am here.'

'You are here about the spirits.'

'My daughter was taken from me.'

This weren't the first time someone had come to me since my retirement, though it was the first in a good long while. But the world didn't forget these things. There was always someone who remembered. Someone desperate. I felt sick to think I used to profit off those poor souls. 'I am sorry for your loss,' I said. 'Truly, Mademoiselle Florence, I am sorry. But I cannot help you reach out to your daughter. I do not say this to be intentionally cruel; if I could help you, I would. But I can no longer call upon the dead.'

I expected pleading to follow. Offers of money, exhortations. Or perhaps resignation. Tears. What I didn't expect was the smile that crossed her face. Not a pleasant smile; it was ghostly in itself. It made the skin on my arms prickle like anything.

'Because you never could,' said Florence.

'I beg your pardon?' Don't let her know she's ruffled you, I thought. Deny it all; she's got no proof. If she wanted to blackmail me, she'd have to do a lot better: I'd had worse in the past, and then some.

'Oh, I mean no offence,' Florence assured me. 'You are a good fake – the best I have ever seen. Which is why I have come to you in the first place. When I said that my daughter was taken from me, I do not mean that she is dead; I meant just what I told you. She was taken. I am not married, you understand. My family were ashamed – furious, rather. My grandfather took the newborn baby from me and carried her away somewhere I would never find her.'

'I do not—'

She shook her head at me, not done yet. 'He tried to tell me that she had died – that she had been born dead. But I held her in my arms! I felt her warmth, felt as she stirred against my chest. She cried as he tore her from my grip. I did not make it up. My baby was alive when he took her.'

She had been speaking quickly, all matter-of-fact till now, but her voice shook in these last words. Florence paused, swallowed. Let out a measured breath through her nose. I got the sense she'd had a lot of practice controlling her emotions.

'Shortly after, I heard voices from the garden below. I had never in my life felt more exhausted, but I managed to struggle over to my window to look down. I had only a moment before my mother caught me and dragged me back to bed, but I am certain I saw my grandfather out there with a cloaked woman. He was passing a small basket to her. I did not make it up,' she repeated, as if I'd been about to say otherwise.

'I cannot imagine what you must have been feeling,' I said. It felt wrong to stand about as she told me all this; I'd half a mind to hold her hand or wrap my arms round her, but I didn't know how she'd take it. In the end, I just sat myself down.

'I tried for months to prise the truth from my family,' Florence went on. 'But they would not admit to a thing. The more I pushed, the worse it became. I was locked in, forbidden from communicating with anyone from my previous life. They insisted I had made it all up – that my senses had been muddled by shock and the laudanum which they themselves had dosed me with! Eventually, they threatened to send me away to an asylum, and I was forced to pretend that I accepted their story. I even came to doubt my own mind, to wonder if my grandfather had been telling the truth. The grief . . . Well, if you have ever lost anyone, then you will know, and if you have not, then I cannot begin to explain it to you. There were days I could barely bring myself to get out of bed.

'For over a year, I lived like this, asking no questions, staying docile. It was easier to be what they told me I was: a helpless, unwell little girl. But despite this, I was always alert for any hint of my daughter's whereabouts.

'Then, three weeks ago, I crept into my grandfather's room to look through his papers as he slept. This had become a habit of mine, although I had long given up any real hope of success.' She leaned forward now, a secretive smile coming over her. 'But this time, I did find something: a discarded sheet of blotting paper. It had been misfiled alongside the household accounts, but it bore the mirror image of a letter in my grandfather's hand to a Mère Ancelot, dated from last year. Although I had drawn back the curtains for some moonlight, it was still too dark to read with ease, but from what I understood, the letter had been written to accompany payment of a generous fee, for . . . What were the exact words? "For your care of the infant, and for your discretion."

'I immediately thought of the tales I have heard of baby farms: those places where unwanted children are sent to be taken care of . . . or, rather, "kept alive". The portion of the letter bearing the address was not legible, but, even so, I could have wept for happiness. Do you see, Charlotte?' And here she beamed at me like we were old friends and it was only right for me to share in her joy. 'This note is proof that my daughter is still out there, being kept by this Mère Ancelot. She is alive!'

I was more confused now than I'd been at the start of Florence's story. 'I am sorry, Mademoiselle Florence,' I said, 'but I'm puzzled. You need me to help you to . . . get your daughter?'

Her eyes glinted, fox-like. 'My daughter,' she said, 'and my revenge.'

Over the next quarter-hour, she described a plan that, truth told, had me starting to think that maybe she was a bit unstable after all. But if one thing was clear, it was that she was willing to risk anything to get her child back – and you had to respect that kind of bravery. That fierce love was what a parent should feel. I'd always known Mama felt it for Sylvie and me. Some days, I could almost convince myself I saw it in Papa, too.

As Florence had continued to pore over the blotting paper for clues, she told me, her grandfather had woken up. But instead of anger, she'd seen that he was terrified of her, clutching his Bible like some holy shield. He'd mistaken her for a ghost. This was what had finally brought all her plotting together into a plan: convince the household of a haunting. Excepting her brother, they were already a superstitious lot, and there was an old family myth about a gory death and a missing fortune – add to that a vengeful ghost, returned to punish the living till they put what they'd done to rights. So they were immune to Florence's earthly implorations? They couldn't ignore a dishonoured spirit and a golden reward.

Florence would sow the first seeds herself, using my expertise to perform a poltergeist, and when her family were convinced of the haunting, she'd suggest they seek the help of a spirit medium. Which was where I came in. Florence, seemingly possessed by the spirit, would tell them the child was alive and must be returned to her mother. By that point, her family (so she said) would be so terrorized they'd have no choice but to reunite her with the baby – which we'd convince them was the only way to put an end to the haunting and receive their bounty. Both carrot and stick.

'You will have the entire medium's fee to keep,' said Florence. 'And I have a small collection of jewels that will be yours also. Forgive me for speaking plainly, but' – she eyed my well-patched apron – 'it seems you could use it.'

I didn't appreciate having it pointed out, even so. And as for her plan . . . Well, it was unhinged, to put things politely.

'I cannot help you,' I said. 'And I still object to being called a fake. But whatever you choose to believe of me, surely you see that what you propose is too much? It would not be a matter of simple trickery, but a large-scale, maintained deception. The longer it went on, the more likely it would be to crumble under scrutiny. I am in no hurry to go to jail.'

'You have skill enough for it,' Florence said, apparently misinterpreting my concern as modesty. 'I really feel that, working together—'

'What would you know about my skill?' I asked.

'I have seen you at work before. Your family held a show; I believe it was in the home of the Comte de Fourbin.'

It was true we'd held an evening's entertainment at the de Fourbins' town house, once upon a time. It was possible Florence had been there, though it would've been three and a half, maybe four years ago, so it was no surprise that I didn't remember her. Still, that didn't explain how she knew our show had been more fiction than phantom.

Maybe Florence saw this question in my face, as she went on to say, 'I had a friend then who was quite obsessed with spiritism. I accompanied her to many sittings although I myself was a sceptic. Of course, I knew that all we saw were charlatans. It was normally so obvious. I often wondered how she could ever be convinced by such poor showmanship. I suppose she wanted to be convinced. But the Mothe sisters – you were different. I never spotted a tell; you were such professionals. That is what I need on my side now.'

'Had it occurred to you, Mademoiselle Florence,' I said, sitting more upright, all officious, 'that you saw no tell because we, unlike those others, were completely in earnest?'

This feint didn't convince her in the least, and she shook her head with another little smile, keeping her eyes on me all the while, so they remained disconcertingly fixed in place despite the motion of her head. 'There is no such thing as spirits,' she said.

'You sound markedly certain.'

'I am.'

'Do you not think it arrogant to assume you can know such a thing?'

Florence raised her brows.

'Very well,' I said, 'let us agree to a moot on this subject. Perhaps I am a fake, perhaps not. Either way, you cannot prove it. And either way, I cannot help you. You are clearly an intelligent young woman, and determined besides, so I want to see you succeed in what is truly a sympathetic aim. But surely there are simpler ways to solve this? You will think of something.'

'There are no other ways,' she snapped. 'You think I have not already tried everything I can conceive? I ask my family, and they lie. I snoop through my grandfather's documents, and find nothing but breadcrumbs. I go to the authorities, and they think me insane; if I take it any further, it is sure to be the asylum this time. I am as a prisoner in my own home. The only reason

I am here now is that, after weeks of persuasion, I was able to bribe the housekeeper to act as an alibi. This is not some impulsive idea, you must understand. I have tried for over a year to make them confess what they have done, and now – for the first time – I finally have evidence and a proper plan. It will work. I know it will. It is all I can do.'

'Have you tried to find Mère Ancelot? I know people who can track down anyone, if you've got the money. I could put you in contact—'

'And then what?' asked Florence. 'My family will not allow me to keep my daughter. And I cannot run away – I have no funds of my own.' This wasn't said with despair; she spoke like she was making a calculation. 'How would I survive? How would I look after her? I need to convince my grandfather to let me keep her, or to pay for me to take her elsewhere.'

'And the only way he will do this is at the command of some supernatural entity?' I pitied her circumstances – how couldn't I? But agreeing to help . . . now, *that* would be true insanity. 'I am sorry,' I repeated.

Again, that sly, fox-like expression came on to her face. 'You know,' she said, 'I do not need proof you are a fake. It would be your word against mine. "Charlatan preys on lunatic gentlewoman."'

The threat cut far too close to the quick, though I was sure it was an empty one. How would she explain why she'd come here in the first place? But, empty or not, I wouldn't stand for being threatened. A cold anger swelled beneath my skin. 'How dare you?' I said, flying to my feet; I couldn't raise my voice due to Papa, so instead enunciated each syllable, steady and furious. 'You sneaky little bitch. You'd better get the hell out of my kitchen, or so help me—'

Florence immediately began to blubber, and on top of this she slipped from her chair and on to her knees on the floor. At first I thought she'd fallen, but then realized she was begging, hands clasped before her, eyes wide.

'Please,' said Florence, voice deep and soft like an echo in a cave, 'please help me. I did not mean to threaten you. I suffered through hell, Mademoiselle Mothe – will you show no pity? I was taken advantage of by a man I thought I could trust – a friend of my brother's whom I had known for many years. He subjected me to . . . horrors, and then, when my brother managed to find me, instead of punishing my attacker, my grandfather locked *me* away, told me I was wicked and sinful! Instead of having him jailed, my grandfather *paid* the man off to keep his silence! Then, when one good thing, one ray of light, resulted from my ordeal, even that was snatched away. My mother and brother stood by and did nothing all the while. Not one thing to help. I know they know more than they will say!'

I looked away, kept my eyes on the far wall. If I looked at Florence, I knew I'd buckle.

'Think of my baby!' she implored. 'My daughter, my little girl. She would have been a year old in December. More than a whole year without her mother, God knows where, living who knows what kind of existence. How can you stand by and let that happen, let a motherless little girl suffer?'

I didn't know – and how would she have found it out? – if she knew my own mother was dead in the ground, if she was saying this to manipulate me. And was this sudden, emotional display down to a brave face finally slipping, or was it another mask put on in its place? I resented the ploy . . . and yet, it was working. I knew exactly what that child would feel. Motherless, like me.

'If I am to help you,' I said, keeping my voice level, 'and I mean *if*, then this needs to be thought through. I am talking about careful consideration. Preparation for all eventualities.'

'What are you saying?' asked Florence.

I couldn't get carried away. This needed a tactical approach. We'd have to consider how to stage a haunting without my being there. Florence said her family were ready to believe, but there were servants, too, that we'd got to think of.

And what about my own safety? If we were discovered, who was to say Florence wouldn't turn traitor and blame it all on me anyway? Christ, it wouldn't be the first time. I needed insurance. A contract was no good, as we couldn't have it notarized. I could demand something of hers in security – but then she could claim I had stolen it off her. What I needed was someone of consequence on my side. Legal protection. And this time I didn't have Sylvie's conveniently love-struck lawyer to hand.

But then I got to thinking: what if I did? My sister's husband had protected me in the past, and surely he'd do it again if her reputation was at risk. I'll admit, my first instinct was that I'd rather go to jail than grovel at Sylvie's pampered feet for her aid. But then who'd help Florence? I looked at the desperate woman in front of me. If I couldn't swallow my pride to help her and her daughter, what manner of monster would that make me?

Persuading Sylvie into our plan wasn't going to be simple, though. Me and Papa were struggling for funds, sure enough, but that'd be of no concern to her – and I couldn't exactly tell her the truth: that I was using her to get to her husband. If she'd been any other person, I'd have been able to depend on Florence's story to move her heart. But you can't appeal to the better nature of a person who *has* no better nature. On top of that, I didn't know a jot about her present life. I'd wondered about it, of course, though it hurt me to do so – like pressing on a bruise just to feel that ache. I didn't even know where she lived; Sylvie had made sure of that. But I'd time enough to think of a way to get to her.

'If I am to help,' I said again, 'I will need my sister.'

'So you *will* help?' A fierce joy blazed across Florence's face. The way she looked at me then – like I'd answered her every prayer – made my heart squeeze.

I cleared my throat and stood, walked round to one of the kitchen drawers and began rooting for a pencil and notebook. My old spiritist's journal was still in there, abandoned midway. I flipped several pages past the last entry – I didn't want the bad luck of that last job to seep through into this one.

Licking the pencil, I began to write. And so the Comtesse Sabine de Lisle was resurrected.

CHAPTER THIRTEEN

13 March 1866

THOUGH I DIDN'T see Florence again for some while, I was bouncing about at the thrill for days to follow. I hadn't told Papa a word of it. He did ask the next morning if anyone had been in the house with me – claimed he'd heard women's voices. But I told him it must've been a dream. He'd only have called me stupid for agreeing to Florence's scheme. Or worse: he'd think I'd agreed to it just because . . . well, because Florence was quite pretty. I didn't need to get into all that again.

And besides, I didn't want him finding out about the money – he'd demand a cut, and why should he have that when I was the one putting myself at risk?

Keeping it from him made it all the more exciting. I'd not had a secret from Papa for a long time. Maybe it was childish to enjoy it, but I didn't care; it was like my whole life had a fresh glow. Even something simple as sewing had a new sheen to it; I'd sit with my threads in the kitchen and think, here's where she dripped all over the floor, there's the chair where she put her cloak.

My latest work was stitching buttons on to shirts. They were of a cheap, rough cloth that made my palms itch like anything, but the soldiers they were destined for weren't exactly in a position to be choosy. The work was dull as you like: line up a button, poke the needle through the holes, trace patterns with thread till it all held together. No wonder I kept drifting off in my thoughts, coming back to find a pricked finger and great cranberries of blood on the fabric. Course, they'd get blood on them eventually, but you hoped it wouldn't be French blood.

Thankfully, Papa didn't seem to notice how daydreamy I'd grown, despite how I must've been walking round half the time with a ridiculous big smile on my face. It was like being in love, only without the heartache.

Then again, Papa had been a tad off-kilter himself these past couple of months. I didn't know what'd got into him – well, besides the usual drink. One day, I caught him putting his shoes on the wrong feet. Another day, he went on and on about the racket of rain at the window, though it was sunny as anything outside – one of those bright February days that hurts your eyes. But he didn't take well to my pointing these things out.

'Not raining? Don't try to be funny with me, girl. I've already got a headache and you know I've no sense of humour. I lost it at a game of faro.'

'Why don't you take a look out the window, then?' I asked.

'Where's my boots?'

Then he went tearing about the kitchen, looking for them everywhere bar the cupboard where they were actually kept.

I had a little fun watching him work himself up, not bothering to help, till he turned on me and it got less fun. 'Where've you hid them?'

'It ain't raining, Papa.'

It was no good; if he heard rain, it was raining. I handed him the boots. They always gave him blisters anyway.

But now, when he was getting at me, I could cheer myself

up and imagine what I'd do with my fee, once I got it. Use it to get away from Papa? But even with the cash to set up on my own, I'd have to find a way to keep myself, going forward. And wouldn't it be lonely, with only my own company? Papa was a bastard to live with, but he was another head all the same. He was still blood.

I'd thought of leaving in the past. I'd got as far as packing my bag once, stepping out of the door. But then I'd stood there in the street and realized I'd nowhere to go. Nobody to go to. And what Sylvie had done – marrying the first man she could capture – that just weren't an option I could live with. I sometimes told people my sister had died with Mama. It was all the same in the end. Both had found a way to escape Papa. Both had left me behind with him.

He was the only person I had left in all the world.

So, if I didn't have him, then what *would* I have? Well, to start with, now I had this secret. Now I had this task.

It was a crisp day, with a breeze that snuck up my skirts like an unwelcome hand as I sallied down the gravel walkways to the Mexican Hothouse. It always struck me as a wondrous structure, oddly burly despite the thousands of windows that made it up. Between the heat-trapping panes and the endless steam, even now it'd be warm enough in there to make you sweat something awful. No time to duck in now, but I'd been enough times in the past with Mama and Sylvie to remember it well: the close air that made every scrap of fabric cling to your body; the greener-than-green light; cacti with their cruel, exotic spines; cloying fragrances rising from the orchids; and Sylvie and me laughing and gambolling about, best friends in those days. I wondered if Florence had ever been.

As I peered through the condensation-slick glass, the reflection of a young man appeared at my shoulder.

'All right, Charlotte?'

'Hullo, Mimi.'

I took in his outfit while we exchanged kisses: a frock coat in absinthe-green velvet, cinched tightly round a corseted waist, with purple-and-emerald plaid trousers, a purple cravat, and a fine topper and cane to complete the ensemble. He'd never been one to disappoint.

'Shall we walk?' he asked.

'You look like a jester fucked a peacock.'

'I try my best.'

We must've looked an odd couple – my shapeless dark cloak next to all that pomp.

'Been a while,' Mimi remarked. 'I was almost ready to believe you really had gone straight.'

I pretended indignation. 'I've not even told you why I'm here yet,' I said.

'I doubt we'd be rubbing elbows if you were truly a reformed woman.'

'Oh, I've reformed all right.'

'Yes, but reformed into what?'

I grinned. 'That's just the question, ain't it?'

Michel – known as Mimi to his associates – was a slender, olive-skinned youth with delicate features like a china dolly. He'd got these gorgeous eyes with thick, dark lashes that he did up with a little black paint on the lids. The sort of eyes that a certain type of man goes mad for. When I'd first met him, he'd been what you call a persilleuse, hanging about the urinals in Les Halles. But he'd since realized there's more than one way to squeeze a man and, while he'd blackmail marks on any basis, his main business was with the same gents who'd been his clients before. Was this cannibalistic approach distasteful? Taste was beside the point; it paid well.

Course, Mimi weren't someone you could actually trust. Only a fool trusts a blackmailer. But I liked him. He was always good for a laugh, and I didn't have to pretend with him. Though we'd fallen out of touch for a bit, I still knew I could count on him with this; he had a truffle-hog nose for scandal and could easily find out anything you wanted to know about the upper echelons.

I explained to him briefly, without revealing more than necessary, that I was after material on my current case. That there was an illegitimate baby and I wanted to know what'd happened to it. I had the name Mère Ancelot and little else to go on.

'How long ago was this?' he wanted to know.

'A little over a year. December of sixty-four.'

Mimi whistled and raised his eyes to the sky, as if scrying the clouds. 'That's a tall order.'

'Too tall?'

'What do I get for it?'

'My gratitude?'

'Go on, Charlotte, you know me better than that.'

I did – which also meant I knew I'd nothing good to offer. I didn't even know the precise sum of money I'd get yet, let alone being able to calculate what cut could go to Mimi. I could always name an amount and hope I had enough to cover it by the end, but you didn't want to cross someone like Mimi, even if you were his friend.

'Listen,' I said, 'I don't know what I'm getting for it yet, but you'll have a fair cut whatever the amount.'

Mimi was inspecting his fingernails – smooth and round and

marvellously clean. 'I need something more concrete than that,' he said, 'and frankly I find it hard to believe you agreed to anything without naming the figure first. Losing your edge, Charlotte?'

'It ain't just about the money, you know. If you'd seen her . . .'

His eyebrows raised in two smooth arches, a twinkle in the eyes beneath. 'Pretty, was she?'

'I mean, it was the right thing to do,' I pressed. Ignoring the goad. Looks had nothing to do with it, though the accusation was no surprise coming from Mimi. Didn't he make his living, after all, based on fleshly desires? Long enough of that and maybe you did start to see everything in those terms. But this had nothing to do with pretty – though Florence was, of course – it was a far more spiritual matter. Ethics. Compassion.

Mimi didn't seem convinced by this. And besides, it still left the question of what I had to offer, as he now reminded me.

'The way I see it, you still owe me, Mimi,' I said. It may have been half a decade ago, but I weren't about to let him forget how me and Sylvie saved his hide the first time we'd met. When the nightly 'poltergeist' disturbances at a manor near Auteuil turned out to be nothing more than a noisy persilleuse sneaking in and out of the eldest son's bedchamber, hadn't we remained silent? Hadn't we convinced the family it was the work of a malevolent spirit? Hadn't we, on one memorable occasion, distracted them as he climbed naked out of the window? And we'd never asked for repayment. Well . . . till now.

Mimi's face soured at this. 'I hadn't realized there were debts between friends.'

'By that logic, there shouldn't be payment between friends either.'

He considered this, eyes flickering calculatingly about my person, and then stuck out a bejewelled hand. 'I get half the cut.'

'A third,' I said and, instead of shaking, took his hand and raised it to my lips, kissing the knuckles.

It worked; he laughed delightedly at the parody and seemed to forget his earlier indignation.

'Oh,' I said, 'and there's one more part to the task.'

A tilt of the head: *Go on*.

'Before all else, I need you to find my sister.'

He lifted his eyebrows again. 'You misplaced her?'

'Yes.'

'A sister and a baby. It's beginning to look like negligence.'

'Can you do it?'

'I'm offended that you even need to ask.'

'Then find her,' I said. 'The address'll be enough. Residence of the Baron Devereux.'

A sly expression crept over Mimi's face. 'Oh, *that's* what she does now, is it?'

'In a way,' I said. 'She married him.'

This titbit came as a surprise; Mimi fluttered his lashes and drummed with reflective fingers against the top of his cane. 'How'd she manage that, then?'

'Devil if I know.'

CHAPTER FOURTEEN

27 March 1866

OVER THE PAST couple of weeks, I'd visited Florence most nights to build on our plans. It weren't too far a walk to her family home – she lived in the Marais, about a half-hour from Belleville – though the streets were muddy as sin on the way.

Since I could hardly announce myself by knocking at the door, I had to creep round the back alley to where there was a garden gate. Florence couldn't easily get out of the house, so we'd come to the solution of speaking at this rendezvous point as she took her nightly walk round the lawn. It wasn't ideal: the gate was choked by plant growth all between the iron bars, and it was dark – Haussmann's installation of street lighting hadn't reached this far yet. Still, I could just about make out bits of the garden beyond when I pressed my face to the bars. Clusters of flower beds bordering the grass, and in the centre a pond mirroring the black sky. Florence appeared as a floating globe of white where her face caught the moonlight. Just like a ghost, I'd joked on the first visit. A will-o'-the-wisp.

I'd started by teaching her how to stage a haunting. All the tricks Mama had shown me and Sylvie as children, things like throwing noises across a room, creating ghost lights and ectoplasm, speaking in tongues.

Florence was a fast learner, surprisingly good at voices. In one of those early meetings, she'd told me proudly of how she already had her grandfather fully convinced the Comtesse was visiting him, how she'd styled herself after a portrait, 'complete with a slash of red at my throat. I went into his room last night and when he woke to my presence, I reached out one hand, like this' – I couldn't really see – 'and said, "Shame."' This last word, she'd delivered in a low, hoarse whisper, at once tremulous and accusatory. 'I do not even know where that voice came from, but was it not good?'

I'd tried to imagine the scene – in my mind, Ardoir was a wizened little creature, lizardly and mean. He slept with a scowl on his face despite his opulent bedchamber. There was a crucifix on his bedside table, and a Bible too. The curtains were open, and it was this – the white glow of the window – that he first saw when he woke up. At first he thought it was the brightness of the moon that had raised him to consciousness. But something about this put him ill at ease. Yes, that was it: hadn't the housekeeper shut the curtains before bed? It was something he specifically demanded. He was rude to the servants and they hated him for it, but they always did as he said. So how, now, did the curtains come to be open? His eyes followed the shaft of moonlight that fell through into his chamber – and it was then he noticed *her*. She'd been standing so still he hadn't seen her straight away, not in the low lighting and with his eyes not what they used to be. But there she was, watching at the foot of his bed. White nightgown, hair loose about her shoulders. So like his granddaughter. But then his eyes found their focus and he saw the bloody line encircling her throat. Not his granddaughter, though she had a face just as familiar. His aunt. The Comtesse. Dead for seventy-two years.

When she saw that he'd seen her, a change came over her

features, a rippling shift of recognition. She began to lift an arm. The movement was a sedate arc, fingers trailing ballerina-like till they came to rest mid-air, exactly level with him, and he realized she was reaching out. She opened her mouth and out of it fell a sound that was as much a death rattle as a word. 'Shaaaaaame.' Her broken throat shuddered with the effort.

Breath catching in his chest, Ardoir groped at the bedside cabinet for his crucifix, but his fingers were stiff and his hand shook, and he couldn't find it by touch. Fearing to look away, but seeing no other option, he turned his head to seek it out. At last, there it was, inches from where he'd been feeling, that safe dark cross with its promise of protection. His fingers closed gratefully about it.

But by the time he looked back, the Comtesse was gone.

'He was clearly shaken in the morning. The day girl dropped a glass and he jumped so hard he spilled jam all over his favourite trousers,' Florence had told me gleefully.

'What flavour?'

'Apricot.'

'Oh God, the yellow . . .!'

This had sent us both into a frenzy of giggles, then Florence had got the hiccoughs and that had made us laugh even harder. I'd been wiping tears off my face by the time I'd got myself back under control.

'You are being cautious, though, aren't you?' I'd finally managed to ask.

Florence had scoffed at that. 'I know my family, and I know how they view me. To them, a ghost is entirely more believable than the idea that I might possess any intelligence or ability for subterfuge.'

'Then they vastly underestimate you.'

'Yes, they do.' A smile in her voice.

I'd vowed in that moment never to do the same. Underestimating your enemies is bad enough; underestimating your allies can be fatal.

In turn, over the course of our meetings, Florence told me of the personalities of her household, to the point that I almost felt I knew them myself. Her controlling grandfather with his head stuck in the past: fanatical, cruel, but bodily weak and dependent. The cowardly mother who only cared about appearance, who'd never stand up for her children, or for herself, who believed any lie so long as it was more palatable than the truth. Maximilien, the brother who loved her but was too convinced she had lost her mind to believe her story. And Florence herself – brilliant and trapped. Creative, brave, intelligent; stifled, unappreciated, unacknowledged. Determined to change her circumstances. None of her family saw her for what she truly was. This was their greatest mistake.

'What about you?' she asked me one night.

The moon was out above us: a clear, crisp disc, like a coin dropped at the bottom of a well. Wintery and far away, its light reflecting off the vapour of my breath. Mama used to call the winter 'dragon days' because of it. Me and Sylvie loved this; we'd swoop round, roaring and razing villages with our ferocious teeth. Sylvie liked to hoard gold; I liked to kidnap maidens.

'What about me?' I asked.

'Your family – it is just you and your father?'

'Yes, since Mama died and Sylvie married.'

I could hear the scuff of something against the earth, maybe the toe of one boot making little circling motions back and forth. I had the sense Florence felt embarrassed, or somehow awkward. 'Charlotte . . . may I ask you something?'

'Of course,' I told her, voice bright to put her back at ease. 'We are friends now, are we not?' I didn't know if that was true, but I'd found that friendship was a bit like a ghost: you could summon it if you spoke its name.

'I am grateful you think of me so warmly,' said Florence – sincerely, I thought. 'Even so, you need not answer if this is too prying. But . . . you lost your mother, did you not?'

'Yes.' I paused. Decided to elaborate. 'I was ten.'

'How did . . . how did it affect you?'

I didn't know what I'd been expecting, but it wasn't this. 'How did it affect me?' I repeated.

'Yes. I know the situations are entirely different, but my daughter—'

I understood it then. She was thinking of that motherless little girl, wondering how she'd have changed in a year, what she'd become. How best to respond? I didn't want to give some meaningless reassurance, a white lie to make her feel better, but at the same time I *did* want to reassure her, to comfort her somehow. There had to be a balance somewhere I could strike.

'Well,' I said, picking slowly over my words as if boning a fish, 'I was heartbroken, of course. There was not – is not – a moment when I do not miss her. I feel it like an absence of warmth, or as if . . . as if I am walking down stairs in the dark, and I go to take the final step only to find it is not there, and for a moment I'm almost falling. I'm not sure that makes any sense. It's about having something you've always believed you can depend on, and then one day you realize you were wrong. But I also know that while Mama was here, I was loved. I know that she loves me still, wherever she is now.'

But Florence shook her head at my words. 'My daughter will not remember me.'

'Of course she will,' I said. 'You're her mother. She may not remember the obvious things, like what you look like, but she will remember that you were there. Your blood is in her even now. She will feel your love for her in every beat of her heart.'

'Do you think, then, that we can truly find her?'

'I am sure of it,' I said. 'And *when* we find her, she will know you at once. She will have her mother back! That is one thing that I will never have.'

Another long silence from Florence. I strained my ears. Caught her breathing – small breaths, sharp on the intake, like somebody trying not to cry. Was she crying for her daughter or for herself? I wasn't nearly vain enough to think she was crying for me.

Where Mama was now was the Père Lachaise Cemetery. I hadn't been by the grave in some while and, after all that talk with Florence the night before, I'd woken up with a sudden guilt. So there I was, doing my daughterly duty.

Mama had a pretty spot near an ash tree. It was peaceful; more peaceful than she'd been allowed in life. There were the noises of birds overhead, their bright chirrups and the faint rust-lings as they vied for position in the ash boughs. The air had a smell of fresh things moving beneath the soil. Worms and roots munching on the flesh of the dead as if taking in the Host. If it hadn't been for these signs, I could've been the only living thing – certainly the only person left this side of the topsoil.

Mama's headstone was neater than I'd expected, flecks of moss scattered at its base, like someone had cleared it recently to read the inscription. Someone searching for their own loved one, maybe. When Mama first died, me and Sylvie used to visit her every week. I wondered – did Sylvie visit still? Or had she forgotten our mother as easily as she'd forgotten the rest of us?

Crouching by the headstone, I thought now about how graves are cut from the ground as rectangles, like horizontal doorways. That implied something, didn't it? Because there are two sides to a doorway: travel ain't one-way. If you can leave via a door, you can also come back through it. Maybe that's why we choke them up with dirt. It's how we make sure the door stays shut.

I traced a finger over the inscription. Papa had picked out the words from Scripture. 1 Corinthians: 'For since by man came death, by man came also the resurrection of the dead.' I'd always assumed it was a joke.

Beneath that quote, and her name and dates, was the gaping space where Papa too would one day be written up – God grant it not be soon – and then my own name, presumably, if I was to remain a spinster, which was by all accounts likely. I sat back on my haunches and tried to picture it. The afterlife. I'd spent so much of my time inventing it for others that I'd lost track of what I thought of it myself. Who was to say it was anything like the stories we spun of veils and gardens and endless summer days? And as for whether the departed could return to walk among us – there was a part of me that wanted to believe this was possible, too, even knowing all the tricks of the trade that I did. I'd never yet seen evidence – and there'd been times in the past, after Mama had left us, that I'd gone out to look for it, trying our rituals and summonses for real. The dead had always remained silent for me. Yet I couldn't go quite as far as the atheists who thought there was nothing at all. How could you make it through the hardships of life without believing there was something better waiting at the end?

Course, there were those who'd claim I was far too much of a sinner to hope for such a thing, and that my own horizontal doorway would lead nowhere but down. But I didn't believe that. God probably didn't care one bit about half the things they called sin – He was much too busy with all the prayers and wars and such to tally up my impure deeds and thoughts.

Speaking of which, it hadn't escaped my notice that I looked forward to my nightly meetings with Florence a great deal – for reasons beyond professional interest. There was some quality to her that pulled me in, a magnetic field, a kind of spiritual attraction. And it weren't just a matter of a finely formed figure. The way her mind worked was endlessly intriguing . . . There was a kind of eccentric genius to her plots. Who else in her situation would have thought, oh, better stage a poltergeist? Who else could have made it work? And she was cunning with it; I'd been both impressed and a tad intimidated when she'd told me how she'd been meticulously moving her mother's possessions about, till the woman had become desperate for help wherever she could get it.

Florence was funny, too, if you drew her out. Whenever she told me about her family, she would do the voices – the pompous, blustering impression of her brother always set me off, even though I'd never met him. I treasured these glimpses into her personality. It was like they were private, just for me. And for the first time in what felt like years, I was having fun.

Mama would've liked Florence. She'd have wanted me to be happy.

CHAPTER FIFTEEN

29 March 1866

'MADEMOISELLE MOTHE?' ASKED a voice.

The newsboy was towering over me, much too close for comfort. I say 'towering' since I was kneeling on the front step with a scrubbing brush, trying to shift the worst of whatever Papa had spewed on to it the night before. God knew what he'd been drinking – lamp oil, from the smell of it. I'd already doused it several times, and was now going at it with carbolic and a brush. I popped those down and straightened up, restoring our height difference to its natural state of me being the one doing the towering.

'Yes?'

'Got something for you.'

'I don't want the papers today, thank you,' I told him. I sometimes bought them to read the news; sometimes out of pity, if it was a particularly cold day and he was looking pathetic. I couldn't help myself: I saw someone in distress, I had to help them. Just like that first time I'd met Florence.

The boy shook his head and whipped out a scrap of paper. 'A note,' he said.

From Florence? No, when I took it, I saw it was just an address on the page. Mimi, then.

I lowered my voice. 'Listen: you get any more of these, they come straight to me,' I told him. 'Not to be delivered to my father – all right?'

The boy saluted. 'Gotcha. How is His Excellency?'

'Drunk as ever.'

'Mine too.'

I gave him a couple of coins and took the note inside.

Nice part of town. Respectable, expensive. Everything she'd ever wanted. I was pleased for her, that it'd all paid off. Imagine the disappointment if you abandoned your family to live in the Faubourg de Mediocrity.

On second inspection, there was a quick message on the reverse side, too:

Dear Charlotte,

I greatly enjoyed seeing you the other day; it had been far too long. I hope you do not mind my saying that you looked tired – I trust you are taking care of yourself? I will get back in touch when I have more news on the other matter.
Yours sincerely and with love,

M.

The address made it all somehow more solid. Suddenly, Sylvie was within my reach. I could go right now, I thought. I could be at her house in an hour or so, and she'd no idea. She was going about her life – her new life, the one she'd purchased at our expense – and I could so easily . . . What? Ruin it? Turn up and tear everything to the ground like some classical god in a fit of pique? Well, yes, I thought – if I wanted. Or I could throw the note away and continue without dragging my sister into all this. Sylvie was a safety net, nothing more. An 'if anything goes wrong' clause in our contract. I could do this without her, in theory. So long as I trusted that nothing'd go wrong.

But I was no fool – I knew better than to trust in luck. Still, I needed a plan to convince her to help.

In the meantime, finish off the step, then lunch for Papa – if he was out of bed by then, that was. I didn't like to wake him. He had a nasty side, did Papa; he could get angry quick as a snap of thunder. Especially when he'd been drinking. It hadn't been like this when we were children. He'd been surprisingly gentle with us back then: rarely shouted, never hit us. Didn't drink, apart from Christmas. I think Mama had stood in his way. I think he'd thought so too . . .

After Mama died, something had stopped working in his head. I didn't know if it was the guilt of what he'd caused to happen or what, but almost overnight he'd become a different man, and if he'd been sober a day since, that would've been news to me. For almost an entire year, he'd barely spoken to me and Sylvie – and that had been the better option, compared to the rages that came later. Looking back, it was a miracle we'd kept up the spiritist work the whole time; our little family business had been waiting to go up in flames. I'd just happened to be the spark that'd finally caught.

Perhaps I *was* a fool, after all: I left Mimi's note on the hall table as I went to refill my bucket from the pump. By the time I got back, Papa was waiting for me. He was wearing his shabby brown coat that I kept telling him needed mending – and which he wouldn't let me touch – as if he was just about to go out. But he was slouched against the wall oh-so-casually, examining his chipped fingernails. Without looking up at me, he said, 'This letter for you?'

'Oh?' I said, closing the door and setting the bucket down.

His eyes flicked sideways at me. 'I picked it up by accident.' And read it start to end by accident too, it seemed. His voice was nonchalant, disinterested – for now. 'You're not plotting something without telling your old father, now, are you?'

'Course not, Papa,' I said. I shouldn't have closed the door – should've left an escape route.

'Of course not. That wouldn't be like my precious little princess.'

'It's nothing,' I said. 'Sewing. A family who need some mending doing. That's the address to pick it up.'

Papa dipped his chin. 'I know when you're lying to me, Charlotte.'

But I weren't going to tell him. Florence was my secret. He didn't get to share her. 'I just thought, what with the bills . . .'

'Is that what you thought?' he asked. He was smiling like the wolf ready to gobble up a little girl in the woods. 'Do you know what I thought?' He paused, clearly expecting an answer.

'What did you think, Papa?'

He held the letter aloft, peering at it as if to reread it. 'I thought that here I held a love note arranging a secret rendez-vous at someone's private apartments. I thought that perhaps my only remaining daughter was trying to do the same thing as her stuck-up sister and slut her way out of my life.'

'I'd never, I swear!' I told him. 'I'd never leave you for some man.'

'But then, I didn't know this was a letter from a *man*, did I?' he asked.

That's when I knew the casual attitude was just for show; he was simmering with anger underneath. He only ever brought these things up when he wanted to hurt me.

'I suspected that it was from that woman.'

He couldn't know anything. He was just testing me. 'What woman's that, then?' I asked.

'The same one you had in our house the other night. The one you've been mooning over.'

My insides clenched, but I kept my voice steady. 'I'd never leave you.'

Papa slowly balled up the letter and dropped it on the floor, then brought his boot down to grind it under his heel. Then he spread his arms, flopping his head like a scarecrow. 'Come here, my loyal daughter, and give your papa a kiss.'

I knew it was a trap, but resisting would only make it worse in the end. I stepped forward, leaning up on tiptoe to kiss his cheek. He needed a wash. When had I last made him wash?

'There now,' he said, patting my hair, 'that was nice, wasn't it?'

Sometimes he was nice. Sometimes he'd sing my favourite songs and tell jokes about the neighbours. He never forgot my birthday or my name day. Maybe he was in a good mood after all.

A dazzling pain as my head was yanked to one side by the hair. I screamed, unable to fight back as the momentum toppled me face-first into the hall table. My forehead connected with the edge. A cloud of dark spots obscured my vision. Flies buzzing, buzzing, buzzing.

I staggered back and saw Papa. One fist was raised, ready to strike. His shoulders heaved like a storm at sea. Pearls of sweat on his brow. He took a lurching step toward me.

'Don't!' I cried out, thrusting an arm between us.

But his expression weren't angry any more. It was confused. He took another step and somehow – I didn't see how – his legs got tangled under him and, like a lead weight in water, he plummeted to the floor.

There was a moment when I thought this was yet another trick, but then the sight of his twitching body brought me to my senses and I got down on the floor next to him. My head throbbed; the skin must've split, and I could feel a warm trickle starting down from where my brow had hit the table. 'Papa?' I asked, pressing a hand gently to his shoulder and giving it a nudge. He groaned in response, telling me at least that he hadn't been struck down dead by God.

'Papa, can you hear me?'

He groaned again, began to lever himself up on his hands and knees. 'What . . . happened?'

'I think you fainted.'

He sat back on his heels, scowling and rubbing his face. 'Get me a damned drink, will you?' There was an ooze of blood coming from one nostril. I watched as the force of gravity grew too strong and the ooze became a droplet, which fell with a plink on to the floor.

'Are you sure you should—'

'A drink!'

If he was well enough to threaten, then he was well enough to drink, even though that was most likely what had caused the faint in the first place. I went into the kitchen and started pouring out gin with one hand, pressing the other against my forehead. The fingers came away sticky and red. Both of us bleeding, then.

'I need a lie-down,' Papa called from the doorway. 'Bring that through to me.' His footsteps were stilted, as if his legs hadn't caught up with his brain yet. He didn't seem to have noticed his own injury, though I didn't see how it could've escaped him.

After taking the drink through, I went and retrieved the balled-up, stamped-on note from the hallway. I wiped up the splashes of Papa's blood – there was more than I'd realized and I started to worry, till a new drip hit the tiles and told me that some of it was in fact my own, mixed in and impossible to tell apart.

CHAPTER SIXTEEN

31 March 1866

A COUPLE OF days later, when I'd started to put the accident out of mind, I was woken in the early hours of the morning by a mighty crash. The sound of something heavy falling in a way it weren't meant to. Then silence. My ears tingled with hollow sound as I listened for anything more. Nothing, nothing, and then a long, low moaning – almost like the wind. Only, it came from *inside* the house.

I pushed back the sheets and slid out of bed, landing soft on the balls of my feet to dull the sound. Slipped my knife out from under my pillow.

The moaning went on, almost phantasmal. I wouldn't have been scared if I'd thought it a genuine spectre. But there are worse things than spectres in this world.

No candle at my bedside – what was I, a baroness? – but there were matches in the chest of drawers by the door. I slid my hands over its wooden face till I found the right drawer, then eased it open as gently as I could. The wood was old and warped from the weight of too much stuffed inside. Despite my care, it let out a shuddering scrape as I pulled it open. I froze. Had the moaning stopped? No, just paused – a second later I caught it again. I ran my fingers over the bric-a-brac in the drawer till they hit on the papery rectangle of a matchbox.

Light a match first, then open the door? Or open and then light? Match first, I decided, fumbling with the box and my knife till I'd struck one on my thumbnail. There was a fizzle and then a tongue of flame, blinding my night-wide eyes. Not waiting for them to adjust, I threw the door open. I'd only a couple of heartbeats of illumination – and I realized too late now that I'd lit myself up like a lighthouse if there *was* an intruder out here. I caught the empty corridor leading to the kitchen door; the kitchen door ajar; the dark, squirming mass on the floor at the threshold. And then the match bit my fingers and went out.

Heart racing, I scrambled with the box, trying desperately to find another stick, but they all seemed to slip away from my fingers like a hive of wooden insects. The moan came louder – nearer? – and then I'd got a match in hand. I tried to strike it, failed. Dropped my knife. Tried again. Dropped the box. Another gasp of brightness. I saw the mass, large and amorphous, a confusion of shapes and textures. Then the moan again and, in the moment before the light died, I recognized it.

'Papa!' I cried, current fear eclipsed by a new one. 'What's happened?'

I crouched down, reaching out my hands to where I thought he was. I got hold of what felt like an elbow, slid my hand up to the armpit and tried to haul him up. He gurgled something in response. Made no effort to help. Was this just the drink again, or was something else wrong? Hit his head, maybe? I let go, took a moment to think. No point doing this in the dark. I felt round on the floor till I'd recovered the matchbox, then fumbled into Papa's room to get his nightlight.

When I went back out, I could see he was lying face-down, arms and legs akimbo, nightshirt rucked up to his chest and only one slipper on. No blood or vomit or suchlike, and – the strangest thing of it – I didn't smell alcohol either; at least, no more than the normal low-level miasma that seeped from his pores at all times.

Setting the lamp down, I went again to lift him, getting a better grip now I could see what I was doing. He still didn't make any move to help, but I managed at least to roll him on to his side and sit him up against the door jamb. He weren't so heavy as I'd have thought – though still too heavy for me to get him any further. I tugged his nightshirt down to cover him back up, trying not to shudder at his concave chest and the network of purpled veins spreading over it. There was a distance in his reddened eyes, like he didn't see me at all.

'Papa?' I asked.

After a moment, his pupils floated toward me and flexed, finally noticing my presence.

'What happened?' I asked him.

He opened his mouth, running his tongue, slow and slug-like, over his lips. Now there was blood: it crept out of his nose, a wriggle of red. He tried to wheeze something – another moan, I thought – but then it turned into a whispered word. 'Hortense?'

I froze at the sound of my mother's name. 'No, Papa, it's Charlotte.' I'd never known him forget about Mama – not even when he was stewed as an apple. 'Mama's gone, remember?' When he didn't respond, I tried to haul him up again. Now he was more alert, I had a better time of getting him on his feet. 'Come on, let's get you to bed.' Something urged me to speak gently, as if to a child. 'Were you sleepwalking?'

It was slow progress, but I managed to shuffle him back to his room. His bedclothes were all scattered across the floor as if he'd been attacked.

'What've you been doing?' I asked.

Once he was safely back in bed and his sheets returned, I sat with him for a time, pressing a rag to his nose to staunch the bleeding. It took a while to slow; almost so long I began to worry. But at last it did stop, and during that time he grew more lucid – or stopped calling me Hortense, at least.

'What're you doing here, Charlotte?' he asked me.

'You were sleepwalking.' I took the rag away experimentally and, when I saw no more leaks, patted him on the cheek. 'Go back to sleep now,' I said.

Papa's snores soon started up again, but I didn't find it so easy to drift off. I kept thinking of those purple veins, and Mama's name spoken in this house for the first time in who knew how long.

As soon as dawn arrived, I sent for the physician. I'd not seen a doctor in many years – even the times we'd been ill, there had never been the money to pay for one where an old wives' remedy would do.

Luckily, Adèle was there to help when I called round next door. 'There's the doctor who treated my lungs last year – I can go and ask for him now. No, no, it's no trouble. Why, the poor lamb must be very unwell; he never misses his Saturday visit to your mama's grave.'

He'd never mentioned this ritual to me before, but now weren't the time to start asking about it.

When the physician arrived, he questioned me and examined Papa, tutting over his body and noting things down in a ledger. He held a candle to Papa's eyes; looked in his ears and throat and nose; felt his pulse; ran gloved fingers over his chest and limbs; listened to his breathing and counted its rhythm; and at long last took me aside to the kitchen to speak.

'Mademoiselle Mothe,' he said, his tone all genteel, 'do you understand what I mean by a "tumour"?'

'I've heard the word,' I said.

'It is a sort of unwelcome and harmful growth in or upon the body, which can keep expanding and interfere with vital organs.'

The physician stepped a little closer to me and drew a handkerchief from his breast pocket. It was only after a moment of it hanging there between us that I realized he was offering it to me. Not sure what to do, I took it.

He nodded glumly. 'I am afraid, Mademoiselle, that this will not be pleasant news. When examining your father's nasal cavity, I discovered one of these "tumours". I was unable to ascertain how far back it extended, but that fact in itself indicates that it must be sizable. I believe that it has been applying pressure to the front of his brain. The human brain is very delicate, and this sort of pressure would cause effects such as reduced motor abilities, confusion, and other trouble with mental function and recall. While tumours to other body parts can sometimes be removed by surgical intervention, I am sorry to say, Mademoiselle Mothe, that the same is not true of tumours of the brain.'

He looked at me again; there appeared to be some reaction he expected from me. Some conclusion I was meant to be reaching. But while I understood what he was saying to me – well, the general meaning, if not the specifics – I didn't see what was meant to come next.

I cleared my throat, which had come over all dry for some reason. 'What're you saying, Doctor?'

The physician removed his spectacles and examined them, as if looking for dust on the lenses. 'Such tumours are terminal when left untreated, and in such a location there is no treatment possible. All that we can offer now will be . . . palliative in nature. I have seen similar cases before,' he went on, snapping closed the spectacles and tucking them into his breast pocket, 'but it is difficult to draw comparisons between them. Often it is impossible even to identify the presence of a brain tumour until autopsy; it is a rare luck that your father's is exteriorly identifiable. I say "luck" because at least with such forewarning you now have time to prepare. I am afraid I cannot specify how much time. Sometimes the tumour takes the patient quickly, sometimes slowly. In many ways, it is more of a mercy for those who go quickly. There is less suffering.' He had small, voleish eyes. 'If I had to name a number – in your father's current condition – I would be counting in months. Half a year at the most. Likely less.' Seeing my silence, he pawed at my shoulder in what I assumed he believed to be a comforting way, and said, 'My condolences.'

'Thank you, Doctor.' My throat and nostrils had a horse-radish sting that made swallowing hard. Months. Months. Months. I kept turning the word over in my head, compre-hending it but not fully *comprehending* it.

'I can speak about options, if you wish?'

'Options?'

'Your father may be more comfortable in the care of the hos-pital. The sisters are well trained, and many find it comforting to spend their last days in a religious environment. Or, if you think he would prefer his own home, I can recommend some excellent nurses.' He went on to name some prices which had me fighting not to wince.

'Thank you. I'll need some time to consider,' I told him.

'Of course, of course, you will want to consult with your father when he is lucid enough for such a conversation, I am

sure. You may call upon me at the hospital any time once you have come to a decision.'

All through the physician's visit, I'd had the odd sensation that I weren't really in my body, that I was watching from outside the window. Then, the moment he left, I was suddenly in myself again – too much in myself. My limbs were heavy as anchors, pulling me down till the pressure on my lungs got too much for me to breathe. I sank to the floor, unable to move.

Papa was going to leave me. No more boots to find. No more brown coat that needed mending. No more favourite songs and jokes about the neighbours. And, yes, no more beatings. But I'd be all on my own. That lurching feeling. The missed step in the dark. I was falling, sinking.

I couldn't – I wouldn't be on my own.

If I'd had any doubts before, they were all gone now. I had to see Florence's plan through to the end. I needed that future. And I needed my sister.

Some hours later, another thought came to me, bringing with it equal parts excitement and shame. I'd been granted my excuse. My reason. Papa, ill – dying – and in need of money. Here was the bait I could dangle over Sylvie to make her join me.

But that was a wicked thing to think.

CHAPTER SEVENTEEN

3 April 1866

THE DAY FLORENCE'S mother sent an invitation to the Mothe sisters, I headed to the address Mimi had found for me.

The rain had set in again, drenching me through, but I didn't have money for a cab. I took the Passerelle des Arts – sticking to the very centre like always, since I'd a fear of going too near the sides of a bridge – then on the other bank I had to ask for directions, which embarrassed me no end, as I'd lived here my whole life. But then, I rarely wandered into areas like these.

When I got to the provided house number, I had to double-check I'd got it right. But yes, this was the building Mimi had pointed me to. It was a beautiful sweeping mansion in limestone, with all these pointed arched windows and baroque carvings hidden at every turn. Devereux was doing well for himself – much better than I'd ever realized. Sylvie knew how to play the long con, I'd give her that. I had a chuckle when I imagined what she'd do if I said that to her face. Well, I'd as good as said it the last time I'd seen her. But what else could it be called? Years of her poring over the society pages in the papers, that shrewd furrow of concentration on her brow as she calculated which bachelors were the most promising. And it'd been her work to get us invited to that ball where she'd met the Baron. 'It will be a lark,' she'd told me. And to Papa,

'It will help us find more people in need of our services.' But what a coincidence that a titled, esteemed lawyer, whom she'd just the previous month observed to be on the rise, was also in attendance. And what a coincidence that they should fall into conversation, and then into love. It did make you wonder – was Sylvie so entrenched in the lie that she'd begun to believe it? Perhaps she really was convinced it was providence that'd brought them together.

Well, in that case, providence looked remarkably like my sister.

Did Sylvie and the Baron really occupy all the floors of this mansion? Even with the servants, it was so much space for just two people. How did they fill it? I was tempted to approach the porter and ask for a look in through the porte cochère to see if they kept their own carriage and horses. But no, I didn't want to attract too much attention. In fact, I couldn't seem to bring myself to move an inch closer; I stood and watched, my feet rooted in the mud, as if I was already returning to the earth from which I was made. The building looked so warm and so peaceful. I tilted my face up so the rain fell under my hood, cooling my cheeks. Paris was beautiful in the rain. Sometimes – when it felt like it.

I cast another look up at the face of the mansion and – there! As if summoned by my observation, there was Sylvie at one of the windows.

An unpleasant, clutching hiccough in my heart. It was like a spirit had plunged its hand into my chest and was trying its level best to crush the organ. Sylvie. Too far away to make out the finer details, but definitely her. She weren't looking out, but stood in profile, speaking to somebody else in the room. Her dress was bottle green, the neckline flattering her plump shoulders with a modern cut. She looked well. She looked rich. She looked like a society lady and not like the girl who used to sit on the dusty floor with me, making up stories and doing all the voices.

As I watched, she lifted something to her mouth. Hard to see at this distance. Something small, cubish, a bright colour. Turkish delight. That's what it was: Turkish delight.

Maybe, if I'd been a better person, I would've ripped up her address then and there, turned away and walked home. I would've been happy that Sylvie had achieved all she ever wanted.

But I'd made up my mind. I'd made it up in the other direction. This weren't about a security net, or giving a believable performance, or any of the excuses I'd made up. I didn't want to be the last one left. I wanted to remind Sylvie that I existed. And I wanted to make her suffer. Why should she – *she* – get out? Leave me crying and bruised on the floor without a second thought? Live without repercussions? The rest of us had to shoulder the consequences of our actions – I'd had to shoulder more than most. Well, I was tired of bearing her cross as well. Even Jesus only carried the one.

Just as I was thinking this, a short, fat, red-whiskered man appeared from the porter's lodge.

'Good day, Mademoiselle,' the man called, once he'd come within earshot. 'May I assist you in some way?'

I took an instant dislike to him. He'd a nasty, pompous, snivelling voice, like he was talking through his nose.

'Thank you, that is most kind,' I said coolly, in my elevated 'talking to the wealthy' accent. 'This is the residence of the Baroness Devereux?'

'Have you business with Madame?'

'Yes.'

'I am afraid Madame is not at home at the present.'

I could see a blur at Sylvie's parlour window, half tucked behind the curtain like she thought that kept her out of sight. 'I can see the madame up there,' I said, raising an arm to point. Sylvie immediately ducked away. Was it possible she'd recognized me at this distance, even under the hood?

The man's face grew flushed and he coughed delicately. 'That is to say, Madame is not accepting visitors at present.'

'She will accept me,' I said, though I weren't at all sure of this. 'Here.' I dipped a hand into my pocket to find one of my visiting cards – though I'd had little call to use them since my retirement. 'My card. Please take this to the Baroness.'

The man took it and turned it upright, about to read the details.

'Wait!' I said. It occurred to me it'd be better if Sylvie's husband didn't know about this visit. 'Only the Baroness is to read that card,' I said. 'You have no reason to obey me, of course, but I promise that she will be most disappointed if she discovers that you have read it before she has had the chance.'

I was treated to a sweeping, suspicious gaze in response, as the man tried to peep beneath my hood. Eventually, he decided there was no harm in following my orders, and turned the card face-down again. 'I will return with Madame's answer shortly,' he said.

I was left outside to the rain. Though I'd been fine up till then, in those final minutes of waiting the chill finally got to me and my jaw was chattering by the time a girl in servant's garb came to fetch me.

The girl didn't take me through the porte cochère to the main entrance, but to a little set of steps at the side of the building.

The servants' entrance. So this was how Sylvie welcomed her sister after so long! We went through a large, warm kitchen filled with the leftover smells of lunch – something rich and meaty, a far cry from the stale bread me and Papa had been nibbling at. From the kitchen, we went up the servants' stair and climbed three storeys. Did Sylvie's husband really own all of them? It was like a fairy-tale mansion. Or Bluebeard's. We went down the next corridor, and then the girl stopped outside one of the doors. She rapped dead on the centre.

A voice from the other side called: 'Enter!'

The girl opened the door and went inside. Again, I followed.

A cosy boudoir. There was a fire blazing in the grate, reflecting all over from well-polished brass and silver. The walls were decorated with clustered flowers in a patisserie pink, so sweet it made your mouth water to look. An elegant mahogany writing desk sat against one of these, covered with writing implements alongside an embroidery hoop and an arrangement of colourful threads. My anger over the Turkish delight frothed up further. All the nights I spent ruining my eyesight over stitches just so me and Papa could eat, and here was Sylvie taking up a needle – for what? Fun? Or just to fill her idle time?

Gooseflesh ran up my arms under my thick, damp cloak: both the rage and the rain taking their toll. I couldn't help but glance at the fire. Cosied up near to it was a tasteful forget-me-not settee, looking all welcoming and warm. Did I have to wait for an invitation to sit down these days? Sylvie was already perched on a Turkish divan, posed in an obviously premeditated manner, her back and neck unnaturally stiff. She'd put on weight – it suited her, but made her look older. Then again, she *was* older.

'Thank you, Virginie,' said Sylvie, not even glancing at the girl. 'Will you take the mademoiselle's cloak for her?'

Embarrassed to have this girl fuss over me, I quickly peeled off the cloak myself and looked round to hang it somewhere. Not fast enough; Virginie plucked it out of my hands and set it by the fire. It began steaming immediately.

'Thank you,' I said to Virginie.

'That will be all,' Sylvie added.

Virginie bobbed a curtsey and retreated, walking backward through the door like she was worried Sylvie'd plunge a knife into her spine at any moment.

At last, Sylvie turned a smile on me. 'So you found me, Charlotte.'

CHAPTER EIGHTEEN

9 April 1866

HAVING SYLVIE BACK took some getting my head round. From that first meeting, to our visit to Florence's family, to the evening we agreed to hold a dark circle, I kept expecting her to disappear again. When I looked at her, it was like she was across a gulf, and in that space between echoed everything that'd happened to the both of us in the years since we'd last known each other. These echoes overlaid the face I'd known and distorted it a little, just enough for it to be unsettling, like catching your reflection in moving water. It made me think of the fairy stories Mama used to read us: tales of changelings, where a child gets taken and replaced with a not-quite-identical copy. When we'd been very small, before I knew my letters, we'd lie on our bellies with the book of Perrault's tales open before us, and Sylvie'd read the stories to me in a right superior manner.

Her favourite had always been 'The Fairies'. Gold and toads. Good sister, bad sister. I thought I could guess which role she'd have cast me in. But we'd never agreed on our interpretations of the story. The problem was, Sylvie always took these things at face value. Perrault said one sister was good and the other bad, so that must have been the truth. But weren't it an unfair trick for the fairy to play, to appear as a young lady on the second day? Being asked a favour by an old crone's not the same as being commanded by some gentlewoman. The test was rigged from the start – even before the fairy turned up, when Perrault labelled one sister as good and one as bad on the very first page, before either got a chance to prove whether this was true.

I hadn't thought of these things in so long, all fond memories tarnished by what'd happened when we'd parted. I was having trouble reconciling them now. How was it that the sister who'd taught me to read, who'd watched out for me after Mama died, was the same one who'd left me when I'd needed her most? Things had been simpler when I'd only remembered the bad.

Before our evening's performance for the de Jacquinots, I'd paid a visit to Mimi to pick up the necessary effects. My old signature candles with the colour-changing flame were a sure winner. Between these and Florence's captivating performance, I thought we were a blazing success.

Sylvie didn't seem to suspect anything yet, but I took the chance to test the waters that night as we prepared to 'keep watch' in Florence's room, needling her about the spirit hand. She thought I was joking – no surprise there. But I could hear the beginning of a doubt under that bravado. This was going to be fun, I realized. This was exactly what Sylvie deserved.

Settling back against the pillows, I caught the smell of Florence's hair: orange blossom and warm skin. I could imagine her there each night, staring up at the ornamental wooden canopy, her limbs resting where mine now lay. This must be where she'd birthed the baby, I realized. Where her newborn daughter had been stolen from her. Bad memories carved into the wood alongside the decorative vines and fruit.

I didn't have to wait long for Sylvie to fall asleep: the tinc-ture me and Florence had put in everyone's wine saw to that. Mimi had called it a sleeping draught, but I'd recognized the bitter, clove-like scent of laudanum, plain and simple. Still, it'd done the trick.

Once she was snoring deeply, I peeled myself back out of bed and crept out of the room, to the library.

Florence was already there. She'd lit a single candle on the reading desk; its flame twinkled across the blades of two garden shovels, propped against the far wall.

As soon as I saw her, I was struck with a giddy wave of excitement. Our plan was really working! 'You were magnificent,' I cried, dancing over to her and – getting a bit carried away – taking her hand to twirl her.

Florence laughed and spun about. 'So were you! Even better than when I first saw the two of you at work.' She was so different from how she behaved round her family, so much livelier now she was free to be herself.

'Oh, but you were the star. Anyone would think you had been taking lessons.'

'From the very best teacher,' she said, looking up at me so earnestly it made my heart twist.

Suddenly aware I still had her bare hand in mine, I let go. Tried not to notice how soft it had been. 'Even Maximilien was spooked.' I pretended to cower, making my voice quiver: '"R-r-rot!"'

My imitation – though nowhere near as good as Florence's were – got another laugh out of her. 'I have been moving things about in his bedroom each day,' she said. 'I think it is getting to him at last. And your sister?'

'In progress.'

Florence drifted over to the wall of portraits, as if to admire the faces of her ancestors. 'You are still determined not to tell her the truth?'

'Not until we have her backed into a corner she cannot get out of. She would never help you with this otherwise, not with something so complicated, and with no obvious benefit to her. Sylvie is not . . . a good person. She does not do things out of kindness.'

I realized, too late, there'd been a flash of real venom in my words. I'd revealed too much of myself. Florence had seen it. She looked at me carefully – curious, but not judgemental. 'She must be the opposite of you, then; you have been very kind to me, Charlotte. Do you mind if I ask . . . what happened between you and your sister?'

My chest felt tight. It weren't that I was ashamed of what'd happened. Though I knew there were those who thought I should be – Papa and Sylvie among them – I didn't feel that way. But I *was* scared at the idea of telling Florence. She might think less of me for it, and I couldn't stand that. But, a small voice in my mind asked, what if Florence understands? What if she doesn't mind? What if she even . . .?

Florence's skirts rustled as she shifted. The silence had stretched on too long, grown awkward. 'You do not have to say,' she told me. 'I only thought – you know so much of my past. And if there is anything of which I ought to be aware . . . that might affect your sister's behaviour?'

She was right: it was unfair, unbalanced. She'd put herself at my mercy, and so I should've put myself at hers.

'I am worried I will lose your good opinion,' I said.

'That could never happen.'

We'd see about that. I closed my eyes and tried to find the start. 'It was over two years ago now. Sylvie had just begun court-ing her husband. We were consulting with a family, a widow and her daughters. For a little extra money, Papa had the idea that

I could train the youngest girl into greater spiritual receptivity. Feed her some claptrap about opening her mind to commune with the spirits, that sort of thing. Eugénie, that was her name.'

I'd never spoken about this, to anyone. But – like my last fight with Sylvie – it was something I'd obsessed over for a long time after it'd ended. There'd been months when I'd felt so cold and hollow that I weren't sure I hadn't died. That I weren't already down there in the grave with Mama.

'We began to have these private tutoring sessions. At first, that was all they were, but then we would get to talking about other things. Our dreams. We had a lot in common – a surprising amount. I grew to really . . . care for her, and she for me. I thought her the best person I'd ever met. And then . . . we got too close. Do you understand?'

It was clear from Florence's silence that she didn't follow me. 'You mean that you told her you were a fake?' she asked at last.

'No,' I said. Swallowed the tension in my throat. My palms were clammy as toad skin. 'Have you heard of the poetess Sappho?'

Florence hummed thoughtfully. 'I think she was a Greek?'

'Never mind. If you do not know what I mean, it is no use.'

'No, go on: say.'

But I'd lost my nerve. 'Never mind,' I said again. 'I just grew too fond of Eugénie and did something silly, that is all, which gave us away. I thought she was fond of me too, but . . . Well, whether she was or was not at heart, she sided against me. Sylvie's fiancé, as he was at the time, was all that kept us from legal repercussions when it all came out. Papa was not best pleased, to put it mildly. I don't think he or Sylvie ever forgave me – Sylvie particularly, as my actions almost threatened her marriage. Almost, but obviously not in the end.'

Florence seemed to consider this, perhaps wondering whether to push for more information. Her eyes drifted to my brow. 'I noticed this when you were here last week,' she said, drawing near to brush a finger over the wound from the hall table, still redly visible up there. 'Was that . . . him? Your father?'

I couldn't stand the thought of her pitying me. 'I just tripped into something, that's all.' Clearing my throat, I stepped back from her touch and slipped the knife out of my reticule. 'Shall we get to work? That lot won't sleep for ever.'

Florence looked at me a second longer, and then nodded and hefted up the shovels. 'Here, these will be more effective.' As she passed one to me, her fingers brushed against mine for a moment again, cool and smooth. If she noticed my instant flinch, she was good enough not to react.

Remaining shovel in hand, Florence stepped toward the wall of ancestral portraits and stopped in front of one of her grandfather. From what I could see in the candlelight, he'd been a much younger man when it had been made, his hair – not yet grey – the same auburn as Maximilien's. In fact, he looked a fair bit like Maximilien all over. Not identical, but similar enough that there'd be no doubt of a family tie.

Florence raised the shovel two-handed and swung. Her technique was perfect: a clean arc down her arms and through the shaft, ending with the spade head embedded in the centre of Ardoir's oil-paint face. A wrenching noise of metal through wood. We both froze, listening out for any sign we'd woken the others. Nothing but silence. The steady tick of a mantel clock.

'That laudanum must have been pretty strong,' I whispered.

A dark expression flitted over Florence's face, reminding me that her family had once used the same drug to keep her placid. 'See how they like it,' she muttered.

When we held up the candle, I saw Florence had driven the spade so far through the portrait she'd also split the frame. I was dumbfounded. She didn't look so strong; I hadn't imagined this'd go much beyond some sliced canvas. But then again, she had enough anger to vent – and especially toward Ardoir. Still, I don't think I'd realized till then just how violently she hated him.

'Your turn,' she said, pulling the shovel clear.

I chose a portrait at random – a haughty woman with thin lips – and struck. My blow wasn't nearly so impressive; it'd take more force than I'd expected to achieve Florence's level of art injury. Besides, the shovel was heavy, and holding it overarm was actually rather a challenge. Maybe it'd be better just to use my knife after all. I tried again, but this time misjudged my aim somehow and hit the wall. A cloud of white-powder dust retaliated, sending me reeling back, hacking up a lung.

'That also works,' said Florence, with a shrug.

Once I could breathe again, I looked up and saw what she was talking about. Where the wallpaper had been struck, it was sliced open and hanging down like the skin from a lanced boil. A large, long chip had been cut from the plaster beneath.

'More of those,' Florence directed.

I adjusted my stance this time, got into a proper crouch with my knees bent and my weight resting on the balls of my feet. A fighting stance, as I'd once been shown by Mimi for a laugh, though I'd never had much call to use it. I swung the shovel again and gouged another chunk.

Florence took her turn, slicing a similar trench. Then – of all things – she let out a cry and hopped from foot to foot in some kind of jig. The silly excitement had caught us again. Before long, we were both giggling breathlessly with it.

'Is this not exhilarating?' Florence said. There was plaster dust in her hair, doubling her resemblance to the portrait of Sabine de Lisle with her powdered pouf. 'I feel so powerful! Like I am not even myself.'

I'd never considered myself drawn to destruction, but, yes, there was something freeing in it. The physical exertion, the satisfying thunk and cloud of powder, the wound left behind in the otherwise orderly library.

We worked at the portraits and the wall some while longer, swinging and slashing and coughing in turns. I got tired long before Florence and had to sit down, sweaty and sore. But she continued; I watched with wonder as she tirelessly defaced the remaining portraits and wall space. Resentment was a right old motivator! The flickering candlelight made the Furies dance across the fresco, a pretty parallel to the scene below them. Mama had told me the story of the *Oresteia* – well, her version of it, which I'd had to take as correct though she may well have changed bits. I'd thought Clytemnestra had had the right idea. Poor, murdered Iphigenia . . . At least her papa had got what was coming to him. Florence wasn't really a fitting Clytemnestra, though you could almost believe it tonight.

At last, Florence laid down her shovel and came to sit in the chair beside me. Her chest was heaving like a panting dog's, and she looked at me with flushed throat and glittering eyes.

She grinned. 'Do you think that will suffice?'

'Goodness, Mademoiselle Florence, we do not want the ceiling to fall in on us!'

'No, I suppose not. Not while we are in here, at least.'

There was a chunk of plaster caught in her hair, a bright flash of white. I debated whether to reach out and remove it. Then I caught the eye of the one remaining portrait – the Comtesse – and under her watchful judgement I thought better of it.

CHAPTER NINETEEN

16 April 1866

IF ME AND Sylvie had still been holding dark circles regularly, I'd have invited Florence to join our act in a heartbeat. She'd a knack for theatrics and could banish the blood from her face as if on command – watching her, even I could've believed that she really had been possessed by another soul.

Sylvie'd been stretched to her limit by our sitting the night before. She'd set about interrogating Florence as soon as it was over, demanding to know where she'd learned to conjure ectoplasm. But Sylvie hadn't slotted me into the puzzle yet, and without me, the image didn't make sense to her. She was tense, watchful, suspicious without knowing where to place her suspicion. Though she'd never been open to believing in spirits in the past – calling my juvenile attempts to contact Mama idiotic and worse – I thought she might even have been half convinced this time. I'd caught her jumping at a shadow as we'd left the de Jacquinots' that night.

Though it'd been past midnight when I'd got in, I was back up at the crack of dawn to start on the chores: there was cleaning, Papa's breakfast, the market to get to, fresh sewing to collect, liquor – as ever – to replenish. I was always damned near collapsing from exhaustion lately. As I dashed about town, my mind skidded between half-formed plans. It was clear I didn't have long before Sylvie worked out what was afoot, and I needed to make sure she was thoroughly implicated by then, if I wanted the guarantee of her husband's legal protection. Besides the haunting, there was also the question of finding Mère Ancelot and, with her, Florence's daughter. I'd not heard yet from Mimi whether his network of scurrilous connections had borne fruit.

And then there was Papa. Who knew how long he'd got left on this earth? I should've been doing my all to make him comfortable in his final months. The dutiful daughter. Like Mama would've wanted. Instead, here I was, scheming behind his back and leaving him with only Adèle's neighbourly charity for company. I'd often told myself he didn't deserve my compassion, but that was nothing but an excuse. Compassion's a moral good in itself; by extension, it ain't something you've got to 'earn', but something you've got to practise regardless. If you're only good when it suits you, you ain't truly good at all, only feigning goodness. *I* was only feigning goodness. Thank God I was better at feigning ghosts, or I'd have ended up in jail many years since.

It was just past lunchtime as I got home. I stood outside the front door without opening it for a minute, breathing in and out. Slowly, in and out. Waited for the dots to clear from my vision. Then I went inside, calling to Adèle, 'I'm back.'

Her wiry head poked out from Papa's chamber, a notched smile on her face. 'Hello, dear. His Excellency's asleep at the minute.'

'Already?' I asked. He normally made it till four o'clock, at least.

'A half-hour ago,' said Adèle. Then, as I walked to my own room, 'Nothing much else to report. He had a walk just before lunch.'

In my room, I'd started shedding my outdoor-wear, leaving the door open so I could still shout out to her. 'Well done you.'

'He's no trouble really. Not at all.'

No trouble to Adèle, maybe. Funny how he could switch it on and off like that. By which I meant not damned funny at all. Damned infuriating.

'Thanks,' I said, a little stiffly.

'I'll be off, then.'

I went back into the corridor and took one of her hands in mine, pressing it gently. 'Really: thank you, Adèle.'

When she'd gone back next door, I looked in on Papa. I wondered if it was the illness that'd diminished him so much, or if he'd always been this small, and I'd just not noticed.

Adèle had left his lunch things in a pile on the vanity table: plate of crumbs, discarded knife, cup with a reddish sediment at the bottom. I went to pick them up, averting my eyes from the mirror out of an old superstition. A long oval looking-glass with a border fashioned to look like leaves – it reminded me for a moment of looking down on the pond in the de Jacquinots' garden. This was where Mama used to sit for getting ready. Me and Sylvie would perch on the end of the bed and watch her – the little rituals of combing out her hair, rouging her lips, holding earrings up to her lobes to test how they caught the light. Shortly after she died, I'd tried everything to get her to appear to me. After that'd failed, I'd developed a terror of looking in the mirror, in case one day I'd see her face there again after all. I don't know why I'd been frightened – weren't that exactly what I'd been trying to achieve? Hadn't I longed to see her features once more?

But, unlike our clients who took comfort in the idea of a lost one returning from beyond the grave, after Mama had refused to answer my call, I'd known for certain she was gone, and – as it followed – if I'd seen her face in the mirror, it wouldn't have been *her*. It would only have been something that *looked* like her. And who knew what that something would've been? For a time, I was too frightened even to enter the room – a fear only intensified by the changes in Papa – so their chamber became a beast's lair. But then, one day, I realized it was stupid to live in terror of a room in my own house. And so, I waited till Papa went out for the evening, and crept in, candlestick in hand. Closing my eyes, I held my breath and stepped up to the glass. I stood there with my heart racing in my ears, sweat tickling in my armpits and at the backs of my legs. I could hear my own breathing – and, after a time, it seemed I heard someone else's as well. A coolness on the back of my neck. I clenched the candlestick till my fingers hurt and forced my eyes to open. A face.

Of course, it was mine. Only mine.

I gathered up the lunch bits now and took them out to the kitchen. After, I sat at the desk to write up my notes from the night before. But all the excitement must've caught up with me, and the next thing I knew, I was waking with my face squashed up against the smooth desktop, nothing but a blot on the paper in front of me where the pen had slipped from my hand. There was someone knocking at the door. I hurried to get up, rubbing at my face, sure there'd be some indentation or even an ink splot there, and went out to the hall. Already the front door was opening, as whoever waited on the other side tried the handle. I half expected Florence; there was a leap in my chest at the thought, like a bird taking flight. But it was Sylvie. Sylvie with red-rimmed eyes and a valise in tow. Sylvie, come home at last.

CHAPTER TWENTY

17 April 1866

'IS THIS THE place?' asked Florence, crooking her neck to look up at the walls before us.

We stood outside a genteel private square, guarded by a porte cochère and all. The outer doors were a stern, dark green; a forbidding barrier to protect the residents from the outside world. They didn't quite meet in the middle, so a crack of daylight showed at their seam. By pressing my face up to this, I could see partly into the court beyond, though the view had that curious one-dimensional quality that comes from closing one eye. Through the gap I could just spy tall, pale-faced buildings fronted with neoclassical columns, looking very modern and even a bit English. Eruptions of flowers pushed through the railings at their feet, vibrant pinks and reds and purples that made the buildings seem like a row of teeth. Smiling ones, I hoped.

Florence was visibly more relaxed now I'd led her here instead of to whatever hovel she'd been anticipating. 'It is really rather charming.'

I shook my head at her, stepping back from the door. 'I must have got it wrong. There's no way he lives here.'

'Are you sure?'

'Let's turn back and retrace the route.'

'We should at least ring and consult with the porter,' said Florence.

Without waiting for my response, she stepped past me and gave a neat tug at the bell, setting off a muted peal from somewhere inside. I began to protest, but was cut short by the porter popping up at his window. He was wearing a wide-brimmed hat, from under which a pair of funny little eyes assessed us — myself more dubiously than Florence. But when he spoke, it was with an incongruously honeyed voice, obsequious and repellent. 'Good afternoon, ladies. How *may* I assist you?' Were all porters this bad, or was it just a coincidence I'd encountered two particularly foul specimens in such short succession?

'Good afternoon,' replied Florence, setting a cool aristocratic smile upon her face, of the sort used by gentlewomen to let you know they're better than you. Smiles like this had been turned on me enough times. 'I believe that a friend of mine is in residence here? His name is . . .'

'Michel Tauret,' I jumped in. 'He will be expecting us.'

'Ah,' said the porter, giving a disdainful sniff that told me, against all reason, that he did know the name. 'Yes, Monsieur Tauret is in residence at Number One. Just a moment, please . . .' And his head disappeared back into his office. A second later, the green doors were pulled open.

Still thinking that somehow there'd been a misunderstanding, I walked through to the gravelled court, Florence in tow. Number One had to be the most luxurious apartment — which only confused things further. Maybe if we'd been sent to a little bachelor's room on the upper floor, I would've thought it more believable.

'I thought you said this person we were seeing was . . . of the underworld?' whispered Florence.

I'd nothing to say to that; I merely bit my lip and headed for the door marked '1'.

A liveried manservant received us and, after listening briefly to our introduction, took us up without complaint. We were delivered into a spacious parlour, where he instructed us to wait. The room was magnificent: high ceilinged and bright from its large windows that looked back on to the court. Its furnishings were the kind of tasteful that comes only at great expense – but definitely masculine. This ebony suite and matching drinks cabinet, the port shade of the walls, the velvet draperies, the hunting scenes in gilt frames . . . I kept expecting the true owner of the apartments to appear and chase us off, up until the very moment Mimi floated through the door. It really was like floating, as he wore a diaphanous jewel-toned robe that wafted about him like the wings of some oversized colourful insect.

'Charlotte!' He took me in his arms and kissed my cheeks. 'And you're Mademoiselle Florence, are you? Charlotte did say you were pretty' – was I blushing? – 'I reckon I'd kill for that hair.'

He exchanged kisses with her too, though it was less an exchange and more an attack, as Florence seemed too dazed by his exuberance to do much more than stand there.

I'd been reluctant when Florence had asked to meet the man I'd tasked with finding her daughter. Partly, it was a risk to have her creeping out of the house when her family might notice, but there was another reason I couldn't quite name. It could be tricky, putting your finger on the cause of an emotion, when in the moment all you knew was that you were feeling it. But maybe it was that . . . well, the way Florence acted when she was in private with me, her real self: that was something only I got to see. It was something special between us. To invite Mimi into it made it less . . . mine. But this was the very reason I should: to stop myself from thinking of anything of Florence's as mine. Soon as you started to think like that, you were already setting yourself up to be hurt.

'Come, sit, sit.' Mimi bustled Florence over to a loveseat, but I remained standing for the moment.

'I've got to say, Mimi,' I told him, 'this ain't what I was expecting.'

He flashed me a feline look of satisfaction. 'It's fantastic, isn't it? Not how I'd have decorated, but I won't lodge a complaint with the bureau over it.'

I refused to laugh at the joke, and instead crossed my arms over my chest and faced him down. 'Are you going to tell me whose rooms these are?' I asked.

'Mine,' replied Mimi with an easy grin, and plunked himself down on another settee, leaning back with his hands clasped behind his head and one leg propped up on the knee of the other.

'And who the hell *pays* for them?'

The grin grew wider and he gave me a wink. 'A friend,' he said.

'You told me you'd given that up,' I said.

'I said I'd given up *whoring*,' said Mimi, slanting a glance at Florence to see if she blushed – which she didn't, to her credit. 'This is a different arrangement.'

I raised my eyebrows and at last perched myself on a nearby chair.

Mimi wiggled the foot that was propped on his knee. 'I can't reveal his name, you understand.'

'Course not,' I replied, giving an exaggerated wink. It was a disconcerting experience, speaking in front of both Mimi and Florence at the same time; I was acutely aware of my voice trying to reconcile itself between the different registers I normally used, and, unable to find the middle ground, it seemed to be wobbling all over the place.

'No, really, don't ask me, 'cause I won't tell you.'

'But he must be wealthy, whoever he is,' said Florence, widening her eyes. To my relief, she looked not scared or scandalized, but amused.

'Oh, yes. He's a vicomte.' Mimi widened his eyes for emphasis. 'And he's madly in love with me. Don't tell his wife.'

We were getting waylaid and I was conscious of Florence's limited time; she was Cendrillon at the ball, constantly listening for the clock chimes that'd tell her the spell was broken, that she had to get back before her wicked family discovered she'd been gone. She'd bribed the day girl to cover for her while she was out, pretend they were on a walk together. In my turn, I'd left Sylvie watching Papa, telling her some lie about needing to pay a bill. She hadn't seemed to suspect anything, though she'd said some odd things about Mama as I left – I reckoned the eviction was messing with her head. It weren't exactly ideal for me either; having Sylvie constantly up my rear had never been part of the plan. Plus, now I had this nagging voice in my mind, saying I was at least partly to blame for what'd happened between my sister and her husband. I kept shushing it down as best I could.

'Have you found anything out yet?' I asked.

Unclasping his hands from behind his head, Mimi used the same motion to push himself off the sofa and into a standing position. 'Now, now,' he said, 'no need to rush straight to business. Can't we talk first? It's been, what . . .?' He waved a hand, searching for an appropriate measurement of time. 'Millennia, almost. We were in such a hurry the other day. Let's have a drink!' He crossed over to the ebony drinks cabinet and opened it, revealing an array of bottles. They made a gentle clinking as he ran his fingers over them, as if choosing by touch which was best to offer.

I caught Florence glancing at me uneasily. 'Sorry, Mimi,' I said, 'but we can't stay long.'

He ignored me, pretending to bend over to peer at labels. 'It's been ages since I got to entertain anyone. Apart from my *friend*. But that's different, ain't it?' He straightened back up, a bottle of gin and three glasses grouped precariously in the crook of his arm.

Now I glanced at Florence, raising my eyebrows. *Can you manage?*

'Well . . . maybe just a little one,' said Florence.

Mimi beamed. 'Excellent! I've got a feeling I'm going to like you, Mademoiselle de Jacquinot.' He set the glasses down on the sideboard and uncapped the gin. It was strong enough that I could smell it from where I sat.

'Florence is fine,' she replied. 'I think we hardly need stand on ceremony. Given . . .'

'Yes, I s'pose we all know each other's deepest secrets,' said Mimi.

'For the most part,' Florence agreed, darting her eyes at me a moment, then looking away when she saw I'd noticed. Was she thinking how I'd refused to say more on the rift between me and Sylvie? Or did she mean that she'd secrets kept from me? Neither thought made me comfortable. But maybe it was no more than an idle comment – a reference to the fact that she was only meeting Mimi for the first time now.

'I like secrets,' said Mimi. 'They breed intimacy, don't you think?' Of course, for Mimi, secrets bred more than intimacy; they were the chief currency he bartered in.

'Go on, then, what ones have you uncovered?' I asked him.

'Well . . .' said Mimi, then broke off to pour out the liquor, doing so slowly, savouring our attention no doubt. When he was done, he recapped the bottle and placed it back on the sideboard – he seemed under the assumption that we'd be staying for more than one drink. Then he passed us our glasses, picked up his own, sat back down on the settee, and took a considered sip. Only once the performance was complete did he continue his sentence. 'It wasn't an easy one to start on, given the time between what happened and now. Really, I didn't have much to go on – just that name you gave me. I'm sorry, but I'll tell you now that I haven't been able to find a Mère Ancelot yet. For all we know, her establishment isn't even in Paris. But I sniffed around a bit, did some asking, and I think I've got something for you. Not a lot, mind you, but something.'

Florence's hands were gripped tightly round her drink, the seams of her gloves straining with the tension. I wished I'd thought to sit next to her, so I could've taken them in my own.

'There's a man who sometimes sleeps in that back alley behind your house, Florence,' Mimi went on. 'I got talking to him, and asked if he'd noticed anything strange going on last year. Now, he couldn't be specific on the dates, but he said it was cold, so that would line up with the wintertime. He's huddling up against the wall for shelter one night, when he hears two people in your garden. So our friend thinks, that's odd, who'd want to be outside in this weather when they don't have to be, and creeps up to the gate to listen in. He hears a man talking, who he thinks is definitely your grandfather. Doesn't recognize the woman. He can't catch all the words, but – and here's the juicy part – he does hear your grandfather tell the woman to "take care of it". Those words exactly. "Take care of it."'

Mimi placed his glass back down on the table and fluttered his fingers in a *ta-dah* flourish.

We both turned our heads to Florence at the same time. Her lips were moving, forming the words 'take care of it', as if it was a phrase in a foreign language she was trying to learn for the first time. She took a thoughtful sip.

'Florence?' I asked her, gentle as possible.

'"Take care of it",' she said, out loud now. 'What was the tone in which it was said?'

Mimi shook his head slowly. 'I didn't ask.'

'But the tone makes the meaning,' said Florence, voice pitching high in frustration. She put her glass down. 'The . . . the emphasis, the way the words are spoken. "Take care" as in "care for", or as in "make it go away"? "It" as in the situation, or as in my daughter?'

'I'm sorry, Florence, I don't know.'

'But this is good,' I said quickly. 'This is an excellent start. Whatever the tone, this means what you saw that night was true: your grandfather did pass your child over to a woman – your living child. Mimi, is it possible that this woman was Mère Ancelot?'

Mimi shrugged. 'There's one more thing – the man thought your grandfather called the woman something like Lucie or Lydie?'

'Lily!' said Florence, perking up again. 'We had a servant named Lily – Lily Masson. She resigned almost immediately after my daughter was born. Grandfather must have made her the go-between with Ancelot, then paid her off to leave us. It has to be!'

'Could be,' Mimi equivocated.

'Well, she'll be easier to find,' I said. 'We've got her full name, and you must have a forwarding address somewhere in the household accounts, Florence?'

'No, we would not normally keep a record of that. God' – she suddenly slapped both hands down into her lap – 'just when you think you have discovered the answer . . .'

If there'd been something – anything – I could've done to make all this easier for her, I'd have done it in a heartbeat. As it was, I only had my words. 'We'll get there,' I promised.

The next step would be for Mimi to track down Lily, who'd know – we hoped – where to find Florence's daughter.

'I wanted to show you something,' said Florence as we discussed this. She fished a scrap of cloth out of her pocket and placed it on the table with a reverential gesture, as if handling something fragile she feared to drop.

'What's that?' asked Mimi.

I craned forward to see as well – Florence hadn't told me about this. I tried not to let it sting.

A square of fabric, composed of broad stripes of white linen interspersed with pale-blue silk velvet ribbons. The linen was decorated with whitework: little blossoms and gambolling rabbits. 'This is part of a blanket that I embroidered for her,' said Florence, with a soft sadness, like she was just then remembering every hopeful stitch. 'An offcut. I wrapped her in the real blanket when she was born. It was what they took her away in – she may still have it in her possession. And she has a birthmark on her neck, just here, below the left ear. That is how you will know her, when you find her.'

With much greater deference than I'd have thought him capable of, Mimi lifted the cloth from the table and held it up, finger and thumb of each hand holding a corner, as if scared to bring too much of it into contact with his skin. He turned it this way and that, eyeing it minutely. I'd once seen a jeweller survey a diamond with much the same attitude.

'I am afraid you cannot keep it,' said Florence. 'It's all I have left . . .'

Mimi nodded absently. 'Of course,' he said. 'Can I take a sketch? I'll be quick.'

'Certainly,' said Florence.

Mimi went off to find drawing materials, leaving me and Florence to ourselves. Again, I'd an urge to go to her, sit beside her and take her hands in mine. Reassure her we'd get to the bottom of this. But I didn't want to scare her off. I knew it could happen, when I struck up a friendship with a girl. My childhood had been a saga of intimate acquaintances who'd turned cold when I'd grown too demanding of their affections. It was always better to keep a distance. Keep up my armour.

My eyes fell on my glass of gin and I picked it up for something to do. It was good and strong, with a burn to it. The smell reminded me of Papa.

'I am grateful you brought me here,' said Florence, who I now realized had been watching me. 'I feel much more at ease, knowing the man behind the name.'

'You are most welcome, Florence.'

'Why do you speak to me like that?' asked Florence.

'I beg pardon?'

'Like *that*. So formally. But not when Mimi is in the room.'

'Well,' I said, taking the time to consider my answer, 'I suppose, when I am working, I have a sort of character that I play. Charlotte Mothe the spiritist. Someone who belongs among her society employers. And I suppose I am so used to playing her in a professional context that, because you are my employer . . .'

'You know that you do not have to be her?' said Florence.

'Not around me. I would like it if you could feel comfortable enough to be . . . well, whichever Charlotte you normally are.' Then, hesitantly, she stood up and came over to sit beside me, so I had to shift over to make room for both our crinolines. 'Would you like that too?' she asked.

I didn't know quite where to look, or what to do with myself. 'Yes, I think I should like that,' I said.

'Charlotte . . .' she said, in a voice you'd use to warn a child who's about to disobey a rule.

I laughed, letting myself relax. Letting myself meet her eye. 'I'd like that,' I repeated. Held her gaze a few breaths longer.

When Mimi returned, he made a quick sketch of the pattern on the blanket. It was reasonably accurate – maybe in another life he'd have put those elegant hands to use as an artist instead. 'This is fine needlework,' he commented.

'Thank you,' said Florence.

'Did you design the pattern yourself? It's pretty.'

'I did. I wanted to incorporate her initials – see, that part represents an "S", and this part is a "J", for the surname.' She leaned forward to demonstrate. 'I thought it would be all the more special for it.'

'Oh, lovely,' said Mimi. 'What did you name her?'

It was at that moment I realized, with a horrified jolt in my abdomen, that I'd never asked that question. Not once had the thought crossed my mind that the child had a name. God, what kind of monster must Florence have thought me?

'A family name,' she replied, with a sudden, bitter laugh. 'Not that they deserved the honour in the end . . . Sabine.'

As we left, Florence took back her piece of baby Sabine's blanket and tucked it into her bosom, as if to wear it close to her heart.

I held back a moment and leaned closer to Mimi to ask, 'Is he good to you?'

Mimi thought for a moment. 'He's good *for* me,' he said at last.

I nodded and tilted my face for him to kiss my cheeks.

'What about her?' he asked as he withdrew, nodding to where Florence was waiting at a distance.

I didn't pretend not to know what he meant. 'I think she's good for me too,' I said.

Twilight was just beginning to dip as we left through the porte cochère. I always liked how it made distances merge like water-colours, so all things seemed to stand on a single plane. The perfect hour for sightings of wraiths and ghouls. Even though it'd been a fair day, the warmth was disappearing from the air now and I'd the beginnings of gooseflesh running up my arms. I hadn't realized how late we'd stayed; by the sudden hurry in her step, neither had Florence, surely now remembering that Willemijn would be waiting to let her back in. She didn't seem to want to discuss what we'd just heard about Lily. Maybe she was scared that if she spoke about it, she'd begin to hope too much.

I wondered what she'd thought of Mimi. I'd told her about him, of course – about what he was and *how* he was. But it was different to confront such people in the flesh. She'd seemed to take him in her stride; she hadn't flinched when I'd named his profession, nor at his references to it. But then, I already knew she'd a steely disposition, that she was good at hiding her true feelings. A calm demeanour didn't tell me what she felt inside. Was she truly not bothered by associating with a sodomite? Or was this tolerance only because he could give her something she needed – a decision to overlook the unsavoury so long as there was a use to it?

But that wasn't the true question, was it? No, I didn't really care what she thought of Mimi. She could despise him, for all I cared. What really concerned me, what I was truly trying to see in her reaction was – I had to admit it to myself – what she'd think of *me*. If she knew *I* was the same. Would she ignore it so long as I remained useful to her? Or would it be different, harder to overlook, due to my closeness? With the light of my inversion cast over them, would my past actions toward her begin to look suspect? What'd be worse – for her to feel disgust, or fear, or . . . even pity? Or – no, I could barely think this; it was ludicrous to place hope in such things – what if she wasn't repelled? What if she . . . Let's not get into that, Charlotte, I told myself. That's the sort of thinking that landed you in trouble last time.

And why did it matter? The fact was, it didn't make a blind bit of difference what Florence would think in the hypothetical, because Florence need never know. Let it remain unspoken. That was for the best.

So why didn't that feel like enough for me?

I only realized I must've been mumbling to myself, or perhaps staring or some other odd activity, when Florence asked, 'Are you quite well, Charlotte?'

I affected a laugh and said I'd been lost in thought, nothing more.

'Yes, me too,' Florence agreed. 'We have much to think upon.'

We were walking along the embankment now, heading for Pont Neuf to cross the river, so I was keen to keep up a conversation to distract myself. A grown woman afraid of bridges was plain silly.

'Were you ever fond of fairy stories?' I asked.

Florence didn't seem put off by this abrupt change in topic. 'I suppose, when I was a child. Our governess used to tell them.'

'I was just thinking about bridge trolls,' I said, 'wondering if one might be about to jump out to ask us a riddle.'

'Oh, I hope so. I do like a riddle.'

I cast my mind back, measuring out meter in my head as I tried to remember any I knew. 'Try this,' I said. '"I have a mouth without a tongue; I travel far but don't advance; I cannot walk, and only run; I speak no French yet live in France; my start is in start and my end is in end; and though I can fall I will never ascend."'

Florence considered, screwing up her nose in thought. 'I do not think I am familiar with this one.'

'It was one of Mama's.'

'She must have been an intelligent woman. Let me see . . . How many guesses do I get?'

'Three's the custom.'

Florence nodded as we mounted the bridge. 'Is it a French horn?' she asked.

'No.'

'"Cannot speak" . . . is it a horse?'

''Fraid not.'

A quarter of the way across. My chest was beginning to tie itself in a knot. Absolutely ridiculous, I told myself; just walk in a straight line from one end to another. Where's the danger? It was no different from walking along any other street. If I just kept my eyes on my feet and made sure not to look to the side . . .

Florence was repeating the riddle to herself. '"Travels but does not advance . . . Unable to speak out loud . . ." Then . . . perhaps it is a book?'

I shook my head. 'I think I win,' I said.

'So tell me the answer, then.'

'It's the Seine,' I said. 'The river has a mouth with no tongue; it travels from Côte-d'Or to Le Havre; the water in it runs; obviously it does not speak French; the "S" can be found in "start" and the final "e" in "end"; and water can fall but never travels upstream.'

'Very clever,' said Florence. Halfway across now. 'So, I have lost.' She sidestepped to jostle me with her shoulder, the unexpected connection sending a jolt over my skin. 'Does that mean you are going to eat me, like a fairy-tale troll?'

I risked a glance at her; she wore a wide smile that animated her features, so her face seemed almost glowing. She was close and beautiful, and I felt more drawn to her than ever, as if the narrow space between us had become magnetically charged. It was the same connection I'd felt in those early days with Eugénie, like I was a compass needle compelled to move toward a spiritist's concealed bar of iron. Surely, surely Florence must feel it too?

'Charlotte . . .' she said.

But I'd stopped looking where I was going, and – though I made it through day after day of walking on a level surface without looking at my feet – somewhere between my anxiety over the bridge and the thrill fluttering in my abdomen and perhaps just poor luck, my foot hit something uneven and I stumbled. A leap of terror went through my heart, an instant of certainty that I was about to fall to my demise, but I was nowhere near the edge and Florence immediately moved to steady me. But in the rush of activity, her gown must've become unsettled, because out of her bodice fell the scrap of fabric she'd brought to show Mimi.

For a heartbeat we both stood frozen, watching the blue-and-white square flit away in the breeze.

Then Florence let out an alley-cat yowl and sprang for it. I scrambled after her, clumsy and helpless. She was almost on it when another flurry caught it up, tossing it into the air as if by the design of some phantom hand. It skittered over the barrier. Crying out again, she dashed over, pressing herself up against the bridge wall to lean forward and look.

'Florence, don't!' I cried. 'It's dangerous – come away!' But she didn't. After a moment, I couldn't fight the morbid curiosity either and, advancing but making sure to keep my feet firmly planted, I too peeped over. I didn't see it at first and thought it'd already been lost completely, but then I spotted the flutter of blue a few feet below us and realized it was caught on one of the stone faces that decorated the outer side of the bridge.

I saw the thought cross Florence's face before she even began to move, and reflexively grasped at her forearm to stop her.

'Let go of me!' she cried, snatching herself away. 'I can do this.'

'Stop!'

'That is all I have left of my daughter, Charlotte. I will not lose that too.' There were frustrated tears welling from her eyes.

'And you'd rather drown?'

But she ignored me and grasped the top of the wall with both hands, and began to hoist herself up. Terrible images shot through my head of Florence falling to the water below. The audible smack as her body hit the surface, knocked unconscious by the impact so she couldn't fight as her clothes became water-logged, weighting her so she was sucked under, down into the darkness and the filth that'd fill her nose and mouth and lungs and steal the life right out of her. And then the horrible discovery in a day or two as some boatman pulled her out, her body now bloated and foul, the skin distended, blotchy, even become blueish if enough time had passed. The final indignity of being presented on a slab for viewing, just one in a gallery of corpses for public titillation at the Morgue, until someone was finally able to recognize her once-beautiful features beneath all that.

'Please, Florence,' I begged, too afraid to touch her again in case I unbalanced her. 'Please, just leave it.'

Again, she took no notice; she was up now, skirts and crinoline in a bunch, hoisting one leg over to the other side, ready to step down on to the narrow ledge which was all that came between the wall and the drop. At least twenty feet to fall before it caught up with you. How much time would that take? Enough time to realize what'd happened? To think a final thought? And what would that be? I wondered. Your final thought of all.

Florence was lifting her other leg now, its arc seemingly slowed by my terror in the moment.

Then a shout from the far bank. 'Hey! What do you think you're doing?' It was enough to distract Florence – she turned her head to look over her shoulder, started in surprise, and then she was toppling, toppling sideways—

I lunged, fingers catching at her skirts, unable to find purchase on the smooth material until by chance I grasped part of her crinoline. There was the sound of seams popping, but it was enough to slow her momentum and she managed to get an arm round my neck. She was heavy – heavier than she looked, what with all those high-quality garments – and I'd time to wonder if we wouldn't both end up in the Morgue, side by side on twin slabs. But then I got both arms about her waist and was pulling her to safety.

I landed on my back, Florence coming down on my chest

and forcing the breath from me. My arms released her from our embrace of their own accord.

As my senses returned, I became aware of a clamour from the right bank and, tipping my head, saw a red-faced gendarme heading our way. Presumably the source of the earlier shout. Presumably unimpressed.

Florence was already on her feet, but I was thoroughly winded and couldn't follow suit. All I could think was she couldn't be caught, else she wouldn't be home in time and her family would know she'd been out. All our plans would be ruined. 'Go!' I wheezed up at her.

There was a twist of conflict on her face, then her eyes flitted to the fast-approaching gendarme and she turned and ran.

The best I could do for her now would be to distract her pursuer. Rolling on to my side – a razor of pain in my ribs that didn't bear thinking about – I managed to get on to my knees by the time he drew level with me, and flung out a pitiful hand to halt him. As I'd hoped, he stopped, grimacing at the missed opportunity to nab his culprit but unable to run by a woman in need of help.

'There now, Mademoiselle, are you hurt?' he asked, stooping over to help me up.

My wince at the pull on my ribcage gave him his answer.

'Do you know that woman?'

'No, officer,' I said, affecting my best bourgeoise voice. 'I was just walking along when I saw her climbing the railing.'

'A madwoman?'

I hesitated. That'd be a convenient story, but the gendarme would surely have to track down a lunatic on the loose. 'No, I think she dropped something over the side,' I replied, hoping that he wouldn't think to question how I knew this.

'As if we don't have enough to do, without fishing imbeciles out the river.'

'Oh, I am sure,' I replied.

The gendarme eyed me, weighing up whether he was being mocked.

'Very well, Mademoiselle,' he said. 'Do you require assistance in reaching home . . . or a doctor?'

I assured him I'd soon be right as rain; I'd just sit on one of the benches over there and get my breath back, and then I'd manage quite well on my own. Satisfied with this, he wished me a good evening and headed back the way he'd come – clearly he saw no value in continuing a pursuit at this point. I waited till he was out of sight before inching back to the edge of the bridge and looking over the side. The square of cloth had gone, likely swept away by the breeze while we'd been otherwise occupied.

Using the bridge wall as a prop, I limped myself back to the sanctuary of dry land. As soon as I regained the street, a fresh wave of terror came over me and I had to collapse on to one of the public benches after all. I could see my hands shaking but couldn't get them still no matter how much I tried; it was like they belonged to another person.

For the bridge had brought the memory of that horrific day creeping back over me . . .

It starts with the puddles: trying not to step in them with my boots, which were a birthday gift recently enough for me still to consider them special. Sylvie holding my hand. A head taller than me, and the six years' difference between us seeming an insurmountable gap at this age. Both of us in freshly blacked dresses. Wrapped in our mourning before it's even been offici-ated. Papa's not one to waste time.

He marches ahead, toward the Morgue, and so we follow,

joined together like two stitches of black thread. That tall, long building looming ahead of us, the three central arches of limestone like teeth in a skull. Inside, thronging tourists obscure the picture windows. All I see over their heads is the back wall: cold, impassive stone, fronted with tatters of clothing that hang against it like some decayed laundry line.

Papa barges past the crowd, heading straight at an orderly. They speak together out of earshot, the orderly nodding and pointing to one of the picture windows. Papa follows his gaze.

'Why're the rags hung up like that?' I ask Sylvie, but she doesn't reply. Chewing her knuckles. Mama wouldn't like this; she's always scolding Sylvie for the habit. But Mama is . . . She's . . . Where is she?

Papa comes back for us and steers us to a window – the one the orderly showed him. A wall of glass which people press up against to look at what's beyond – and as we draw nearer, I see what that is. Slabs in a row, tilted at an angle to show us what lies upon them: people, all lined up at attention, like soldiers on parade. But unlike soldiers, they're naked – in public! I can see the breasts and private bits, and the members on the men right there in front of me. And then I start to spot the injuries. The slashed neck on one, the missing foot on another, the bruises.

There's a female one in front of us and Papa is looking at her with a strange expression.

I tug at his cuff. 'Why're we here, Papa?' I ask.

He nods at the dead woman. 'To see your mother.'

After the initial lurch of panic, my second feeling is relief. Because that ain't Mama. It couldn't be clearer to see. This bulbous, blued creature, with its peeling skin and ragged clothes; with its left cheek split to reveal maggot-like teeth; with its mud-matted hair and staring dark eyes – how could anyone mistake it for Mama?

The orderly hushes something to Papa, who nods once, curtly, then says, 'It's her.'

Sylvie lets out a high whimper and clutches at my shoulder, her fingers pressing into me so hard that later I'll find a set of bruises ripe as grapes.

'I am sorry, young ladies.' The orderly has a kind face. He stoops a little and pats me on the head. And I think, why's he saying sorry? Is it because he's caused us all this worry by leading us to some stranger's corpse, and now he's realized his mistake? 'It is hard to be without a mother,' he says. 'You must be sure to cherish your father all the more for it.' Maybe he doesn't look so much kind as simple. Yes, a very small forehead, which is well known to be a sign of idiocy. 'I will give you a moment, Monsieur,' he says to Papa.

As he steps from the room, I look up to my sister for reassurance. In a whisper, so Papa won't hear and get cross with me, I ask her, 'What's he talking about? Course that ain't Mama.' But Sylvie doesn't offer a comforting word; she stares at me blankly, her eyes filled with little red lines like cracks in a pot. 'That ain't her,' I say again.

'Don't be so stupid.'

Stupid! If anyone is being stupid, it's Sylvie, and Papa and the orderly, who're all too stupid to realize they've made a mistake. 'But . . . it ain't Mama!' I say. A bubble rising in my chest. It suddenly seems very urgent we find the *real* Mama, before it's too late, before she's gone for good. 'She ain't here, Sylvie!' My voice now breaking out of a whisper, rising in volume and pitch as I work myself up. 'We've got to find her. She'll be at home. We've got to go home right now, before she leaves. What if she gets lost? We've got to go! That ain't her!'

So fast I don't see it coming – just hear the sharp noise

of connection, then feel a blooming smart across my cheek –
Sylvie's struck me. 'Shut up!' she says. 'Shut up, shut up, shut
up!' and she keeps on shouting it, louder and louder, until it's
a roar that's crushing the breath from my body.

And then Florence at my side, and her gloved hand brush-
ing for a moment against my cheek. 'Are you hurt, Charlotte?'

'Am I . . .?' The street had returned to me. I was in the
present again, no longer ten years old, but a fully grown woman
quaking in fear of a bridge. 'Florence! What are you doing here?
The gendarme . . . And Willemijn! You have to get back.'

'I will. But I . . . I had to be sure you were not injured.' She
was flushed from running, loose hair slipping out from under
her bonnet.

I scrubbed my eyes swiftly with a sleeve. 'I'm fine. Really.
Please go.'

Her eyes flicked away from me, off in the direction she
should take. She seemed to be weighing her desire not to be
caught against her desire to . . . to what? To make sure I was
unharmed?

'Yes, I have to go,' she said at last.

But instead of getting up, she shifted closer on the bench.
I felt her breath on my face. Like a cautious vixen leaving her
earth, she glanced swiftly from side to side, then darted in to
press her lips against mine. I was neither expecting it nor prepared for it; I let the kiss happen to me as if I'd no more feeling
than a bust of marble. But then the feeling did arrive, surging
hot through my blood, and I kissed her back.

It lasted no more than a moment, and then Florence was
dashing away.

My hands continued to shake.

CHAPTER TWENTY-ONE

18 April 1866

I SPENT THE next day veering between obsessing over and trying *not* to obsess over what'd happened between me and Florence. A kiss – but what did that mean? Was it a kiss between friends? A kiss of passion? A kiss of gratitude for distracting the gendarme? A kiss in the irrational heat of adrenaline that in fact meant nothing at all? One moment I'd be certain Florence wanted me as much as I did her, and the next I'd have convinced myself the whole thing had been a hallucination.

I had this fantasy of being the one to find Florence's daughter. If our plan worked, and her family were convinced of the need to keep the child, I could deliver Florence from all of this; see her happy, and safe, and reunited with the person she loved most in this world . . .

But – a horrid, selfish thought – if Florence and daughter were reunited, she wouldn't need me any more. I felt sick with myself for even thinking it. Simultaneously: foolish for not thinking of it sooner. What'd I imagined? That her kiss was some kind of promise of a place for me once this was all over? Or had I hoped it'd never be over, that I could keep Florence dependent on my help for ever? Both were equally stupid, and the second – reprehensible.

It was near impossible to listen to Sylvie going on about her husband all day while I was in this turmoil. I wanted to scream right in her face: 'Well, at least you can talk about your problems! I've got to keep my mouth shut like nothing's wrong.' Like the bad sister holding back her toads. How was that fair? Who'd decided that was the way things should be?

I couldn't stand not knowing. Soon as Sylvie and Papa fell asleep that night, I slipped out of the house. I needed to see Florence. I needed to ask her what she'd meant – or I'd never sleep again. My veins were fizzing with a strange, excited energy, like the air before a storm.

I didn't see a soul on my walk, though it was almost two miles. The moon hid away behind banks of cloud, every now and then giving a ghost-glimmer of light, but not near enough to brighten the way. A fine mizzle was hanging in the air. The emptiness of the streets seemed an enchantment. I was thinking of the fairy magic in Perrault that sends an entire castle to sleep after the Beauty pricks her finger.

Course, I did spot the problem with my plan when I reached the garden gate and found it locked, with no Florence waiting there to greet me. Well, I'd come this far, and surely the wall could be climbed. Slinging my reticule round my neck so I'd have both arms free, I set about it.

It weren't exactly dignified, and I suffered the casualties of a grazed knee and a torn glove, but eventually I gained the top. Then down the other side, and I looked about for something to throw at Florence's window. If she was still awake, that should be enough to catch her attention. Eventually I found a twig on the lawn and aimed it up, counting carefully to be sure I had the right room. My missile skittered off the wall about a foot below and to the side. I found another stick and tried again. On about the sixth attempt, I got it dead on, and – after several tense

seconds – there was motion behind the glass. I waved and wondered if I could be seen well enough. Another few seconds, and
then the window sash went up, and Florence's head peered out.
I waved again – I didn't want to start shouting and wake anyone
else. It seemed Florence had a similar thought, as she began a
mime, pointing at me and then spreading her hands. *What are
you doing here?* A good question – and not one I could answer
at a distance. I tried to indicate two people talking, using my
hands like sock puppets. Florence considered this. She held
up her hand, palm forward. *Wait.* Then she disappeared back
into her chamber.

I stomped from foot to foot, too pent up with nervous
energy to be still. It was an age before I finally heard the creak
of the garden door, and the next moment Florence had joined
me. She was bundled up in the same blue velvet cloak she'd
worn at our first meeting – a parallel that made my heart swell.

'Come inside quickly, before you are seen,' she hissed, already
tugging me to the house. 'Please try to be as quiet as possible
on the stairs.'

She led me to a side door, which, it turned out, opened
into the servant's stair. The cramped vestibule was warm and a
little muggy, its walls painted flesh-dark so you had the impression of stepping into the depths of a living creature. A set of
bare wooden steps wound upward, barely visible. As soon as I
closed the door behind us, they disappeared completely. Maybe
I should've felt nervous and hemmed in, but in fact I found the
vestibule's smallness and darkness cosy – soothing, even. I let
myself relax a little.

When we reached the top, we emerged into the main corridor of the de Jacquinot apartments, right next to the door to
Florence's own chamber. Still struggling to see, I let myself be

led. She seated me on the soft coverlet of her bed, then, after a time, there was a tiny hiss and the leap of a match flame, followed by a more sedate newborn-candle glow.

Florence's face was summoned by the light. She stepped over and sat by me on the bed, both hands holding the candle in her lap.

'Now,' she said gently, 'are you going to tell me why you are here?'

I hesitated. Suddenly I was frightened, unable to ask her about the kiss or any of the rest of it. What if she said something I didn't want to hear? What if she said something I *did* want to hear?

Instead, when I opened my mouth, what came out was the story of Sylvie's return. I hadn't told Florence about it the previous day, but now it all spilled out – the bad memories Sylvie had brought with her; a fear I was to blame for the breakdown of her marriage; the guilty sense of relief that at least it weren't just me looking after Papa on my own now; the ghost of Mama hanging over us all. What would she think of how I was today?

'Although I never had the pleasure of meeting your mother,' said Florence, 'I do know that if she was a woman of any sense, she would be highly proud of you, Charlotte.'

But that could only be a platitude, for what'd I done to make anyone proud?

'I'm scared that . . .' I began, but the thought faltered.

'Yes?'

I was thinking of Sylvie: had there ever been a good, logical reason for why I'd needed to bring her into all of this? And even *if* there had been – then what'd been the rationale for doing it in such an underhand manner, for keeping her in the dark about my true designs on the de Jacquinots, even allowing her to begin believing in the ghost I'd created? Some hazy excuse that she wouldn't help me if she knew the extent of the game. But how did I know that? What if, instead of all this subterfuge, I'd just *asked* her? But by now it was, of course, too late. To reveal the truth to Sylvie would outrage her. It'd be the end of our plans. I'd never know what it might have been like, in that hypothetical, if Sylvie had been working with us this whole time.

'I'm scared I haven't done the right thing,' I said in the end.

To my surprise, Florence winced away from me, as if I'd caused her some harm. Her eyes, when they looked into mine, were wounded. In a quiet voice, she asked, 'You mean, in helping me?'

I realized my error too late, and leaped to correct it. 'No! Never in helping you, Florence. I'd make the same decision over again, a hundred times.'

'You really mean it.' It weren't a question; she was describing what she could read so easily on my face. I expect she read much more – I must've been doing a poor job of hiding all I felt at that moment.

The candle in her hands was tilting gently to one side, sending a pearl of wax rolling down its column. With the trail solidifying behind it, it was as if the drop was racing against paralysis; the paralysis won about midway down.

'If I tell you something silly, will you promise not to laugh?'

'I'd never laugh at you, Florence,' I said. It occurred to me, suddenly, this was the first time since the night we'd destroyed the library that we'd been truly, unrestrictedly alone together, without a wall or a family member or the need to get back to Willemijn coming in between us. It occurred to me there was nothing to keep me from kissing her myself . . . Nothing but what might happen if I did.

'I know that,' said Florence. There was the warmth of a smile in her tone. I could see it in profile: that gentle curving of her lips that brought her features to life. 'Sometimes,' she went on, 'I almost believe in her.'

It took me a moment to follow along. 'In the Comtesse?'

'Yes. No. Of course, I know her ghost is not real. That I am the one who . . . But sometimes, when I am being her, it is almost as if . . .' She laughed quietly. 'I said it was silly.'

'As if what?' I asked.

'Well, I know that I am doing and saying these things – it is not as if I am not in control of my own actions – but I feel almost as if there is something else, something . . . moving through me. Or . . . For example, there used to be a sister, some years ago, who distributed bread in the square. I would talk with her sometimes, and one day I asked her how exactly it was that God spoke to her – I was very young at the time – and she told me that it was not so much like hearing a voice as it was a sensation as she was performing an action, sometimes, that there was something larger than her telling her to do it. Not forcing her, but . . . hoping that she would.' A pause. 'I am not making sense, am I?'

Sense or not, I'd gladly have listened to her speak for an eternity. 'You mean, something's hoping you'll act as the Comtesse?'

Florence sighed. 'I do not know. No, I do not really believe that. I just mean . . . I had not thought about it before, but . . . I wonder where I got the idea for all this.'

'Well,' I said carefully, not knowing what she wanted to hear from me, 'you're a clever woman. It's no shock you'd come up with a decent plan.'

'But that is the thing,' she replied. 'I did not really . . . come up with it. It just occurred to me one day. Like a bolt from the blue.'

I knew what she was implying, but it would've been irresponsible to give her false hope – I'd been hurt enough myself by that line of thinking in the past. Instead, I shrugged. 'Then maybe it *was* God.'

A long pause, so long I started to worry I'd said something wrong. Then she smiled again and said, 'Thank you, Charlotte, for humouring me.'

She was too close. I stood up quickly and went over to the window, exaggerating the motion of stretching my legs, like that could explain my abrupt need to walk about. Something hard as a cherry stone lodged in my throat. I tried to swallow it away, but it wouldn't move. 'I . . .' I started, but then realized I didn't know what it was I wanted to say, and my words were stuck round the cherry stone in any case.

'Yes?' asked Florence. The word was urgent, expectant, and she leaned forward on her perch, as if trying to impart something to me by mental effort alone.

'What comes after all of this?' I asked.

'I beg your pardon?'

'We find your daughter, we punish your family . . . and then what?'

'Oh.'

Had the question really not occurred to her? Through all her patient scheming, had she never thought of what she wanted at the end of it?

'I suppose,' she said, 'I suppose I will go away with my daughter. Yes, I will run away. I have jewels I can sell – I know I said I would give them to you, but, perhaps, I could keep a few for myself, and raise some capital, and then . . .'

'I'll help you,' I said, the decision arriving without any deliberation. I knew I should've cared more about losing part of my fee, but somehow it didn't seem to matter any more.

Florence replied with something too soft for me to hear.

'What was that?' I asked.

'Come with me.' There was a flash of nervousness in her smile, but then she jutted her chin and said again, with more confidence, 'Come with me. It will be easier, travelling together; I will be less likely to attract unwelcome attention. And . . . my daughter – I will need help to look after her.' She spoke slowly, as if each word required a process of evaluation before it could be released, but with a growing current of excitement. 'Yes, and . . . and you are not happy with your life as it is, so why not leave it behind? Oh, Charlotte, is it not a good idea, though?'

My heart had leaped at the first words, but now that'd been replaced with a strange sinking feeling. It was almost disappointment. Because, I realized, I didn't want her to ask me along because she needed me . . . I wanted her to ask me because she wanted me.

'We can find somewhere to live, all three of us,' she went on. 'It does not have to be grand – we will fill it with beautiful embroidery together and it will feel like a palace.'

'I don't know, Florence,' I said. 'I'll have to think about it.' I turned to the window, looking at my face reflected against the night. Though I could see myself clearly, I felt almost insubstantial – maybe the exhaustion was finally catching up to me.

'You have nothing to stay for,' said Florence. Was there a chord of bitterness in her voice? I turned back to look, but she was examining a loose thread in her nightgown, her features angled illegibly downward.

'What about my father?'

'And does he deserve your loyalty, after how he has treated you?'

'I'm not thinking of his soul; I'm thinking of mine.' Because no matter what he'd done, he was my father, and to abandon your father was . . . Well, it was something that someone like Sylvie would do. 'I should go, Florence,' I said. 'I don't know why I came in the first place. I'm sorry.' The most ridiculous thing: there was the threat of tears at the corners of my eyes. Stupid, stupid; would I never learn? Because I'd done it again – hadn't I? Letting my desires run away with me and imagining reciprocation where it didn't exist. Imagining passion in a kiss that was no more than – what? A bone thrown to a loyal dog? I was nothing more than an employee to her. I was useful, that's all I was.

As for Papa, Florence didn't know the half of what he'd done. Oh, she knew how he'd punished me after what'd happened with Eugénie, but really, that could be forgiven. It weren't like I was blameless. I'd been stupid enough to fall in love and get us all found out. No, the heart of it had been that night, eleven years ago, when he and Mama had gone for an evening walk and only one of them had returned.

It'd been one of Mama's low weeks – the ones when she obsessed over all the bad things that might happen, hid from the neighbours, cried if Papa didn't take her seriously. She hadn't left the house in days. But Papa had lost his temper that evening, said she had to get some fresh air, even if he had to drag her the whole way. Ignored her pleas.

Me and Sylvie had been left waiting up, reading a story from Perrault. Toads and gold. It'd got later and later, and then later still, and then finally the sound of the door. Only one set of footsteps, and in walked Papa. Face grey, nose red. The smell of alcohol rolling off him in ripples – the first time I'd ever known him drink like that. Not the last – not by any stretch.

He'd stopped at the door. 'Go to bed, girls. There's been a terrible accident. Your mother tripped and fell off the Pont au Change. She is dead.' Then off he'd staggered, off to their room – *his* room now – as if he'd not just pierced us both straight through the heart, shattered our world in the space of one breath.

I didn't know better at that age – I was just a grieving child back then – but I've been up the Pont au Change since. I've seen the railings. They're high and they're sturdy. It'd be near impossible for you to trip and fall by accident over the side. To fall over the side, you'd need to be pushed.

'Charlotte?' Florence's voice, tethering me back to the present again. I really needed to sleep. 'I hope I have said nothing wrong?'

'No,' I said, the word so hurried it was more a gasp.

She pursed her lips. 'No. I know you, Charlotte; I can tell that something is the matter. Please tell me.'

'Really, it's nothing. And of course I'll come with you, for as long as you need me. If I'm useful.'

Now she seemed to understand my mood. 'Charlotte, I do not give a damn if you are useful. I *want* you to come.'

A swoop in my stomach. 'You do?'

She held my gaze, her eyes brilliant jewels in the candlelight. Something hung now between us in the air, heavy as lead.

Then our silence was torn by a tremendous creak just outside the door – so unexpected I nearly yelped in surprise. A moment later came a light knock, then a man's whisper. 'Florence, who is that in there with you?'

Maximilien.

Florence shot a wild, terrified look at me, then at the door. 'There is nobody here, Max,' she said, at the same moment waving a hand at me to show I should hide. I cast around. The only decent place was her wardrobe. Moving on tiptoe, I rushed toward it.

'I can hear you talking,' said Maximilien's voice.

Florence mouthed 'hurry' at me, and then, full-voiced, said, 'I was talking to myself. I am sorry – I hope it did not wake you?'

I eased open the wardrobe door, wincing at every tiny protest from the hinges. There was just enough room among the gowns – so many bright, fine gowns I'd never seen before, dresses which Florence must've worn in the days before she'd been stolen away from the world – and I pressed myself inside, scrambling to close the door behind me.

'I am coming in,' announced Maximilien. Thankfully, the noise of his opening the chamber door concealed the creaking wardrobe hinges as I finally sealed my hiding place.

'There really is no need,' said Florence, sounding perfectly relaxed.

How did she manage it? My own heart was clanging like a blacksmith at an anvil. I strained to hear past it for some clue as to what was happening. There was the shift of floorboards as someone – Maximilien? – approached my hiding place. Was he going to search the room? I cast about for a sensible explanation of why I was hiding in Florence's wardrobe, but my imaginative powers were all worn out. If he found me, I'd have nothing to say for myself. No matter the quibbling over whether Florence 'needed' or 'wanted' me, for either way I'd be locked up for sure. The wood and fine fabrics seemed already to harden around me into the stone walls of a jail cell.

'I was speaking to myself,' said Florence again. 'I was . . . reading aloud.'

'Then where is the book?'

I could picture the movement of Florence's throat as she swallowed back her fear. 'I just . . .'

'I heard another voice, Florence.'

It'd never occurred to me to look up which sentences came with my various crimes. I'd always had a superstition that knowing would invite bad luck, but it would've been comforting now to be able to say to myself, 'It'll only be five years – five years is manageable.'

'Was it . . .' began Maximilien. He paused to clear his throat. 'Florence, was that *her*? Was that the Comtesse?'

I could've sobbed with relief! Oh, thank you, good and merciful God, for delivering through Maximilien the means of his own deception.

Florence must've nodded, because the next moment there was the sound of Maximilien sitting down heavily on a chair. 'My God,' he said. His voice was a rasp.

'I did not think you would believe me,' said Florence.

'My God.' He stood again, and walked a few paces – toward her, I thought. 'She really . . . I am so . . . I am *so* sorry. I have been the most awful of—'

'Do not apologize, Max. I know that you have only ever wanted to protect me.'

'Flo, you have to believe me—'

'Peace, dear brother. There is nothing to say that cannot be said in the morning. Go back to bed. I will be quite safe; the Comtesse is gone now, and in any case would never harm me.'

There was some protest from Maximilien, suddenly reluctant to leave his sister alone with a spirit he'd not believed in only five minutes ago, but eventually Florence managed to coax him out of her room. Then came a protracted silence before she cracked open the wardrobe door.

'Are you all right?' she asked.

My pulse had slowed but I was still quivering all over with the pent-up stress – what with that and my exhaustion and the conversation Maximilien had interrupted, my emotions were up and down like a jumping jack.

'Christ, that was close.'

'You had better leave now, before he decides to come back and check on me,' said Florence. She reached into the wardrobe and snatched me out by the hand. 'Of all the nights for him to be wakeful – normally he sleeps like a hibernating bear. Come along.'

She led me to the bedroom door, then motioned for me to halt as she peeked out, candle held aloft. 'I think it is safe,' she whispered, and took my hand again and led me to the servants' stair.

We both bundled in, squeezing together on the top step, and Florence drew the door closed. There was hardly room for both of us, but I didn't descend. Not just yet. Her orange blossom smell crowded the air.

Florence pressed the candle into my hands. 'Take this down with you so you do not trip. You can leave it in the alcove at the bottom.' Her pupils flitted over my face, as if trying to absorb my image. No – not so much absorb as consume. 'Well,' she said, 'goodnight, Charlotte.'

My arm shot out to stop her leaving. I didn't mean to; it was like instinct.

We both looked down at where my hand had closed round her wrist. I could feel her pulse, like raindrops on glass.

Then she looked back up to me, amused curiosity in the motion of her eyelashes.

I didn't know if it was the excitement or the tiredness or just the simple fact of her body so close to mine, but I suddenly felt brave. Braver than I'd felt in a long time. 'I want you too,' I said, and drew my mouth to hers.

She was expecting it; her lips moved against mine without hesitation, soft and magnetizing. Her body, warm and so solid, so real. The scent of her hair. Her wrist, her pulse. Then she pulled back. A punch of disappointment at the separation – soon melting away when she took the candle and purposefully placed it a few steps down, out of the way.

CHAPTER TWENTY-TWO

20 April 1866

'WE THOUGHT WE would sit in the dining room today, if that is acceptable?' I suggested. 'The library has been proving too potent.'

Not that the move from one room to another would protect them; Florence had grand plans for us all. It was time for the Comtesse to speak.

As the family left us to unpack our equipment in private, I kept snatching glances at Sylvie, disturbed by the far-off look to her expression. I tried to place myself in her mind, to imagine her thoughts. She'd been through a lot lately, after all: the reappearance of her sister, the return to an abandoned life, being kicked out by her husband, and – of course – now ghosts were real too, according to Maximilien. I'd hardly believed my eyes when he'd turned up at our house the previous day: I'd been sure – *sure* – that he'd come to confront me about my nighttime visit to Florence. Of course he'd figured it out in the light of dawn, of course he'd realized everything. The threat of prison flashed before my eyes. Worse: the threat of never seeing Florence again. But then, by some miracle, he was apologizing for his disbelief and spilling all Florence's secrets over our kitchen table.

He weren't here this time, an absence that pricked my guts

with foreboding. I'd been horrified to hear that bastard Vasseur was back in Paris, but Maximilien's reaction had been stronger still. Who knew what state of mind he was in.

Sylvie was handling the storm glass, turning it to and fro so the liquid lapped up the sides. I'd the sense she was unaware of what she was doing; if she tilted it much further, the chemicals would mix together prematurely and ruin the trick.

'Sylvie, is everything all right?' I asked her. She didn't reply; I thought maybe she hadn't heard me, and moved closer. I put out a hand toward her shoulder, but then hesitated, unsure whether a touch would be welcomed. 'What is it?' I asked her.

This time she flinched at the sound of my voice, the storm glass slipping a little in her fingers so she had to lurch to stop it falling to the floor. She placed it carefully on the table and looked into it, as if waiting to see what crystals would form. 'Yes,' she said. 'I just . . . What are we doing here?'

I cleared my throat, mulling over the question. Course, I knew why I was there. Always for Florence. 'Our jobs,' I said at last.

Sylvie gasped out a breath – a tad hysterical, if you asked me. 'I keep thinking – it's mad – but what if . . .? What Maximilien thought he heard . . .'

Had I pushed her too far? I squashed down a pang of guilt; she hadn't cared enough to feel guilty when she'd walked out on me! So what if she was unsettled? As long as she could keep her head in front of Florence's family. I squeezed my hand round her shoulder, whispering gently, 'It's you who's always said there's no such thing as spirits, remember?'

She nodded. 'I know, I know. I just—'

'I need you to hold it together.'

There was the sound of a throat being cleared: Florence at

the door. A look of panic flashed over Sylvie's face. But we'd been speaking quietly, and anyway it didn't matter if Florence did overhear us – not that I could tell Sylvie as much.

Florence gave me a questioning look, head tilted, chin raised.

'Yes, we are ready,' I said. *I have the situation in hand*, was the message I hoped she'd read in this.

Florence fetched her family in and we set about our acts: me and Sylvie as spiritists, Florence as the spirit. As we took on our roles, my earlier fears slipped away; Charlotte Mothe was effaced by her masks. I watched us almost as if from the outside as we moved, dancer-like, about each other. Florence in particular was mesmerizing: her timidity to begin with, then the violence of possession. She was incredible. Surely there was no other person quite like her in the world.

The performance had a strong effect on the family. They were enraptured, eating the whole thing up as we served it to them. But then there was some shift – I didn't notice the moment it happened, the moment the balance tipped, but once it passed there was fear in the air. Fear bred anger.

Florence was mid-keen when the anger snapped. Ardoir ripped his hands from the circle and stood. His shoulders heaved with the deep breaths of a lost temper. 'Stop it!' he snarled. 'Stop it, girl!' Then he was up, lurching at her with his hand raised.

The hatred that flashed over me was so strong it left me breathless. I lost all sense of who I was and what I was doing, and before I knew it I was saying stupid, reckless things that were sure to get me and Sylvie in trouble. But I weren't in a state to consider the consequences; all I could think was I wouldn't let that man hurt Florence ever again. In that moment, I swear I was ready to murder him, if that was what it took to keep her safe. And I think Ardoir saw that in my eyes.

But before I could send us all down a terrible path with no return, we were interrupted by the news that Maximilien had been injured. It killed me to see the effect that hearing Vasseur's name had on Florence – I could barely wait for her family and Sylvie to leave the room before I threw my arms round her. She was trembling something awful. Hiding her face against my chest, I heard her say, 'This is all my fault, this is all my fault.' I stroked her hair, making shushing noises and wondering what to do. What possible help could I be to her now?

'No, no,' I said gently. 'How can it be your fault?'

'Max is . . . Max . . .'

'Your brother's a grown man and makes his own decisions, Florence. It's not your fault he's gone after that swine.'

'But it is! It is all in my name!'

'Anyone could do anything in your name,' I said. 'That doesn't mean you've caused them to do it. I could take my blade and stab myself right now, and claim it was in your name, but that wouldn't be your fault, would it?'

After a moment, I felt Florence shake her head against me.

'Right,' I said, moving a little away from her to give her space, producing a handkerchief.

Dabbing at her nose with this, Florence said, 'Do you think he has been injured badly?'

'That man – he was a friend of your brother?' I asked.

Florence nodded gently. 'Clement is a student of medicine.'

'Well, then, that sorts it. He wouldn't leave Maximilien's side if his life was in grave danger, would he? The fact he came personally must mean the wound's not fatal. Max will be fine.'

Florence took a deep breath in. 'I only hope you are right,' she said. 'God, I need to get out of this blasted chair.' She shoved it away, standing up and taking a few paces to lean on the table.

'There, much better.' As she spoke, she arched her back, spine curving to ease the ache of sitting so long – which brought to mind the vivid memory of her body moving against my touch, just the night before. There was sudden heat in my face, and I turned so she wouldn't see it, but of course she did.

'Charlotte . . .' she said, in a soft, tugging voice.

And because I was suddenly unable to talk about what'd happened between us, I said, 'I'm worried about Sylvie, too.'

A blank, confused expression. 'Sylvie?' she asked.

'If I overestimated her nerve. I think she's started to believe in Sabine. I wonder . . . Is it time we tell her?'

Florence winced, circling one of her feet backward and forward in thought.

'I know,' I went on, when she didn't respond, 'but what's the alternative? Leave her to have some kind of breakdown? What if she gives us away by accident?'

'Can we trust her not to give us away on purpose?'

Surely Sylvie would realize she was implicated as well and hold her tongue? That'd been the whole point of bringing her in in the first place: make her complicit so we could count on her husband's help if things got tricky. But could I still depend on Alexandre interceding now, given what'd happened between him and Sylvie?

'Charlotte.' The soft voice again, this time accompanied by Florence reaching out to me. I'd not realized I'd been mumbling to myself till she placed a finger to my lips. She gave a small tug, and I obediently stepped closer. 'We will see this through together. You and I.' Her eyes, ordinarily so pale, seemed as dark and drowning as the garden pond. Her finger trailed to my chin. I felt her breath on my face.

When her mouth met mine, that was dark and drowning

too. I was aware of nothing but her: the push of tongue on tongue, the crush of chest on chest. The air felt colder when we parted.

'You and I,' Florence said again.

Before I could gather my thoughts together enough for a coherent response, there was the sound of the door – damned Sylvie back from her quest for water.

I took a quick step away from Florence, for decency's sake, and said, 'Did you find it?'

But Sylvie's hands were empty, her hair disarrayed and her cheeks red. She stormed toward me, finger pointing. 'You!'

A chord of fear went through me. Absurd – because how could she possibly know? But it didn't matter how she knew; it was clear she did.

Then I looked at Florence and the fear melted away. Sylvie's words passed over me – oblivious to my protests – but they couldn't touch me now. How often had insults like these been hurled at me? I wouldn't take it, not any more; I was *not* deranged; I certainly hadn't done anything wicked to Florence.

I was just about to say all this to my sister, when Florence cut in: 'Oh, shut up, Sylvie.'

Who was more surprised: me or Sylvie? But I shouldn't have been; this was Florence alight with the same blaze of fierce, protective, righteous love she'd kindled through her suffering – the love which had galvanized her to defy her family; which gave her the power to shatter walls, to lie and perform and plot, never to falter in pursuit of the justice owed her; the love she had for her daughter, her Sabine . . . and now this love was turned to my defence.

'Good,' said Florence. 'Now, listen very carefully. You will not ruin this for me. Do you understand? If you breathe a word, then I will go directly to your husband, the Baron Alexandre Devereux, and I will tell him all about your plan to defraud my family . . . and give evidence of your affair with my brother.'

Sylvie, in a gesture that was almost theatrical, clutched a hand to her chest. 'How dare—'

'This is no empty threat, Baroness,' said Florence, cutting off the protest.

I could see the cogs moving in Sylvie's head now, like clockwork winding closer and closer to the chime. With each turn, her face grew more mottled.

'Sylvie, I swear I never wanted to hurt you with this,' I said. 'You've got to understand, this is all for Florence's baby; she's alive out there! Maximilien was wrong. Ardoir sent her to a woman – a baby farmer, we think.' I knew I was gabbling. 'But we've got a plan. You can't ruin it now, please! We're so close to frightening him into telling us where she is, to confessing where he sent her . . . The spirit – I mean Florence; the Comtesse ain't real – she'll tell them she can't rest till the baby's reunited with the family, and they'll have to give her back. D'you see? This has nothing to do with you at all.'

Sylvie was trying to reply, the syllables a mere wheeze. 'You . . . you . . .' I could see she was far beyond convincing. Her nostrils flared like an agitated bull's. Sucking in the air required to form words. 'You *toad*.'

I caught the reference to 'The Fairies' – it had always been her favourite. But she'd always had it wrong. 'And that makes you the golden one, does it?' I asked. 'You're gold, and I'm toads, and that's all there is to it? God, you don't even see what a hypocrite you are, do you?'

Florence put out a hand to me, rested it on my upper back in comfort.

As ever, Sylvie either didn't, or chose not to, understand me. 'Are you saying you think you have done nothing wrong?' she asked.

'I'm saying there's more than one way to look at a story. There's more than one point of view – but that's always been your problem. You can't see from anyone's perspective but your own.'

I may as well have slapped her, she looked so incensed. 'Do not dare call me selfish,' she snarled – though I didn't believe that word had actually passed my lips. But this seemed to unleash a new, merciless resolve in Sylvie. Her eyes narrowed like chips of glass and she tossed her head, as if casting something away. 'You would tell my husband?' she said, turning upon Florence. 'Very well: tell him. I have already lost all. What more hurt could it cause me? But *I* can still cause you hurt, Mademoiselle Florence. What if I tell your family what I have learned tonight? That you and Charlotte have been scheming to defraud your own flesh and blood? That the two of you engage in depraved passions? That you have been laughing at them all along? I wonder what would happen – I think you would get off lightly, Florence; you would simply be locked in your room for the rest of your life. That or the asylum. Charlotte, my dear sister, I think they would not be so kind in your case. Without my husband to intervene, how do you think the law would look upon you?' She had the air of a child that's pinned a bug beneath its finger and knows it now has sole power over that life – to free or to squash.

Me and Florence looked at one another.

'That is what I thought,' said Sylvie. 'So now I will tell you what is going to happen, and you are both going to do as I say.'

The terms were simple and clear: I'd leave with her now. When we came back next, we'd 'exorcise' the spirit. We'd claim our fee – which Sylvie would keep as sole recipient. Then we'd go, and never return to the lives of the de Jacquinots ever again.

It was like an axe to my heart: blow after blow, severing the organ from its fleshy surrounds so that all that remained in my chest was a cavity. Bloodied and hollow.

At some point – was it when we were still in the room with Florence, or did I keep my dignity till we'd at least reached the stairs? – I began to weep and couldn't stop. Sylvie was forced to prod me along, as I couldn't see where I walked. I wanted to kill her. I wanted to place my hands round her neck and squeeze and squeeze, or else take my knife and plunge it deep into her abdomen till the blood bubbled from her throat like a laugh. But Mama wouldn't have wanted that.

I weren't scared for myself. It didn't matter to me if I went to jail. What was the difference, if I'd never see Florence again either way? Freedom wouldn't comfort me at all. But Sylvie's threats against Florence – they were a different matter. I couldn't condemn her back to the miserable existence she'd endured; I had to see her freed, so she could still someday find her daughter. For her, there was still hope of escape from it all.

And so, for Florence, I complied with the sister who dared think herself golden.

CHAPTER TWENTY-THREE

25 April 1866

THE DISTURBING THING about Maximilien's new state weren't the wheeled chair, or the bandages showing through his shirt, or even his milky complexion; it was the silence. We'd been gathered in the parlour for at least half an hour, and in that time I hadn't heard him say more than ten words in total. No smart retorts, no interrogations, not even a scoff of disdain. It weren't that he couldn't speak; he'd greeted Sylvie and me politely enough on our arrival. But he seemed to have lost the willpower for it. As if the gunshot had wounded him in soul as well as body.

'The doctor says he is most lucky not to have been hit in the bone,' Madame de Jacquinot was saying, using her coffee cup to gesticulate, 'but it will still take some time for the flesh to heal completely. My poor boy – he has always been too headstrong for his own good. Thank heavens Clement was there to help.'

It was like a kind of torture to be sitting in this stuffy, claustrophobic room with Florence mere feet from me and yet utterly out of reach. She kept trying to catch my eye, but I could scarce so much as look at her; every time I did, I was struck with fresh pain.

Yet the past five days without her had been their own kind of agony, too. I'd suddenly known how condemned women at the Grande Roquette must've felt, waiting in their cells for an appointment with the guillotine's blade. Counting down the hours till my life was over. Or at least, the glimpse of life Florence had given me, when she'd talked about escaping together. Our palace filled with beautiful embroidery.

I blinked back the tears from my eyes.

'In any case,' Madame de Jacquinot was saying, 'Maximilien has insisted he is well enough for this sitting, even though I am not so sure he should be out of bed.'

'Do not fuss so, Mother,' said Maximilien, but his words were flat, with none of the bite that would've accompanied them in the past. Was he not even annoyed his mother spoke like he weren't in the room? He'd never have let that slide before. Maybe he felt emasculated, ashamed at being bested by Vasseur again, or at failing to protect Florence. I'd never thought much about him one way or another, but now I experienced a spurt of fellow feeling over this one thing we shared in common. The both of us had let her down in the end.

'I am glad that Maximilien could join us,' said Sylvie, with a charming smile. I did wonder sometimes – was there any truth behind her husband's accusations? Course, she'd never actually engaged in an affair, but maybe she harboured a secret attraction to the young Marquis. That'd make her a bit more interesting, at least. 'I do not want to tire him, however, so perhaps we should be getting along with it? If you are all ready for the task?'

At Madame de Jacquinot's agreement, we formed a ring. We hadn't sat in the parlour before, but there was a certain neatness to its being the location of this final circle – it completed the set, the last of the three interconnected rooms.

'I think it best to warn you,' said Sylvie, speaking primarily to Madame de Jacquinot and Ardoir, 'that this may be noisy or alarming. It may even be dangerous. After the previous session, I am in no doubt of the spirit's powerful potential.'

Madame de Jacquinot was wringing her hands.

'We must be brave for this short time,' said Sylvie, 'in order to make your home safe for evermore.'

'We will take the utmost precautions to protect everyone,' I assured the family, as I'd rehearsed with Sylvie. The only times she'd spoken to me these past days had been to make these preparations. Beyond that, I'd had nothing from her but a cold, judgemental silence. Like she had nothing left to say to me at all.

We set to burning sticks of sweet church incense about the room, placing Florence at the centre. As I marked out a loop of salt round her, her orange blossom scent kept finding me, twisting my stomach to knots. When I reached her feet, I left a gap for Sylvie to fill when the spirit appeared, to close the ring and trap it. I shut the lid on the salt box. Finally, I let myself look up at Florence's face. She met my gaze with a soft, reassuring expression, like I was the one needing comfort.

This done, we all assumed our places.

Sylvie took the lead this time, speaking the words of summoning. Then a long pause. A stretching expectancy. I almost started to wonder if Florence was rebelling, refusing to participate in the plan – but then there was a shift, and the spirit was with us.

'To whom am I speaking?' asked Sylvie. Straight to the point; there was no time for play.

Florence returned her gaze for a moment and then, very precisely, said, 'Sabine.'

This weren't what we'd agreed – Florence was meant to reveal that the spirit had been an imposter all along. Sylvie glanced at me; I could almost hear the race of her thoughts as she tried to work out if this was an act of insurgence or just part of the pantomime. I didn't know which it was myself. I looked forward to finding out.

'You and I both know that is not true,' said Sylvie. 'You are found out – there is no point in continuing with the deception. So, tell me, spirit, what is your *true* name?'

A pause. Then, firmer still: 'Sabine.'

Ardoir spat. 'Liar!'

Sylvie's only response was to close the ring of salt.

'It is best we do not engage her,' I said in an undertone to Ardoir. 'We are not here to question her, just to send her from this place. We must not make her angry.'

'I am not frightened of her,' said Ardoir.

'But you should be.' This was Florence. She smiled a slow, spreading smile, like treacle. Though I knew it was an act, the sight still made my breath hitch in discomfort.

'Do not engage with her,' I repeated, louder so all could hear.

Sylvie thrust her chin forward and clutched Papa's old Bible in one hand. She'd marked a page with a ribbon, which she opened now – though, of course, we'd both learned the exorcism by heart many years ago. It was from Ephesians 6: the words of Saint Paul. She cleared her throat and began to read: 'My brethren, be strong in the Lord, and in the power of his might. Put on the whole armour of God, that ye may be able to stand against the wiles of the devil.'

Florence began to laugh at this, an unpleasant, harsh rasp.

Sylvie looked up at her briefly, but continued. 'For we wrestle not against flesh and blood, but against principalities, against powers, against the rulers of the darkness of this world, against spiritual wickedness in high places.'

The laugh was more of a growl now. Madame de Jacquinot looked from her daughter to Sylvie with uncertainty. Was this how it was supposed to happen? Why did the spirit laugh?

'*Wherefore*,' said Sylvie, emphasizing the word to make herself heard over the noise, 'take unto you the whole armour of God, that ye may be able to withstand in the evil day, and having done all, to stand. Stand therefore, having your loins girt—'

Florence, who'd begun to writhe about in her seat, let out a particularly loud yap at that – I'd got to admit, I also appreciated the irony of the phrase.

'Having your loins girt,' Sylvie said again, 'about with truth, and having on the breastplate of righteousness.'

'Why is she doing that?' asked Maximilien, the worry almost returning his voice to its normal levels of animation. 'Why is she not scared?'

'And your feet shod with the preparation of the gospel of peace.'

'I do not fear your words!' cried Florence.

'Stop, stop! It is not working, do you not see?' This was Madame de Jacquinot, tugging wide-eyed at my sleeve.

'That is what she wants us to think,' I replied, though I'd no idea whether this was the truth. I was beginning to wonder whether even Florence knew what she was doing.

'Above all,' said Sylvie, her voice rising further, ringing impressively about the room, seeming almost to combine with the incense smoke in the air, 'taking the shield of faith, wherewith ye shall be able to quench all the fiery darts of the wicked.'

Finally, there was a hint of panic from the spirit. She gnashed her teeth and said, 'Shut up! Shut up, you fool!'

Sylvie was almost done, hurrying her words now to finish:

'And take the helmet of salvation! And the sword of the Spirit! Which is the word of God!'

At His name, Florence let out a horrible, ear-splitting wail, like the scream of a fox, or a child in pain. I cried out, forced to cover my ears. The screaming went on and on – how did Florence's throat take it? I could see cords standing out in her neck.

'Florence!' shouted Maximilien, and he even managed to get halfway to his feet before letting out a sob of pain and falling back into his chair, helpless.

Ardoir had also risen – but Sylvie was quick to block him with an outstretched hand. 'Do not cross the salt,' she said, 'so long as she is in the salt, we are safe. Now begone, demon! I command you in the name of God.' And she crossed herself.

The screaming stopped. Florence swayed in her seat for a second, eyes distant, and then she collapsed sideways, down on to the floor, her body colliding with the salt line and scattering it like dust.

I can't say what caused the thing that happened next. Perhaps one of the incense sticks had burned too low and, in the change to its balance, toppled over and touched against something dry – fabric or paper. All I can say for sure is that in the exact same moment Florence slumped from her chair, there was a strange whooshing noise, a flash of heat, and then all was panic as the settee burst alight.

Madame de Jacquinot immediately began to shriek, flapping at the flames with a handkerchief – only succeeding in spreading them further. I looked round wildly for something more effective, but in the next instant was nearly knocked to the floor by Ardoir as he rushed to leave the room, the whites of his eyes flashing in terror. Maximilien was blocking his path in any case, trying to call the servants for help.

Then, just as suddenly as it'd begun, it was over. Florence had emptied the remaining contents of the coffee pot over the blaze.

We were all struck silent for a moment, looking from the smouldering fabric to Florence and back again. After the turmoil of the exorcism, she was now completely placid. As if she was a different person altogether.

Some hours later, when me and Sylvie returned home with the scent of smoke in our hair and garments, I recalled I'd been careful to place the sticks of incense each on their own china plate, precisely to avoid such an accident. And I thought, what if there'd been another presence in the room with us after all? A presence both unseen and angry.

CHAPTER TWENTY-FOUR

16 May 1866

I SHOULD'VE FOUGHT Sylvie; I should've railed against her till she was forced to let me see Florence. Maybe there was a time I'd have done so, but I still feared what she'd do, feared the power of the secrets she held over our heads. She weren't about to let me forget it, either. Practically every waking minute of the day, she was there, breathing down my neck, questioning each little thing I did. It was all, 'What do you need ink for – are you writing to someone?' and, 'Why did your boots move? Did you go out while I was at the market?' The worst part of it was, she was imagining the lot of it. I didn't even try to escape her. I just gave up.

When she wasn't guarding me, Sylvie spent most of her hours composing long, densely written letters to her husband. I didn't know what was in them. He never replied as far as I was aware.

Time passed. A series of unseasonably cold, despondent May days. I sewed shirts for a pittance. I tended to Papa, watching helplessly as he wasted away. There was a constant ache right at the centre of my chest.

Then Mimi came to call.

I was in the middle of changing Papa's sheets when we heard the knock, and so it was Sylvie who went to answer. I paid it no mind at first; the only person to visit us was Adèle, though she normally walked right on in. But then I recognized the voice in the hallway, cast the bedding aside and rushed out before Sylvie could send him away.

'My, my,' Mimi was saying, 'what a long time it's been!'

Sylvie didn't respond with such fond nostalgia. 'What on earth are you doing here?' She'd angled her body to block the corridor.

Mimi looked her up and down. 'Some way to greet an old friend,' he said. 'I could ask the same of you, Baroness.'

'This is my family home.'

'Well, that's *wonderful*, 'cause I'm here to see your family. Specifically, your sister. Charlotte, I can see you there in the depths! Will you call off the guard dog, please?'

'Oh, for Christ's sake, Sylvie, let him in,' I said. 'Or ain't I allowed *any* visitors?'

It was quite possible this was Sylvie's intention, but Mimi grew tired of waiting and squeezed past while her attention was on me.

'Excuse me!' snapped Sylvie – but it was too late; Mimi was already in the house. I saw her deflate as she realized it'd be more trouble than it was worth to expel him.

Kissing me in greeting, Mimi used the activity as cover to whisper, 'What's all this, then?'

'Not now,' I hissed back, eyes on Sylvie. Hassle be damned, Mimi would *definitely* be ejected if Sylvie realized his involvement in our scheme.

Mimi winked in understanding. 'Let's leave the Baroness in peace, shall we?' he said, already setting out toward my bedroom.

'Wait a minute,' said Sylvie. 'You cannot mean to speak to her in private?'

Mimi turned back and pursed his lips. Rouged, of course.

'Oh, I'm sorry, Sylvie, but didn't you just say this is your family home?'

'Yes.'

'So it *ain't* the Bastille?'

Sylvie's mouth formed a tight little line, emphasizing the hairline wrinkles that were beginning to assert their presence. She crossed her arms but didn't say anything further.

Mimi smiled at her and turned to continue on his path.

'At least—' said Sylvie, before cutting herself off. A blush for some reason climbing her cheeks. 'At least not the bedroom. Sit in the kitchen, if you must.'

It took a moment, but when I realized why she was blushing I couldn't help but laugh. ''Cause it would be inappropriate for me to be alone with a man in a bedchamber? My God, Sylvie, what do you think we're intending to *do*?'

The blush grew brighter.

'We can use the kitchen,' said Mimi, with a shrug. 'A table or a bed – it's all the same to me, darling.'

Without another word, Sylvie stormed into the kitchen, letting the door swing behind her with a decisive *crack*. Giggling like schoolfellows, me and Mimi went through to the bedroom.

Once the door was closed, though, I realized now I'd got to tell Mimi all that'd happened. A sobering thought.

Quick to make himself at home, Mimi swung down on the bed, sprawling out like a cat in the sun. 'So . . .?' he said.

Perching on the bedspread next to his toes, I told him how Sylvie had discovered me and Florence were working together – that is to say, I told him only *that* she'd discovered this, rather than the circumstances of it – and her reaction. The 'exorcism', the end to communications, how I was now prisoner in my own home. Mimi listened attentively; he was a good listener.

Sometimes when I spoke to men, I got the sense they weren't so much engaging as waiting for their turn to speak – as if they didn't see conversations with women as an exchange, but just a backdrop to show off against, or an opportunity to impart a lesson and assert themselves as the higher intellect. Not with Mimi: he made you feel like what you'd got to say had intrinsic value. I was never sure if this was a personality trait or a skill learned from the years of men whose own showings-off he'd had to endure. Whatever the cause, he knew exactly when to nod, when to make a noise of comfort.

Then, when I'd finished – and only then – did he speak. 'What're you going to do about it, then?'

I blinked at him. '"Do about it"?'

Mimi propped himself up on an elbow to look me in the face, one eyebrow raised in a curious arch, elegant and interrogative at once. 'You don't mean you want to give up?' he asked.

This made me cross for some reason – the simplicity of the statement, as if it was somehow a failing on my part. 'Don't say it like that! There's no question of "want to" in it. What choice have I got?'

'Of course, of course, Mademoiselle Maudlin,' he replied, nudging me with a toe.

I chopped one-handedly at his foot, but he moved it out of reach too quickly so I ended up thumping the bed instead.

Sighing, Mimi swung his legs down to the floor so he was sitting upright beside me. 'All I mean to say is I don't see why it has to be over. So Sylvie's upset with you. What's new? She's got no actual power, you know; she can't stop you from doing what you want.'

'She could tell Florence's family what I am,' I replied. 'A fake.'

'Not without implicating herself.'

'A sapphist.'

Mimi snorted. 'I don't think Sylvie's capable of thinking the word, let alone saying it.'

I leaned my head against his shoulder. Let the bright scent of his perfume comfort me. 'What am I going to do?' I asked.

Mimi patted my arm. 'Well, that's a decision you'll need to withhold till I've told you why I'm here.'

It hadn't occurred to me that Mimi had a specific reason to visit – besides wondering why he'd not been paid yet, that was. I tilted my chin to look up at him.

'I've found Mère Ancelot.'

This made me sit up straighter. 'And?'

'We had a little chat. A couple of years ago, Florence's grandfather writes to her, looking for someone to take a baby off his hands. Mère Ancelot gets an annual payment, Ardoir gets rid of a problem – everyone's happy. Apart from the baby, 'cause I've seen the state of that place and no child is thriving there. But no matter: they're just unwanted bastards, right? Now, this servant, this Lily, is meant to bring the baby when it's born. But she never turns up. All right, thinks Mère A, so he's changed his mind. It happens. Until she gets her fee from Ardoir all the same.'

'So the Comte still thinks the baby's with Mère Ancelot?'

'She's hardly going to point out the error, is she?'

'And, what, Lily *stole* the child?'

Mimi shrugged. 'I really don't know. But we're going to find out, if we can track her down. After all we said about her being the easier one to find, it's like she's disappeared without a trace. Can you share all this with Florence?'

I shook my head. 'Out of the question. Sylvie . . .'

'Even for this?' asked Mimi, eyebrows rising. 'Yes, she must feel betrayed, but can't she put that aside?' He regarded me, eyes flickering over my expression. 'Unless . . . there's something else?'

I hesitated – but who was Mimi to judge? 'It weren't just the lies about the spirit. Florence is . . . *was* my sweetheart. Sylvie knows.'

'And she found this out . . .?'

'In the worst way.'

Mimi let out a long sigh and patted my hand. 'Then I'll try to find Lily,' he said, 'and let you know as soon as I've got anything new. Listen, Charlotte: Sylvie will back down eventually. Nobody can stay mad for ever.'

But if anyone could, it'd be my sister.

CHAPTER TWENTY-FIVE

22 May 1866

AFTER MIMI'S VISIT, Sylvie did in fact let up on some of her rules; she'd clearly realized she couldn't keep me under lock and key for ever. Suddenly, I was allowed out of the house on my own – though only on specific errands.

One such trusted mission was to call on the physician at the hospital. It'd been almost two months since he'd come out to examine Papa, and things had deteriorated so quickly since then. Papa barely left the bed any more. He couldn't feed himself – couldn't seem to line up his hand with a spoon, a spoon with his mouth. Some days, when he looked at me, it was clear he'd forgotten who I was.

'Charlotte?' he'd said, when I'd reminded him that morning. 'No, I was just playing with her in the park. Oh, you should see her little ribbons.' Then he'd smiled so tenderly, like I hadn't seen him do in over a decade.

When I told the physician all this, the first thing he did was hand me that damned handkerchief again. It turned out his initial estimate of 'half a year' had been over-optimistic. Each patient was so different, he said, you just couldn't predict with full accuracy. But if he were going to make a new guess now, the figure would be in weeks.

I took the handkerchief.

This was the first time I'd properly cried about it all, and once I'd started, I couldn't seem to stop. I sat myself down on a bench in the corridor and let these great, heaving sobs take me over. It wasn't just Papa – I'd let everyone down. I'd failed to save Florence and her baby. Sylvie couldn't stand me. Even Mama would've been disappointed: a spiritist was meant to *help* people; that's what she'd always taught us. All I'd done was cause problems. And now I was right back where I'd started: about to be left all alone.

'Is everything all right, Mademoiselle?'

I'd barely registered the approaching footsteps. Quickly giving my eyes a scrub, I looked up to see a young man standing over me. He seemed familiar somehow . . . but I couldn't think why.

He must've been wondering the same thing, as he drew up short and said, 'Ah, have we met before?' Then a flicker in his eye as he worked it out. 'Yes, you are the sister of Madame Devereux, are you not? I do not believe we have been introduced. I am Clement Diagne.'

I placed him at last: he'd been the one to bring news of Maximilien's duel on that fateful night, though I was surprised he'd recognized me from then. Maybe I resembled Sylvie more than I'd thought. I let him take my hand, slipping into character by reflex even as my chest tightened at the reminder of my time with Florence. 'Charlotte Mothe.'

'May I sit?'

At my nod, Clement perched on the bench at a polite distance. He didn't say anything further. Still, it was comforting to have some company. In the silence, I tried – and failed – to blow my nose discreetly.

After a few minutes, Clement nodded in the direction of the physician's office door. 'I hope you are not unwell?'

'No – my father.'

'I am very sorry to hear that.'

'Thank you. And yourself?' I asked quickly. If we got into all that, I'd only start blubbering again.

'I was attending a lecture. I am a medical student, you know?' Florence had mentioned something like that, now that it came to it.

'And you are a friend of Maximilien's?'

'His closest.' There was an admiring warmth in his voice, more than Maximilien probably deserved. I was just trying to work out a way to ask after Florence, when Clement added in an undertone, 'Forgive me for bringing this up, but I believe you were there that night he got himself shot. I hope it did not cause you too much distress? It seemed to me that I was interrupting some kind of gathering.' His words were casual, but I could tell what he was angling at. So I weren't the only one that wanted information.

'Not at all,' I said.

Clement waited a moment for me to say more, then decided to try head on: 'Look, Maximilien is my dearest friend, so I know when he is hiding something from me. What is it exactly that you have all been up to in secret?'

'I am afraid I have no idea what you mean, Monsieur Diagne.' Truth told, I did consider telling him all of it; let the gossip spread and see Florence's family and Sylvie down in the muck. But it would've been poor revenge – many members of society dabbled in spiritism, and the ghost was officially gone now, in any case. Besides, hadn't I done enough damage to everyone's lives already?

'Of course not,' he replied. 'And I imagine you have no idea why the family have suddenly decided to open their doors to society again?'

My ears pricked at this news. 'I beg your pardon?'

'The party to celebrate Florence's twenty-first birthday. Forgive me – I assumed you had been invited. It seems just about everyone else has.'

'A party? Then she is well?' I felt like a starved man snatching at crumbs.

Clement considered this. 'She has been in much improved health this year, it is true, although I fear she has been set back by what happened to Max. She has not been herself at all, these past few weeks.'

Another tightening in my chest as I wondered if it was all Maximilien, or if it was partly down to her missing me. 'Did he get a shot in himself?' I asked in the end.

'Max has always been a lousy aim.'

'And your friend Vasseur?'

Clement shook his head in disdain. 'Any friendship I once had with Vasseur was ended the moment he behaved in such a reprehensible manner to Mademoiselle Florence.' He looked at me askance. 'You know something of Max's quarrel with him already?'

'I have had the story from Florence in full.'

He raised his eyebrows at this; clearly he knew enough of the unsavoury details to be surprised I'd know them too. 'Indeed? Then you must be aware that once Vasseur refused to do the so-called honourable thing and propose, he was strongly encouraged to leave town by Comte Ardoir.'

That was one way to put it.

'As far as we were all concerned, he was gone for good. Then Max learned Vasseur had returned . . . Now, I adore Max, but I am not blind to his flaws, and I will say that rashness is one of them. He immediately tracked down Vasseur and demanded satisfaction. The first I heard about it was when Max appeared at my door telling me I was to act as his second – he would not even name the opponent! I tried my utmost to talk him out of it, but in the end I had no choice but to agree and hope I could at least keep him from bleeding out when he got himself shot.'

Clement stopped talking as a nurse hurried past, then lowered his voice further. 'That afternoon, we took a cab to the Bois de Vincennes. It was then that I learned the identity of our foe. I could not believe Max's lack of foresight: if Vasseur turned up dead, it would surely come back to us, given our history. I think Vasseur was counting on that insurance when he decided to return to town. But again Max refused to listen to reason. He had it in his head that he had failed Mademoiselle Florence before, by allowing her attacker to get away so lightly, and of course she has had such a hard time of it since.' He paused, sighing. 'I have always regretted what happened to her. I was also unwilling to see Vasseur for what he was until he hurt someone I cared about . . . But Max seemed to think that if he could just kill Vasseur this time, everything would go back to the way it had once been. How he thought it would help Mademoiselle Florence to see her brother jailed for murder, I have no idea.

'Anyway, he took his paces and Vasseur immediately got him in the ribs. Max wounded an innocent tree. I should not say that – I should pretend he put on a good show, but anyone who has seen him shoot would know I was telling a lie. I went immediately to Max's side and tried to staunch the bleeding. Do you know what the idiot asked? "Did I kill him?" When I told him the truth, he became entirely insensible. I had to enlist Vasseur's man to help carry him to the main road so we could send for an ambulance.'

'And what of Vasseur?' I asked again.

'I reported him to the authorities for attempted murder. The last I heard, he had been arrested and was awaiting transportation. So I suppose, in a way, we did manage to achieve some form of justice for Mademoiselle Florence.'

'Good. She deserves some peace.' I couldn't keep the passion from my voice.

Did Vasseur's arrest make up for all the times Maximilien had refused to listen to her? For the pain he'd let her suffer? I wondered if she'd forgiven him. But then, it must be hard not to forgive someone who'd go to prison in your name.

'Are you a close friend of hers, then?' asked Clement. 'I saw you at her side, that evening.'

'Her friend, yes.' The understatement bitter as bile on my tongue. 'And you? You said just now that you care for her, too?'

This flustered him like anything. 'I did not mean . . . That is to say, she is a very special young woman, but I was referring to—'

'Maximilien?'

There was a moment – just a moment – of panic in his eyes, as if he'd given away more than he'd meant to. Someone like Sylvie probably wouldn't have caught it, but I recognized it; I'd felt the same thing plenty enough. I saw Clement realize I'd understood him, then understanding me in return.

'I see,' he said, with a slow smile. 'If you will excuse me, Mademoiselle Charlotte, I really must get back now, but you should come to Florence's party. It is the Tuesday after next. I am sure you would have received an invitation had she been the one to write them. Come as my guest, if you like.'

With that, he was away, and I hotfooted it back home as well. As I marched through the streets, I wondered why Madame de Jacquinot would want to host a party after all that'd happened. All I could think was that it was a statement. The family were announcing to the world: 'Those times are over; this is a new time.' The epigraph to a new chapter. Hadn't we ourselves told them a poltergeist was attracted to the negative energies in a house? So now they were bringing life back into the dwelling. Hell, maybe my joke at the beginning of all this – that the Comtesse would convince the family that true wealth was located in the love they had for one another – had come to pass.

Whatever the case, a party was the perfect way to speak to Florence without her family getting suspicious. And I *had* to see her again, even if it was only to tell her what Mimi had found out, to ask if she'd got any idea where to find this Lily. I had to help her. But that left the problem of how to get there. No point in lying to Sylvie – she'd see right through that – and her threat to expose Florence still hung too heavy over my head to risk sneaking out. No, I'd have to find a way to convince her instead.

'Of course we cannot go.'

A slicing disappointment cut through my chest at Sylvie's verdict: the same cold, gasping feeling that comes after running too fast on a frigid day. It'd been stupid to expect anything else, but I'd started kindling a hope in my heart even so.

'But isn't this good news, Charlotte?' Sylvie went on.

'How d'you mean?'

'I know you were . . . attached to Mademoiselle Florence. But now you can see that she is moving on with her life, and you can move on with yours.' She smiled and patted my hand.

I resisted the urge to slap her. 'Move on?'

'You see why they are hosting this party, do you not?' I must've looked suitably mystified, as she said very slowly, as if speaking to a child, 'They are seeking a suitor, of course. For Mademoiselle Florence.'

Of course. What better way to solve the trouble both with Florence *and* with their finances? This party was a second 'coming out' – a reminder to all the bachelors of Paris that Florence was as yet unmarried.

Florence married.

I only just made it to the sink in time.

'Oh, really!' said Sylvie, turning away as I retched. 'Well, what did you think would happen?'

What *had* I thought would happen? That if I gave it enough time, all would be well? That the rules of the world would change overnight?

Turning away from the basin, I wiped my mouth with the back of my hand. 'I need to go,' I said.

'You know we cannot. We have not even been invited.'

'Clement invited us.'

'Clement is not the host. Honestly, Charlotte, I am only thinking of what is best for you.'

A bitter laugh escaped me.

Sylvie pressed her lips together. 'Why do you find it so hard to believe?'

''Cause you never think of anyone but yourself. You don't care about my feelings at all.'

'And what about you? You seem to have forgotten that I have just lost someone very important to me too. Alexandre threw me out because of something that I did to help *you*. Because you asked me to do it. Even though you were lying to me the entire time! So do not think that I cannot understand how you are feeling; I have lost my *husband* because of you.'

So she was blaming me for all this mess! Like a river bursting its banks, the full anger I'd been suppressing for years swept over me. 'I remember how you left me for him!' I cried. 'Left me with Papa. Even though I begged you not to. When you'd seen him beat me all to bruises. When you knew what he was like. What he did to Mama.'

Sylvie shook her head at me sadly – almost pityingly. 'You have to stop blaming him for that. God knows, I blame him for so many things, but—'

'Stop blaming him? The man who pushed our mother to her death?'

'Charlotte, you know that's not what happened.'

'I am no—'

'She jumped, Charlotte.' Sylvie's voice was softer now. She moved closer to me, took my hands in hers. 'I know that it is hard to accept, but you have to face up to the truth.'

'No,' I said. My head was shaking back and forth of its own accord.

Sylvie was still speaking. 'Maybe Papa made her miserable. Maybe *we* made her miserable, too. I do not know; I have tried and tried to understand what she was thinking, but I cannot. All I do know is that she jumped from that bridge. She *chose* to jump.'

Yes, Mama had had her bouts of melancholy. Her sudden terrors. The premonitions of horrible things to come. But she'd also had us – me and Sylvie. She wouldn't have left us on purpose, would she?

In my mind's eye Mama was watching me, and on her face was the same pitying expression as Sylvie wore. 'I am sorry, Charlotte,' she said.

'No!' I said again. I yanked my hands free from hers – but then Sylvie was hugging me, keeping hold even when I struck her with an elbow in the chin.

'Shh,' she said. 'Shh. I know, Charlotte, I know.'

To my embarrassment, I was crying again, ten years old, in the arms of my big sister. I let my head fall against her chest.

'I have not always been perfect, but you must know that I love you. Everything I have done, I have done out of love. To protect you and keep you safe. I never would have left you if I had truly thought Papa was responsible for Mama's death.'

And I think she really did believe herself. I lifted my face to see her properly. 'Then please, Sylvie. I need . . . to say goodbye to Florence. Just let me go to the party, speak to her once more. Then it will all be over, I swear.'

Sylvie gave me a long look.

'I swear.'

Perhaps people really could change, because, maybe for the first time in her life, Sylvie surprised me. 'Very well, then,' she said. 'If it was Alexandre, I know that I would ask the same of you. But, Charlotte, listen: you speak with her, and then we leave. And then you never, ever stir this up again. You must see that there can be no other ending to this story?' Her face softened. 'Believe me, I wish for your sake that there could.'

CHAPTER TWENTY-SIX

5 June 1866

ARE ALL HOUSES like the families that live in them? As I stood looking up at the de Jacquinot house, I got to thinking that it was like the de Jacquinot family. Not Florence, of course – never Florence – but the rest of them. Antiquated, for one thing. Steeped in the mud of the Marais – all that historic dirt clinging to them like muck on a toad. The grand mansion now diminished, shrivelled into a single floor. Secrets partitioned away behind dividing walls. Crumbling plaster and the smell of dry rot, poorly concealed with lavender bags.

So which came first? Had the de Jacquinots transformed to fit their home, or had their home transformed to fit them?

Our home had transformed. When I looked back on my childhood, I remembered the range lit and candles burning, always bright enough and warm enough to chase out the rain. The comforting haze of paraffin. Mama showing us how to tourniquet our arms till the veins leaped up and our fingers swelled. A quick dip into the bowl of hot water and wax, then plunge into the bowl of cold. Mama loosing our bindings and gently peeling off the fresh-made spirit moulds, her sleeves turned up and that raven hair gathered under a cap to keep it off her face. Papa whittling in his big chair. Solid walls, well-kept furnishings – nothing expensive, of course, but all clean and polished and tidy. I used to imagine this was how bees felt in their hives, cosy and safe, far beyond the reach of anything that could hurt them. And then later, after Mama, those rooms had become disorganized and dirty. Small and mean.

But now, the interior of the de Jacquinot apartments was like I'd never seen it before; suddenly the dead house had been reanimated. The closed doors were thrown open, the dark dusty corners swept out and illuminated with yet more lanterns, the drab furniture polished to a gleam. It was like the de Jacquinots thought this was enough to expel anything that still haunted them. Exorcizing their morbid isolation along with their ghost.

I was looking for Florence from the minute we entered. Was she well? Was she safe? Was she missing me?

'Be careful,' said Sylvie. For a moment I thought she meant emotionally, like she had seen into my thoughts – but then I realized she was warning me about a close-passing waiter with a tray of drinks.

I stepped aside, swiping a glass of wine as I did so. I drank down half in one mouthful. I was very ready to have a fuzz between me and the world.

In the week leading up to the party, I'd thought long and hard about what I'd say when I saw Florence again. But then Mimi had complicated my plans. That very morning, he'd sent a note:

> Found LM. When can you get away from S? Need to see you
> & F together. Name time & place.
>
> M.

Had we found Lily Masson, and therefore baby Sabine? Could we reunite Florence and her daughter at last? I'd immediately

298

sent a return message with the newsboy, telling Mimi to find Florence and me in the de Jacquinots' garden at ten o'clock. Whatever happened, we had to make that rendezvous. It was eight o'clock when me and Sylvie arrived, so that gave me a couple of hours to locate Florence, lose my sister, and escape into the garden to meet Mimi.

I felt time dripping away like candlewax. How long had it been already? Five minutes? Ten? Sylvie was guiding me about by the elbow like she didn't trust me to choose my own movements. Yes, she'd allowed me to come here to say my goodbyes, but she'd be damned before she left me to run free.

In the dining room, the table had been pushed against one wall to make a sideboard and the chairs were lined up on the edges, leaving a space that threatened to be used as a dance floor later.

We twisted round a circle of men in friendly debate, and now I finally caught a glimpse of our hosts. The whole family was in a cluster over by the garden window, Florence at the centre, like they'd closed ranks about her.

It was enough to stop my breath, finally setting eyes on her again after all these weeks. She had on a sapphire gown, low at the shoulder and elegantly silhouetted. She looked beautiful, a splash of brightness against the daguerreotype of the room: the deep blue of her dress, her pale face and fair brow, her glowing red hair coiled and gemmed.

I tried to catch her attention, but she was preoccupied, looking away from me and out over the garden. Losing Sylvie aside, it seemed like an impossible task to get Florence away from her family and this thicket of party guests. I wondered where they'd found all these friends after so long hiding from society. But then I noticed the answer. There were lively discussions – but not with the de Jacquinots. People laughed – but they didn't laugh round the de Jacquinots. It was as though instead of ending the house's self-imposed quarantine, the family had merely withdrawn the radius to just around them. Like an invisible ring of salt. And the guests, just like spirits, weren't able to cross. Of course, they acknowledged the de Jacquinots – people cast them nervous half-glances, or passed a word or two with them – but no one was here to spend time with the hosts. No, these guests were here to observe. To see the fabled family and their house that'd been shut up for so long. To carry titbits back to their own households like a mother bird to her chicks. *Oh yes, the Dowager Marquise was looking old. They say the girl is no longer a lunatic but, my word, I could still see it in her eyes. The son was shot, did you know? Yes, that is why he has that cane in hand. And did you see the fresh plasterwork in the library? I wonder if they have had the damp. Well, I heard there was a fire! I wonder if the whole house is secretly rotting around them. They are an attractive family but there is something stand-offish about them, and really, I am very glad that they only host once in a blue moon.*

Not that any person was saying such a thing out loud; but it was there all the same, bubbling beneath the surface conversation.

Sylvie tugged at my arm. 'Come on, Charlotte.'

'No.' I dug in my heels like a donkey that refused to be led. 'I want to speak to her.'

The tug became a pinch. 'You will have to wait until you can catch her alone. Be sensible; we do not want to risk the others sending us away, do we?'

'Let go!' I said, this time louder. The circle of debating men slid their eyes curiously in my direction, but I hadn't time to see if Florence had noticed me before Sylvie won out; to protest any more would've required a proper brawl, and I didn't want to get into that. Not yet, at least.

Back in the parlour, I grabbed another glass of wine before we got ensnared in conversation with some poet who kept quoting himself to us. After that, it was a disagreement on Mexico, and then Victor Hugo's latest novel – though our companions were less concerned by its literary merits than whether or not it was unpatriotic to read an exile's work. I was well out of my depth with these people; the way they carried on was enough to make me consider fleeing to Guernsey myself. Now, there was a thought. A little cottage on Guernsey with a view of the sea. That'd be plenty big enough for two women and an infant.

Focus, Charlotte. Don't get carried away.

A fresh couple soon appeared in our proximity – a lavishly dressed woman and a plain man.

'Sylvie, darling!' cried the woman. Wriggling away from her partner, she dashed forward. 'I did hope you would be here!'

In the flurry, I managed to slip my arm away and gain a small freedom.

'My, what a delight to see you,' replied Sylvie, her voice taking on that plummy drawl she used to show rich people she was one of them.

I cleared my throat; if my sister insisted on having me at her side all evening, let her acknowledge me in her social circle for once.

'Oh, yes,' said Sylvie, with only a trace of alarm. 'May I introduce . . . my cousin, Mademoiselle Charlotte Mothe. Charlotte, these are my dear friends, the Vicomte and Vicomtesse Coupart.'

'Cousin?' asked Madame Coupart, smiling widely. Now she was up close, I realized that what I'd taken for a fur muff had big watery eyes and a lolling tongue, and was in fact a dog. It caught me looking and let out a low grumble. Madame Coupart rocked it a little to quiet it down, and said, 'And this dear baby is my little Gévaudan. Now we have all met. But Sylvie, you have never mentioned family before!'

'They live in the countryside,' said Sylvie, and glowered surreptitiously to let me know just what'd happen if I contradicted this story.

Madame Coupart examined me curiously, no doubt noticing I was in one of Sylive's gowns – its hem let down and the waist far too loose. It was clear I didn't fit with the other guests. 'Is that where you have been, then, Sylvie – staying with family? We had no idea what had happened to you – only that strange letter, and then it was as if you had disappeared from the face of the earth! Your husband simply refused to tell me. He just said you were on "a trip". There were rumours that you had been packed off to some sanatorium.'

'Well, I . . .' Sylvie swallowed. She was hiding it well, but I knew this conversation must've been torture for her. I'd been so caught up in my own misery, I'd barely stopped to feel too guilty about my hand in ruining her marriage, but here was the reminder. 'Yes, I have been with family. I am not sure why Alexandre felt the need to be so mysterious about it.'

Madame Coupart tinkled a laugh and placed a hand upon Sylvie's shoulder. 'We have so much to catch up on, my dear. Mademoiselle Mothe, you will not mind if I steal away your cousin, will you?'

Sylvie glanced at me, torn between the demands of friendship and her job as my jailer. 'My cousin is—'

'I would be pleased to keep Mademoiselle Mothe company if you ladies wish for a moment in confidence,' said Coupart.

This seemed a fair solution, and after a few ticks Sylvie slunk off with her friend, leaving me to Coupart like they were guards changing shifts. Well, at least this guard might be easier to slip.

I smiled thinly at him. 'Would you be so kind as to remind me how you are acquainted with my cousin?'

Coupart launched into a dull and muddled story about some estate in Lozère and a belligerent relative, from which I gathered he worked with Sylvie's husband. I let my eyes wander about the people in the room, not taking the trouble to hide my opinion of his conversational skills. At least the other guests provided a varied distraction. A woman in a lurid pink gown, so tightly laced that veins showed stark on her pushed-up bosom. Two red-faced men smoking and whispering together. A milk-white old lady letting out owlish shrieks of laughter. And there – Clement Diagne. His eyes lifted and met mine, which he must've seen as an invitation, as he began to weave across the room in our direction.

'Most strange to see the rooms so full of life, is it not?' he asked by way of greeting.

Coupart looked round to see who'd spoken, then beamed in genuine pleasure. 'Clement, my dear man!'

'Wonderful to see you,' said Clement, pumping Coupart's hand. 'And Mademoiselle Charlotte, so pleased you could make it.'

Angling himself to cut me out of the conversation, Coupart interrupted, 'Now, Clement, I promised my wife I would ask you all about how the young de Jacquinot got that injury of his. I hear it was a duel, and you were his second, no less?'

Clement's smile didn't quite reach his eyes. 'Only after trying my utmost to convince him out of it.'

Coupart nodded sagely. 'Quite so. Such a spirited young man, but it is no way to solve a problem. Now, take my trouble with the Lozère estate—'

It seemed Clement was as tired of hearing about this as me, as he quickly cut in to say, 'Yes, you make an excellent point, Guillaume. Look, sorry to do this, but actually I have promised Mademoiselle Charlotte to show her something in the library. I will find you later and tell you all about the duel; I give my word.'

I could've kissed him, if it hadn't been for the fact that neither of us would have enjoyed that.

'You looked like you needed saving,' said Clement, once we were out of earshot of Coupart.

The workmen had done a good job repairing the plaster in the library – once the paper had been remounted, nobody would be any the wiser about what'd happened in here. I could still summon the satisfying feeling of smashing up the walls, still see the look on Florence's face. Her heavy breathing, her delight that glowed bright as moonshine.

'I must confess to an ulterior motive,' Clement went on. 'You never did tell me what you were doing here, the night of the duel?'

No point keeping it from him at this point, and I did owe him one – or two, now I thought of it. 'All right,' I said. 'If you really want the truth? We were consorting with the dead. I am a spirit medium.'

Clement stared at me for a number of seconds, and then burst into laughter.

'You don't believe me?'

Wiping his eyes, he waved the other hand to dismiss the question. 'No, no, that is not it at all. It is just that now I understand why Max would not tell me anything about it! Oh, he would be so embarrassed if anyone were to find out.'

'You won't tell, will you?' I asked, suddenly worried this would get back to Sylvie.

'He would never forgive me for that. The secret is safe in my hands.' He'd sobered up a bit now he was over the surprise. 'I really am glad that you could make it tonight. Have you managed to speak with Florence yet?'

I shook my head.

Clement raised his eyebrows. 'But then why on earth are you still talking to me? Go and find her!'

I didn't need telling twice. Thanking Clement, I headed for the last place I'd seen her, the dining room, eyes searching for a flash of red. She wasn't there; in fact, I couldn't see her in any of the rooms, not unless she was moving between them too. Maybe she'd slunk off to her own chamber. We *had* to be in the garden at ten; Mimi wouldn't risk sticking about.

When I finally found her, she was in the balcony area, leaning against the balustrade to look down over the spiralling steps and arriving guests. At her side was a young man with an ill-fitting moustache. They were speaking – or rather, he was speaking, and she was giving the appearance of listening, nodding her head every so often but saying nothing much back. The man didn't seem put off by her silence. I wondered if he was one of those suitors Sylvie had mentioned.

With that thought, I had a quick glance about for any sight of Sylvie – her friend was keeping her blessedly busy, it seemed – and I stepped over to Florence and the man.

'. . . all down to the Prussians,' the man was saying, 'and it has resulted in far too much power for Germany. If we do not keep an eye on them, France will surely be in for an unpleasant surprise.'

Florence replied with a low, noncommittal, 'Mmm,' at the same time turning her head and spotting me. Her eyes widened and she pushed herself upright from the balustrade.

'Mademoiselle de Jacquinot,' I said, hoping there was passion enough in my gaze to excuse the cool greeting.

'Mademoiselle Mothe,' said Florence. 'I am . . . so glad you could come.'

The man, somehow unaware he was an unwelcome third in this meeting, summoned an easy smile and put out a hand to me. I didn't bother to listen as he gave a name.

'I have much to discuss with you,' I said. 'There is news from our good friend Michel.'

Florence glanced at the man and said, 'Monsieur, I would have a moment alone with my friend. If you do not mind?'

He did seem to mind, but as he couldn't exactly object, he gave a polite bow of the head and withdrew.

We both began to speak at once.

'Florence, I need to—'

'Wherever have you—'

The sentences dropped off and we stood before each other, blinkingly uncertain how to proceed.

'After you,' I said.

Florence passed a hand over her face and glanced about. 'Where have you *been*?' she asked. 'It has been weeks! You promised you would not give up.'

'And I haven't. I'll never, never give up on you. I swear it. With all my soul.' It felt as if hairline cracks were trickling over my heart, like on a roughly handled bit of porcelain. I'd spent these weeks in purgatory, but how much worse had it been for Florence, who'd had no idea where I was, or whether my loyalty and feelings were still with her? 'Sylvie's had me trapped, but I've been biding my time. I knew something would come my way eventually. And now it has, Florence!' Gripping her hand, I told her quickly of Mimi's note, of my promise to meet him in the garden.

'Can it be true?' asked Florence. Her voice was so light with hope that I felt my heart swell in response.

'You must get away from your family. Can you find an excuse?'

Florence's eyes flashed with that familiar determination. 'God Himself could not prevent me.'

Twenty minutes before ten, and I knew I couldn't evade Sylvie for that entire time. Better find her now on my own terms, then try to get free again just before the hour. Even she couldn't stop me going for a piss, after all.

I located her in the parlour, where some of the chairs had been arranged in a strange echo of our dark circles. She was sitting with Madame Coupart, the dog and the woman in the pink gown I'd noticed earlier.

I sloped over, glad they were in a group – hopefully that'd protect me from Sylvie's scolding, at least for the time being.

'Your cousin has been looking all over for you,' said Madame Coupart. 'Here, there is a seat next to her – do please sit down with us.'

'Yes, please *do*,' said Sylvie, with pointed emphasis.

I took the chair, letting their conversation flow round me, nodding occasionally, my eyes on the mantel clock more often than not. Time was stretching like warm dough. Though the second hand chased itself round and round the clock face, the minute hand barely seemed to creep forward at all.

When it was at last five minutes to the hour, I interrupted Madame Coupart's speech on her dog's dietary preferences and said to Sylvie, 'I will just step outside for a moment to take some fresh air.'

Sylvie was having none of it: she gave a swift frown and shook her head.

'Just to powder my nose,' I said.

Madame Coupart, overhearing us, said, 'Oh no, you must not just yet. I have heard there is to be a cake served at ten! You must stay to see it. Monsieur Maximilien was telling us earlier about the sugar-work. Apparently, it has been got up to look like a swan. Is that not most delightful?'

As if in support, there was a glassy tinkle from the open doorway into the dining room: the sound of a spoon being struck against a champagne flute. Then came Ardoir's voice, too distant to make out words, but it was clear he was calling a toast.

Madame Coupart hefted up her dog. 'That must be it. Come on, let us go through at once!'

I considered running then and there – after all, what could Sylvie do about it? But could I trust that Florence had managed to get away herself?

As if she'd heard my thoughts, Sylvie snared my forearm and began to pull me along behind her. I decided I'd go with her just long enough to check for Florence, and then I'd get away whatever it took, and social niceties be damned. Unlike Sylvie, I wasn't scared of what people thought of me – nor was I afraid to use my fists.

Following the flow of bodies, we went through to the dining room. It was heaving like a net of fish. At the centre, Ardoir held his glass aloft, waiting for his audience to let him start. But what about Florence? I craned my neck to see past the gathering crowd, but couldn't spot her. It was now too dark through the garden windows to say if she was already outside; all I saw was the mirror image of the interior. Was Mimi out there, looking up at all of this? How long would he wait for us?

'Ladies and gentlemen,' Ardoir was saying, 'my dear friends. Thank you so much for joining us on what I hope to be the first of many such evenings. It is such a delight to have you all here . . .'

Florence must've gone already. I tried to slip out of Sylvie's grip without her noticing, but no such luck.

'I'm going,' I hissed at her, 'and you'd better let me if you don't want a scene.'

Sylvie simply frowned. 'Shhh.'

Ardoir was saying something about a fresh beginning, a new era for the family. I twisted my arm round sharply and managed to free myself. The crowd was so thick I had to shove people out of the way to exit the room. Ardoir was asking us to toast his loved ones: his dear daughter; his devoted grandson, the Marquis de Jacquinot; and, of course, his beautiful granddaughter – but now, where was Florence? Florence? Come forward and say hello, my dear.

But Florence didn't come forward, and everyone was still looking round when we heard the wailing scream. Shrill, protracted, unbearably awful. Inhuman.

An unnatural hush fell across the packed room.

Then, from somewhere in the crowd: 'Did that come from the garden?'

There was a sudden buzz as the people nearest to the windows bustled to try to see out. Fighting the other way, I finally got to the parlour door, only to hit a bottleneck with Maximilien and Clement, all three of us getting tangled up as we tried to fit through at once.

Ardoir's voice, uncharacteristically calm, resonating above the hubbub: 'Ladies and gentlemen, please, please, I assure you there is no need to worry. It is most likely no more than urchins playing in the street beyond. My grandson and I will take a look. Please continue to enjoy yourselves – Caroline, some fresh champagne for the guests?'

I didn't hear the rest, as I now finally got through into the parlour.

'Both of you, stay back here,' said Maximilien, not pausing to see if we'd obey. 'Clement, I need you to keep the guests calm.'

Clement hesitated, lower lip between his teeth, but then nodded and turned back.

'I'm coming,' I said.

Maximilien looked at me oddly, before waving a hand that said he didn't really care. I followed him into the gallery, where he turned to the right, heading for the main stair.

'Wait.' Without thinking, I grabbed his shoulder to hold him back.

He looked down at my hand in something between disbelief and anger.

'The servants' stair will be faster,' I said.

A flash of annoyance, till he saw I was right and changed direction.

As we rushed that way, I noticed a shift in the air: a draught at my heels, sighing over them in the same spot that had felled Achilles. Sure enough, when I pushed the stair door it swung open with ease. Someone had left it ajar.

We flew down the coiled steps, moving far too quickly in the dark for safety, jostling and clumsy in the narrow well and Maximilien all the more ungainly with his stick. The pink walls seemed closer than ever, as if the house wanted to slow our pursuit.

Reaching ground level, I could hear the sounds of a scuffle.

Another yell – Florence. This was all my fault; I'd sent Florence out alone and now . . . If she was in pain . . . If someone was hurting her, I'd kill them; I really would.

'Get away from my sister!' roared Maximilien.

It was Mimi. He'd got his arms wrapped round Florence and was trying to hold her still as she struggled. At Maximilien's shout, he looked up and panic swept over his face. 'I'm trying—' he began, but was cut short by Maximilien's fist colliding with his cheek. The blow sent him reeling back, his arms thrown up for balance.

Maximilien went after him, throwing another punch. This time Mimi was ready; he ducked to the side just in time. Maximilien pinwheeled forward under the force of his own momentum and couldn't keep his footing. He landed heavily on his hands and knees, stick flying across the lawn to rest some-where in the dark. Between his injury and the champagne in his bloodstream, it was remarkable he'd even made it this far.

I dashed to Florence's side and touched her cheek. Half her hair had come down, gems glittering loose on the ground. I was vaguely aware that others had come out through the main set of doors behind us: Comte Ardoir and Madame de Jacquinot, followed by Sylvie.

'What happened?' I asked quickly, before anyone else was in earshot.

Florence leaned into the embrace, one arm crooked round me, her hand trailing over my hip. But just as I was putting my own arms round her, she suddenly pulled away from my touch. She leaped back and – to my surprise – she had my reti-cule in hand. This little thievery was so unexpected I didn't react at all, just watched in confusion as she began to run. I thought she must be minded to get away from Mimi or even from her brother, but she weren't headed back to the house, nor the garden gate; she was going right for the pond.

Realizing what she was up to a fraction too late, none of us could do anything to stop her before she reached the water's edge. She didn't even try to wade; she threw herself into the water in a half-dive, half-crawl, splashing toward the centre.

'Florence!' I called after her, desperate. I made it to the edge of the pond, but as soon as it started lapping darkly at my feet, I saw again the drowned, inhuman corpse left by Mama; the terror swept over me, fixing me in place.

'She is trying to drown herself!' came a voice from behind.

Maximilien, upright again but missing his stick, stumbled past me in a blur. He didn't even pause to remove his expensive garments – just plunged right in.

The rest of us watched in wide-eyed suspense as Florence reached the centre of the pond. Giving a single glance back, she plunged her head under the surface. Maximilien shouted her name, ducking underwater himself, though how he hoped to find her, what with the murk and the darkness, and how he hoped to carry her out in his state, I couldn't say. But I wasn't so worried about what'd happen to Florence now; I was more concerned about what Florence would make happen – because in that last glance she'd thrown back, I'd recognized the twisted face and glinting eyes of our poltergeist. With her red hair in the moonlight, she looked like a banshee, a bad omen. But so, *so* beautiful. It did something physical to me, like a spirit hand clenching itself round my internal organs. I loved her. I didn't know what she was thinking, but whatever happened, whatever she did, I'd go along with it. There was nothing else I *could* do.

Madame de Jacquinot had recognized the expression too. 'My God, she is possessed again!'

A heartbeat later, Florence broke the surface, rivulets streaming down her head and shoulders. The pond bit at her upper chest, just below the collarbone. Seconds later, a couple of feet away, Maximilien also emerged. He spluttered and tried to smear the pond scum from his eyes.

'Get out of there, the both of you!' shouted Ardoir.

Maximilien held his dripping arms out to Florence, like a supplicant at a shrine. 'Come on, Flo,' he said. He took a step toward her. All in a flash, Florence's arm shot out of the water and above her head, and in it she held a knife. *My* knife. It glinted in the moonlight and the glow from the house, the brightest thing by far in the dark garden. The blade was pointed up to the sky, the handle gripped firmly by Florence's white-gloved hand. So that was what she'd wanted with my reticule – and this little premeditation was how I knew that whatever she was doing, there was a plan behind it.

'Get back,' Florence snarled. Lit in a stark white beam by the moon above, her face was a skull, her wet hair flowing down her chest like blood.

Maximilien faltered. His arms dropped dumbly to the water, a defeated slap heralding the moment they reached it.

There was a press on my hand that almost sent me leaping in shock: Mimi's fingers against mine. 'I'm so sorry,' he said. His breath was heavy, not recovered from the struggle. 'When you didn't get here . . . she made me tell her . . . I *had* to tell her.' I realized there was something in his palm – folded paper. I took it swiftly so the others wouldn't see.

'I promised to restore this family.' The words seemed to force their way past Florence's vocal cords: this was the rasping, guttural voice of the poltergeist. 'I promised to see you get that which you deserve. There is no bond greater than name and

313

blood. You wish for your repayment?' A glint of mischief – that mocking smile from Sabine's portrait. 'You shall have what you are owed.'

I turned for a moment from Mimi and my eyes met Sylvie's. Her face – bloodless with horror – asked a question: did I know what was happening? I shook my head, tried to ignore the burble of panic in my own chest.

'Please . . .' said Maximilien. It was unclear whether he addressed his sister or the spirit.

'For so long I have been unheard,' said the voice of Sabine. 'But no more. Now I will speak, and you will listen. I will tell you how I died. I was murdered by my own family.'

There was a gasp from Madame de Jacquinot, and I saw her clutch Ardoir's arm, like she needed paternal protection. Ardoir was shaking his head, white brows beetled in a frown.

'I was defenceless. Scared. Betrayed.'

'No, it was a common woman. I will not believe it!' said Ardoir.

Maximilien extended an arm to Florence again. He was shaking enough that I could see it. 'Please, Florence, if you can hear me . . . Please, Auntie.'

'I was murdered by my family,' she repeated, 'and what remained was hidden away so it would not be discovered. You wish to claim your reward? Very well: look to the bottom of this pond. Your treasure awaits you.'

At that moment, Maximilien pounced. I think he meant to wrest the blade away from her while she was distracted – but she was stronger than she looked, as I knew all too well. They tussled for a moment, one of Maximilien's hands closed round Florence's knife arm, his other fending off her attempt to bat at his face. There was the even balance of two matched strengths, and then some extra reserve came to Maximilien and he twisted a shoulder into Florence's chest in a powerful barge. The force drove Florence back one step, two, and then – suddenly – they were both down in the water. It was almost like Florence had tripped over something – something hidden on the bed of the pond.

'Jesus!' cried Maximilien, flailing to get his footing again.

Florence was coughing up pond water. 'There is something here,' she managed to splutter, herself once more.

I looked round for Mimi, for an explanation, but he must've slipped away. Only the paper in my hand remained as a clue.

'Come out, darling,' said Madame de Jacquinot, holding out her arms. 'Come, let us get you a towel.'

Maximilien was ignoring all this, his attention now focused on prodding his foot at whatever had tripped Florence. 'It feels solid,' he said. 'Like . . . a box. A wooden box?'

I was surprised saliva weren't dripping from Ardoir's mouth, he looked so much like a dog watching a bone. 'This is it!' he cried. 'We have found it!' He launched himself into the pond, striding toward Maximilien.

'Found what?' asked Madame de Jacquinot.

'Auntie's treasure!'

Florence picked her way over to us, her dress clinging damply to her body, in places turned translucent. I hurriedly offered my shawl. 'What're you doing?' I whispered to her. She held my gaze for a moment – long enough for me to see fury there – but didn't speak.

'Come inside,' said Madame de Jacquinot, pushing me aside with a sharp glance. 'I think the Mothe sisters have done quite enough already. Let us get you a hot bath and a blanket.'

Florence shrugged her mother off. 'No, the box – I must see it.'

But if it was the treasure, then how'd Florence known where to find it?

As much as I'd have liked to ask, it was impossible to speak to Florence for the time being – she was heavily guarded by Madame de Jacquinot. Instead, I moved closer to Sylvie, thinking I'd take advantage of her lamp to investigate the paper Mimi'd given me.

'What is she up to?' hissed Sylvie on my approach. It was clear she thought I was involved in whatever had just taken place.

'I don't know,' I replied. 'Let me alone a moment.' The paper, when I unfolded it, was thick, expensive stuff – I guessed Mimi had taken it from his lover's apartment. The hand was Mimi's but, when my eyes skipped ahead to the bottom, there was a signature in another – the crude, messy scrawl of someone unused to holding a pen. *L. Masson*. I realized what I held in my hands was Lily's confession – written with Mimi's assistance, so it seemed.

'What do you have there?' asked Sylvie.

I shushed her and held the paper closer to the lantern, angling my body so the others wouldn't see. It was too difficult to read quickly in the flickering low light, and then I was interrupted by a cry of success. Ardoir and Maximilien had hoisted the box free. It was a small rectangular wooden crate, and, from the men's gait as they hauled it on to dry land, it must've had heft to it – between Ardoir's age and Maximilien's injury, it took some effort for them to get it clear of the water.

Despite how long the family had awaited this moment, now it'd come they didn't know what to do with themselves. Here at their feet was either a box of treasure – a birthright that'd restore them to a glory most couldn't even remember – or there was a box of nothing. To open it would be to discover the truth. And whichever truth it was, their lives would be irrevocably changed. Nobody moved to hoist the lid; each was trying to prolong the present moment, before it shifted and was lost for ever to the past. But I'd got no such qualms. The night was growing cold and I was conscious of Florence's sodden dress and felt tired of all this carry-on. 'Well?' I asked. 'Is anybody going to open the damned thing?'

The suspense was broken. Ardoir stooped over and placed his hands on either side of the lid. His fingers slid against the wood for purchase; I could see now that, beneath the sludge that coated it, the wood was painted in something dark – perhaps a pitch – that would've preserved the box, preventing the water from rotting it. 'I cannot get a grip,' said Ardoir. 'Someone help me lever the lid. Keep at it, Maximilien.'

Madame de Jacquinot offered to fetch a spade for her father. As she waddled off to the tool store, Florence melted to the ground like silk. Maximilien and I reached her side simultaneously. We tried to lift her together, but she let out a low wail and slipped from our arms.

'What is it?' asked Maximilien. 'Are you hurt? We need to take you inside and—'

'No!' said Florence. 'I want to see.'

Maximilien glanced at Sylvie – seeking her opinion, or maybe just reassurance.

'She should be all right out here for a little longer,' Sylvie said. 'I do not think the spirit will come back again.' I knew what she was really thinking – that we should follow Florence's lead if we wanted to avoid recriminations. I was thinking it too.

Maximilien nodded sharply and removed his hands from Florence, slowly and carefully, as if from a piece of expensive china he'd only just managed to set to balance. 'I will fetch a blanket.'

'No, you will help your grandfather, boy,' said Ardoir, jabbing a finger. 'Let the women help your sister. Unless you consider yourself one of their number?'

Maximilien's cheeks reddened, but he held his tongue and strode over to take a trowel his mother had managed to find. He carried this across to Ardoir, and they tried to wedge the blade into the box's seam.

In the meantime, Madame de Jacquinot went inside to reassure the guests and locate blankets.

Left alone with Florence, I rearranged my shawl more carefully over her shoulders – it'd already become wet from her hair, and I feared was doing more harm than good. As I knotted the fabric over her front, my hands felt a strange bump at her breast. She hadn't – as I'd assumed – lost my knife in the pond scuffle, but had rather tucked it into her bodice. The realization gave me an unpleasant shiver. 'What's this about?' I whispered to her, keeping my voice low and my lips as still as possible. I thought Sylvie caught me nevertheless, as her brow began to crease. It didn't matter; Florence still didn't respond. 'I'm on your side,' I said. But she wouldn't say a thing, just stared wordlessly ahead, her face shining with tears or pond water – I couldn't say which. As I peeled off her gloves and breathed on her hands to warm them, I wasn't even sure if she registered that I was there. Sighing, I finally moved away, back over to where Sylvie stood, nearer to the men at their work. They were having difficulty finding purchase on the slimy wood.

Then a sharp crack. The trowel had slid in at last. Exchanging an excited glance with Maximilien, Ardoir applied pressure to the shaft and, after a moment's strain, the box lid growled open – just an inch or so, but open nevertheless. Throwing the trowel to the ground, Ardoir let out an unexpected whoop of achievement. We all crowded forward – with the exception of Florence. She remained where she'd fallen, huddled in my shawl. For all her talk of wanting to see, now she weren't even looking in our direction. I felt a squeeze in my heart: worry, fear and anticipation combined. What was in this chest, and how'd Florence known about it? Whatever she'd been leading us to, this was the moment, the climax, the reason we were all there.

'Let me look! Let me look!' Ardoir was clamouring. He pushed Maximilien aside and laid his hands on the chest, fingers spidering grotesquely over its dirty surface till he found a grip and tugged the lid open the rest of the way.

My first thought was that the contents were held in a sack, but then I saw the texture of the fabric and the pattern on it. At the same time, I caught the smell rolling off it. It was dank and decayed, reminding me of the drowned gallery at the Morgue. Holding one sleeve over his mouth to block the stench, Maximilien moved to lift the fabric aside when Ardoir wobbled backward, a strange rattle coming from his throat. 'Stop!' he said, but his voice cracked so the command sounded more like a question.

'What?' said Maximilien, flinching his hand away. 'What is it?'

Whatever it was, it'd drained all colour from Ardoir's face. His lower lip was trembling. Strangely, though I'd never seen much family likeness before, the person he most resembled at that moment was Florence in the middle of a possession.

'We . . . We should leave it. This was a mistake.'

'What do you mean, leave it?' asked Maximilien. 'This is what you have been looking for, for decades!'

'You will do as I say!'

But Maximilien wouldn't. He turned back to the fabric and peered down at it, then beckoned Sylvie closer with the lantern. He brushed his fingertips against the weave. 'This cloth . . .'

'Come away, Maximilien,' said Ardoir, sharper even than before.

'Does this cloth not look familiar?' asked Maximilien. 'I know this pattern. Surely this is like the fabric for—'

There was a sudden lurch in my stomach, because I also knew this pattern. It was white linen striped with silk velvet ribbons – the colour hard to make out in the low lighting, but something cool and pale. Blue. The linen was bumped in places with whitework. Blossom and rabbits. I'd last seen the design as it had fluttered away from Florence's fingers, over the side of the Pont Neuf.

When Florence had accused her family of her murder, we'd not been speaking to the Comtesse. We'd been speaking to the other Sabine.

I glanced at Florence now, and what I saw was enough to chill me to the quick. This wasn't the woman I knew; she'd been replaced with a mask of raw emotion, her teeth bared in the parody of a grin and her face crinkled up, something between glee and grief, laughter and tears. 'For the baby,' she said.

'I forbid you to touch it,' said Ardoir.

Maximilien dropped his hand. His jaw was twitching as if something was trapped beneath the skin, some awful parasite wriggling to escape. 'I do not think I need to,' he said.

He was right. We were all quick enough to understand – if not the entire situation, at least what was under that blanket, that little bundle just the same size as a loaf of bread, or a cat . . . or a newborn baby.

'You told me she was born dead,' said Florence, 'but I saw her, I *heard* her as you took her from my room. I watched you pass her to Lily to take away.'

And Ardoir clearly believed this was what'd happened – the shock on his face now was genuine. He'd never have opened the box if he'd known what it contained. How many lies had been told? How many layers had this child been buried beneath?

'Well, Grandfather, would you care to defend your position?' asked Florence. 'Or perhaps I should lay out my findings first? Charlotte, give me that note.'

All eyes turned on me and I froze, unable even to swallow down the bile rising in my throat.

'Do not play the dunce – give it over.'

I did so.

'This is from an old friend, Grandfather,' said Florence. 'Here, let me read it for you: "*I, Lily Masson, do hereby detail the true events of Thursday the fifteenth of December in the year of our Lord 1864. I hope the Lord will forgive me for the part I played in these unhappy events.*

"'*I had been in the employ of Comte Ardoir for some years before that date and, at this time, I was responsible for the sole care of Mademoiselle Florence de Jacquinot, who was with child although not wed. The Comte had faith that I would keep his granddaughter's secret, which I have done up until today, and reveal now only as I believe that it is a greater sin to keep the truth concealed on this matter.*

"'*On the night the babe was born, the Comte called me into the garden. It was a bitterly cold evening, with ice upon the ground. I saw that there was a basket in which was a bundle of cloth. I realized it contained the sleeping babe.*

"'The Comte told me that he had arranged suitable and discreet accommodation for the child, and gave me the address of a woman named Mère Ancelot, where I should take her. I asked if he should like to wish her a final farewell, but he replied that she was as good as dead to him and he did not care what should happen to her past this moment. He told me to take care of it.

"'When I was alone, the Comte having returned to the house, I picked up the bundle; I felt that she was very still, so I pulled back the cloth. I was horrified to see her face, for she had clearly expired and there were marks all about her neck and chest from rough handling.'"

Ardoir was trying to shout over her, but Florence in turn raised her voice and continued, undeterred:

"'God forgive me for what I did next, but I feared the Comte had killed the child on purpose and wished to pin the crime on me. In the garden was a box of gardening tools, and I enclosed the child inside it. Then I walked her into the middle of the pond.

"'I spent the following weeks in dread that the gendarmes would come calling. As time went on, I realized that either the Comte did not know the child was dead, or he did not care enough to frame me for it. I do not know which is worse. I only hope that God will forgive—'"

'Well, you can imagine the rest. So which was it, Grandfather? Were you heartless enough to murder my daughter on purpose, or incompetent enough to do it by accident?'

A normal man would've been struck dumb by this, but there was no force on earth that could have stopped Ardoir's tongue. 'How dare you moralize, you shameless slut?' he spat. 'You will speak to your grandfather with the respect he deserves. A lesser man would have turned you out for what you did. Do you not see that all of this was to protect you?'

Florence let out a toad-croak of laughter. 'To protect me! From what? A defenceless child?'

'A child that would have brought you nothing but shame! It could not have lived here. You would have been out on the street. It would have died anyway. And what would have been left for you? A short future whoring yourself out until you perished nameless and diseased in some squalid gutter.'

'You monster!' I cried, unable to keep my resentment inside any longer.

'*You* keep out of this,' said Ardoir. Then, turning back to Florence: 'That child was a wretched thing in any case, crying and crying – until I held down its face to shut it up. If it had had any fight in it, it would have survived a little pressure like that.'

Then everybody was shouting, our words all tangling together in a meaningless melee, each of us still fixed in place in a ring round this tiny salvaged coffin, as if performing an absurd mockery of a funeral. A parody of a dark circle.

'It is better that it died!' roared Ardoir, and maybe this was what pushed Florence past the brink, or maybe she'd been building to it all along, but she leaped at her grandfather like a wildcat, digging her nails into his face with enough force to draw bloody lines across his cheek.

Ardoir staggered back under her momentum with an animal yell, but then the element of surprise was lost and his larger bulk won out. He twisted from her grip and in turn took hold of her, one arm crooked round her neck in a choking clutch. Her face was red and bright with terror and I was sure in that moment he was capable of killing her. Without a thought, I rushed forward, closely followed by Maximilien. At the same moment, Ardoir unleashed Florence, who collided with Sylvie.

'Leave her alone!' Maximilien shouted.

The Comte twisted his head to glower at us. On his other side, I spotted Florence pulling something from her dress, though I didn't fully register what she was doing. All my attention was on Ardoir, who, turning back to Florence, raised an arm, ready to swing again. I reached him just at this moment of instability and I shoved him. And Florence chose the exact same moment to extend her hand – just as a warning – with the glinting object it held.

It happened in a blur. An unfortunate coincidence of angles. Perhaps an engineer or an architect – some Brunel or Haussmann – could have produced a technical drawing to describe it. The velocity of my movement, the fulcrum of Ardoir's feet, the angle which Florence held my knife at: a Pythagorean turn of fate.

The next thing I was conscious of was the *thunk* as Ardoir hit the ground. The same spot where Sabine may have breathed her last – either Sabine, I s'pose. He remained there, twitching, as blood and something that wasn't blood hurried out of the place where his eye should've been. The place where a knife hilt was now lodged.

And after that, Madame de Jacquinot's scream. The blankets falling from her arms. Too late now to help any of us.

Sylvie was scrambling to her feet, dress sopped in mud. I could feel my limbs shaking out of my own control. Me and Florence had just murdered a man. With witnesses. There was no way out of this crime scene; I'd be executed for it. All I could think was that I'd got to protect Florence. I raised my face to look at Madame de Jacquinot, at her warped, ululating mouth.

'I did it.' It was Sylvie who spoke. 'It was me.'

EPILOGUE

15 July 1866

I RISE AT five a.m. I pray. I sew gloves. I do not feel any anxiety as I await my sentencing. I know that I will not be an inmate of Saint-Lazare for much longer.

I have a good lawyer: not Alexandre, but Guillaume. Sarah has sent him; a true friend even now. Florence and Charlotte are nowhere to be found – disappeared from Paris like smoke from a blown-out candle – but Maximilien has agreed to testify. After all, I spared his sister this same fate, although that was not what was going through my head when I made my confession. As I saw that little waterlogged body, as I tried to imagine the grief Florence felt for her lost daughter, I was thinking of Mama. The promise I had once made to her that I would protect Charlotte, and how I had failed her – had failed them both. I will admit, it was an impulsive decision; I do not know that I would make it again. But I do not regret it.

Charlotte's friend Mimi visited me a couple of weeks ago. It was the day after Papa's funeral, which he had attended. He said he wanted to describe it to me, as I had not been there, and in fact had not even learned of his death until that very moment. I was not upset by the news, but I was not pleased either. There was no sense of loss, of relief, of anything – it was just another piece of knowledge that I absorbed without emotion.

There had been a small procession: the hearse at the head, then an unostentatious mourning coach swagged in black, in which Mimi had ridden with Adèle. Adèle had wept. Perhaps, after all, there was at least one person who would miss him.

Two mourners and two vehicles – that was the valuation of Papa's life in the end. And, looming over the procession, the twin spires at the end of the road, shards of neo-Gothicism that rose out of their shared church like sisters.

After the ceremony, Papa was taken the short distance to Père Lachaise, where he was buried alongside our mother. I hope for her sake this does not mean she will be stuck with him in the hereafter.

Yesterday, another visitor. There is never a warning; just a sister calling one's name, leading one to the visiting room where a guest waits on the other side of the grille.

This time, it was Alexandre. As soon as I saw him, I wanted nothing more than to collapse into his embrace and weep like a child. But all I could do was press close to the bars between us.

'Good morning, Sylvie,' he said. 'I trust that you are well?'

We both winced at the formality, then – miraculously – shared a smile over that. He looked grey, wrung out like an old cloth. I did not imagine I looked much better.

'I do not know what to say. I am sorry that I have not visited you before now.'

'Why have you come today?' I asked. It felt faintly ridiculous to have this conversation in the presence of a nun; the sister had remained to stand guard.

'I received this.' Alexandre pulled a folded letter from his breast pocket, but did not hand it to me, just held it to his chest. It had obviously been much read and reread, the paper

326

crumpled and grubby. 'It is from your sister. She has . . . confessed it all.'

'All?'

He dipped his head. 'That she blackmailed you into returning to spiritism; that she enlisted Mademoiselle de Jacquinot to help falsify a haunting; that she stabbed Comte Ardoir, not you. That you are, in a word, innocent. Of all of which I – and others – have accused you.'

As he went on to detail how Charlotte had begged him to return to me, to show me forgiveness, I wondered what she hoped to gain. What benefit was there to her? But I came to realize that there was no angle: it must have cost Charlotte nearly everything to write the letter – not least her home, for she could not enjoy freedom in France after this. She had risked Alexandre detaining her, and she had done it only to save me.

'Sylvie . . . why did you tell me none of this?' asked Alexandre. 'Why protect her?'

I shook my head, unable to give an answer that he would understand. Instead, I latched on to something else: 'Can you do as she asked – can you forgive me?'

His features softening, Alexandre stepped closer to the bars, reaching out to clasp my fingers in his own. Tears threatened me once more.

'I see now that there is nothing to forgive,' Alexandre murmured. 'If anything, it is I who should be asking you.'

'Alexandre, I . . .' But what use was there in arguing the point? Thanks to Charlotte, the story ended with me as the victim: the good sister tricked by the bad. It was simpler that way. I returned the welcome press of his fingers. My Alexandre, my home.

'Let it all be forgotten,' I said. 'Let it be done.'

My trial is in a month. With Charlotte's confession in writing, Alexandre is certain that I will walk free. My sister, on the other hand, will never be able to set foot in France again. Her letter closes with how she has decided to leave Paris, taking Florence's jewels and fleeing with her – she does not specify where. They plan to start a new life together, somewhere they are not known. I can see the appeal in that.

I know that I am unlikely ever to see my sister again, but then I had thought the same thing not long ago, and look at all that has since come to pass. One cannot predict the future – not even if one happens to be a highly commended spiritist.

Then again, perhaps I can predict one small element of it. I have suspected it for a couple of months, though I have not yet spoken it aloud, for fear I was mistaken. But now I notice myself growing, and I am sure. A flicker inside me. A girl, I think. I sew and I wonder what she will be like. If she will be toads or gold. But I do not think I will read her the Perrault story. I think I will let her decide for herself how a girl should be.